The Queen of Smiles

ALSO BY CHRIS TULLBANE

The Murder of Crows

See These Bones
Red Right Hand
One Tin Soldier

Stories from a Post-Break World

The Stars That Sing
The Storm in Her Smile
A Sure Thing

The Storm Who Rides

The Queen of Smiles
The Queen of the Road *

The Many Travails of John Smith

Investigation, Mediation, Vindication
Blood is Thicker Than Lots of Stuff
Ghost of a Chance
The Italian Screwjob
A Dead Man's Favor *
Godswar *
John Smith Doesn't Work Here Anymore *

*Forthcoming

THE QUEEN OF SMILES

CHRIS TULLBANE

NEVADA

First published by Ghost Falls Press 2022

GHOST FALLS PRESS

Publisher's Cataloging-in-Publication Data
provided by Five Rainbows Cataloging Services

Names: Tullbane, Chris, author.
Title: The queen of smiles / Chris Tullbane.
Description: Henderson, NV : Ghost Falls Press, 2022. | Series: The storm who rides, bk. 1
Identifiers: ISBN 978-1-955081-13-9 (paperback) | ISBN 978-1-955081-08-5 (ebook)
Subjects: LCSH: Superheroes--Fiction. | Revenge--Fiction. | Self-actualization (Psychology)--Fiction. | Voyages and travels--Fiction. | Fantasy fiction. | Apocalyptic fiction. | BISAC: FICTION / Superheroes. | FICTION / Thrillers / Supernatural. | FICTION / Science Fiction / Apocalyptic & Post-Apocalyptic. | FICTION / Fantasy / Dark Fantasy. | GSAFD: Fantasy fiction. | Science fiction.
Classification: LCC PS3620.U45 Q44 2022 (print) | LCC PS3620.U45 (ebook) | DDC 813/.6--dc23.

Book cover design by ebooklaunch.com

FIRST EDITION

For Nami,
the reason for everything

Acknowledgments

Thank you to everyone who helped make my eighth book a reality:

My angel-wife, Nami.

Claudia, Charity, Cory, Jamie, Johanna, Keith, Kerri D., Kerri K., Mark G., Mark M., Mitch, Montie, Reid, Sam, Shawn, Simon, Tom, and Ziggy.

And always last but never least, my parents.

This book would not be what it is without your support!

The Post-Break World

On an otherwise uneventful night in the mid-1980's, one man's dream changed the course of history. When he woke, his dream had become reality. Cities had vanished, topography had transformed, and ordinary individuals were discovering they had strange powers lifted straight from the comic books: powers to heal, to build, and, perhaps inevitably, to destroy.

Humanity's reaction was predictable. The period of anarchy and bloodshed that followed would come to be known as the Break, and by the time it was over, the so-called dream had birthed a nightmare. In the decades since, new regimes have sprouted, propped up by those superpowered individuals known as Powers and replacing the splintered fragments of long-dead nations.

In the Badlands, however, people focus on survival instead of politics. They build their town walls higher with each passing year, they hoard weapons and ammo, and they sleep with one eye open and fixed upon the horizon…

For they know there are worse things than Powers walking the night.

1

I was born full-grown in the middle of a highway, standing six feet, two inches tall from the top of my helmet to the soles of my riding boots. No mother and no father, unless you count the bastard who dreamed me into existence from a thousand miles away.

I died, seconds later, when an eighteen-wheeler hit me going eighty-five. Its driver was one of those unlucky thousands who had just found themselves with powers thanks to that same bastard's shitty dream. Turns out it's hard to focus on the road when every creepy crawly that's ever lived in your truck is coming to pay you a visit. He lost his life in the resulting wreck but taught me two lessons in the process.

First, that this shell I was born in, this body that means so much to the world, is just a container for the storm within. Cut me and the world bleeds.

And second, that nothing—nothing at all—lasts forever.

I'm reminded of *both* lessons as I see thick plumes of smoke in the sky above the only town I've ever called home.

○○○

When I first encountered Eclipse, it was a nothing little town in the broken remnants of a nothing state, notable only for how far it was from damn near fucking everything. In the years since the dream and the Break that followed, the hundred or so inhabitants had turned it into a walled outpost, a trading hub that existed in an uneasy no-man's land between the nomad clans to the north and the few remaining outcrops of so-called civilization to the east and south.

It's not somewhere I would have ever stopped if my ride hadn't been out of juice. In fact, I'd already been pushing my motorcycle for miles before their wall came into sight. Eclipse was a nothing little town in the middle of nowhere, yeah, but damned if they didn't have two solar panels on the roof of their tallest building, gleaming like black gold in the summer sun.

I stayed overnight to get a full charge and then an extra week to do a job for Eclipse's then-mayor that paid off my debt. Because that was the third lesson I'd learned, not long after my birth: existence is transactional. Especially mine. Every job requires a payment. I could no more accept charity than I could give it, and once again, it was the asshole who dreamed me into existence who was responsible.

When that job was done, I'd gone on to the next one, crossing the continent like I'd been doing since my first death. Looking for truth. Hunting for that dreaming bastard, for the man who was the closest thing I had to a dad. Dr. Nowhere, who had broken the world and dreamed me into existence in the same damn night.

Decades of searching. Decades of doing the worst kind of jobs in exchange for scraps of information that would bring me closer to the only person who had real answers for me. Who and what I was, yeah, but more importantly *why.*

When I finally found him, those answers were every bit as disappointing as the man himself. And soon afterwards, he, like so many other people, was dust on the wind, a casualty of his own actions.

Fucking poetry.

But I was talking about Eclipse.

Turns out Nebraska's damn near the center of what used to be the United States, and over the decades, I'd come back through Eclipse more than once. Get a charge, do a job, bump uglies with a new sweaty townie happy to make sure the sexual giving equaled the getting… and then rinse and repeat over a span of thirty or forty years.

When Dr. Nowhere died, when I lost my reason for doing what I did, somehow Eclipse was the first place that came to mind. A nothing little town in the broken remnants of a nothing state, but also a place to hole up in. A place to figure out who I was and what came next.

And now, almost three years later, someone had answered that second question for me.

○○○

By the time I made it into the burning town, the crows were as thick as the smoke. A gate that had been strong enough to give a howler pause now lay in pieces across the dirt road. Inside that gate, the town's only inn was a shell of itself, a single wall somehow still standing, empty windows looking out and in upon destruction.

As for the streets? Bodies. Bodies everywhere. Burned and stabbed. Broken and torn. Every one of them a face I knew, a face I had come to recognize over the past years. Whoever had done this had taken their own dead with them, had possessed enough manpower to not only destroy a town, but to then clean up afterward.

Numbers and discipline. Even that much was a clue, though I wasn't sure what to do with it yet. My search for Dr. Nowhere had started out like that: gathering data, narrowing my search. Put enough pieces together and you start to understand the puzzle. Understand the puzzle and maybe then you can solve it.

The mayor's house, just off the town square, had mostly fallen inward, those two precious solar panels nowhere to be seen. I waved aside a crow as large as my bike and ducked through the half-standing entryway to find the mayor's body, sprawled atop that of his wife and child. Nathan, Mina, and their son, Duke, who'd been too young to fear me, who'd pouted for days when I told him that, as a queen, I outranked his scrawny little ass.

I looked down at their bodies and the storm inside me howled and gnashed its metal teeth.

Mina's thirtieth birthday had been just a week away, and in the Badlands, that meant something, so Nathan had found me on one of my infrequent trips into town and asked a favor.

I didn't do favors. I *couldn't* do favors, but I *could* accept something equivalent in trade—another charge for a bike I rarely rode anymore, and a home-cooked meal that I'd secretly dump out in the plains, because eating was something other people did. A deal was struck and then I was gone.

And while I was away… this.

I took the bolt of silk from my saddlebag. Five yards of emerald green, purchased down in Wichita. Enough to make a dress fit for the mother of a duke. The nicest thing Mina would have ever owned. Now, just a burial shroud.

Maybe a true mercenary would have kept it. The ones I'd ridden with certainly would have. But I'd taken payment for this job, and I would finish it. I wrapped the family in the silk of Nathan's gift, in the dress that would never be. I kicked down the last wall of their house and built a makeshift pyre atop their silk-wrapped remains. And then, when one last fire was burning bright, adding its smoke to the greater mass, to angry clouds that blotted out both sun and moon, I took up my saddlebags. I headed back to the bike I'd left on the outskirts, brushed ash from its frame, reformed my shell so that both riding leathers and helmet gleamed free of blood and soot, and peeled off into the darkness.

A town was gone. My adopted home was gone.

Balance in all things, in the giving and the taking.

And that meant someone had to pay.

2

I'd never been much of a tracker. I didn't have the patience for it, but the woman who tried to teach me said I also lacked the necessary perspective. Whatever the fuck that meant. I had seen enough to know that Eclipse's attackers had gone east, but half the damn continent was east, and that did shit-all to narrow things down.

So, instead I went north.

Fall had come to the Badlands, less a season than a warning that winter was on its way with ice and snow and the return of terrors that buried themselves in the earth until the cold brought them forth to hunt again. Winter, the killer that lies in wait, that lulls you into an endless sleep with false promises of crackling fires and peppermint dreams.

I love winter. But fall? It's just a tease.

My bike is a shit ton quieter than the old combustible engines that were still around when I was born, but that's a low bar to clear. As I traveled, it made plenty of noise: the electric hum of the motor, the tires on dirt, even the air's moan as I forced my way through. There's nothing silent about speed, and the prey animals of the plains heard me coming and scattered before me.

As for the predators? They watched and they waited, lurking high above, or pacing alongside me for a mile or two before finally falling away. Most killers are lazy. Only a few species in the Badlands had the malice to track their targets for hundreds of miles.

Howlers. Humans. The Great Terrors. And me.

Midway through the next afternoon, I let my bike roll to a stop. The poor excuse for a road I'd been following had petered out, so subtly you'd almost think it had happened naturally. Scrubland dotted a nearby hill, but to the east were the plains themselves, wide and open. To the west, distant storm clouds gathered in black and green ranks like an army preparing to march.

I lowered the kickstand of my bike and dismounted, leaving the saddlebags behind as I leaned back on the handlebars and waited. The wind was cold, even through my riding leathers, kicking up dirt as it swirled around me, but I kept still. I'd never had the patience for tracking, but hunting? That was a whole different thing entirely.

An hour passed, then two, and the sun disappeared behind the coming clouds. I spent the time listening to the storm inside me, watching its naturally born sibling creep closer across the sky. Fall is just a tease, yeah, but there's a kind of peace to be found in its chaos. I let that crackling energy filter through me, waited as one storm communed with the other, and then waited a little bit longer.

Finally, I sighed.

"You already know I came alone, as usual. You also know I mean no harm, and that even if I did, you and your clan could just melt away and disappear. Assuming, of course, that your elders didn't send their Powers to fight me instead. I don't intend to set another foot in your territory, but I have business and I have questions."

There was another long pause and then a man materialized out of the twilight shadows, dark-skinned and stone-faced, thick black hair bound in braids. He wore clothes fashioned from deer hide and decorated in beadwork, and the spear in his hand had two feathers bound to its shaft. I had no idea what those feathers signified, if anything, but I knew he could use that spear like he'd been born with it in his hands. I was also pretty sure he was a Power; his clan elders weren't so dumb as to send a Normal to watch me.

He didn't say anything, but then, he never had. Just stood there, dark eyes fixed on my helmet's visor, as if trying to see past the smiley face decal to the face that lay beneath. Or maybe he knew enough not to bother, and simply waited, like I had been doing all these hours.

"There was a town named Eclipse," I told him. "Almost two days to the south. Someone wiped it out. Left the bodies where they fell, so they're not animals or cannibals. Didn't steal the organs or the heads, so they're not cultists. Took their own dead away with them but burned the whole place to the ground."

More silence. Lightning flashed, close enough now to feel as well as see, and thunder rumbled like the eighteen-wheeler that had been my welcome to the world. The storm inside of me shifted, metal whirring and grinding against itself.

"I'm looking for the ones who did it," I said to the silent nomad. I had no idea what his name was but had dubbed him Two-Feathers in our very first meeting, on account of the spear. "They went east, but your clan knows everything that goes on around here." I motioned to the saddlebags on the bike behind me. "I've come with items to trade."

He regarded me in silence, as the skies opened and fat drops of rain fell to the ground in sheets, and then finally moved, braids swaying as he looked to his left. Another nomad materialized next to him, not quite as smoothly as the first. He met Two-Feathers' gaze, nodded, and scampered off into the darkness.

This was new. My jobs had taken me through nomad territory in the past, but this particular clan had only ever sent single representatives to deal with me: first, a scarred man with eyes like broken flint, and then, when the years turned into decades and the old generation died out to be replaced by their descendants, Two-Feathers himself, strong-armed and silent as a ghost.

Whatever had changed, the storm inside me didn't like it, but it was control that distinguished us from base animals. I ignored its grumblings, ignored the other storm too; rain that soaked my leather-clad shell, the spatter of water hitting chrome and rubber behind me. The bike was as weather-proofed as I could make it, batteries tucked away and safe from the elements, and if Two-Feathers wanted to get into a staring contest with me, he'd learn soon enough that I didn't blink.

I sensed the new arrivals, long minutes later, moving quietly enough, but with none of the almost supernatural stealth I associated with my usual contact. First was the younger nomad Two-Feathers had sent away, followed by an older man: gaunt, grey-haired, and hook-nosed, with burn scars across the left half of his face. He rested one wrinkled hand on Two-Feathers' shoulder and stepped forward to address me.

"We greet The Storm who Rides."

"Greetings… elder," I returned, my guess rewarded with an almost imperceptible nod. "I come seeking information. I have brought items—"

"To trade, yes."

I waited as the storm swept by overhead, and the three of us—plus however many more had come in silence with the old man—stood there and got wet. I respected the nomads, respected anyone who could not only survive but thrive in places like this, but I sure as hell didn't understand them.

"We know of those you seek," the elder finally said. "They have yet to dare our lands, but that day will come and soon." I could feel the weight of his gaze, heavy with foresight and hard-won wisdom, for all that I was older than he was. "Unless it can be delayed."

"Delays are temporary," I told him. "Death is forever."

"Some of the time," he agreed, turning to Two-Feathers.

The silent warrior extended his spear, butt-first, and dragged it along the ground, digging into the fresh mud. Within moments, he had drawn a crude image of a skull that appeared to be dripping blood on a pile of bones.

"This is the banner they march under," said the unnamed elder. "They come from the east and their numbers are legion."

"Not for much longer." I committed the image to memory, even as rain filled in the freshly dug channels, like blood welling to the surface of a razor-thin cut. If there were as many of them as the elder said, that banner would be all I needed to find them. It was worth as much as a name.

I motioned to my bike and its saddlebags. "I have seeds and gold and a few pieces of steel. You are welcome to as much of it as you wish."

He shook his head. "The land gives us what we need, and we thank it for its bounty. This information is offered freely."

I shook my head slowly. "I can't accept. It must be an exchange of equivalent value."

For the first time since I'd met him, something like interest sparked in Two-Feathers' black eyes, but he remained silent. The elder at his side nodded, as if he'd anticipated my reply. After a moment, he spoke again.

"There is a tale among the clans about a one-handed stranger who speaks to the spirits. A man who walks with an army of ancestors."

Of its own volition, the storm inside me went quiet, and I heard the change in my voice, the absence of that metallic snarl.

"Bakersfield. I didn't know you two had met."

"We have not," said the elder, "but this individual shared fires with another clan and the story spread, as stories do. We would know what became of him when he left our lands. If you have knowledge to share, consider your debt fulfilled."

There was a whole lot I could say about Bakersfield, about the boy I'd escorted to superhero school, the man I'd rescued in bloody Reno, and the Power who went crazy and wiped a town not unlike Eclipse right off the map. And yet none of it mattered anymore.

"He went south. Into Tezcatlipoca's domain."

"Ah." The elder's face closed itself up like a fan. "Do you know why?"

I didn't. I'd already left him at that point, left because I wasn't sure what I'd do if I stuck around, wasn't even sure who I was anymore with all my questions answered in the least satisfying way possible. But I *had* known Bakersfield before he became what he became. Something told me that even powers-given madness hadn't changed his core.

"I think he was trying to make something good of his death," I finally said. "Maybe buying time for those he loved in the Free States."

"A delay of the inevitable." The elder nodded knowingly.

I didn't miss the synchronicity.

○○○

With our exchange done, the elder stumped his way back into the night, to a warm fire and what I could only hope was an equally warm bedmate. He didn't invite me to the nomad camp, which was just as well because I wouldn't have been able to accept. It hadn't been part of our deal, after all.

Night in the Badlands is all-consuming. Nothing but darkness and the cries of creatures you'll never see in the daylight. Predators and prey and all too often it's hard to tell the difference. I knew what my next step was, what it had to be, but even in the Free States, post-Break roads weren't compatible with nighttime riding. Out here in the Badlands, it was so much worse. I'd survive the almost inevitable wreck, but the nomads called me *The Storm Who Rides*, not *The Storm Who Walks Away From a Mangled Frame of Rubber and Steel*… and I'd hate to disappoint them.

So instead, I made myself cozy right there. No fire because you never knew what would set the clans off. Just me, stretched out on the wet earth next to my bike, saddlebags under my helmet as a pillow.

I gave it a good ten minutes of lying there in the night, as the thunderstorm dwindled to a disappointed shower, before I turned to the darkness and asked:

"Do you have a name?"

A soft rustle was my only response.

"Guess I'll just keep calling you Two-Feathers then." If there'd been light to see, I'm guessing the smiley-face on my visor would have looked particularly maniacal. "You know, your predecessor never smiled—I'm not sure he even knew how—but he did remember to occasionally speak."

More silence.

"Fair enough. It's been a pleasure. Let's talk some more in the morning."

When the sun rose, he was gone.

I was a fan of the strong and silent type, especially when they had shoulders like Two-Feathers, but there was such a thing as taking it too far.

I'd make sure to tell him so the next time I rolled through.

3

It took me two days to reach Kansas City, although most of that was because of the mess the storm had made of the route. I was starting to wonder how many more years my bike would remain viable as a means of transportation. Not because of wear and tear—I babied the thing, and there were a handful of engineers in the Free States willing to work on it when necessary—but because the roads themselves were vanishing throughout the Badlands, having long since gone from asphalt to dirt. Some of the larger communities with access to rock quarries still put down gravel or even stone on their local throughways, but they were more the exception than the rule.

Riding a horse around the Badlands wouldn't be my idea of fun, even if there was a horse alive that wasn't troubled by my presence.

I passed a couple of merchant caravans on the way in, men and women with balls of solid brass headed to Wichita or Texas or even the Free States now that international trade was becoming a thing again. Every year, a few of those caravans ended up as so much trash scattered across the Badlands, only to be replaced by the next would-be entrepreneur, ready to make their fortune.

I ignored the little rugrat hanging off the side of one wagon and spared a nod for his parents as I sped past. The rifle in the woman's hands wouldn't do much good against the Badlands' horrors, let alone someone like me, but that was the risk they took. If merely human bandits came along, maybe it would be enough to keep them safe. The fact that they were leaving Kansas City alive and with their possessions suggested they weren't complete victims.

An hour later, the city itself came into view. Even before its demise, Eclipse had been a sleepy little town. Kansas City was the opposite, a sprawling lesson on what depths humanity could sink to when freed of its morality. It was a great place to get fucked or stabbed. Or both if you were dumb enough to visit one of the cheaper brothels.

I wove through the shanty town that served as the city's first unofficial district, coming to a stop as a patrol of bandana-clad guards slid out from between the tents to surround me.

"I heard you were dead," said their leader, Lily, a woman with a face not even her mother could have loved. "Killed fighting Capes in the Free States."

"You heard wrong." I flipped Lily a coin, one of the city's own minted bits of currency, and accepted a brightly colored bandana in return, my pass through her cartel's district. "What's new?"

"Same shit, different day," she replied. "Are you looking for a job or here to finish one?"

"Just taking in the sights," I told her.

"Fair enough." She walked her horse carefully out of the way. "Have a good one."

"Fair enough? I don't think so." One of the other guards pushed his way forward with a scowl. "Where are you headed, and what's the reason for your visit?"

The woman rolled her eyes. "I don't think we need to bother with the script today, Kev. Just let the woman be on her way."

"This is why you've been stuck out here on patrol for years," Kev retorted. He turned to me. "As for you, I asked you a question."

"Two."

"What?"

"You asked me two questions."

He spat, the wad of tobacco and saliva charting a slow arc from the top of his horse all the way down to splatter in the dirt. "That's right. I did. And I'm still waiting for an answer."

Technically, he was still waiting for *two* answers, but I doubted Kev would appreciate a second correction. Instead, I just fixed him with a stare he could feel if not see.

"Where I'm going and why are my business, not yours."

"And if I make it mine?"

I held up a second coin, and watched his expression turn greedy, but when he reached for it, I pulled the coin back. "This isn't for you. It's for the lieutenant who will have to fill your suddenly vacant position."

"What?"

"Might need something in a smaller denomination," said Lily. "Not sure our lieutenant has enough change to make it a fair trade."

"Get the hell out of her way, Kev," added the third guard, who had been quiet until then. "The queen here is practically one of ours, and it's a sure bet that the bosses value her more than they do you."

I didn't think too highly of being claimed by anyone, let alone one of the piece-of-shit cartels that ruled the city, but that was a battle for another day. Instead, I just waited, a patch of darkness in the otherwise sun-dappled road.

Eventually, Kev moved aside, and in doing so, bought himself another day of existence. I restarted my bike and rolled forward.

"See you around, Lily."

"With all due respect, I kind of hope not."

Kev had been so busy pointing out that Lily had been stuck on patrol for years that he hadn't stopped to realize how impressive it was that she'd stayed alive all that time.

Either he'd learn from her example, or he'd end up a lesson to the rookie brought in as his replacement.

ooo

I passed through two more districts, collecting each cartel's passes as I went, before finally reaching my destination on the other side of the river. The house was a shirtwaist, even older than I was, with a limestone first floor and a porch that would have been inviting if it hadn't been entirely bare. It fit neatly into a neighborhood free of trash and corpses. Most of the residents here were persons of value to the district's cartel and the community was a far cry from wilder districts like the Zoo.

I pulled onto the remnants of a driveway, dropped my kickstand, and headed for the house's cheery yellow door. There weren't many places in Kansas City where you could leave a bike like mine unattended, but this was one of them. Thieves got the same penalty as traitors and child molesters, and that penalty was death. Usually preceded by torture. Unless there was a war going on, shakedowns and shakeups were something that only happened to other districts.

I was a step from the door when it opened, revealing a small but cozy foyer and the similarly small, if not at all cozy, woman standing inside. Somewhere along the way, Raya had gotten old—wrinkles and frown lines, grey hair now dominant among the black—but her skin was still golden, her eyes as hard as railway spikes. She scanned me from head to toe and I let her do it.

"It's been a long time. Been out west?"

"What gave it away?"

"Mud on your bike. Heard there were some storms out that way recently."

"You heard right." I nodded past her. "May I come in?"

"We both know I couldn't stop you if I tried." She moved aside and waved me through, throwing in a bow that was ninety-percent mockery. "I'd offer tea and scones, but I'm doubting you've gained an appetite after all these years."

"Not that kind of appetite anyway." I followed her to her sitting room, where a comfortable couch and significantly less comfortable chair had been set up with a coffee table between them. "Very domestic."

"We can't all ride the roads forever."

"It's still just you?"

"Had a man. Loved a man. Lost a man." She flipped her hair as if she was twelve. "Turns out I'm not the catch my mama always said I was."

I stifled a laugh. Raya's mom had been a cartel enforcer without a kind word for anyone, least of all her daughter.

"So, what can I do for you, your Ladyship?" she asked. "I'm guessing you didn't come around just to count the grey hairs on my little old head."

"You've always been a spectacularly sarcastic bitch."

"That's why we get along. Insofar as we do get along."

There wasn't much I could do but nod. "I have a job for you."

"On whose behalf?" She arched an eyebrow. "You know that working against my own cartel's interests would be problematic."

"And?"

"And it'd cost you extra." Her smile was as cold as her eyes.

"I'm the client. This one is personal."

That smile disappeared. "Personal's never a good thing. You taught me that back when I was just a child."

"Yet here we are, sitting, talking, and not drinking tea." I scanned the living room. It was empty of décor, of any trace of personality or those little touches that said someone lived within its walls. Honestly, it was a lot like my old house out in the wilds near Eclipse.

I wasn't sure I'd been the best of influences.

For a long minute, I watched Raya watch me, and wondered what was going through that clever brain of hers. Finally, she shrugged.

"What's the job?"

"I'm looking for raiders," I told her. "Burned out a town west of here less than a week ago. No survivors. They march under the banner of a bloody—"

"Skull and bones," she finished for me.

"You know them?"

"Yeah. If you hadn't disappeared off the face of the planet for the past few years, you would too. There's a new empire in the East that's been pushing their way into the Badlands."

I'd heard something about a warlord but hadn't put two and two together. "The red queen or something?"

"Crimson Queen, but yes." That smile came and went. "Between the two of you, that's an awful lot of royalty for one little region."

"What can you tell me about her?"

"She's supposed to be a Power, but nobody knows what kind. Her empire's been buying other Powers off slavers. Adding them to an army that might already be bigger than anything short of the Free States'." She shook her head. "That much is free. Honest. Anyone on the street could tell you the same."

"And if I want more?"

"I'd circle back to the part about the woman building an entire *army* of Powers, and suggest, based on our past relationship, that you might want to let things go."

The storm gnashed its metal teeth and raged inside of me, the whirr and buzz of metal filling the room's small space.

"And then?"

"And then I'd charge you triple. And do my best to get the hell out of the way."

"I don't care about this so-called queen," I told her. "Or her plans for the continent. Tyrants come and go, and hell claims them all eventually. I just want the name and locations of the people who destroyed my town."

She chewed on that for a bit and then pulled out the electronic tablet I'd brought her from the Free States, years earlier. Without access to a network, it was little more than a glorified notepad, but that was valuable all on its own.

"What was the town's name?"

"Eclipse. In what used to be Nebraska." I gave her the general directions and what information I'd put together about the attack itself.

"From the sounds of it, those were troops from the general army, and not third-party slavers." She tapped on her tablet. "That will make it easier for me but harder for you."

"Names and locations and I'll handle the rest," I said.

"I wouldn't have it any other way." Raya tucked the tablet away. "It'll take a few days. Maybe even a week. And because I know you, I know that now we'll have to talk about my fee."

"Yeah. I have some local currency but nowhere near enough, especially at triple your rates. So, what do you want? Gold? Seeds? A second tablet?"

She shook her head, and this time, the smile that spread across her face almost looked genuine, a match for the permanent smile across my visor.

"I want to hire you for a job. Something personal."

○○○

An hour later, I was on my way back out of town, a letter added to the mix of items in my saddlebags. It wasn't the first time I'd played courier. Given my bike and my powers, I was uniquely suited for the task; a one-woman substitute for the armed caravans I'd passed on my way to Kansas City.

The sun was low in the sky behind me, sending my shadow flitting ahead as I headed east. I could have waited until morning to leave, but Raya and I didn't have that kind of relationship, and even in its quieter moments, her city had a way of preying on my mind. Not sure if it was the people or the politics or just one more quirk Dr. Nowhere had hardwired into my personality when dreaming me into existence. Not sure it mattered either. It was the road for me, and after all those months in semi-isolation near Eclipse, it felt good to be tearing across the landscape again.

Figuratively or literally, I was born to ride.

When darkness fell, I followed a small trail down into a gully that ran parallel to the road and set up camp. If another storm came through, I'd be in a bit of trouble, but I hadn't seen a cloud all day, and in the meantime, the walls of the canyon would hide my campfire.

Technically, I didn't need a fire, of course. Cold wasn't going to kill me anymore than heat exhaustion or dehydration. Still, I *did* feel temperature, and there was no reason to rough it if I didn't have to. There was plenty of wood in the gully, some of it dry, and within minutes, I had a cheery fire burning away, sending shadows dancing across my bike and the rocky walls behind me.

This was what my life had been for decades. In the days before hotels and motels disappeared, I'd been too new, too uncertain of my existence to risk staying at one. And by the time the world had finished breaking, well let's just say the tourism industry wasn't what it had once been. Some towns, like Eclipse, had inns, but travel had gone from a leisure activity to something you only did if you had to.

Above me, a large and unseen creature moved along the lip of the canyon, sending pebbles and clods of dirt bouncing down, but whatever it was didn't seem interested in working its way around to me. As it shuffled away, I turned back to the fire. For the first time in years, I spared a thought for my future. Once the debt was paid and Eclipse became just another memory, avenged and buried, what then?

People needed the necessities to survive. Food, drink, and shelter. Some might add nebulous concepts like love and fulfillment to that list, but overall, humans and animals weren't so different; each scratching and clawing for another day in the face of a death that could only ever be delayed.

Where did that leave me? I didn't eat, didn't drink. Hadn't fucked in too damn long. I'd achieved what I thought was my life goal, and the disappointment of that moment had made me a hermit. I was doing jobs again now, but for what purpose? Revenge would keep me going for a while, but just like the fire I'd set, it couldn't burn forever.

That's the downside of being on the road; when you're your only company, it gets that much harder to avoid the questions that come creeping in from the shadows. I toyed with the zipper on my riding jacket—the jacket that was as much a part of my shell as the flesh and bone beneath—and stared into the fire. Three years and I still didn't have any answers to replace the ones Dr. Nowhere had taken with him to his grave.

Some hours later, the dawn broke early on a horizon I couldn't see, rays of light struggling to penetrate the gully's depths. Two handfuls of dirt put the fire the rest of the way out, and I was ready to go. I didn't ever sleep, not really, but there was a release of sorts: quiet, empty stillness where the storm and I pretended to be separate thoughts, where the heart in my chest was flesh and blood and not the endless spiral of a tornado about to touch down.

Raya's envelope was still safely tucked inside my saddlebags. I didn't know what she'd written or why, but she'd given me the name and town of the recipient and that was enough. Two days there, and two days back, if it all went according to plan. By the time I returned, she'd have the information I'd requested, and after that, well, Eclipse's raiders and I would have ourselves a reckoning.

And when that was over?

Hell if I knew. I'd been born a creature of action and violence. Introspection was best left to other people.

If only I could remember that.

4

Eastwood wasn't near a forest and it wasn't particularly far east either. Whoever had named the town clearly hadn't been concerned with accuracy. I'd passed the place once before, in the early decades after the Break, but what had then been a small collection of shacks atop a hill had since grown to a thriving town, complete with a wooden palisade surrounding it. The path up to the town's only gate followed a series of switchbacks, and guards atop the wall watched me coming the whole way. For such a small place, the defenses were impressive. They wouldn't stop anything that could fly, of course, let alone a Power or two, but most animals and raiders would move on to softer targets.

By the time I made it up to the gate, a crowd was waiting for me, most of them armed and on the wall. An older man stood outside, bald pate shining in the sun and hands twitching at his sides. I let the bike roll to a halt and regarded him in silence, the smiley face on my visor golden in the afternoon sun.

"Welcome," he said, voice cracking like a boy just entering puberty. "I am Mayor Jonas Grawley. May I ask the purpose of your visit to Eastwood?"

"I'm here for a job," I told him.

He licked his lips nervously and the men on the wall shifted and muttered among themselves.

"We are a law-abiding town. If someone has done something that merits killing, we ask only that you tell us what that was." He swallowed. "Maybe we can offer restitution or—"

"A delivery job," I interrupted, sparing a second to scan the gunmen looming over us. "Nobody needs to die today."

"Oh, thank God." Grawley wiped the sweat off his brow with gnarled fingers. "Please, enter and be welcome."

I parked the motorcycle just inside their gate and pulled my saddlebags over one shoulder. Eastwood didn't look all that different from a lot of towns sprinkled throughout the Badlands and adjacent territories. Hard-packed dirt roads, wooden houses, and a faint sense of desperation hanging over everything, like morning fog on the ocean. Up close, the armed force that had greeted me on the wall looked even less impressive: exhausted and worn thin. A few sported bloody bandages, suggesting that I wasn't the first threat they'd faced down recently.

I didn't ask what had happened. Even discounting the Crimson Queen's armies, conflict was a fact of life out here. The town's business was none of mine; I had a job to do for Raya and I would do it.

"Who are you looking for?" asked Mayor Grawley. "I'll show you to them, or have a message passed if they're down in the fields."

"The fields?" Eastwood's position on top of the hill made it defensible but didn't leave much space for agriculture.

"On the other side of our mountain," he said, dramatically overstating the size of the town's molehill. "To the north. We have a small lift that provides access, and half our town works those fields on a daily basis."

I nodded, impressed despite myself. It left the town's food supply vulnerable to attack but kept the town itself secure. If they had sufficient stores, they'd be able to wait out what passed for sieges these days. Raiders weren't exactly known for traveling with their own supply trains. "My delivery is for Han Jae-Sung."

"You're in luck then. I believe he's home today."

I followed the mayor down one of the town's side streets to a small house two rows from the exterior wall. Like its neighbors, the building was showing its age—paint peeling, and shingle roof bulging with one too many patch jobs—but the large window that flanked the front door had a flower box mounted below it, and that box had daisies planted in it.

"This is Jae-Sung's house," said the mayor, clearing his throat before continuing. "When you are done with your delivery, maybe we can talk over tea?"

I shook my head. "I'll be heading back out. Miles to go before I sleep and all that."

He didn't get the reference. There were times I wasn't sure *I* got it either. I'd been born with knowledge I hadn't earned; places I'd never seen, people I'd never met, and words I'd never read. For the first few decades of my existence, I'd tried hunting those strange memories down, thinking they were clues that might lead me to my past, but the Break had buried more than just a world. Half the stuff in my brain didn't exist anymore.

Grawley wanted to say something more, but I was no longer in the mood to listen. I left him behind, taking three long strides to the house's wooden door. One knock. I could hear Jae-Sung inside, along with another voice, high-pitched enough to be a child or woman. Then footsteps. A moment later, the door swung inward to reveal a moderately tall Asian man with gentle eyes, wide cheekbones, and short-cut hair as black as my leathers. He wore the same roughspun clothing as the townsfolk I'd seen, pants rolled up to the shin to expose bare feet.

"Can I help you?" he asked. His eyes went wide as he took in my appearance, darting past me to the mayor as if looking for reassurance.

It was hard to imagine anyone less like the sort of people Raya had once rolled with, making me even more curious about the letter she'd sent.

"I have a—" My words trailed off as the owner of the second voice I'd heard came into view, dragging a poorly crafted doll behind her by one long bunny ear. The girl, who couldn't have been more than four, was wearing a dress too large for her, the hem tangling in her feet as she walked.

"My daughter," said Jae-Sung when he realized where my attention had gone. He held the little girl to his leg as she drew near, ruffling her hair.

I just nodded, drawn to the small face now turned up in my direction. She had cheekbones like her father, if still waiting to emerge from childhood fat, but her eyes… her eyes were one hundred percent Raya, right down to the flecks of gold in their darkness. Without the years of bloodshed, effort, and pain that colored the older woman's every expression, those eyes were almost beautiful.

"I have a letter for you," I told the man, finally tearing myself away from his daughter. And then, because I couldn't help myself… "And some questions."

He looked from his daughter to me and something in his face shifted. He offered a short bow, eyes never leaving my visor.

"Please, come inside."

○○○

The house was homier than I'd expected from the outside, a far cry from the empty shack I'd spent years in outside of Eclipse. The little girl who looked too much like Raya for comfort ran in front of us to curl up in a badly upholstered chair, pulling a heavy blanket up to cover her and her rabbit doll.

I took the letter from my saddlebags, and let Jae-Sung escort me past his daughter, into the room that served as their kitchen, complete with a wood-burning stove, and a bubbling pot of something that looked like onion soup. There he turned, eyes drawn to the envelope in my hands. "What does Vo Binh Raya want?"

"How do you know it's from her?"

"My life is here in Eastwood," he told me, words flat. "My friends are here, my daughter is here. Raya is the only person beyond this wall who would even remember we exist, let alone have the resources to find us. And," he added, gaze reluctantly leaving the still-unopened letter as he looked me right in the visor, "she told me stories about you."

"Good stories?"

"Stories."

I let the humor drain from my metal voice. "She never told me about you. Or her," I added, nodding back to the living room where the small child was now singing to herself.

"I was a mistake," said Jae-Sung.

"And your daughter?"

"Cho-Hee was a gift. To me, at least."

"So, she *is* Raya's daughter?"

"Yes."

Despite decades of observation, I didn't really understand families. But Raya's daughter living here, days away from the woman who had given birth to her, made even less sense than normal. Especially if you considered the relative opulence of Raya's lifestyle back in Kansas City. Which left only one possibility.

"You ran."

"Yes. Of course, if you know Raya at all, you know we could never have made it to the city limits unless she let us go."

That much was true, but it didn't answer the bigger question. "Why?"

He shrugged. "Why did we leave, or why did she allow us to? The answer is the same, I think."

"Cho-Hee."

"I did not want that life for our daughter. That I am still alive tells me some part of Raya agreed. I spent the first two years here waiting for her to walk through the door, never sure if she would come to join us or to take her daughter back. Eventually, I convinced myself that she truly had let us go, that we had become just two additional threads in the tapestry of her past." He shook his head and looked pointedly at the letter I still hadn't given him. "I do not know whether to be relieved or distraught at my continued naïveté. May I?"

I passed the letter over without a word and stood there in silence as he scanned its contents, watching emotions chase each other across his features. By the time he was done, his mask was back in place. He shook his head again.

"She has not changed."

"Bad news?"

"A mixture of admonishments, apologies, and threats," he said, "followed by directions to a treasure somewhere south of here, so I might raise our daughter in the manner she deserves. Classic Raya."

"For a guy who is about to be rich, you don't seem happy."

"What use is treasure in a place like Eastwood? It has been months since the last merchant caravan deigned to grace our town. Cho-Hee needs a mother, not a benefactor."

"She *had* a mother," I said, pointing out the obvious.

"Did she?" He shrugged. "You knew the woman who raised Raya, didn't you?"

"Yes. Bian and I did a few jobs together, back in the day. I was with her not long after Raya was born."

"And was she a good mother?"

"No." My voice had gone as flat as his. Bian had been many things, but loving mom wasn't one of them.

"And that is the second reason I think Raya let us go. She remembered her mother, and knew that if we stayed, she might repeat that woman's mistakes."

I chewed on that—metaphorically, of course—for a long while. Then, it was my turn to shrug. Three days ago, I hadn't even known Raya had a man… let alone a daughter. As revelations went, this was a big one, but it was also irrelevant. I would walk out that door and these people, much like the town itself, would become echoes in the past: blurred faces and half-remembered words.

If Raya wanted to talk to me about it, I'd listen, but for now, I'd done my job. It was time to return to Kansas City to reap the rewards.

"Luck to you both," I finally said. "But I need to get back on the road before the light is gone."

"If that is your wish." This time, his bow was a little bit less perfunctory. "However, the sun will be down well before you make it to the base of the hill, and I would not recommend trying that route in the dark. Instead, you can stay the night here. The soup is—"

His nose wrinkled, and he rushed to the stove, pulling the pot off the hotplate, and setting it aside on a metal rack.

"The soup is slightly burned," he admitted, "but still better than whatever rations you would eat on the road. Cho-Hee and I would welcome you as our dinner guest."

"Why?"

He was silent for a moment. Finally, he sighed. "You knew Raya. Before everything. I would enjoy hearing of the woman she was."

A lot of things clicked just then. "You still love her."

"Yes." His smile was bleak and cold. "Sometimes, love means letting someone go, and sometimes it means leaving while you still can."

I shook my head. Despite the shape I'd been born into, the shell that walked this broken earth, there were times humans confused the shit out of me.

He took my gesture as a reply and bowed again. "So be it. I wish you fair travels. When you see Raya next, please tell her we are well, and that Cho-Hee will be raised knowing that her mother cares for her, in her own way."

In the living room, the little girl was still curled up on the couch, now whispering secrets in her doll's floppy ears. I started to move past, toward the door, when those eyes, bright and shiny like another girl I'd known, decades earlier, darted over and up to my helmet. Her smile, missing a tooth, but beautiful all the same, spread to match the decal across my visor.

One night wasn't going to change anything.

"I don't eat soup," I told Jae-Sung, the snarl in my voice missing for the first time since I'd left Kansas City, "but you're right about those switchbacks."

○○○

It was strange, lying awake in a stranger's home. I couldn't let go of my shell for fear of what the storm might do to the interior, to handmade furniture and the handful of heirlooms Jae-Sung had brought with him to the town. I couldn't wander, for fear of waking up the man and his daughter, and since their primary bedroom, currently shared to give me my own space, was on the way to the front door, I couldn't go outside for the same reason.

Instead, I lay there in my shell of flesh and leather. I listened to the sounds the house made in the darkness, listened to the rustling from the other bedroom, the occasional high-pitched complaints when Cho-Hee woke to find herself in a strange room and was then soothed back to sleep, listened to the muffled noises of the world outside. Eastwood didn't have solar panels or a generator and most of the town shut down with nightfall, but there were guards on the wall, and the occasional night owl wandering the street; I listened as they came and went, mentally charting their course around us.

I've had better nights. Worse ones too.

When dawn broke, I was up and ready to go, but the house woke up around me before I could make good my escape: Cho-Hee padding past me on bare feet, eyes half-closed as she made for the outhouse, Jae-Sung starting a kettle in the kitchen. He sent me a tired smile as I came in to say goodbye.

"Headed out?"

"Job's done. It's time I left." And then, because I'd stayed under his roof, and that required recompense, "I'll pass on your message to Raya when I see her."

"Thank you." Jae-Sung was clearly not a morning person. No doubt it made being a single parent that much more challenging. "Safe travels and quiet roads to you."

I didn't tell him that both things were fantasies and had been since the Break. As someone who had shared a life with Raya and then fled that life, he already knew as much. Instead, I just nodded and headed for the door. I was ready to be gone. Ready to be back on the road.

Too bad Eastwood had other plans.

5

Mayor Grawley was waiting when I stepped into the street, the old man already sweating, though the sun was a grey orb in the sky and the morning wind brought a cold I could feel through my leathers.

"I was hoping to catch you," he said.

I ignored the way the storm shifted and raged. "Be careful what or who you try to catch, Mayor."

He cleared his throat, dabbing at the sweat beading on his forehead. "A poor choice of words. I do apologize. There is… there is a band of raiders who moved into the area recently. Some of them mounted a preliminary strike on our town a week ago."

"And you drove them off." The wounds I'd seen on the guards made more sense now. "Well done."

"Yes, quite." He sighed. "Only, my scouts say they're coming back. Tonight, and with numbers, including at least one Power. We don't have the manpower to hold them off."

"You might want to make nice with them then."

"It's too late for that, I think. And the last town these people hit ended up in a pile of ashes."

That got my attention. "Do they march under a bloody skull?"

"The Crimson Queen's banner?"

I took one long step until I was towering over him. "You know her?"

"Of her, at least. Who doesn't?" He shook his head. "Word is she's bringing order to the land. If she'd come north instead of going west, she'd have no doubt stomped out these raiders long before they became a problem. Instead, my town is facing annihilation."

A part of me wanted to tie him to my bike and drag him out to what was left of Eclipse, just so he could see the order he was so desperate for. But my fight was with those responsible, not some minor official in a nothing little town.

"What does this have to do with me?"

"We have guns, but no Powers. We're a simple community with little to offer, but we were hoping to hire you."

"To drive away the raiders."

"They'll just come back once you're gone." He swallowed again. "We want you to kill them."

Behind me, Jae-Sung had come out on what passed for his home's front porch. I couldn't see Cho-Hee but could sense her moving about in the living room.

"I don't work for free," I told the mayor.

"We have food. A few heirlooms. A spare weapon or two."

None of which I needed, especially when Raya would be waiting for me with answers. I swung my saddlebags back over a shoulder. "I can't. I'm sorry."

"You'd just walk away and let us die?" For the first time, something other than fear and worry had entered the mayor's voice.

"Everyone dies, Mayor Grawley. Even Dr. Nowhere himself." I stepped past the outraged little man. "I can only be what I am."

"Wait." I turned to find Jae-Sung coming my way. His daughter's face was briefly visible in the window behind him, and I felt something inside of me twist as if in pain.

"Jae-Sung—"

"I know. Raya told me. There's a need for balance, right?"

"Something like that, yes."

He pulled a familiar envelope from his waistband. "How many deaths will this buy? Raya said there was enough to see us comfortable for the rest of our lives. Given that we'll be dead by tomorrow without your help, a treasure doesn't seem worth holding onto."

"What treasure?" squawked the mayor.

Ignoring him, I took the letter from Jae-Sung's outstretched hand. There were directions at the bottom, but Raya hadn't given any details about the treasure itself. It might be a single bag of currency, worthless outside of Kansas City, or a hundred bars of gold. There was no way to know whether the offer was sufficient.

Still, when I'd been searching for Dr. Nowhere, before he'd died at the hands of a boy just becoming a man, I'd done worse jobs for less, for information or favors that I didn't know if I would ever need. Sometimes, value was subjective.

I gave Jae-Sung back the letter, and watched the mask settle over his features, hiding his disappointment. "Give the letter to Cho-Hee," I told him. "So that she has something to remember her mother by in the years to come."

He blinked. "Does that mean you'll do it?"

My sigh was a snarl of shrapnel and steel. "If the treasure proves insufficient, I'll require some additional form of compensation." A favor would be of limited value, given his skills and lifestyle, but I told the storm we'd find a way to make things balance.

"Anything is worth my daughter's life."

"So be it." I walked past the gaping mayor and dropped my saddlebags onto Jae-Sung's porch, the smile on my visor matching that of the little girl inside. "Let's see what we have to work with."

○○○

The raiders came that night, after the sun had sunk below the distant horizon, somewhere far beyond the city I should have already been returning to. I added the cost of a day's delay to my mental tally as I watched armed men and women creep up the line of switchbacks toward Eastwood.

There were several dozen of them, enough to overwhelm the town's remaining defenders even without the Power who towered over her fellow raiders, seven feet tall and as wide as one of Eastwood's primary roads. In a meaty hand, she carried a metal pole even taller than she was, barely recognizable as the mangled remains of a pre-Break streetlight.

The Free States called her type Titans, and most of the continent had adopted the term in the decades since. Strong, big, and durable as fuck, Powers like that usually found enforcer roles in larger organizations. This one appeared to have taken on a leadership role instead. It meant she was either the only Power around or the strongest. I'd find out which it was in just a few moments.

I waited for the Titan to start up the path to Eastwood. Twenty raiders had preceded her, slipping up the road like hungry shadows, and the final ten followed close behind, a train of armed men snaking their way towards their unsuspecting prize.

I slipped out of the night behind them, the rattling tail to their venomous serpent, and went to work.

Three quick steps took me to the base of the path and then my shell fell away. The storm filled the night air, the shrapnel and steel and tangled wire that formed my core bursting forward to carve through meat and bone. Seconds later, I reformed my shell, black leather reflecting the cold light of the stars above, and stepped past what was left of the first few bodies.

The storm is chaos given shape, and chaos is rarely silent or subtle. Ahead of me, raiders were already turning to address the threat I represented. One particularly fast draw had a bullet winging my direction almost before I'd taken that next step. I felt it tear through my riding leathers, through the shell I'd just created, and then the storm was loose again, howling forward to teach these predators what hunger truly was.

Far above us, I sensed more than saw the light that suddenly appeared. It had taken some doing to get my bike up on the town's narrow wall, but its headlight cut through the darkness in a way that simple torches couldn't, a second moon picking out the figures streaming up the path below.

And that gave the people of Eastwood something to shoot at.

I reformed my shell in the midst of another clump of attackers, twisting to drive a woman's knife into her companion's chest, as I looked about for the Titan only I could stop. Then, I was the storm again, cutting my way through the chaos of gunfire and blood. The narrow quarters worked for me, bunching up my targets as they'd been designed to do, and the storm tore through them with ease. Before I knew it, the sizable mass of the enemy's only Power loomed directly ahead.

She was quicker than something that size should be. The streetlight-turned-club swept through the storm in a rush of motion, but it was like driving a car through a cloud of assassin mosquitoes. A dozen fragments were knocked away, but the greater whole slipped past the strike, above and below and around, swarming the Titan as she pulled back for a second attack.

Her skin was tough, but I'd encountered tougher. As barbed wire wound ineffectually about her limbs, and steel fragments scored superficial wounds on flesh increasingly exposed by the shredded remains of her clothing, the storm drove twisted columns of rebar toward her face. One eye disappeared with a wet noise I wouldn't have heard over the storm, even without the riotous gunfire, and then she pulled her arms back to protect what was left of her face.

In doing so, she gave the storm full access to the wounds it had already been carving into her torso.

There's nothing pretty about what I am, despite the shell Dr. Nowhere gave me, and there's nothing pretty about what I do either. I reformed just long enough to kick the dead woman's club off the road, and then the storm tore into the raiders still standing on the path above.

○○○

There's no sense of time when the storm is free, but it was still dark when the last gun fired. I reformed my shell, alone in my bike's spotlight, surrounded by the death Jae-Sung's re-gifted treasure had bought.

My first step was more of a stumble; I hadn't recovered the fragments that the dead Titan had tried to send into orbit—some pieces scattered in the woods at the base of the hill, one embedded in a tree trunk, thirty feet above the ground—and without them, my shell wasn't quite whole, the heel on my right boot too low, the decal across my visor half-formed, the zipper on my riding jacket a misshapen line of unformed aluminum.

For a moment, the storm inside of me was quiet and calm. *Satiated. Quiescent. Passive.* Words I was born knowing even on that first night, when the storm was still learning it had been forced into the shape of a woman. I let my consciousness drift to those other pieces of me, the tiny fragments of self that were momentarily separate from the greater whole, and then they were winging their way to me, scraps of storm that embedded in my shell and were once again absorbed.

My next step was stable, or as stable as possible given the sheer mess of fluids staining the earth around me. I walked out of the motorcycle's circle of light and further up the hill, up to the men on Eastwood's wall. Moans of pain came from the wall where return fire had left its mark, and the survivors' breath sounded harshly in the suddenly quiet night. My voice, by contrast, was soft and thick as liquid honey.

"I'm going to need my bike back."

6

Two uneventful days later, I was back in Kansas City, entering through the east gate this time, my saddlebags still mostly empty. According to the letter I'd left behind, Jae-Sung's treasure was in what used to be Arkansas, and that was entirely the fucking opposite direction of where I needed to go.

It'll wait, I told the impatient storm. *Blood first, then money.*

The cartel that watches the eastern gates tended to be less antsy than the one to the west, and this day was no exception. I was in and clear after only the briefest of conversations, and not long after that, I was three districts north, parking outside Raya's cute little home.

The woman herself was there to greet me, opening the door and inviting me in before I could knock.

"Tea?" she asked over one shoulder, as we made our way back to the sitting room.

"You get funnier every time we see each other." She'd chosen the opposite seat this time, so I shrugged and took the couch. "It's done."

I waited for her to ask about Jae-Sung or her daughter, but she just nodded, passing me an envelope significantly thicker than the letter

I'd delivered to Eastwood. The cartel had a paper mill out there somewhere, but I was still amazed how freely Raya gave the stuff away.

"The information you requested," she said. "The man in charge is Silvers, Colonel Raymond Silvers. He heads up the Crimson Queen's 2nd Brigade."

Even the Free States' army was a shell of what it once was, so I knew this pretender queen's army couldn't possibly be as large as she wanted it to seem, but even so… a brigade wasn't small.

"Most of the troops are still stationed east," Raya continued, as if divining my thoughts, "but the Colonel himself, along with a detachment of soldiers, came through Kansas City about a month ago, heading west. Word is they've been building a fort."

"Word?"

"I still have my sources." Her smile flickered, there and gone. "Some of the cartels bury their head in the sand, pretending that Kansas City is all that matters, but the rest of us, well—"

"A city's only as good as its defenses," I quoted, "and the first of those defenses is actionable intelligence."

It was something her mother, Bian, liked to say, but for once, Raya didn't rise to the bait.

"I've included the location and blueprints of the fort," she said instead, taking a sip of tea. "Along with what I could find on troop dispositions. He'll have some Powers with him, but nothing you can't handle."

Something was off. Maybe it was that Raya was holding her teacup more tightly than usual. Maybe that, other than the joke about the tea, she seemed subdued, even for her. She had always been a secretive little shit—it's one of the reasons we'd gotten along after she hit adulthood—but I'd known her long enough to know when something was wrong.

And I had a pretty good idea what it was.

"You didn't tell me you had a daughter," I said, the words almost gentle.

She paused, looked away, and then those hard eyes swung back around to drill into my visor.

"Does it matter?" she asked.

"She has your eyes, but my smile." The joke fell flat in the strange distance between us, and I tried again. "She looks well. She and Jae-Sung both."

"Good." She looked away again, as if blinking away tears, but her eyes remained bone dry.

I mentally shrugged and let it go. There were some things I would never understand about humans, even after living among them for decades. The many permutations of familial love clearly belonged on that list.

"I'm going to steal a charge from your generator out back," I said, rising to my feet even as the storm rumbled inside of me.

Raya waved the hand not gripping her teacup but said nothing. I left her to her silence, her empty house, and the lonely life she had chosen.

She was still there, an hour later, when the current battery had been topped off. I remained one battery down but had ample extras to make the trip into the Badlands and back and wanted to be clear of Kansas City by nightfall. Something had changed between Raya and I, after all these decades, and I needed space and time to think on it. She'd been retired from wet work for a while now, but still had enough pull with her cartel to make life difficult for me if she wanted.

"I'm headed out," I said, startling her from a quiet contemplation.

"So soon?"

"There's a debt to be paid."

"I won't keep you then." She placed her cup of tea, still only half-drunk, on its coaster, and showed me to the door. "Stop by when you're done, and we'll talk."

I nodded, trying not to tower over the other woman in her own foyer. We'd known each other a very long time, and that meant something, even to someone like me.

"I'll do that."

ooo

My departure from Kansas City was swift, helped by the fact that I'd already collected my access badges from the various cartels for the week. A mixture of scavengers and street trash eyed my bike as I drove through, but none were dumb enough to try to claim it.

It was a pity really. Even with the carnage back in Eastwood, that conversation with Raya had been enough to get the storm gnashing its metal teeth. A little bit of righteous bloodshed might have settled things down, maybe taken my mind off whatever was going on with the spymaster.

The world was a toilet, but some people got shit on more than the rest. Raya had had a hard life, but that was true for most people in the Badlands. She'd survived, and in some ways, even thrived, and yet, all that success didn't seem to matter. Was she just marking time now, in the little house? Counting the days and waiting to die?

I shook my head as the city receded in my mirrors. Truth was, I didn't know if it was Raya I was worried about or myself. In a few more decades, she'd be in the ground, but I'd still be riding through the hellscape of my creator's making. I'd spent my whole life wondering *why*, and now was faced with an even bigger question: *what next?* I'd spent three years on the outskirts of Eclipse, hiding from that question, letting the storm's noise drown out my own questions and doubts.

Maybe Raya and I had more in common than I'd thought. And maybe I'd suggest a family reunion when we got back. Maybe leaving the cartel behind, maybe starting over in a shitty little town with her blood and her love would fill that void inside of her.

Or maybe she'd tell me to go to hell over a cup of lukewarm tea. It was always hard to know for sure.

I set those thoughts aside as I left behind the shanty town that ringed Kansas City and stepped on the accelerator. Raya's directions would take me almost back to Eclipse, only veering off to the south in the final day of travel. I'd spent more than a week on the road to find an enemy who had been only a day's ride from my initial starting point.

Even with Dr. Nowhere dead, it sometimes felt like we were all rats, running through a maze for his amusement.

○○○

I found the road leading to the fort long before the fort itself; a path wide enough for two wagons side by side that had been hacked and slashed out of the forest. Apparently, the Crimson Queen's colonel was a student of history and knew logistics mattered. Of course, that same road also told me where I could expect guards, so it worked in my favor too. I stashed my bike out of the way a mile or so back, Raya's blueprints stored in the saddlebags with my other possessions, and crept through the woods after nightfall, taking a wide arc to approach from what those plans told me would be the back.

In the old days, I might have just gunned it down the road and killed everything that got in my way, but the past decade or two had reminded me that there were meaner things than me in the post-Break world. Most of those things were on the coasts, down in Texas, or in the wreckage of other countries, but proper reconnaissance remained the order of the day, even *with* the wealth of information I'd already secured.

The fort itself was deceiving in appearance—a rough stone wall with guard towers at the corners and a handful of buildings enclosed within. Only one of those buildings rose above a single story, but I knew from the blueprints that the architects had built down rather than up. Most likely with an Earthshaker doing the heavy lifting, which also explained the exterior wall being crafted from half-ton stone blocks.

I looked for a vantage point on a nearby hill—then settled for a worse one, when I realized the colonel had placed eyes on that first hill—and settled in to watch.

I don't have eyes, but my eyesight works just fine. Maybe better than fine. Even from the lesser hill, I could make out the soldiers moving about in the fort: guards on patrol, watchmen changing shifts, stablemen vanishing into a long, open-air building to feed the horses inside. Even the grooms were in fatigues, the skull and bones patch on their left breast telling me I'd come to the right place.

What I didn't see was anyone who looked like they were in command. If the Crimson Queen was anything like the dictators further east, her army would be big on rank insignia, medals, and ribbons… all the indicators a stranger needed to pick out the officer in charge. But everyone below me seemed like a grunt.

Of course, even the new recruits would have to die; I just wanted to make sure I got Silvers first. The people who lived long enough to become officers in modern militaries tended to be weasels; slicker than shit, and quick to flee. The last thing I wanted was to have to chase the asshole down a second time.

By the time the sun was up, I'd mapped out the guard rotations, but there was still no sign of the colonel. I burrowed deeper under my blanket of leaves and continued my vigil. Sometimes, not having to sleep worked in my favor.

In the daylight, the camp came alive with movement and noise. I watched soldiers emerge from the barracks, descend into the mess hall, and then come back out again. Some formed work details to improve defenses or continue widening the road while others vanished into what Raya's blueprints had identified as the command structure. Still no sign of Silvers, but at one point, an aide made a bee line for the mess hall to retrieve a tray of food that they took down into the command center. That told me the colonel was likely camped out inside.

I wasn't wild about heading underground. Tunnels made it all too easy for a solo operator to find themselves outflanked, and that could mean death, even for someone like me. My original plan had been to wait for Silvers' appearance and to strike while he was out in the open, but by the end of that first day, I knew I couldn't afford to wait. The hill I was observing from was remote, but the defensive perimeter was already widening. At some point, they'd post watchmen here as well. And while I could kill those soldiers as they came, it risked setting the whole fort off.

I was going to have to go in after the bastard.

I gave it another few hours, listening to the quiet hum of the storm just to keep myself sane. Sometime after midnight, I crept out from under my camouflage and slipped toward the other hill, the one that held the watchers I'd almost tripped over a night earlier. I didn't know if they'd been posted to watch over the fort, or to keep an eye out for people sneaking up on it from behind, so I split the difference, wishing—and not for the first time—that Dr. Nowhere had dreamed me into existence wearing something quieter and more practical than leather.

I crawled up the hill until I heard the low voices of the two men on watch. I don't have ears either, but my hearing is good enough to get by when I'm in my shell. Once I'd picked out the soldiers, solid shadows huddled together for warmth, I moved in. The one on the left was talking about the two women he'd left behind in New Memphis, while the one on the right…

Well, he didn't get much of a chance to respond before I was there, a glove over his mouth. I pulled the knife from the second man's belt and drove it into his companion's throat, wiggling the blade around a little bit, just to be sure that Lover Boy was dead. Then, I pulled that same knife out, shifted my squirming captive just enough, and drove the blade into his chest.

Two men dead in a matter of seconds. It wasn't quiet—death rarely is—but it was a hell of a lot less noisy than if I had killed them with the storm. A quick glance showed me nobody in the fort seemed any the wiser. I had a clear path down to the wall and its almost-hidden rear gate.

Virtually any Power would have had an easier path into the fort, from building handholds in the stone to convincing a tree to fall over and crush the wall to just flying right over the damn thing. All I had was the storm. I timed my run to match the now-predictable change-of-shift and made it to the wall without being spotted. The position of the watchtowers didn't offer their inhabitants the right angle to see someone pressed flat against their gate, but extraneous motion could still give me away. That made for a long and boring two hours standing perfectly still, waiting for the next shift change.

When it came, I took my second real risk of the night. A leap brought me within a foot or so of the gate's top edge. Before I could drop back down, I let the storm loose. My momentum gave the storm direction, and then a second or two later, I was back in my shell, my hands now high enough to grip the gate and pull myself over and into the fort.

I was as quiet and as quick as I could be, still a long way from the assassin-like Powers that the Free States called Stalwarts, but stealthy enough to avoid detection from the guards at the watchtowers.

The guards standing just on the other side of the gate though? The ones I dropped on even as they were turning to look up?

They *definitely* heard me coming.

ooo

They shouldn't have been there. The previous night, guards had only ever walked *past* the gate and only during the patrols I'd already mapped out and timed. But I didn't have the luxury of wondering how things had gone to shit. Instead, I let go of my shell and the storm surged downward, tearing the two soldiers apart.

I couldn't tell if they'd gotten any shots off first and wasn't sure it mattered; their deaths would have been loud enough to attract the attention I'd been trying to avoid. I reformed my shell and sprinted forward as shots rang out from the two towers along the rear wall, bullets pinging like music off the building in front of me.

So much for a stealth mission. Now, it was all about reaching the colonel before he could escape.

A half-dozen steps and then the storm surged forth again, tearing through a squad of soldiers as they came around the corner. Alarms weren't going off yet—maybe they hadn't had enough time to get their local grid working—but the gunfire filling the air was more than enough to roust anyone who had been sleeping. I cut behind the barracks, through the alley between it and the stables—horses screaming and bucking inside, agitated as much by my presence as by the chaos outside—and then I was shredding the guards outside the command center and rushing into the tunnel Raya's blueprints had told me to expect.

Either the colonel hadn't brought any Powers from his brigade, or they were considered too important to serve on night watch. Either way, it was a mistake that was going to cost him. It had taken less than a minute to breach his command center.

Things were looking up.

Those same blueprints had told me the first two rooms off the tunnel were for meetings. They were empty as I rushed past, the pathway descending with almost every step. At an intersection, a second tunnel branched off to the left and right, but the colonel's office and living quarters were straight ahead, so I pushed on and downward. I didn't like the near certainty of troops gathering at my back, but there wasn't a damn thing I could do about it either.

I kicked a door off its crudely made hinges and pushed down another hallway. Voices began to fill the passageways behind me, but they were far too late; I thundered into the colonel's office, letting go of my shell and setting the storm free to do what it did best.

The lack of targets was my first indication that something was very wrong. The lack of any actual furniture was the next. I reformed my shell, finding myself in an empty room, ten by ten and hewed right out of the stone. No desk or chair. No door leading into the colonel's private quarters as had been indicated on Raya's blueprints. Just an empty space with a dirt floor and a ceiling so high it had to extend into one of the buildings that flanked the command center. Below that ceiling, but still fifteen feet above my head, rough stone jutted from the chamber's walls to form a kind of walkway.

I didn't need eyes to recognize a trap when I saw one. I spun about, just as a door boomed shut behind me. From the sound it made on closing and the wave of air that rushed before it, it was metal, at least as thick as the bike I'd parked over a mile away, and so solidly set in its frame that not even air could get through.

And that's when I knew Raya had betrayed me.

7

A moment later, there was a soft pop, and I was no longer alone. The newcomer was a woman, young and reasonably pretty, in a long-sleeved red blouse and black pants. She had blonde hair dangling to her shoulders in curly ringlets and a mouth that stretched a little bit too wide as she began to speak.

I didn't hear a word that she uttered because the storm was already emerging from its shell, crossing the empty space in a hummingbird's heartbeat to fall upon the woman in a wave of chaos and cutting edges.

Where it did *nothing*.

Barbed wire, saw blades, rebar, and old rusty railway spikes all slid off the stranger's form, leaving her untouched and unbloodied, her clothes unmarred, even her hair still in perfect curls. She waved a hand about in the middle of the storm's mayhem and gave a sigh I felt instead of heard.

I reformed my shell several feet away.

"Shall we start over?" she asked, her now-audible voice melodic with a slight southern twang. "Or do you need to get more of that out of your system? Hells, if you can hear me when you're shifted, go right ahead. It don't matter none to me what you're doing just as long as you listen."

If any of the data Raya had given me was true, Colonel Silvers was a man. Which meant this was either one of his Powers or… I tilted my helmet to one side as I took in the red blouse again. She was smaller than I was but had a confidence about her so strong it was almost physical. "The Crimson Queen?"

"You better believe it." She made finger guns in my direction and then laughed, the noise ringing like bells through our too-small space.

"I thought you'd be older."

"I know, right? It's amazing what a woman can accomplish when properly motivated." She beamed a smile, wide and apparently genuine. "And you would be our continent's other monarch, the so-called Queen of Smiles, on account of that adorable little decal on your riding helmet. When I heard you were looking for info about me, I couldn't help but ask one of my Immortals to fly me out so we could have ourselves a little chat."

"Immortals?"

"You like that? I took it from a history book. Lots of good ideas in books, no matter what most people will tell you these days. And now here we are, two queens together in one room, almost like it was meant to be."

"All I want is your colonel," I said. "And whichever of his men burned Eclipse to the ground. Give them to me and you can carry on with your empire building."

"Oh, bless your heart! That is so sweet! But I didn't fly all this way just to say hi, you know? I came to make you an offer of my own."

I was studying her as she talked. She looked like a mundane late teenager, but if that were the case, she'd already be in so many pieces on the chamber floor. A Power then, as the traitorous Raya had so helpfully warned. Too slender for a Titan and too durable for a Stalwart… and neither power explained her clothes being as invulnerable as her flesh. A one-off, maybe, like me, Tezcatlipoca, or Grannypocalypse?

"Oh, I can practically see your brain whirring away inside that helmet," she said. "*What can this delightful young lady have flown all the way out here to offer me?* Well, I'll just go ahead and say it: I want you to join me. You'd have to take a teensy bit of a demotion, on account of there only being room in my empire for one queen, but the Countess of Smiles sounds almost as good, don't you think?"

"Why would I do that?"

"Because you could be part of something great, of course! We've already come so far, bringing civilization to this terrible land. I suspect it's been a while since you traveled east, but you wouldn't believe how nice things have gotten within our borders! Law and order where once there were just a bunch of jacked-up tyrants all thinking they had the biggest dicks in the land. Clean water. Electricity in more than just a few towns. And if you still wanted to ride around on that dusty motorcycle of yours, you'd have some real roads to travel. That's got to be better than dirt, dirt, and more dirt!"

"And if I say no?"

Her smile flickered. "Well, that would be a shame now, wouldn't it? We watched you come in—and it was truly a sight to see—but it's not like you can fly. And from what I hear, you're tough, but you ain't indestructible." She waved a hand up at the ledge high above us, and a handful of people appeared. "More of my Immortals, don't you know? All of them ranged specialists, because I don't think they want to tangle with your other form. And really, the fact that I had so dang many of them flown out here with me should be taken as a compliment."

One of the men up on that ledge had smoke curling from his nostrils, which told me he was probably what the Free States called a Pyromancer. He was flanked by two women and a scrawny fellow in a black-leather muzzle, but I had no idea what their powers might be. Either way, there was nowhere for me to hide down below. If they had any strength at all, it would be like shooting fish in a barrel.

"You're down here with me," I reminded the Crimson Queen.

"Only so we can have this little chat. Depending on how it goes, Pierre up there will pull one or both of us out."

"The man in the muzzle?"

"Oh honey, you don't want to mention that where he can hear." She shot the man in question a radiant smile and lowered her voice. "He has a little bit of a biting problem after being left to an overeager technician for just a hair too long. But even with his limitations, powers-related and otherwise, he's a total sweetheart and just about as gosh darn useful as you could imagine!"

A Teleporter then. And, given that the queen has said she'd been flown out here, one who had only limited range.

At least it explained how she had appeared in the room with me. That pop I had heard must have been air being displaced by her arrival.

Not that it did me any good. Pierre and the other Powers were well out of my reach. I didn't carry weapons normally, because they never survived the storm, but right then I'd have literally killed for some sort of gun.

"I guess I don't have much of a choice," I allowed, "but I do have a few conditions."

"And I have a feeling I know at least one of those conditions." She looked up to the ledge again. "Say hi, Colonel Silvers!"

An older man in full military regalia leaned over the edge, scowling. "Your Majesty, could we please hurry this—"

"Say goodbye, Colonel Silvers!"

The Pyromancer exhaled and the officer went up in flames, arms pinwheeling as he plummeted through the air. He was still screaming when he contacted the hard stone floor, the impact audible over the crackle of the quickly fading flames.

"Join my army," said the Crimson Queen, not even looking at the man who had died three feet to her left. "Become one of my Immortals, and I'll give you the company that burned your little town to do with as you wish. Frankly, they have it coming. They were supposed to just make an object lesson of a few of the people in charge, and maybe invite the rest to become citizens. Now, a town is dead, you're mad as hell about it, and we didn't get a single recruit in the process. Boys will be boys, sure enough, but my soldiers need to be smarter than all that."

"If you're okay with them dying, then why bother with any of this? I would have handled the issue for you on my own."

"Don't I know it, but it's like I said; I wanted to come meet you. And it's not like I can really afford to have you running free, making all manner of mischief. Once Kansas City joins my little empire, we'll be making a serious push west. Better to hash things out now than some time in the future. Plan for what is difficult when it is easy, don't you know? That's Sun Tzu. Wish I could have met him, but life doesn't always work out that way."

I ignored the way the storm rumbled inside of me, still studying the woman in front of me.

"Now, if you don't mind, I'm gonna need an answer. Sooner you join up, the sooner we can head off to civilization. It's Free Beer Friday back at the palace!" She smiled again and extended a hand in my direction, the nails painted a red that matched her shirt.

That impressed me as much as her apparent invulnerability. Cosmetics were hard to come by outside of the Free States.

"I guess I don't have much of a choice, do I?" I reached out for her hand with my own, and watched the smile grow on her face until it almost matched the decal on my visor.

And then, as we clasped hands, I set loose the storm again.

She shook her head, but I wasn't listening. I was watching pieces of the storm rebound from absolutely nothing, a bare inch away from her bare skin. When I reformed my shell, I saw our hands weren't making contact at all… that same invisible layer was between us, more solid than steel.

"You're a Telekinetic," I finally realized.

"Got it in one." She made a small moue of disappointment. "Well, more like in *two*, but I'm feeling charitable. And you're a Shifter like I've never seen before. Most Mineral Shifters just replace their bodies with their element, but you… wowee, you are something special indeed." The smile fell away, leaving her face curiously plain and blank of emotion. "And that's why I'm giving you one more chance, despite your admittedly underhanded attempt just now. Join me or die."

I didn't know if the offer was legitimate, but it didn't matter. I wasn't aligning myself with someone who sent her troops out to make *object lessons* of people like Nathan and Mina, to say nothing of little Duke.

"Watch your back," I said, "because I'll be coming for you."

"Well, ain't that a crying shame. Not entirely unexpected, but still… very, very disappointing. You would have made such a cute countess."

The man in the muzzle gibbered and suddenly the queen was standing on the ledge above, gone even though I'd still been holding onto the shield of air around her. She propped her elbow up with one hand and rested her chin in the other, beaming down at me as her earlier disappointment fled like rain before the resurgent sun.

"Have at her, Immortals."

○○○

Fire rained down from above in fat liquid globules, but the spears of radiant light were even faster, the shock wave from their passage visible as water vapor being forced aside. One of the female Powers was a Lightbringer? There was no dodging those strikes, so I set the storm free even as light tore through me and what seemed almost like napalm splattered against and pitted the stone walls and dirt floor.

The storm rushed for the door, but it was every bit as solid as I'd feared, as strong as any individual piece of the storm, and a dozen times more durable. Even the attacks from the Pyromancer and Lightbringer, which I'd intentionally pulled to my only potential exit, did little but scar its surface. It would take minutes of concentrated fire to break through that door, and I didn't think either Power would oblige.

And then the third Immortal went to work.

I didn't notice it at first, the hissing inaudible over the sound of the storm, the mist lost in the smoke and flashes of light. It wasn't until I felt it settle on the whirling fragments of the storm that I even knew it was there. Some sort of air-based poison, coating my shards with a film that looked almost as virulent as it no doubt felt to breathe.

If I could have laughed, I would have. The storm doesn't have a mouth, for all that it howls and rages, and my shell doesn't breathe any more than it eats. Whatever poison the third Power was dumping into the chamber had as much effect on me as dew on a raincoat.

That was just about the only good news though. Iron has a melting point of 2,800 degrees, with steel roughly the same, and the fire was at least that hot, with the Lightbringer's beams even hotter. Pieces of me were melting to slag, the ever-spinning storm shrinking with every revolution.

I drove some of my few remaining fragments deep into the earth, angled to penetrate under the wall I couldn't breach or climb, and reformed what was left of my shell in the center of the room. I faked a deep racking cough, as if the poison was already at work, only to realize such theatrics were unnecessary. The storm is something I carry with me, but it is also the foundation for the body that the world sees. With so many pieces already gone, my shell was a mess, one leg missing from the knee down, my helmet misshapen, the decal across its visor entirely gone. I crumpled to the rough floor, deep rents in my leather and the rarely seen flesh underneath. With an effort, I pushed through the pain, propped myself up on my one working hand, and turned my cracked visor in the direction of the Crimson Queen and her immortals.

"Say goodbye, pretender-queen," she whispered.

And then fire and light crashed down to obliterate me.

8

"I." It wasn't a thought. Not really. There wasn't enough left of me for thoughts. Just a few fragments of the once-greater whole, clinging to existence because chaos isn't something you can stamp out, not with all the money or guns or gods-fucked fire in the world.

"I." *Still* not a thought, despite the way it echoed.

It was… at best… a silent declaration.

But it was enough.

There were seven pieces of the storm remaining, each buried under the wall of my would-be tomb where I'd sent them scant moments before incineration. One by one, they dug themselves out of the ashes, flopping like dead, rotten fish across the space. When they were close enough to touch, when whatever was left of me was that much closer to being whole, the shards settled back down again. Not enough to form even a scrap of shell, but enough, just barely, to let me move beyond the simple statement of self.

I have never been human. I've always known that, even if the so-called Crimson Queen did not. I'm not a Shifter, because Shifters are people with powers, while I am a thing who presents as a person. I'm not even sure if I *can* die, but I do know I'd never come so close to finding out for sure as I did in that shitty little fort, a half-day's ride away from a dead little town.

Those seven fragments that had once been a storm waited, a pile of steel and iron in a pit of dirt and scrap. Together, they were enough for basic thought, but little more than that, and time passed in units I couldn't perceive let alone count. Eventually, an eighth fragment dug itself out of the dirt, a length of metal scrap regaining its edge, reclaiming its shape from the greater mass of cooled slag.

Because even though I wasn't a Shifter, I did have one thing in common with them: I healed. I'd never had to heal quite like this, not even after my showdown with Red Dragon in Reno, or a battle with a Hydromancer and his bestial brother in Mobile, but as more pieces of the storm began to form, sometimes out of their own remains, sometimes out of nothing at all, as my consciousness expanded past single syllables, I knew my rebirth was just a matter of time.

The first question on my mind, once I'd regained the ability to *ask* questions, was what came next. Colonel Silvers was dead, even his corpse lost in the face of the conflagration that had obliterated the storm. The Crimson Queen and her Immortals had likely flown back to whatever town the bubbly bitch called home, but the men directly responsible for burning Eclipse remained, somewhere above me. I could extract my payment in their blood and flesh and return to the road and my endless wandering.

But what about the young warlord who had read too many books and was carving her way across the continent, the woman who hadn't officially sanctioned Eclipse's burning, but *had* ordered the soldiers to deliver an object lesson to its leaders?

What about Raya, who had known me since she was a child, yet had betrayed me as easily as a snake shedding her skin, sending me into a trap that should have killed me… that for all anyone else knew, had done so?

I added both women to the mental tally and waited for that transactional part of me to protest, to warn me that I was exceeding the guidelines of the job I'd taken on, the set of rules that bound the storm's chaos in chains of order.

Nothing. No twinge. No censure. Just fury and hunger, and for once, I couldn't tell whether it was the storm's or mine.

I was still hours or days from being able to form my shell, let alone the helmet that was my face, but I felt the smile, cold and hungry, that was waiting to form.

Sometime later, I was whole again. I let my senses drift upward for any sign of people on the ledge above, but the pit was empty except for the pile of metal and steel that would become the storm, a pile that shifted and shivered with every passing moment. The storm's natural state was chaos, and now that it had reformed, it wanted to rage, to howl across the chamber in a cacophony of noise and violence.

Instead, I formed my shell, shiny leather and equally shiny helmet, and looked for a way out of my would-be tomb. The floor under my feet was hard-packed dirt, covered by ash and patches of glass formed from the Lightbringer's rays, but below that was rough stone. The ledge above me was far too high to reach, even with the tricks that had gotten me over the fort's exterior wall, and the door near me was every bit as imposing as I remembered, its surface barely scarred by the combined fury of the storm and the Crimson Queen's Immortals.

Stone above, below, and beside. It would take time, but I could work with that, whether I carved handholds to climb up to the ledge, or attacked the walls around the impenetrable door's frame. The question was which would be faster, and which was less likely to be heard. This remained, as far as I knew, an active fort, and I didn't want to alert whoever was out there, giving them time to summon additional Powers and start this whole cursed cycle over again.

I had just picked the ledge route, hoping that whatever door was up there would be less durable than the monster down below, when the question became moot. I could sense people coming toward me, down the same path I'd followed in my ill-considered race for Colonel Silvers' quarters. There was a muffled grunt, and the sound of something being turned, and then the door began to open, one slow inch at a time.

"Are you sure it's safe, Ziggy?"

"It's been a week. Sarge says Venom's poison doesn't last more than a few days."

"I can't help but notice *Sarge* isn't down here with us."

"And he won't help clean the place out or turn it back into a storeroom either. Welcome to life on the bottom of the pile. Now, how about you quit bitching and help pull? This damn thing weighs as much as your mom."

"You've never even met my mom."

"Then who the hell kept me up all the way past Reveille?"

Snickers from both men slipped through the growing gap. The door they were struggling with opened outward, giving me no place to hide, so I let go of my shell, whispering sweet nothings in the storm's ear as I tried to keep its pieces quiescent, a misshapen tangle of shrapnel spread across the dirt floor.

Finally, the door opened wide enough to admit the two shit-talking soldiers. They stopped dead at the sight waiting for them.

"I thought they said there wasn't nothing left of the bitch?" muttered the one who'd answered to Ziggy.

"Maybe you're thinking of *your* mama—"

"Shut the fuck up, Cory." Ziggy took a careful step into the room. "Something ain't right."

But of course, by then it was too late. I'd made sure there was nobody else nearby and seen enough of these two to feel confident neither was a Power. That meant they were just meat for the grinder. The storm surged to life around them and the soldiers' much maligned mothers were swiftly each missing a son.

I reformed my shell in the hallway.

I'd already seen how easy it was to find myself trapped in the tunnels, so I was cautious on my way out. Thankfully, the rest of the space matched the blueprints I'd been given. I took a right at the first intersection and made my way to a small chamber with a ladder leading up to the only building inside the fort that was more than one story tall, what those same blueprints had labeled the radio tower. There was one soldier inside, and the lazy bastard was asleep, so I kept my shell and cut the man's throat with his own knife. Then, I used that knife to perform open heart surgery on the electronics spread across the desk in front of him.

I'd never been much of an engineer, but I was pretty damn sure it would take a Technomancer or a miracle to put the radio back together.

There was no point in letting Raya or the Crimson Queen know I was still alive. Eventually, they would figure it out, when the reports stopped coming, and the queen sent one of her so-called Immortals out to see why. But by then, I'd be in Kansas City, and the second of all too many dominoes would have already fallen.

But first, Colonel Silvers' merry men.

I watched the fort from its own radio tower. The level of activity was distinctly different from what I'd originally observed, another sign that they'd been waiting for me, that the whole thing had been a play staged to lure me into their deadly trap. There were soldiers everywhere, drilling, marching, shoring up walls of interior buildings. Sergeants barked at their men, listened carefully to the lieutenants that came by with their own orders, then went right back to barking. The towers that ringed the walls each held four men instead of two, and they maintained a careful watch in every direction.

More than a hundred men and women were in sight, most of them armed, all of them reasonably well trained. If I'd seen the fort like this during my initial observation, I wouldn't have pressed my assault. I'd have waited for the colonel to depart, hopefully at the head of a column of soldiers I'd be able to ambush somewhere less well guarded. But that had been then and this was now. I was already *in* the fort, and the only way out was through. More importantly, I hadn't seen signs of a single Power in all the hours I'd been watching; just a shitload of Normals, the grunts of the Crimson Queen's superpowered empire. I didn't see anyone down there who could stop me.

Also? I was pretty fucking pissed.

The radio tower didn't have windows, just empty frames, because glass was expensive to transport. I dismissed my shell and the storm surged through one of those openings, spreading as it fell to the streets below, right on top of the patrol making their most recent pass.

And then there was gunfire and smoke and the howling of a storm that was always angry.

○○○

Long minutes later, I reformed my shell in the last of the watch towers, stepping over the bodies of two men and a woman to look down at their fourth, who had thrown himself off the tower to escape the storm's reach. His head was twisted to the side at an angle human necks were never supposed to turn.

The fort had held multiple companies. I didn't know which had been responsible for Eclipse's destruction, and it didn't really matter anymore, because I'd killed every person I'd encountered, from the officers all the way down to the unfortunate privates who'd ended up buried in the latrines they'd been tasked to clean.

I dropped over the exterior wall, let the storm loose, and reformed my shell as I landed. From outside, the fort still looked whole, its front gates solid and untouched. By the time the smoke of guns fired in futility cleared, the scavengers would have arrived to take their fill. In a matter of days, there would be nothing left but bone. Bone and an empty-walled monument to my new enemy's hubris.

I avoided the woods this time, following the road the colonel's men had carved out of the forest and letting it lead me from checkpoint to checkpoint. Several of those were empty, soldiers who had heard the battle, and charged back down the road to their own deaths, but the last couple had guards present, anxious but unwilling to leave their posts. I left them in shreds and pressed on until I reached the place I'd stashed my bike, tucked inside a grove of trees a few hundred feet off the old path.

It wasn't there.

I spent way too long standing in the woods, looking at that empty space, at the leaves that had fallen atop the depression where my bike had laid. Dr. Nowhere hadn't seen fit to grant me a motorcycle as part of my shell, but the truck that hit me had been carrying a dozen, and the bike I'd chosen had been one of the few to survive the crash. I'd ridden it until gas became an issue, then hunted down a Technomancer willing to convert it to something I could recharge wherever a generator was found. That bike and I had traveled from one end of the continent to the other. It was unique, as much a part of me as the storm or my shell, the one companion I'd had since the day of my birth.

And now it was gone.

Even though I'd never been much of a tracker, I knelt to look for signs in the grass. Footprints were obvious, leading deeper into the forest instead of back to the road, and there was the faintest hint of a tread that suggested my bike had been taken the same way. I followed that trail for as long as I could, and then kept going when it vanished, my senses peeled, looking for any hint of where the bike had been taken.

Instead, I ran into someone I hadn't expected, a man waiting in silence, shoulders as broad as ever.

"Two-Feathers?"

The nomad, per usual, nodded but said nothing, dark eyes never leaving the visor of my helmet. In one hand, he held the feathered spear I'd named him for. He turned and led me deeper into the forest, quiet as a whisper next to the noise I made in my leathers, to a small clearing where a dappled horse stomped its hooves nervously at the sight of me. Sunlight streamed down through the curtain of foliage to reflect off the magnificent chrome of my treasured ride.

I ran my gloves over its frame, looking for new dents or dings and finding none, and then turned to the nomad.

"If I could kiss you right now, I would. I thought this might be gone for good. But why did you move it? And how are you even down here? We're a long way from your clan's territory."

He held his hands to his face as if they were goggles, then waved in the general direction of the fort I'd just emptied.

The storm rumbled, its dissatisfaction filling the clearing.

"If you knew where the fort was, you could have sent me here directly, instead of starting me on a wild goose chase of my own." I wouldn't have had to reach out to Raya, which would have saved me a week, *and* allowed me to reach the fort without the Crimson Queen being any the wiser.

Two-Feathers shook his head, tapped his own chest, and then, with fingers pointed down, pantomimed walking.

I was starting to think his whole not talking thing was a matter of necessity, not choice. "You came on your own? To search for them?"

At his nod, I felt the storm subside, just a bit. “I should have just hired you from the start.”

He shrugged, face impassive, but I got a sense of satisfaction from him anyway. Smug bastard.

“And the reason you took my bike?”

He extended his spear, pointing south of the clearing. For the first time, I saw dark stains on the weapon’s shaft. Dried blood.

I pushed through the tree line in the indicated direction. Three bodies in fatigues were heaped in a pile, far enough away to not disturb the horse, and deep enough in the forest that the Crimson Queen’s men would have had to hunt to find them, had there been any men left to search.

“They came for the bike,” I said, returning to the clearing, “and you killed them, moved both the bike and the bodies, and then waited around for me to find you?”

He nodded again.

“It’s been a *week*. What if I had never come back?”

For the first time in our shared history, he cracked a smile. It looked good on that normally severe face. He planted his spear in the earth and then held both hands out, palms down, and rotated the right one, as if to control an invisible throttle.

“Glad I made it back then.” I ran a hand over the still-secured saddlebags. “Even so, I owe you. I have places to go and people to kill, but what can I do to repay you?”

Two-Feathers took up his spear, pointed in the direction of the soldiers he had killed and then turned and pointed a second time in the general direction of the fort.

“Yeah, they’re dead. For whatever that’s worth.” He gave a me a long look and I elaborated. “This was just a small part of the Crimson Queen’s army. It’s probably not even the only fort this side of Kansas City. Tell your elders that this woman isn’t just another warlord raiding for resources. She's looking to build an empire, and she's gathering Powers to help her do it. I'm going to see if I can cut the head off that snake, but the clans should be ready if it doesn't work out."

He nodded, dark eyes still riveted to my helmet, and then, for the second time, pointed at the unseen soldiers he'd killed and the fort. This time, he held his left hand out, palm down and patted the air.

"We're even?" At his nod, I shrugged. "Some people would say you got the better end of that deal, given that you only had to kill three soldiers, and I took down a hundred. On the other hand, you saved my bike. If you say there's no debt, I'll take it."

I raised the kickstand on my bike and pushed it through the woods back to the path, Two-Feathers and his horse on my heels. Once we reached what passed for a more typical Badlands road, a far cry from the wide and even causeway the Crimson Queen's men had laid, I swung a leg over the saddle, and said goodbye.

"It's been fun. Spread the warning to your elders, and maybe we'll see each other again someday."

My bike turned on with its usual hum, a melodic counterpoint to the storm's ever-present snarl. I eased it forward at low throttle, winding my way around a root system that had decided to make itself a home in the middle of the path.

Two-Feathers' horse stepped right over the same roots, the nomad astride and easily matching my pace.

If I could have frowned, I would have; as it was, I'm sure the smiley-face across my decal had gone a little less sunny. "Not to tell you where to go, but isn't your clan north of here, not east?"

He nodded, guiding the horse with his legs in the nomad style, and then tapped his broad chest, pointed at me, and then wiggled all the fingers on his hands in the same direction.

This fucking game of pantomime was already getting old, but once again, I understood what he was getting at.

"You're coming with me?"

Another nod.

I thought about protesting, about listing all the reasons it was a bad idea, but let it go instead. Taking out a fort of Normals was one thing but taking on the Crimson Queen and her so-called Immortals was beyond even my abilities. Especially given the power she'd displayed. I had thoughts about where I could find people with the special skills I needed, but I wasn't in a position to turn down extra muscle. Especially when the person offering was almost definitely a Power and capable as hell in the countryside we'd be traversing.

"Welcome aboard," I said, "but if we're going to be companions, I need an actual name to call you by."

He tilted his head, dark eyes glittering with what I thought was amusement, and then tapped the feathers on his spear.

Apparently, his name really *was* Two-Feathers.

Sometimes, you just had to laugh at the world.

9

Traveling with Two-Feathers slowed me down some, but I didn't hate having company on the road. Silent company, admittedly, but the nomad had a presence to him, solid and comfortable. Even better, he was great at taking care of his own needs… all that stuff like food and shelter I habitually ignored.

He wasn't bad to look at either, but we kept to opposite sides of our nightly campfires. I had things to think through regarding our current destination and what I would do when I got there, and he… well, I don't know exactly what he was doing when not hunting, cooking, cleaning, and sleeping.

Maybe communing with the sky, the way I did with the road.

Even after decades of encounters with the nomad clans, I didn't know much about them; just enough to stay on their good side, and vice versa. I spent those quiet hours of travel trying to puzzle out the mystery of why he'd invited himself along.

By the time Kansas City rolled into sight, I still didn't know. I had never played cards—any form of gambling seemed like something that might drive that transactional piece of me off the deep end—and maybe Two-Feathers didn't either, but the man had one hell of a poker face.

I turned to him as the ever-growing, ever-chaotic tent town on the city's borders came back into view. "You might want to wait here. Cartels have been leery about your kind for a while now, and security was amped up even further because of some incident that happened a few years ago. I've got business inside, but I'll be back afterwards. Shouldn't be more than a day. Two at the most."

He studied my helmet, nodded, and turned his horse to ride into the forest. In addition to the spear lashed to his saddle, he'd added three guns from the soldiers he'd killed: genuine assault weapons instead of the hunting rifles most people used in the Badlands. Those weapons were one more sign that the Crimson Queen's operation was organized and had some serious technological backing. Or a weapons supplier in the Free States, maybe. Either way, whoever I brought with me to the eventual party would need to be similarly armed, or better.

For the third time in as many weeks, I went through the tired old ceremony to enter Kansas City. No Kev this time, even though his cartel was still guarding the western gates. No Lily either, which was a shame, as I'd have liked to ask her a few questions. Instead, I bought my weekly badge and moved on, making it to the district that held Raya's house just as the sun began to set.

In retrospect, I probably should have left the bike with Two-Feathers. If Raya was now the enemy, her old cartel might be too. That made parking in their territory a risky proposition, even in the dark. On the other hand, it would have taken me three to four times as long to make the trip on my feet, and this reckoning of ours was already days overdue.

I hadn't quite reached Raya's house when light came from around the corner, strong and steady unlike anything that came from fire, and I heard the rumble of an engine in a city that hadn't seen cars in decades. I pulled to the side, in between two houses with peeling paint and empty window boxes, and peeked out as the vehicle drove through the intersection.

It was an old military jeep, whatever paint it had once worn having long since been replaced by primer gray. It was dumping out noxious fumes in thick black smoke and cruising along like neither it nor its riders had a care in the world. In the rear seats, whooping and hollering, were older men and women bearing the district cartel's colors, and in the driver's seat was the man who almost had to be their current leader, teeth gleaming gold and white as he smiled.

But riding shotgun next to him? It was the woman of the hour, Vo Binh Raya, hair flowing in the nighttime wind like she was some kind of fucking fairy tale princess.

It didn't take a genius to guess how the cartel had gotten their hands on a functional combustion engine, let alone enough gas to waste it on city joyrides. I'd have sensed the Crimson Queen's hands all over the scenario, even if Raya *hadn't* just sold me out to the woman.

I let the car drive out of view and headed on to Raya's vacant house. I didn't have a beef with the cartel—not yet anyway—so it made sense to keep our forthcoming conversation as intimate as possible. I'd charge my batteries and wait inside Raya's house for her to return.

I parked my bike in the back yard and my ass on the living room sofa where we'd last spoken, thinking about what I'd seen. There hadn't been a single vehicle in the entire fort I'd murdered, which told me the Jeep that had just torn through the streets was less common than the Crimson Queen wanted them to think. And that meant she was likely still in the process of wooing the cartel with gifts and half-truths. Was that how all her conquests went? Was every town bribed to open their gates and then conquered once it was too late for resistance?

Hell if I knew for sure. Politics wasn't something I spent a lot of time on. Governments came and went, and I had nothing to do with any of them. That was one more reason I loved the Badlands. People out here lived as they wanted to, without the watchful eye of the Free States' Capes or the outright tyranny of a Legion or Steel. And yet, where I saw open land and people living free, those burgeoning empires just saw territory free for the taking.

Humans, as a rule, pretty much sucked. Individually, there were a few gems, of course, but as soon as you gathered the species in numbers and removed personal responsibility, they became a bunch of tyrants, a thousand crowds screaming obscenities in one voice.

Maybe Dr. Nowhere hadn't broken the world quite enough.

I sat in the darkness of Raya's living room, waiting as thoughts spun through my head. The minutes turned into hours, and soon the storm wasn't the only thing itching for action. Eventually, I climbed back to my feet and did something I'd never done in all the years I'd known Raya.

I went snooping.

The former spy would tell me what she knew before the end, but she had grown up hard and cold, and any information I could find beforehand could help me corroborate a deathbed confession. Problem was, the rooms I searched were immaculately kept, and the only paper I found was a blank notepad, yellow and lined, sitting next to one of those disposable pens that had once been manufactured by the millions. There was no sign of Raya's tablet, what the Free States called a Glass, and no poorly hidden manifesto spelling out her reasons for betraying me or offering a twelve-step plan for what came next.

There was nothing I could use.

I shook my head and went out to the back where I switched batteries on the charger. The yard behind Raya's house was tiny, much like the others in the neighborhood, but almost half of that available space had long ago been allocated for a storage shed, now barely visible as a shadow in the night. I'd never seen Raya use that shed, even once, but it *was* a place I hadn't searched yet.

The discovery of a brand-new padlock on the shed's beat-to-shit door told me I was onto something. I looked at the neighboring houses, at the dark windows that suggested nobody was home, and I let the storm come, tearing through wood almost as old as I was.

After reforming my shell, I left the padlock—bright, shiny, and whole—hanging from its latch and stepped through the hole the storm had eaten in the attached door.

It was pitch black. With a growl, I went and fetched my bike, slapping in a new battery so that the other one could keep charging. A flip of a switch turned on the headlight we'd used as a spotlight on the wall in Eastwood, and the interior of the shed lit up.

The back wall had a row of shelves, and the left wall a series of metal lockers, but my gaze went to the chest freezer to the right. Without electricity, chest freezers were basically just boxes, but this one was big, and by the size of the cloud of flies hovering above it, Raya had stashed something perishable in it.

I waved aside the flies, tugged open a lid whose seal had dissolved at one corner, and found a corpse curled up on itself inside. The organs had already started to liquefy, which told me it had been at least several days since the person's death. Probably more, given the cooler. Fluids were leaking everywhere in a display that made me grateful I didn't have a stomach or a sense of smell, but I was pretty sure whoever it was had been a woman. Not just small but *petite*, with delicate bones, and—

I frowned and reached into the gore, scraping putrefied flesh away from the body's upper torso and shoulder. The woman's left collarbone showed signs of an ugly old break, years before her death. The fracture had long since rejoined, its edges rounded and smooth, but the jagged lines remained visible. I would never have seen that break if I hadn't been looking for it, if I hadn't known someone who had taken an injury just like that as an adult, leading her to seek a desk job with the cartel instead of running their espionage network from the field.

Raya. And if I had to guess, if decades of dealing in death told me anything, she'd been a corpse for over a week. Maybe even since shortly after she'd sent me off to her husband with a letter and a treasure map.

So, who the hell had I just seen riding with the cartel?

○○○

There were more than a hundred different types of Shifters in the world, but scientists during the Break had lumped them all into three general categories, and their egghead successors in the Free States had adopted those same categories when publishing the magnum opus that was their attempt to codify superpowers in general.

There were Beast Shifters, from the werewolves of ancient myth to the Weaver up north and all manner of animals—live or dead, mythological or real—in between.

There were Mineral Shifters, like Steel in the northeast, or Avalanche in the Free States, who could take on humanoid versions of their given mineral, ore, or alloy. It was a group most people, the Crimson Queen included, assumed I belonged to.

And then there were Body Shifters, fewer in number and mostly weaker too. The vast majority were barely Category Ones or Twos by the Free States' ranking system… able to change some minor aspect of their appearance on command but nothing else. Most of that group ended up in the western nation's vid scene, leveraging their ability to adjust their weight, hairstyle, or hair color while acting opposite real Capes.

As for the handful who could do more, who could take on entirely new appearances to the extreme of being able to replace someone with nobody the wiser?

I was pretty sure I'd already met one.

And that meant this woman, whoever she was, if she even was a woman at all, was almost certainly another of the Crimson Queen's Immortals. A weapon sent to assassinate the cartel's spymaster, and then replace her, making the eventual conquest of Kansas City that much easier.

As I returned to the house, I thought back to the conversation I'd had with Raya on returning from Eastwood. She'd been cold, but she was always cold. Still, hindsight highlighted all the minor changes in her reactions and behavior: the offer of tea that probably *hadn't* been a joke, the lack of interest, concern, or even knowledge about Jae-Sung and Cho-Hee. So many damn clues, but I hadn't caught a single one, had happily accepted the altered blueprints, and ridden off to get trapped in a well, like in that pre-Break dog show everyone had loved.

Raya must have already been dead by then. Given her value to the cartel, she could have even been a target before the inquiries on my behalf provoked a response that she, for once, hadn't seen coming. There was nothing I could have done to save her… but that knowledge did fuck-all to make me feel better.

Considering I'd come all this way to kill the woman, I was almost surprised by the depth of emotion I felt, knowing that she was gone. The storm spun in angry circles, hot within my shell, and my gloved fists clenched as I sat there in the darkness of a house whose owner hadn't betrayed me… who might in fact have died *because* of me.

And then I heard a key in the front door. I pushed all that shit aside, got up, and went to work.

I waited for the door to close, for the fake-Raya to take a few steps deeper into the house, and then I was on them, slapping the weapon out of their hand, and tossing them over my hip and into the living room where they'd so recently fed me fake intel.

By the time they were back on their feet, they were eight inches taller, with arms rippling with muscle and fingers that ended in claws of sharpened bone, but the storm didn't care, sweeping in to devour the flesh thrust into its midst. They pulled back bloody stumps, turned them into curving bone hooks, and the storm tore through those as well, shredding limbs and carving away the mass their power desperately tried to add.

Finally, they went limp. I reformed my shell with one hand pinning a fleshy blob with facial features to the hardwood floor, blood and bone spread in uncertain patterns around us.

"You're supposed to be dead," the Body Shifter said, in a voice that changed and warbled with every syllable. The mouth they had formed lacked teeth, just a cavity in the inhuman mass, and a small part of me wondered if they had formed new lungs or if they too spoke without them. An extra two pairs of eyes squeezed their way out from that flesh and cast about wildly, looking for an exit.

"Always verify your intel," I said. "The real Raya knew that."

○○○

I never learned the Body Shifter's name. Not because they weren't willing to tell me, but because I never asked. Didn't care at all, really. As far as I was concerned, they were just my second step on the way to payback. They *were* happy to answer every question I asked though, and the loss of more of what appeared to be their core mass put them back on the straight and narrow whenever those answers started to stray into the realm of fiction.

Nobody in the Badlands had time for fiction, least of all me.

As I'd expected, they were one of the Crimson Queen's pet Powers, the so-called Immortals, and had plenty to say about my young adversary's empire. Where they were based out of, what their numbers were like, even how their communications worked, although that last bit wouldn't do me much good, given that the protocols changed on a weekly basis.

I forced myself to listen to every detail, ignoring the constant shifts in the organic blob beneath me and the muttering of a storm that was far from satiated. I let them talk until the words went dry, until a second mouth formed to start begging for freedom and mercy. And then I let my shell fall away, let the storm come forth to take what it wanted.

When it was done, there was no piece left larger than a thumb, and not a single scrap scattered around the living room so much as twitched. But I had never encountered a Body Shifter this strong before, and if there was one thing everyone knew about Shifters, it was that they healed. So, I piled up furniture in the middle of the room, got the hotplate in Raya's kitchen going, and lit the whole place on fire, using pieces of the imposter I'd carved off as kindling.

Even then, I wasn't done. I stuffed the tablet the fake Raya had brought back with her into my saddlebags and dragged the chest freezer with the real Raya's corpse into the street in front of a house already showing signs of the fire inside. I left that freezer open, with Raya's body exposed, and a note written on the yellow notepad.

You've been lied to, it read. *The Crimson Queen killed one of your own, Vo Binh Raya, more than a week ago, and replaced her with a Body Shifter. That Shifter's death was free, but it's on you to clean the rest of your fucking house.*

I didn't bother signing it. Just hopped on my bike, and drove into the darkness, Raya's house a bonfire in my mirror.

10

I wasn't sure if Two-Feathers would still be there when I made it back from Kansas City, but sure enough, he rode his horse out of the woods to meet me, ignoring the looks from passing wagon trains. With Wichita and Kansas City having both been recognized by the Free States, trade between the two cities was at an all-time high, but few merchants had expanded their routes into nomad territory.

I dismounted from my bike just long enough to release and reform my shell, dispersing the ash that had dusted me in grey flakes on my way out of Raya's former district. There was nothing I could do for my bike, but we had a long way to go, and by the time we arrived at our destination, that ash would be indistinguishable from the more usual road dust.

"All done here," I told Two-Feathers. "And I got some new information. Looks like the Crimson Queen is headquartered out of New Memphis. That's a few weeks to a month from here by horse."

He nodded and said nothing, as usual.

"But we're not going straight there," I continued. "I'm sure you're hell on two legs with that spear, but even if we could figure out a way past the queen's army and into her palace, she's got dozens of Powers with her at any given time." To say nothing of her telekinetic forcefield. "We're going to need help. There's a group of Powers—let's call them mercenaries—that I know. Last I heard they were operating out of Texas."

He nodded a second time and started to turn his horse to the southwest, but I raised a hand to stop him.

"Unfortunately, *because* they're mercenaries, they don't work for free. So, we're headed over to what used to be Arkansas, where I have a line on a possible buried treasure. And there's someone else I need to look up in that area. If he's still alive, he might be useful."

This time he waited to make sure I was done, but as I turned my bike to head southeast, charting a course that would skirt Kansas City, the nomad and his horse fell in behind me.

I still didn't know why he was coming along, but I had to admit Two-Feathers was growing on me fast. Decent looking, great shoulders, didn't talk a woman's ear off, and best of all, he took directions like a champ.

We didn't run into any problems on that first day out of Kansas City, nor had I expected to. Proximity to one of the Badlands' few major cities was itself a deterrent for anyone other than the cartels who ran that city. As we headed southeast, we left behind the few remaining merchant trains and rode on into the emptiness that typified the region. Dr. Nowhere's dream had done more than just give random humans superpowers; it had reshaped the world entirely. Topography had changed, whole cities had disappeared, and creatures I'd never found in any pre-Break books had come into being and flourished.

The years after the dream, that time period humans called the Break, had only amplified those changes. Places that survived the dream fell to the chaos that followed it, even in the Free States, one of the rare places where Powers worked *with* the government to maintain order. In those early years, I'd ridden through bustling cities that would become little more than corpse-filled ruins by the following winter. A continent that was already mostly empty had become even more so, miles and miles of open land, with only a handful of cities dotting the expanse, each a far cry from what they had historically been.

The nomad clans seemed the only ones truly happy with the change.

As we rode, I filled in Two-Feathers on what I'd learned from Raya's killer. The Crimson Queen's army wasn't huge, but she'd made the recruitment of Powers a priority and that had made all the difference. In the Free States, Powers were citizens, like everyone else, and the choice of career was an individual one. Even those who eventually became Capes did so as independent contractors, working alongside the government instead of under it, paid through endorsements and celebrity status.

The Crimson Queen, on the other hand, operated like one of the Eastern warlords, if on a scale none of them had managed. Every Power within her empire's borders, whether born there or purchased from slavers, was property of the state, drafted into the military and fully weaponized on its behalf. The Immortals were a subset of that larger group, an elite shock force of Powers who could reshape battlefields all on their own.

As things stood, I was confident the Free States would win any conflict between the two nations, but that balance of power would shift as time went on, as the Crimson Queen added to her growing collection of Powers. Dominion, on his own, was enough to forestall any invasion of the Free States, but last I'd heard, he was dying, and the country didn't have another Full-Five waiting in the wings to replace him.

Not that the other nation was any of my concern. Beneath all the pretty words and high-minded sentiments, the Free States had their own methods of exploitation; *freedom* was something only available to those who worked within that system. Eventually, they would expand into the Badlands too, just like the queen was currently doing, and while their conquest would be less bloody than hers, I wasn't sure the result would be any better.

But geopolitical cage matches weren't my concern either. Nations would rise and fall, and I would survive and even thrive in the chaos both actions brought. Despite all I had learned, my interest wasn't political; it was personal. Which brought me right back to the Crimson Queen and her growing empire.

I didn't know the first thing about fighting an army, let alone one that included more Powers than I'd seen in decades of existence, but that had never been my goal. I'd leave that sort of thing to other nations, to trained militaries. My focus, the job I'd taken on behalf of the dead, was on balancing the scales, and that meant bringing down the bubbly little psychopath herself.

Maybe the Crimson Queen's burgeoning kingdom would tear itself apart in the aftermath of her death. Maybe it wouldn't. I didn't care much one way or the other. I wasn't in the business of empire-building.

"It'll have to be a small group," I told Two-Feathers over the campfire that night. "People with the skills to get in, take down the queen, and get the hell back out."

He just nodded, his horse making more noise than he did as it went to town on the grass buffet nature had thoughtfully provided.

"Getting in may be the easy part. Killing the woman will be harder, but I've got some thoughts about that too. It's getting out that's going to be bloody, especially if we can't keep a lid on things. Are you sure you want to be a part of this?"

That earned me a flat-eyed stare, and I shrugged.

"Alright then. Wish you could tell me why, but I don't hate the company. Get some sleep. I want to be gone as soon as the sun's up."

○○○

The second day out of Kansas City started a lot like the first: quiet wilderness and empty space. Two-Feathers' horse had finally gotten used to my presence, and we rode side by side on trails that might once have been roads or even highways. We stopped beside a stream to water the horse and refill the nomad's canteens, and then were back in the saddle again, counting the passing miles by the sun's ever-changing position in the sky.

One afternoon, we crested a hill and almost plowed right into a herd of deer, hundreds of them filling the space ahead of us. Instead of scattering at our approach, they turned to watch us with eyes that showed far too much intelligence for comfort. A few does stepped aside and a buck moved toward us, his wide rack of antlers crackling with a visible electrical charge. He bowed until those antlers were pointed in our direction, and then swung his head to the side.

I'd never been ordered about by a deer before, but I'd also never seen one that used lightning as decoration; we left the path in the indicated direction and took a long detour around the stag and its herd.

"Have you ever seen anything like that?" I asked Two-Feathers, once we were back on what passed for a road. "Smart deer with lightning powers?"

He shook his head.

"Me neither. There's always something new."

Our second encounter was less peaceful. We were riding through yet another forest—or maybe the same one; I couldn't quite tell—when a roar from ahead brought us both to a stop, the nomad's horse shifting nervously from side to side. We parked both bike and horse and advanced on foot, Two-Feathers ahead of me because he was a damn ghost in the woods, and I was anything but.

As we crept through the trees, the roars continued, followed by the occasional scream of what I figured might be a horse or two. By the time the source of all that noise came into view, I already knew what to expect.

What had once been a wagon was now on its side and in several pieces, the horses that had pulled it dying or dead. Two human bodies, merchants or settlers by the looks of them, lay strewn across the open space, and a creature as big as the wagon was devouring a third. The beast looked like an unholy blend of bear, shark, and wolf that had been turned inside out. In addition to six eyes and an extra set of legs, it had red and white pebbled flesh instead of fur.

This was something I *had* seen before, and such encounters never, ever ended well.

"Fucking howlers," I murmured. "Let's avoid it if we can."

Two-Feathers met my gaze and then gestured back down to the ravaged wagon.

The howler was looking straight at us. Its roar shook the trees of the forest, exposing a maw that was almost all teeth.

"Ah hell," I managed to say, and then it was on us.

○○○

I took half a breath to make sure that Two-Feathers was safely out of the way and then dismissed my shell. The howler charged right through the storm, taking a hundred cuts in the process, but didn't slow, kicking a tree over as it spun back around. It pawed the ground like a bull preparing to charge, claws digging furrows as wide and deep as a wagon's wheel, then paused and lifted its grotesque head.

I looked at the trees around us. The wind had shifted and was now blowing from the way we'd come. And that meant the howler had caught the scent of fresh meat.

With another roar, it spun again and ran, not so much fleeing the storm as chasing after a far more appetizing meal: Two-Feathers' horse. The storm surged forward in pursuit, but for sheer speed, the howler was in a different league entirely. There was no way in hell I'd catch it before Two-Feathers' horse became just the memory of a two-bite snack.

Thankfully, the nomad himself was already in action. A spear lanced out of the woods, driving into the howler's broad chest with inhuman force, and then Two-Feathers himself was there, not chasing the howler like I was, but standing in its path. The assault rifle in his hands started a conversation I couldn't hear over the storm, bullets tearing into the howler's snout, maw, and eyes from a hundred feet away, then fifty, then ten.

Much like the storm's attacks, all that gunfire barely inconvenienced the howler. It did veer to the side, however, crashing through one tree, then another as Two-Feathers continued to pour ammunition into its passing form, and *that* let the storm catch up and attack from behind. Jagged steel slashed through tendons as thick as suspension bridge wires, savaging anything that seemed pivotal to keeping all that mass up and moving.

The first rear leg went slack, and as the storm moved to encircle its target, the howler turned on us both, paws lashing out to send Two-Feathers tumbling.

The beast's hide was too thick to penetrate on a single pass, but the storm was an organism with a thousand teeth. Those teeth dug into wounds made on previous passes, burrowing deeper until the blood truly began to flow, even as the howler's own triple rows of teeth closed on air or swallowed the occasional metal fragment that did even more damage from the inside.

And yet still the creature wasn't done, multiple tons of fury with only the kill on its miniscule brain. It tore down another tree, and branches swatted aside fragments of the storm, creating rifts in the cocoon of steel I'd created. I pulled back the pieces that were left, focused them into a tight ball of shifting malice, and waited.

A shape in the forest resolved itself as Two-Feathers returned to the fight, leaping down from one of the few trees still standing to land atop the howler. He tugged his spear free of the creature's chest, and then, balancing on the ever-shifting mass of muscle, drove it back in, just behind the skull. The howler staggered but its next turn threw the nomad back into the woods, spear still in hand. I could feel its angry roar even if I couldn't quite hear it.

Which was when I sent the remaining mass of the storm straight down its throat.

When it was done, it took an almost embarrassingly long time to dig back out of the dead howler's belly. I let the storm hover for a moment above its kill, as disparate pieces rejoined the greater whole, and then reformed my shell a few feet away, bright and shiny like the day I'd been born. Two-Feathers was further down the path, battered but not broken, standing next to my bike and the horse who had stood its ground through the whole damn fight. He mounted that horse and waited.

"You're a Stalwart?" I asked, before remembering the nomads didn't use the Free States' naming system. "You have strength, I mean? Strength, speed, and agility?"

He nodded.

"And you can ride and cook? How the hell are you still single?"

Something like a smile flickered in his night-black eyes.

ooo

We stopped early that evening, next to another stream, this one shallow enough that we could see the bottom and verify nothing was hiding in it. Freshwater was less dangerous than the oceans, but it only took one tentacled horror to ruin an evening.

Two-Feathers' canteens didn't need much refilling, but his horse was happy to drink some more. The real reason we stopped was so that the nomad could head downstream and wash the filth and gore off first himself and then his clothes. Some people didn't have the luxury of instant laundry by way of reforming their shell.

I waited by the campfire but can't deny that my senses were oriented in Two-Feathers' direction the whole time. This wasn't the first howler I'd killed—although a pack of the monsters was normally enough to drive even me away—but the post-battle high was more pronounced than usual. Maybe because it hadn't just been me. Even if I hadn't won the fight, I could have walked away from it, eventually... but Two-Feathers and his horse?

There was a special kind of adrenaline rush when the stakes were truly life and death. I'd experienced it before, traveling with others, and more often than not, it led to the same thing.

Two-Feathers returned from the stream to find me waiting, the fire painting my naked body in shades of crimson. Clothes were as much a part of my shell as the figure beneath, but I could choose not to form them. Only my helmet remained, and that was because Dr. Nowhere, being a man, had focused on what I looked like from the neck down, and left shit undone from the neck up. In a very real sense, the helmet and its decal *were* my face.

The one person who'd seen me without it had taken two steps away and vomited, and that had damn sure put an end to any thoughts of sex that night. The helmet was weird and maybe a bit off-putting, especially during sex, but I'd found it was rarely a deal breaker for men confronted with a 6'2" naked woman whose body had literally been built by God.

"Since we stopped early for the night," I said to Two-Feathers, in a voice free of the storm's usual snarl, "I thought we might want to celebrate still being alive."

His eyes wandered across my naked form, then he shook his head, almost as if to himself, turned, and went to check on his horse.

The fire popped and crackled in amusement. I coughed, clearing a throat that didn't need it, would never need it, and reformed my shell a second time, bringing back the clothes I'd been born in, as a whole new feeling crept in to displace the usual post-combat horniness. I didn't have teeth to grind, but the storm made a noise all its own.

Next time, I'd just let the howler eat his damn horse.

11

Over the next week, we crossed from Missouri into Arkansas. Not that either state existed anymore, of course, except as inaccurate lines on out-of-date maps. The town my next recruit lived in was deep in the mountains and only a day's ride to our south, but I had decided to head straight for the treasure instead. I'd lost a full week of time thanks to the queen's Immortals and couldn't help but remember the interest Eastwood's mayor had shown in Jae-Sung's treasure. The last thing I needed was to show up late and find he'd sent someone down to steal it away.

Relations between Two-Feathers and me were a little bit chillier after his rejection, but by the end of the week, I'd put it in my rearview mirror, just like the howler corpse that even buzzard-sized crows knew better than to scavenge. It wasn't the first time I'd been turned down, and it sure as shit wouldn't be the last. If life had taught me anything, it was that fewer things were worth making a fuss over than most people realized. If something reached that bar, you fought and you bled for it, but everything else? You had to let that shit go or it'd eat you up from the inside.

Even the people who *didn't* have a storm living inside them.

The sun was an hour or two from setting when we forded our first serious river, a tributary from the lake that straddled the former state border to our northeast. For once, I was the one slowing us down, following the river downstream until I found shallows where I could carry my bike across. The motorcycle was fine for driving through rain but submerging it in water was a sure-fire way to have some bit of electronics go wrong, and the Technomancer who'd originally retrofitted it for me was long dead.

As I set the bike back down, Two-Feathers was giving me a considering look.

"You're not the only one with muscles," I told him, reforming my shell to repair whatever damage I'd done carrying a bike that weighed three times my own weight.

That river was the first landmark that Raya had mentioned in her directions to Jae-Sung. We camped nearby, far enough from the water that we'd hear if anything crawled up out of it to come for a midnight snack. The next morning, we headed east, directly into the rising sun. For as long as we could, anyway; the terrain had turned mountainous days earlier, and while the roads had long since gone to shit and now wove about the landscape like teenagers after an all-day bender, they were better than trying to forge our own path over the increasingly steep peaks.

On our fifth day in Arkansas, just after the mountains had transitioned back into hills, we came across Raya's second landmark. This one was also a river, but instead of crossing it, we followed it south. The Badlands were generally considered to be everything west of Kansas City and east of the Free States, but Arkansas was just as empty. Maybe even more so. We passed only two towns on our journey into the state, and the people there hid behind their walls, guns at the ready.

It felt kind of like home… which was enough to remind me that home didn't exist anymore, stirring up the storm even mid-ride.

By the time we spotted the rusted old water tower that was Raya's final landmark, we were only a few weeks' ride from the Crimson Queen's capital city and stronghold. The irony wasn't lost on me… we'd traveled to my target's doorstep just so we could turn back around, go to Texas, then turn around *again*, and head to New Memphis.

There were times I wished Dr. Nowhere had made me a pilot instead of a rider. Hadn't been any airplanes in a very, very long time, but maybe I could have found a helicopter or something and paid that same Technomancer to make it fly.

We camped at the water tower because the sun was already disappearing behind the distant mountains, the increasingly early sunsets one more reminder that winter was on its way. Two-Feathers set a small fire while I unleashed the storm to drive away the bat-like things who had taken up residence in the water tower's decrepit shell. There was no sign that anyone had been here recently, even to the nomad's vastly superior tracking abilities, and that eased some of the tension I'd been feeling since first realizing this treasure had become a necessary part of my still-forming plan.

Assuming the treasure was as valuable as Raya had said, anyway. In the letter to Jae-Sung, she had described it as loot from a failed mission that she'd never made it back down to claim, but that description left a wide range of possibilities, and the men I was looking to hire would want something that spent easily.

I settled in next to the fire as Two-Feathers took up a spot beyond its light. The big nomad had insisted he share the watch every night, even though I didn't need sleep, and I'd stopped trying to fight it. Instead, I lay back, helmet on my saddlebags and looked up at the stars just now making their appearance in the cloud-stricken sky. Their light had struggled for thousands or even millions of years just to reach our tired old shithole.

I had to wonder how disappointed they were with what they found.

The next morning, we counted our steps from the base of the water tower to one outcrop of rock among many on the nearby hill. I used Two-Feathers' spear to break up the dry earth beneath, and then dug down almost a foot, until I found something hard that echoed when I tapped it.

It was the work of another few minutes to unearth the object, but when it was done, we had a metal box, half as wide as one of my saddlebags, and several inches deep. It was heavy as hell too, even though my shell made me significantly stronger than the average person. I set it down on the mound of dirt we'd recently excavated. A latch and a lock held the lid shut.

"Want to do the honors?" I asked Two-Feathers. I could have bashed the thing open, or maybe even torn through it with the storm, but didn't want to risk damaging anything delicate inside.

With a nod, he took hold of the padlock with one hand, pushing down on the box with the other, and exhaled in a short, sharp breath as he pulled away. The padlock stayed whole, but the latch proved less durable, tearing out of its frame with an audible squeal. He tossed the padlock aside and carefully opened the lid.

Raya hadn't been lying.

On the left and right side of the box were stacks of thick gold coins, forming columns like you'd see in pre-Break houses. Each coin was embossed with symbols I didn't recognize, and twice as heavy individually as Raya's tablet in my saddlebags.

Prior to the Break, gold had reportedly served as a kind of alternative currency to the US dollar. The collapse of the federal government, and the eventual rise and fall of city-states and fledgling nations had birthed a whole new set of currencies. Few of those currencies were recognized outside of their respective borders, and that had brought gold back into prominence as a universal standard.

Many of the smaller towns throughout the Badlands still worked on a barter system, but for the rest, even the metropolises on the coasts, gold was worth far more than it weighed. These four stacks of coins represented more money than I had ever seen in my life.

They weren't the box's only contents either. In the middle, flanked by those stacks of coins, was a faded velvet pouch, pulled tight with a corded drawstring. I loosened that string and fished out a handful of glittering gems, rubies, emeralds, and diamonds, their cut edges refracting the morning light.

"Holy shit. This is a fortune." In fact, it was far *too* much, and I didn't even need the twist of metal in my core to tell me so. Jae-Sung had hired me to kill Eastwood's raiders, yeah, but a handful of coins would have more than covered that service.

I couldn't take the treasure for myself. Not all of it. But I didn't want to rebury it either, when Eastwood's mayor might succumb to greed at any time and send some of his own men on the weeks-long ride to collect the treasure. Most of these riches weren't mine to take, but they weren't his either. This treasure was for Jae-Sung and his daughter, and I would make damn sure they got what they were owed, especially since I'd cost them the life of the woman who gave it.

"We'll take it with us," I finally said out loud, just in case Two-Feathers cared. "But it's not all mine to use. When we're done, I'll make sure it gets to where it belongs."

The nomad shrugged, which could have pretty much meant anything, but at least he didn't protest. I dropped my handful of gems back into the bag, tossed the bag into the box, and then stopped. Below the muted clinking of precious stones, there was another sound, an echo of the bag's initial thump. I dumped out the coins and the gems, ostensibly emptying the box. Except… the interior base of that box was a good half-inch higher than it should have been, based on the width of its walls.

Secret compartments inside buried treasure chests?

I already missed Raya.

I ran a gloved finger around the edges of the box's false floor but couldn't find the entry-point. Next, I examined the exterior. There wasn't much to recommend it: four unadorned metal walls and a base, remarkable only for their relatively pristine conditions. A seam near the bottom of those walls indicated where the bottom had been attached or welded or… whatever it was pre-Break factories did to make the thousand and one meaningless items the citizens of the time had been unable to live without.

Part of me just wanted to smash the thing open or have Two-Feathers stab it with his pointy best friend, but I forced myself to keep searching. Whatever was in the false floor had to be significant if Raya had used gems and gold-fucking-coins as mere distractions.

Finally, I found an almost imperceptible vertical ridge in the seal, and then a second on the opposite side of the box. Putting pressure on both ridges triggered a soft click and the floor of the box popped open to reveal the compartment I'd been looking for.

I didn't have to breathe, but I held that breath anyway as I slowly eased the compartment open.

No gold this time. No jewels. Just paper. Stacks and stacks of paper, in surprisingly decent condition, and covered in hand-drawn charts and diagrams and tiny text. That text was in English, I thought, but very little of it was intelligible, and even the pictures resisted interpretation. As best I could tell, these were plans or manufacturing schematics, but I couldn't tell what the end products were supposed to be.

This was the hidden treasure?

Two-Feathers seemed as mystified as I was, so I tucked the pages back into their secret compartment, pressed it closed, and then put the gold and gems back in on top. I was many things, but an engineer wasn't one of them. I'd have to find someone trustworthy with the skills to decipher those plans before I knew what we had found.

In the meantime, there was work to be done.

I shut the lid and turned to my saddlebags, emptying the contents of one bag into the other so that there'd be space for Raya's treasure. Even then, the weight distribution was a bit off, but I had no intention of splitting up the gold coins when it would only double the chances of someone seeing them.

Two-Feathers' horse raised its head as we carried the saddlebags back to my bike. The grass around the creature had been cropped low while we dug, and the beast looked rested and halfway complacent. Sometimes, horses were as dumb as humans.

"Hope you enjoyed your break," I told it. "Because we're leaving again in ten."

Much like Two-Feathers himself, it didn't bother to respond.

○○○

Days later, we reached a town in the mountains. If it had a name, I'd never learned it. There was no wall, even though it was larger than Eastwood, but the place was so remote that the only thing its residents had to worry about was wildlife, and even then, only during the annual migrations.

With winter on the way, our visit had come right in the middle of those migrations, but I hadn't had much choice. By the time we returned from Texas, these mountains would be clogged with snow. It was now or never, and I'd chosen now. As we rode in, Two-Feathers kept an eye on the skies above us, looking for both storm clouds and winged terrors.

There were a handful of people on the streets, but none of them confronted us as we moved past. This was the sort of place where people kept to themselves, coming together only when survival was at stake. Two strangers, even a nomad and someone who looked like me, didn't really rate.

I led us to the far side of the town, took a right, and looked for a house with blue shutters, only to almost ride right past it. Two decades had made their mark and the once-blue shutters were now as worn as the rest of the place, bare fragments of peeling paint clinging to wooden frames. I put down my kickstand, dismounted, and crossed the dusty street to bang on the door with a gauntleted hand.

At first, there was only silence, but then I heard footsteps inside. The door swung open to reveal a single room with an unmade bed, a hotplate on the floor, and a small, older man in rough spun clothing. His eyes, almost lost in a maze of wrinkles, widened as he looked up into the helmet that was my face.

"You." His voice was a whisper.

"Hello, Evan."

12

The little man straightened up, spine stiffening. "That's not my name. It was *never* my name, not really. These days, I go by Miles." He paused, glancing past me to see if anyone was nearby, eyes barely even pausing on Two-Feathers, and his voice dropped even further. "Were you just in the area? Decided to stop by?"

I shook my head. "I'm calling in that favor you owe me. You're going to help us out."

"With what?"

"A job."

Any color left in his face fled for safer territories.

"I'm not a killer."

I let the storm creep into my voice. "There are a lot of people who would say otherwise, if they could."

"That was—"

"One favor," I said, cutting off whatever meaningless defense he'd been about to mount. "Whatever I needed, and no questions asked. Those were the terms."

"That was twenty years ago!"

"Sixteen years, eight months, and a handful of days." To be honest, I was guessing on that last part. It's not like we traveled with a calendar or anything.

He gave me the sort of look harder men had failed to master. "And if I say no? You'll kill me?"

I let his angry glare slide off my helmet and its cold-faced smile. "Death wouldn't balance things out at all now, would it? I'd take you back instead. They still remember you, you know. The official story is that you were allowed to leave, but in secret, they still wonder how you got away. Pretty sure they've still got room for you in the Hole."

Resistance crumbled like sugar in a rainstorm, taking the steel in his spine with it. He turned away and sighed as he bent to drag an old rucksack out from under his bed. "Fine. Where are we going?"

"West," I said. "To pick up some reinforcements. Then back east again. And Evan?"

He looked back over one shoulder.

"Pack whatever you want to keep. You're not coming back here when we're done. I'll find you someplace a little bit more cosmopolitan."

"That's the first halfway decent thing you've said," he muttered. "Did you know they have a rule here? *You only eat what you grow.* Who does that?"

"I'd think you'd be happy to get your hands in the dirt."

"I'm not a Druid. Growing things isn't my specialty *or* my passion. Lately, I've even found myself missing sim-rations. *Sim-rations!"*

"You'll get your share of meat on the road," I promised.

"Next time, maybe just lead with that?" He dumped an armful of loose clothing into the rucksack, along with a few other possessions, and leaned past me to look out into the street. "Hello there, young man. My name is Miles. I'm sorry she dragged you into whatever this is."

Two-Feathers, as was his wont, said nothing at all. I took the rucksack from Evan and held it out to the nomad.

"Miles will ride with me until we get him a mount, but you and your horse will have to carry his gear."

He sketched a lazy salute and took the bag from my hands.

"That's Two-Feathers," I told Evan. "He doesn't speak and he's not even half as funny as he thinks he is."

The nomad was already turning to position Evan's rucksack on the back of his horse, but I saw one corner of his mouth crook upward.

ooo

We left town the same way we'd come in, following the path as it curved its way down to older and flatter peaks. Some things hadn't changed in sixteen years: Evan kept a death grip on me as we rode, as if one bump would send him flying off the bike to his death. If he'd been stronger or I'd needed to breathe, it might have been a problem. As it was, I just ignored the human-sized tick on my back and focused on keeping his fears from coming true.

It took us days to make it back over the mountains, headed west this time instead of north. We had more hands to work with when we stopped each night, but everything seemed to take longer anyway, Two-Feathers now hunting for two instead of one, as Evan pitched a tent that had to be almost as old as I was. I'd burned through several batteries going up and down mountains, and Evan's extra weight, minimal as it was, added to that mounting cost. I wasn't truly worried—I had more than half my bag of batteries left—but memories of the early days, when I'd had one charge and no option but to push my motorcycle to the next town if I ran out, kept me conservative. We'd need to stop at one of the towns ahead of us with generators or solar panels so that I could recharge.

Many towns in the Badlands had energy these days, despite the lack of a grid or ready access to fuel. Most of that was courtesy of the Mission, who had been touring the countryside for years, bringing charity—including solar panels and generators—from the Free States to the unwashed masses. The leader of the Mission had been a friend, insofar as I had friends, but he was dead now, and I found myself wondering whether the Mission itself was still running.

My hermitage for the past three years had left me more than a bit ignorant about the world at large. In a way, I'd been doing the same thing as Evan… hiding away from a world that didn't make sense anymore. And now here we both were, together again, getting ready to assassinate a monarch.

I was pretty sure there was a lesson in there somewhere, but what that lesson was remained elusive.

Do the job and move the hell on. That was the plan. It had always been the plan, and if this one job was both personal and a hell of a lot larger than most, it didn't change the basic math.

"So, what exactly *are* we doing?" asked Evan for the twentieth time. The little man was warming his hands at a campfire that seemed more and more insufficient as the nights grew longer and colder.

"I told you already: heading west, then back east."

"East where?"

I borrowed a page from Two-Feathers and said nothing. After a moment, he turned back to the fire.

"I just don't get why it's a secret," he grumbled.

"Someone needs to die."

"I figured as much. But you don't need *me* for that."

"You're part of the plan to get us in." I waved off whatever he had been about to say in response. "Or out. But the specifics of that plan depend on information I don't have yet. Once we've hired the rest of our crew and reached the target, I'll know better how you fit. Now, eat your damn rabbit and get some sleep."

Not sure exactly why I didn't just tell him we were going to New Memphis, other than the knowledge that he'd truly lose his shit if I did. Evan had a thing about cities—with reason—and I didn't want to risk his protests turning into outright insurrection. I was pretty sure I'd need him when all was said and done, and despite my threats, I had no intention of turning him in.

I rose and left the camp behind, dropping my shell as soon as I was at a safe distance, but the man's complaints chased me into the darkness, somehow audible even over the storm's metal and fury. I was starting to regret not waiting to pick him up on our way back through, coming winter be damned.

The next morning reminded me why I hadn't. I reformed my shell to find the skies above us thick and dark. Two-Feathers nodded to the western horizon where we could see a wave of rain making its way in our direction. When that storm reached the peaks we'd just left, it would become snow and that narrow path to Evan's former town would turn deadly.

Even at our current elevation, we were only a few weeks away from snowfall. As it was, the coming rain would make for muddy trails that would slow us even further.

"You really fucked up this world, didn't you, *Dad?"* I asked the distant sky, hours later, as rain came down around us in sheets.

The only reply was the wind whipping past my helmet, and the squelch of tires through increasingly wet dirt.

ooo

The rain fell for three days, the offending weather system content to stall out above us and pound the earth until streams were overflowing their banks and trees were collapsing under the weight of their own branches. After the first day, conditions became too dangerous for travel, and Evan and Two-Feathers huddled in the darkness, waiting on higher ground next to a cold fire not even the nomad could get started. I eyed the smaller man, wondering if he was going to do anything to build a better shelter than the tent he'd brought with him, but he appeared resigned to cold, damp misery instead.

I had already removed my motorcycle's battery and tucked it away inside the weatherproof saddlebags. Now, I released my shell and set the storm loose to greet its natural-born cousin—steel and rain, thunder and iron, each relentless and implacable in their own ways.

I didn't have eyes to see the picture we painted across the sky, but the storm was satisfied and so was I.

By the time the rain finally broke, Evan had been reduced to a mess of snot and slobber. Two-Feathers had eventually stashed some wood inside the tent to keep it dry and had a fire lit as soon as the rain was gone, but our little companion didn't seem to feel the heat, red-nosed and shaking even when seated a hair's width away from the crackling flames.

Travel was a young man's game. It was all too easy for me to forget that. After a day, everything had dried out, but Evan's condition stayed the same. Just a cold, I was pretty sure, but it was far too easy for minor illnesses to turn into something worse, something that could prove fatal to humans in all their fragility.

Two-Feathers wrapped the smaller man in one of his own blankets, red and black with a star pattern picked out in thread. Once I was mounted on my motorcycle, he tied Evan to my back before retreating to a horse whose rolled eyes and dancing hooves made it clear he was more than done with our shit.

"Why didn't you build a better shelter?" I asked my passenger.

"I don't use my power anymore."

"Ever?"

"Ever." He sneezed and sent a wad of phlegm flying past my shoulder. This was going to be fun.

"You know you'll have to for this job, right?"

"Yeah." His voice dropped even further. "But only when I must. And you'll be the one to blame when it all goes wrong."

"I can live with that."

We stopped at the first town we found, some shithole I'd never been to before that had both solar and something they tried to pass off as an inn. Two-Feathers and I traded manual labor for the price of a room for Evan and battery charging for me, and spent the next week there, helping the dozen or so families repair their town wall and dig a new well. Two-Feathers even pitched in with diagnosing the intermittent issues they'd had with their solar harnessing, leaving me to approach the nomad after the day's work was done.

"I didn't realize you knew your way around solar panels."

He said nothing, as usual, but his body language was pure, unadulterated smugness.

"Did you go to school in the Free States, or were you taught by someone in the clans?"

Two-Feathers nodded.

"You do realize that wasn't a yes or no question?"

He nodded again, and this time, his smile came fully into view.

If I had eyes, I'd have rolled them like a teenager being told to do her chores. Instead, I just shook my head and ignored the way that smile once again softened his otherwise chiseled features. I'd already been down that road and it was a dead end.

"Fine. Keep your secrets… but if something goes wrong with my bike, you better believe I'm going to come to you to fix it."

Dark eyes flicked to where I'd leaned the motorcycle against the wall and came back to my visor. The nomad shrugged, which could have meant anything at all.

By the end of the week, Evan was not only back on his feet, but ready to go. And that, of course, is when we ran into more problems, in the form of a small crowd of men standing between us and the newly fixed gate.

Their leader was named Thomas, although I hadn't figured out yet whether that was his first name or last. He'd been the person I negotiated our labor exchange with, and I didn't like how greasy his smile had become in the days since.

I was pretty sure I knew what this was about, and equally certain it was going to end in a different fashion than Thomas expected.

"Can we help you with something, Thomas?"

"It occurred to me," he said, confident as only someone backed by another half-dozen men can be, "that we let you stay in our lovely town for a week, taking care of your man, and feeding the three of you, and all you did was address a few maintenance issues we could have addressed ourselves. Does that seem fair to you?"

"That was the deal." I didn't bother pointing out that I hadn't eaten a thing. That wasn't what this was all about anyway.

"Yes, and part and parcel of the hospitality we chose to offer to simple travelers. But then, you're not just simple travelers, are you? Not when you're carrying enough wealth to buy a whole block in one of those fancy cities back east?"

And there it was. I'd been pretty sure someone at the inn had gone through my saddlebags while we were out working but hadn't made a big deal about it given that none of the contents were missing. Seems that had been a mistake.

"Most of that isn't mine to give," I said, "and the rest isn't yours to take."

"Please," said Evan, stepping between me and the crowd. "Just let us go. This is not a fight you want."

The storm shifted inside of me, gnashing its metal teeth, but I stepped back and let the little man say his piece.

"The woman behind me," he continued, "is a Power."

Some of the men behind Thomas shifted and muttered, but he shrugged. "So?"

"She doesn't eat, she doesn't sleep, and I swear on the life of my mother that if you get in her way, she will not stop until every one of you is dead and left in pieces too small to merit burial. Please," he added, "for your sake and mine, don't invite that evil into this place."

The mutterings intensified, one man going so far as to shake Thomas' shoulder, but their leader looked unconvinced. I stepped past Evan to stand visor to eye with the suicidal townie.

"We had a deal," I said, letting the storm's fury grow around us like the buzzing of a thousand hornets.

He tried to look through the visor, like everyone does, and when that failed, looked past me instead, to the small man standing behind me, whose sincerity was so genuine even I could feel it.

Finally, Thomas stepped back and nodded.

"You're right. We did have a deal. Be on your way."

I rode until the town had faded in my rearview mirror before pulling off into the grass. "You never told me your mother was still alive, Evan."

"It's *Miles* now, and she's not." His voice was slightly muffled against my back, unaware that we had come to a stop. "But I don't think she'd mind me using her memory to prevent a massacre."

Two-Feathers leaned out of his saddle just far enough to pat Evan on the shoulder.

"Yeah," I agreed, speaking from a place of motherless ignorance, "I guess she probably wouldn't."

13

Travel in the Badlands was always a challenge, but doing so on the cusp of winter really had me regretting my life choices. The storm that tried to drown us out had come out of the west, and as we moved in that direction, we found the countryside's rivers and streams filled to the point of bursting. Some days, we spent more time looking for spots to ford those rushing waters than we did making progress toward our ultimate destination.

Not that I knew exactly where that was. Last I'd heard, the mercs I was looking for had found a town down in Texas to call their own, but Texas was a big damn place. A woman could spend half her life running around in its expanse, and I didn't have that sort of time to waste.

That's why we'd gone straight west once we cleared the mountains of Evan's one-time home, avoiding the eastern edge of the enormous former state that could swallow a person whole, and aiming instead for a town I knew well.

Between the rain and the flooding and the need to make campsites that were sheltered from the wind so Evan didn't catch pneumonia, it took weeks to make a trip I could usually do in a matter of days, but Lawton eventually came into view, thirty shacks and a three-story building set inside a well-guarded wall. That wall was a hell of a lot better made than anything inside of it, which pretty much summed up the town as a whole.

"Keep your hands and your eyes to yourselves, boys," I told my companions, as we headed down the hill to Lawton's only gate. "But if someone tries to start something, make enough of a spectacle of their death that others take it as a warning."

I wove my motorcycle around the body of a man who had clearly been dead *before* someone tossed him over the wall and nodded at the guards on gate duty and the handful I couldn't see but knew were watching us from above.

"Gentlemen." It was a comical overstatement of character, but I didn't think they'd protest.

"Well, if it ain't the Queen of Smiles," said one of them. "I heard you were dead. Killed by cabalists."

"It didn't take," I told him, the smile across my visor jagged and maniacal.

"Never seems to," he agreed, rolling his eyes as someone inside the town yelled at the top of their lungs. "What brings you to our humble establishment?"

"The usual," I said. "Entertainment and pleasure."

"And which one are these two?" He nodded to Two-Feathers and Evan.

"So far, mostly the first. The Old Man still in charge?"

"You know it."

"And that guy?" I waved a gloved hand at the body we'd passed.

"Thought it was time for new leadership. He tried putting together a posse to claim the town." The guard grinned, exposing yellowed teeth and a front gap where someone's punch had gotten through his guard. "It didn't take."

"It never does."

"True enough. You know the drill. Leave the horse and the bike with us. We'll have someone take them to the stables."

"Same amount as always?"

"Only if you want to be sure nobody rides off with them."

That was a given, so I paid the price out of the small bit of money I'd had *before* digging up Raya's treasure. Then the three of us retrieved our possessions—the security fee only covered our mounts, after all—and the guards waved us through.

"What is this place?" asked Evan, doing the very thing I had warned him not to, eyes wide as he took in the bacchanalian mess that had spilled into the streets, a few dozen people drinking, fighting, and fucking under the dim light of the cloud-stricken sun. It was a cornucopia of organs and orifices, a scene that changed every time I visited the town, and yet somehow remained the same.

"This is Lawton," I told him.

"Are you sure? We've been here a minute, and most of what's going on is illegal everywhere but the worst parts of Kansas City."

"You never even saw the worst parts of Kansas City," I told him. "And the town took the name from a pre-Break city as a joke. There's only one real law here and it's the Old Man's: don't rock the boat too hard or you'll end up like the body we passed outside. Beyond that, anything goes. Why do you think people like it so much?"

Two-Feathers stood impassively next to us, but I was pretty sure he was doing his level best not to blush at the sights before us. Sweet summer child.

"Anyway, we're not here for the revelry," I reminded them. "And stop staring, Evan. You're practically screaming *victim* to anyone paying attention."

And people *were* paying attention, I knew. Beneath its mask of amiable debauchery, Lawton was a gathering spot for predators. By the next morning, the streets would run red with the blood of those who couldn't keep pace with the pack.

It wasn't my *favorite* place in the Badlands, but there was no question it made the list.

I led our group to the epicenter of the ongoing party, the three-story building we'd been able to see from outside. A cracked sign hung from the rafters of the expansive porch, bearing the painted image of a mug filled to its brim with bullets.

"Welcome to the Last Shot," I said, pushing the saloon doors open. "I don't recommend the beer."

○○○

The inn's common room was a shithole, but it was a comfortable shithole; a fire roaring away in the hearth, a game of cards in the corner that was liable to turn ugly sooner or later, and Big Ed waiting behind the bar.

Big Ed was not, in fact, big, and it was anyone's guess whether his name had ever been Ed. Maybe an inch or two taller than Evan, he prowled back and forth on the raised platform behind his bar, dispensing scowls and dirty glasses of alcohol with equal fervor. He gave me the former as I approached.

"I'd heard you were dead," he growled. "Spider food for the Weaver's children up north."

"They didn't like how I tasted."

"I can believe that." He poured a mug of what might charitably have been called beer if not for the chunks floating in it and sent it rocketing down the bar to a waiting hand. "What will it be? I know *you're* not here for drinking."

"I'm looking for information."

"You on a job?"

"Always."

He blanched, just a bit, but rallied enough to nod. "Who's the dead man?"

"It's a woman, actually, but that's not what I'm here about. Not specifically, anyway." I leaned over the bar, pitching my voice to carry over the sound of the fight that had broken out in the corner, right on schedule. "I'm looking for Jules and his crew. Any idea where they've holed up lately?"

"I might have some thoughts," he allowed, "but a man like Jules is practically family, and I don't—"

His words cut off as I pushed a small gem across the bar, its polished facets glimmering in the inn's shitty light.

"I'm just looking to hire them on," I said. "Nothing more."

With a cough, he covered the emerald with one hand as he pretended to ponder. "In that case, pointing you in his direction seems the neighborly thing to do. Last I heard, they were down in Texas."

I waited, letting my silence speak for me, and he kept going.

"Remember the spot where McAllister and his men bought it? Back when they were trying to take down that Flamebringer?"

"Yeah." Guns were a wonderful thing, but a flamethrowing Power had taken McAllister and his band down in a heartbeat. "It was an old church, right?"

He nodded, casually tucking the hidden gem away. "Yeah. Word is, Jules set up shop in a town about twenty miles further south."

"Word?"

He spat to the side, his scowl deepening as the fight behind us turned ugly. "From Jules himself. Stopped by this past spring to knock back a few and sell some merchandise." He shrugged. "That's as much as I know. Honest."

If there was one thing Big Ed wasn't, besides big, it was *honest*, but I let it go. He hadn't lasted as long as he had in this shithole by selling bad info. Bad beer, yes, but info? Not so much.

At the same time, that sliver of emerald I'd given him was worth a hell of a lot more than just basic directions.

"We'll take a room for the night," I told him. "But for now, why don't you pour my companions some whisky. And *not* that shit you make in your bathtub."

"I'll have you know that *shit*," he said, voice all nasally like I'd offended him, "is gin, not whisky."

"Call it whatever you want; I need them alive. And not blind."

"No promises." He gestured past me. "Especially given how things are going."

I turned to find Evan crowded into a corner, Two-Feathers in front of him. The nomad was dodging strikes from what felt like a veritable sea of arms and legs, though this was just a crowd of Normals instead of another Body Shifter. I wasn't sure if one of my people had started things or if they'd been pulled into the larger melee, but either way, something needed to be done before Big Ed got involved… let alone the Old Man.

I caught Two-Feathers' eye, the nomad somehow still stoic as he redirected one man's punch into another man's face. "You don't have to kill them, but at least put them down!"

Evan didn't respond, but I hadn't expected him to. Two-Feathers, on the other hand, took my words to heart and decided to show his opponents what a Power could do.

I turned back to Big Ed as bones started to break behind me.

"How about that whisky?"

Two-Feathers ended up taking out a few men—and one woman wearing face paint, a leather tail, and absolutely nothing else—in a manner of seconds before a ring of empty space opened around him even as the brawl kept on going, the mob somehow aware, in that mindless way of all single-celled organisms, that to approach the nomad was to invite pain and injury.

Evan gulped down the whisky I brought him in one breath, and I was pleased to see Two-Feathers accept the second glass.

"I was starting to worry you were some sort of choirboy," I told him, as we settled in around a table near the bar. Alcohol wasn't much of a vice, but at least it was something for me to work with.

Of course, then he cocked his head, and I was left explaining what the hell a choirboy was, since, like all too many things Dr. Nowhere had crammed into my head, they weren't a thing anymore. Not out here in the Badlands anyway.

By the time I finished that explanation, Big Ed had finally lost his temper with the remaining brawlers. The little man pulled out a shotgun almost as big as he was and fired it directly into the melee, the noise of the gunfire as much of an attention-getter as the rock salt he used for ammunition.

"Take it outside, reprobates," he said in the ensuing silence. "The Old Man doesn't want this place destroyed and neither do I."

Drunk or sober, that was enough to get people moving, leaving a small army of unconscious or dead people spread across the floor. None of those bodies came from the shotgun blast—at that range, rock salt was little more than an irritant—and Big Ed shrugged and tucked his shotgun back under the bar, as new customers streamed in through the saloon doors to order drinks.

Lawton was never, ever dull.

○○○

We had settled into our room on the third floor, Evan taking the bed and Two-Feathers taking the vastly cleaner floor, when a knock came at the door. I undid three deadbolts and cracked it open.

"The Old Man wants to see you," said a man who looked like he chewed rocks for breakfast. Kyros, the town's chief enforcer.

I'd expected as much, and so I dropped off my saddlebags and left with Kyros to go see Lawton's head honcho. At night, the town truly came alive, buildings and streets overflowing with neighboring townies here on a lark or guns-for-hire looking to let loose. They scuttled aside for Kyros, but I felt eyes on our backs as we crossed to the single-story home set up against Lawton's rear wall.

More guards waited out in front, but neither the enforcer nor I stopped, pushing through the door, past the foyer, and into the dining hall that doubled as the Old Man's audience chamber. There were another few guards along the walls, and a woman in white silks bustled about in back, but my attention was reserved for the individual sitting front and center.

Old Man had long ago progressed from a *nom de guerre* to a simple statement of fact, but the man across from me looked like he'd aged a decade for every year of my sabbatical. The barrel-chested man I remembered, with steel-grey hair and eyes that could cut at a hundred paces, was now just a bag of bones and loose flesh, propped up in a chair with wheels crudely mounted to its sides.

If I'd had a human face, there'd have been no way to hide my reaction. As it was, even the decal on my visor lost some of its smile.

"I wondered if I'd see you again," he said, in a voice like torn sandpaper. "Or if your road would continue to lead you elsewhere."

"You didn't think I was dead?"

He gave a cackle that quickly turned into a body-wracking cough, waving away the woman who came to wipe the blood from his lips. "I always said we were both too mean to die. Turns out, I was only half right."

"Sounds like the kind of thing a quitter would say." I let the storm leak into my voice, metal and anger clashing like swords on a battlefield. "Are you a quitter, Omaha? Have you forgotten your own creed?"

One of the guards took a threatening step forward, only for the Old Man to turn on him, finding the strength somehow to unleash the glare that had carved out this small sliver of intentional chaos. "Don't be stupid, Rahim. This woman could kill everyone in our town and there's not a damn thing you or I could do about it."

I shrugged and said nothing, disinclined to test just how true his statement was now that his fearsome prime was little more than a memory. I'd come for information, after all, not blood.

"*Omaha*," the old man continued, his smile revealing more gum than tooth. "It's been years since anyone called me that."

"Even longer since the city fell," I agreed.

"As for the creed and quitting?" His shrug was more of a wiggle, two sharp-edged shoulders rippling beneath a head that seemed too heavy for its own neck. "You'll still be you when the sun burns itself out in the sky and humanity's bones have crumbled to dust, but for the rest of us, time is not so kind, I'm afraid."

"You've become a poet in your dotage?"

"I may have found a book or two," he wheezed.

I shifted from side to side. I'd walked the earth since the dream, seeing more death than I could recall, but something about the Old Man's plight troubled me in ways few others ever had. Death was never dignified, no matter what the stories or vids said, but this… this was somehow even worse.

I was ready to be gone.

"What did you need from me, Omaha?"

"Nothing that you can't give; I remember your rules." He cleared his throat noisily, fighting off the cough that followed. "You never sleep, and I can't manage more than an hour a night these days. I was hoping we could chat before you headed down to Texas."

I wasn't surprised he already knew where I was going. Even a few inches from the grave, he was still the Old Man. "What did you want to chat about?"

"The past, the future, anything at all. There's nobody left who knew me before I became Lawton's lord. Nobody except you. And I strongly suspect we won't have this chance again."

Seeing the condition he was in and the nervous way his would-be nurse hovered in the background, I knew he was right. So, instead of heading back to the inn like I'd have preferred, I waited for the guard named Rahim to bring in a chair. I sat across from the old man, the Badlands' singular *Old Man*, keeping him company through the empty night, through the unexpected naps, the pained fits, and the careful hours of reminiscence.

And when it was done and his next breath became his last, I walked away under a morning sun that spread its light across the uncaring world.

14

One unexpected development from our brief stay in Lawton was that Two-Feathers and Evan appeared to have bonded. I wasn't sure if it was because of the bar fight or if something else had happened while I was gone, but it was the nomad who lifted Evan onto our freshly purchased second horse, and who, through both gesture and example, helped the older man improve his seat on his new mount.

I wasn't sure what to think of that, but by the time Lawton had vanished from my mirrors, I decided it didn't matter. Team spirit wasn't a requirement for the job, but I doubted it would hurt any either.

We stopped for the night a careful distance away from the banks of yet another river whose name I didn't know. We'd brought fresh rations with us from Lawton, and not needing to hunt had given us an extra few hours of travel. Even so, we were days, if not weeks, away from our destination.

"What happened in Lawton?" asked Evan, wrinkled hands almost touching the fire. Two-Feathers was asleep on the other side of that fire, getting his forty winks in before the night watch he still insisted on helping me keep.

"That's what I want to know."

"I'm sorry?"

"First, you and Two-Feathers get in a fight in the half-minute I'm not paying attention, and now, you're practically best friends after barely even speaking to each other over the past few weeks."

The little man shrugged, thoughtful expression almost buried under all those wrinkles. "He's a good kid. I guess I realized I shouldn't be holding him responsible for my situation."

"True. The only person to blame is you."

"I guess so." He sighed. "When I promised you a favor for smuggling me out of the Free States, was this what you had in mind? Traipsing across the Badlands?"

"The value of a favor is that it stays undefined until needed."

"I'll take that as a *no*." He took a drink from his canteen. "Back to what I was saying earlier then: what happened in Lawton?"

"I don't remember you being this annoying."

"That was sixteen years ago, and I was going through some things at the time, as you well know. Since then, I've had an awful lot of time to myself to think."

"And?"

"And I realized life is short, and that I might as well ask questions when I have them. You can answer or not, as suits you… but you were gone all night and you've been *off* all day. Two-Feathers can't ask, so I figured I would."

"The Old Man, Lawton's leader, died last night."

He swore, his words heartfelt enough that Two-Feathers shifted in his sleep. "And they let us ride away?"

"What?"

"He can't have been your primary target, or we wouldn't still be traveling south. So, I have to ask: what did he do that merited killing, and why didn't you wait until the rest of us were away and safe? I don't know about Two-Feathers, but I'm pretty sure I'm allergic to bullets."

"I didn't *kill* him," I growled. "I'd known him almost as long as you've been alive. He was aware his time was short and wanted to spend it reminiscing."

"Oh." Despite all that had happened to him and the years that had passed since, I guess a part of Evan still wanted to play hero, because he couldn't help but ask: "Do you want to talk about it?"

"Fuck no."

"Guess I'll get some sleep then." He groaned. "Who knew riding a horse could be so awful? I ache in places I didn't know a man could ache."

"It'll be worse tomorrow."

"At my age, it usually is." He paused, face hidden in the darkness as he turned away from the fire. "I hoped I'd never see you again, you know."

"One favor," I reminded him. "It was always coming due."

"Maybe so. And it does beat another winter in the mountains, eating dried-out tubers and shriveled vegetables, but…"

"But?"

He lowered his voice until I could barely hear it over the crackling of the fire. "But that's me. I'm almost sixty years old and I've more than earned what's coming my way. Two-Feathers has his whole life ahead of him. Maybe think for a second about what it is you're dragging him into?"

"You're not my conscience, Evan, and Two-Feathers is a grown man who decided on his own to come along."

"Fair enough. Not like there's much I can do about it anyway." He was halfway into his tent before he turned about. "But my name's Miles, not Evan."

"Right. Somehow, I just keep forgetting."

Within moments, he was asleep.

I found a seat away from the fire and the old man's snoring to keep watch, but for once, the world seemed content not to throw any new horrors our way. The skies were clear, leaving an endless expanse of stars and a crescent moon that showered silvery light onto our campsite and the surrounding foliage. Even the sound of the nearby river was almost soothing.

As I'd told Evan, the Old Man and I went way back. He'd been around long enough to feel like a fixture in my life… rarely seen, but comforting nonetheless, a piece of permanence in an ever-changing world. Now, he was one more reminder of that second lesson I'd learned at birth: nothing is forever. Even the stars, whose rage spread light across the expanse of space, would one day dim and die. Might have already done so long before we even saw them.

And for what?

I was no closer to knowing that than when I'd started.

○○○

On our fifth day out of Lawton, we reached the burned-out church Big Ed had mentioned. The area around the town's ruins had long since been picked clean—first by the birds and wildlife, then by the scavengers who ran on two legs instead of four—but the shell of the church remained, its steeple blackened and crooked, raised like a middle finger to all who saw it.

"Please tell me that's not where we're headed."

"We've got another day or two's ride to go," I told Evan.

"Good. Because I don't want to meet whatever lives there, assuming anything does."

We swung wide around the church ruins, just in case. The Pyromancer—or Flamebringer, as Big Ed had called him—was long-since dead, but as Evan had unwittingly pointed out, that was no guarantee that someone else hadn't moved in since. The ominous atmosphere would appeal to some of the things that made their home down here in Texas.

And speaking of those things…

I pulled off to the side of what was more a suggestion of a path than an actual road and waited for their horses to come up alongside me. "A few days ago, we crossed into Texas. Probably should have had this talk then, but we're having it now instead. Neither of you have ever been to Texas, right?"

I aimed that question more at Two-Feathers than Evan. There weren't any clans down here, but I'd learned that the nomad went wherever he damn well pleased.

Both men shook their heads.

"It's not really Texas anymore, of course, thanks to the Break and the disappearance of most of its inhabitants, but everyone calls the place that anyway, as much to differentiate it from its surroundings as anything else. Texas isn't part of the Badlands. It's worse."

"The Worselands?" grinned Evan, who was getting entirely too comfortable with our group, despite the saddle sores.

I waited as his joke crashed and burned, the expression on my visor never changing, then shook my head.

"There are things in Texas you won't find anywhere else. The White Wail. Terrorbirds. The Hunger that Walks."

"There's a *whale* here? I didn't even know Texas had lakes, let alone an ocean."

"A quarter of the former state borders on the gulf, but the White Wail's not named after the sea creature. It's named after the sound. If the trees start rustling even without a wind, and you hear the slightest hint of a baby crying, turn and ride north as fast as you can. Both of you. Chances are your horses will be way ahead of you on that front."

"And the other things you mentioned?"

"Keep an eye on the sky, and a hand on your gun. In fact, you might want to borrow one of Two-Feathers' rifles if he has any ammo left to spare. There are a lot of things here guns won't help against, but anything is better than nothing."

"Lovely."

I shrugged. "Plenty of things can kill you in the Badlands too, and we made it through there just fine both times. Texas has predators and it has full-on *terrors*... I just need you all prepared should we run into the latter."

"Prepared, she says," muttered Evan to the nomad. "Like I'm ever going to sleep again after that?"

Two-Feathers slapped the smaller man on the back, but even he looked discomfited, scanning the terrain around us, spear in hand instead of at his side.

I nodded in approval, and we rode out again, a little bit slower, and a lot more paranoid. I preferred *cautious* to *scared*, but I'd take either one over *dead*. Especially with Evan still having a part to play when we made it to New Memphis.

Most of the terrors roamed further to the south, last I'd heard, but the route we took was more circuitous than any we'd followed since the mountains, avoiding possible hot spots and terrain that looked even vaguely suspect. I'd encountered the White Wail once, decades earlier, and while I was one of the few who could truthfully claim they survived the experience, it wasn't one I had any desire to repeat. Especially with two fragile meatbags at my side.

Despite my warning, the next few days were almost idyllic, passing by in a blur of fields and streams. Eventually, our destination—the next of many—came into view. The small town was as much rubble as buildings, but that wasn't uncommon, even in the Badlands. A wall encircled the parts of the town that remained standing, and smoke drifted up above that wall to mingle with the clouds that had recently swept back in.

"Oh, thank God," said Evan, on seeing that smoke. "Four walls, a roof, and a warm fire. I don't even remember what my toes feel like anymore."

Two-Feathers frowned, black eyes tracing the smoke from the sky to the town below. He had noticed the same thing I had; it wasn't coming from any chimney.

A few moments later, a sound we all recognized reached us.

Gunfire.

The town we'd finally arrived at, the town Jules and his crew had turned into their headquarters, was under assault.

ooo

The attackers were easy to pick out as we neared the town, half-naked maniacs screaming at the tops of their lungs as they threw their own bodies at the shabby fortifications. A few had weapons, but most seemed content to stick with tooth and nail… despite, as far as I could tell, not being Beast Shifters.

I'm not sure they'd have made any headway at all if it wasn't for the sheer number of them… two to three dozen humans assaulting a town guarded by less than ten.

The *thing* in their midst was probably helping a bit too.

As big as a Titan, it had black horns curving outward from the forehead of a face that had never been human: skin the color of ash, three eyes, two mouths, and a vertical slash that might be taken for a nose if it didn't have teeth of its own.

I shook my head even as we crept forward. Okay: *three* mouths and no nose.

"Is that a *demon?"* asked Evan, his voice rising to a squeak.

I wanted to tell him that demons didn't exist, but the visual evidence before us suggested otherwise. The wooden wall trembled every time the creature hit it and was starting to sag inward as its structural posts were forced out of the ground, screaming maniacs climbing the sharp incline.

One of the defenders popped his head over the wall, made a gesture, and the half-dozen naked climbers fell to the ground, their screams suddenly silenced, but the demon didn't even slow.

That was the bad news.

The worse news? I recognized the guy on the wall as the person I'd come to Texas for. And that meant I couldn't just hang back and watch the mayhem unfold.

"Stay here, watch the horses, and try to keep hidden," I told Evan. "If you're not going to use your powers, then at least shoot anyone that comes near you. And try not to miss; the naked ones look hungry."

As for Two-Feathers… I traded glances with him, and he just nodded, taking his spear in both hands as he dismounted and sprinted towards the melee.

Ahead of us, the splintering of old wood told me time was running out. I couldn't run like a Stalwart, but my bike put even his acceleration to shame; I rode down the hill toward the scrum, jumped from the seat as I charted a course past the rubble, and dismissed my shell to set loose the storm.

The biggest advantage the half-naked crazies had was numbers, but those numbers did nothing to protect them from the swirling avalanche of steel that ran right through them, tearing through flesh and bone alike with equanimity. In fact, their crazed state only added to the slaughter, as an increasing number turned from the wall to charge our two-person counterattack.

I couldn't see how Two-Feathers was doing, but every fragment of the storm was covered in blood and tissue and the idiots kept rushing in, like lemmings marching into a pre-Break blender. The storm's momentum carried it onward, and finally the demon took notice of the death that had crept up in its shadow. It roared from two of its three mouths, grabbed a post from the wall it had just finished smashing to pieces, and swung it like a club through the storm's midst.

First the Titan out at Eastwood, now this demon in a no-name town down in Texas? Hitting things with a big club seemed to be the go-to move for opponents of a certain size. I'd have thought it an attempt at overcompensation if the Titan hadn't been female and the demon wasn't both aggressively naked and terrifyingly over-endowed.

Once again, the storm swarmed past a strike that would have splattered even the average Power. The creature's size and lack of pants made my choice of targets that much simpler. Its hide was tough, but less so than the howler's, and a part of me wondered if that was true everywhere, or if demons were just especially vulnerable between the legs.

If it was the latter, you'd think they'd have learned to cover up.

I couldn't hear the roars over the storm's own music, but I *could* tell when they turned to screams and then again, when they cut off entirely, as the storm finished cutting its way through the creature's midsection. Without a pelvis to keep its legs attached, they fell in alternating directions, while the torso and head dropped straight down into my ever-spinning abattoir of iron and steel.

More blood splashed across the wreckage of the town's wall.

For the first time, the attacking Normals—the handful who still lived, at least—showed signs of self-preservation, turning to flee now that their otherworldly enforcer was a pair of twitching limbs on the blood-drenched earth. I reformed my shell in the middle of that charnel house and watched as they were shot down by defenders in the fort.

When the last body dropped, two heads poked over the wall to examine the slaughter.

One immediately turned away, the sound of his retching audible over the moans of the few people still engaged in the business of dying.

The second, the one I recognized, looked at what was left of the demon at my feet and shook his head.

"Damn, Queenie. Why am I not surprised you went straight for its dick?"

"It's every man's vulnerability, Jules," I said, the smile across my visor wide and maniacal. "One way or another."

"Not that we don't appreciate the assist—because I promise that we do—but what are you doing all the way down here?"

"I'm here on a job."

"Fuck." The blood drained from his face. "Is it me, specifically, or one of my crew? Because I'll be honest, after the past month there ain't that many of us left. Fucking cultists might have already done your killing for you."

"My target sleeps like a blonde-haired angel on a feather mattress a thousand or more miles east of here," I told him. "I came to hire help."

The second head, the one who'd so recently puked all over the inside of their wall, popped back up, eyes wide.

"Well shit," said Jules, waving at people down in the town behind him. "In that case, why don't you step into my office."

I could hear a latch being lifted, but the gate, ten feet from the section of wall the demon had been beating on, refused to open.

"Once we get the door working again," Jules amended.

"Tough times?" My laughter was its usual snarl of metal.

"Let's just say a thousand miles sounds pretty fucking rosy."

"I'll remember that when it comes to negotiations."

15

It took almost twenty minutes to get the gate open, and even that required Two-Feathers' help from the outside. I reclaimed my bike, Evan joined us from his spot on the hill, and we were escorted into the part of town Jules had turned into his base. One glance told me it hadn't been worth whatever effort he'd spent on it. The place was a dump, even by the already-shaky standards of low-end career criminals.

"It's not much to look at, but…" He trailed off.

"But?"

"Couldn't think of anything positive to say, to be honest."

"We have a well," pointed out one of his crew, as skinny as he was tall, a rifle slung loosely over one shoulder.

"There you go; we have a well. Thank you, Tom. Even better, the water's drinkable." Jules turned back to me. "If your men want, they can refill their canteens there while you and I talk business."

Talking business, in this case, first involved entering one of the nearby houses. Both of its windows were missing, and the back half of the house was caved in, but the front room was spacious enough and the furniture was covered in a vinyl that might still be decades away from decomposing. I lowered myself into the chair, and like true professionals, we both ignored the noise made from leather kissing its synthetic cousin.

I took a long look at the man across from me. Jules, much like his town, was looking considerably worse for wear, dark curls thinning to reveal the scalp beneath. His face had gone the opposite route, fleshy cheeks and the hint of a second chin swallowing the bone structure that had once left a trail of broken hearts behind him. Only his eyes remained the same—cold and green, glass mirrors instead of windows to a soul whose existence had long been publicly questioned—and even they held a fatigue I'd rarely seen.

"You look like shit," I said.

"And you look the same. As always." He shook his head. "People tried telling me you were dead, you know? Captured and transformed into another of Legion's monstrosities."

"And what did you tell them?"

"That they were idiots. There's no way in hell you'd go anywhere near Old Baltimore again after ripping that freakshow off."

"I didn't *rip him off.*"

"You stole an entire bag of his disgusting creations!"

"He's a Technomancer. He can always make more." I shook my head. "And that was *after* he reneged on payment. I did the job, and I took what I was owed. End of story."

"End of that story anyway." He sighed and ran his hand over his scalp. "Where *have* you been? Nobody I spoke to had seen you in years."

"I quit the road for a bit. Took some time to myself to think."

I expected him to laugh. The Jules I knew would have laughed. Instead, he just nodded. "I can't say the idea doesn't have some appeal."

"Thinking or quitting?"

"Maybe a bit of both."

I let the frown I couldn't show express itself in my voice. "What the hell happened to you?"

"What do you think? Time doesn't pass us all by like it does you. I hit forty last year and it's like every part of me is competing to see what will go to shit first. Knees hurt in the morning, back hurts at night, hands aren't as quick as they used to be. This is what time does to the rest of us."

"I know how age works, idiot. I was asking about your crew, not to mention the legion of flopping dicks I caught trying to tear down your wall with their faces."

"Our new neighbors. Cultists from the Church of Shabaa."

"I've never heard of Shabaa."

"He's a Summoner. Got driven out of south Texas a few years back by a bunch of kids, if you can believe it. If this world had any justice, he'd have died with the rest of his original crew. Instead, he made his way north, found some bombed-out city on the brink of starvation and fed the survivors with the meat of his own summons. That was the start of the Church of Shabaa and it's been spreading ever since. About a month ago, some of their evangelists reached us."

"And you decided not to change religions."

"This world only has one God, and he's the asshole you've been searching for since before I was born. I'm not going to worship Dr. Fucking Nowhere, and I'm not going to worship some creepy Summoner either. So yeah, we said no, and when they tried to force the issue, we killed their pushy asses. It wasn't until a few weeks later that we found out just how many of them there were."

"Demons and enraged cultists. The former are his summons?"

"Yeah. Never seen Shabaa himself or the Powers said to be in his inner circle. They're smart enough to sit back and wait for us to be overwhelmed by sheer numbers." He scowled. "Back when we found this place empty for the taking, I thought it might be the start of something good, you know… a nest egg to carry me into retirement like the Old Man. Instead, Shabaa's been grinding us into the dirt. Getting the hell out of here sounds like a damn good idea."

"Will your crew feel the same way?"

"Hell, yes. There were *twelve* of us last spring. Five left now, after the sixth and seventh died making a run for it last week. If you can get us clear somehow, you'll have bought yourself some muscle."

"Those are words I like to hear."

"So, what's the job? And who's it for?"

"You'll be working for me."

"You're the client and the contractor?" He frowned. "I didn't think you operated that way."

"Times change. Someone burned down the town I was calling home. Killed everyone in it, men, women, and kids."

"And? Don't tell me you need *our* help to get revenge."

"The people who did it are already dead."

"Like I figured. So then…"

"It wasn't enough to balance the scales. I'm going after the person ultimately responsible."

"And this walking corpse of a woman lives out east?"

"New Memphis."

"Huh; I wouldn't hate finally seeing the place, truth be told. I've heard things, but I've never been that—" He paused. "Wait. Isn't that the home of the new warlord everyone is talking about?"

"The Crimson Queen."

"Yeah, her. Not sure she or her *literal armies* are gonna be too enthused with our particular brand of mayhem."

"Then maybe her men shouldn't have burned down my home."

Jules' eyes widened.

"Queenie—"

"Two queens might be one too many for the continent."

○○○

I gave Jules time to digest the news as we sat in our respective chairs and the shadows crept across the floor. Finally, he rubbed his face. "You're asking us to exchange one death for another."

"Maybe so."

"I'm afraid that changes things."

"If we hadn't shown up, you might be dead already."

"You know that and I know that. Not sure anybody else will care though." He thought for a while longer as I listened to the storm inside me and shook his head. "Tell you what. Get us all out of here and I'm in."

"And your crew?"

"You can broach the subject when we're free and clear, but they're not dumb and they're not suicidal. Most of them, anyway," he allowed. "Be prepared for them to walk."

"So, you're buying their lives with your own?"

"Price of being a leader, I guess? I got them into this mess. I'll pay to get them out."

That was new. When we'd ridden together, Jules had been a hellion, more interested in drinking, fighting, and fucking than anything approaching responsibility. I wasn't sure if it was the age or the miles that had changed that, but it worked in my favor. Jules was the one Power I *knew* I needed. And I might not even have to pay him.

On the other hand, it meant my decision to retrieve Raya's treasure before coming down to Texas might have been a waste of more than a month of travel, but that was okay too. Sometimes, that's just how shit went.

"Speaking of my crew," he said, "Why don't I give you the rundown so we can head back out before they get too frisky with yours?"

"It'd be a mistake if they tried anything."

"Because of the nomad?"

"Name's Two-Feathers. He's a Stalwart who invited himself along for the ride."

"I bet he did." Something ugly glittered in Jules' eyes. "Broad shoulders, young, and easy enough on the eyes. Is he the new me?"

"How could he be? He doesn't speak, and from what I remember of you in your mid-twenties, you never shut up."

"You know what I'm saying, Queenie."

"Does it matter?" I read the answer on his face and shrugged. "I wouldn't say no if he offered, but he hasn't."

"Then he's dumb as well as mute."

If I had eyes, I'd have rolled them. Jules and I had shared some good times, but those days were ancient history. I didn't need or want his opinion on my sex life. Especially when it had been complete shit lately.

"What about the little guy?" he pressed.

"He's *definitely* not the new you. Or the old you, for that matter."

"Again, not what I meant." He frowned, looking out the window at our respective groups. "Something about him feels familiar."

I wasn't surprised by that. After all, Jules had grown up in the Free States before a brush with the law had convinced him of the Badlands' allure. Still, sixteen years had left their mark on Evan, and if Jules didn't recognize him anymore, I wasn't going to share that secret.

"He's my insurance."

"An old man? Seriously?"

"Seriously."

"That's all you're gonna say?" He cocked an eyebrow and grinned, dropping a decade's worth of age in the process. "You ain't gonna give your old pal Jules any more than that?"

"You'll know when you need to. *If* you need to."

"Always did love your secrets." He waved toward the window. "Meanwhile, I've got Havoc, Cross, Tom, and Selene. Cross is my second, a Normal, but rock-solid under pressure and decent at damn near everything. Tom's a Normal too. Bit of an asshole but magic with a rifle in his hands."

"And Havoc and Selene?"

"Both Powers. He's a Titan, as you might have gathered from his size. Got the appetite and the durability but only a bit of the strength. And Selene… well, she's different."

It was my turn to give him a look. "Is she the new me?"

"Not if I want to keep breathing." His laugh rose and fell on its own, like something wild. "We brought her on as our thirteenth member about a year ago. Seemed to hit it off with one of my enforcers, a real smooth-talking son of a bitch. Eventually, they started finding their own spot to spend the night."

"And?"

"And one morning, we found him spread-eagled on his back, dozens of stab wounds in his chest and face, and a gaping cut stretching from one side of his stomach to the next." Jules drew the jagged line across his own stomach, like I'd asked for visual aids. "Selene said she gave him a second smile because the first wasn't honest enough for her tastes."

"And you let her stay?"

"She's… useful." He licked his lips nervously. "We learned not to touch her, and she's been peaceful enough ever since."

"What is she?"

"A Crow." He held up both hands as if warding off my objections. "Not a powerful one. Not like that walking nightmare who took Mexico. She can't raise the dead or anything… just talks to ghosts, and even then, only when they're willing. But sometimes they give advice or even warnings. Saved our asses more than once."

Apparently, my silence had spooked him, because he started rattling off specific instances when Selene had proven herself useful. Truth was, I wasn't listening at all. Eventually, I cut him off.

"What are you talking about, Jules? Mexico? Tezcatlipoca's not a Crow. Not sure *what* the hell that creature is, but I know it's not that."

He stared at me. "You mean you haven't heard? I know you said you were taking some time to yourself to think, but even so..."

"Heard what?"

"Tezcatlipoca's dead. Word out of the Free States is that one of their own, a Crow they tried to make a Cape, was responsible. Raised an army of the fucking dead and killed the so-called lava god with it." He shrugged. "Not sure it's much of an improvement, swapping one horror for another. The new guy is called—"

"Walker." My voice was just a breath, and I added the second name in almost without thinking. "Bakersfield."

"Never heard that second name but yeah, they call him Walker, among other things." He frowned. "You've heard of him then?"

"I was there."

"In Mexico? Really?"

I shook my head. "In the City of the Sun, just north of the border. Bakersfield was down there with the Mission because I'd called in a favor he owed me."

"You mean you *know* the Lord of the Dead?"

"I'd been searching for Dr. Nowhere for more than sixty years," I said, not really answering. "Bakersfield found him in a matter of months. And then the town was attacked, and baby Crow lost his shit. Killed Dr. Nowhere. Killed damn near everyone, townsfolk and Mission included."

By this point, Jules' eyes were dinner plates in his face, his usual calm demeanor well and truly abandoned. He started to speak, swallowed, and tried again.

"You finally found Dr. Nowhere, and this Walker killed him?"

"Yeah."

"Shit, Queenie. I'm sorry."

I shrugged with a lightness I didn't feel. That I hadn't felt for three years. "Anyway, I got the hell out of there. Made it all of an hour before I stopped and turned around to have myself a little talk. Problem being that a man named Tyrant had had the same idea."

Jules whistled. "I've heard *that* name too."

"Yeah. Top-five most dangerous people I've ever met. Cold as a razor blade and possessed more powers than I could count. Didn't keep him from becoming worm food when Walker was done with him."

"And then?"

"Bakersfield headed south. Crossed the border into Tezcatlipoca's territory. I watched him go from a distance and figured that was it, that he was trying to make something of his death."

"You sound like you almost pity him. Even after he killed the man with all your answers."

I didn't bother telling him that Dr. Nowhere hadn't had any real answers. That my creator had been a scared man hiding away in a desert town, in some ways as much a victim as the rest of us.

Instead, I let my thoughts turn to Bakersfield.

"He wasn't a bad kid. Lived through more shit than someone his age should have faced but kept on going anyway."

"I'm sure that'll make everyone feel better when he leads his undead legions north to kill us." Jules snorted. "Luckily, it sounds like *I'll* be dead in New Memphis long before that. And now I know you're alright traveling with a Crow, should Selene decide to join us. Things could be worse."

I nodded, taking whatever the hell I was feeling about Bakersfield's survival and packing it away for the nights when the world slept. The Crimson Queen was my immediate future. Everything else could wait until the killing was done.

"Anyway," Jules continued, "that's my crew. Me, a Titan, two Normals, and a significantly less murderous Crow than the kind you're used to. Some of them will have heard of you, and all of them are probably wondering what the hell we're talking about."

"Then by all means, let's go fill them in."

I made just as much noise standing up as I had sitting down, but once again, we both chose to ignore it.

16

Jules' crew was waiting with mine when we came back out, the woman—Selene—standing off by herself, back against the wall in the shade of a building almost older than I was. She was the only person who didn't turn to look at us as we emerged.

"For those of you who don't recognize her from the stories," said Jules, his voice carrying easily in the otherwise empty town, "this here is the Queen of Smiles. First name Queen, last name Smiles."

"I also answer to Your Majesty," I added.

"I'd heard you were dead," said a small, wiry man with hard eyes and close-cropped hair. Cross, I assumed, since I'd already met Tom and the hulking blonde behind him had to be Havoc. "Pissed off Grannypocalypse and went boom."

Unconsciously, almost half of us looked to the northeast, as if we could have even seen a mushroom cloud all the way over in the irradiated remains of West Virginia.

I shook my head, all the laughter gone from my voice. "Granny and I have a strict no-interaction policy."

"Queenie's crew is going to get us out of this mess," said Jules.

"Music to my ears," rumbled Havoc. Like most Titans, he was a big man, with a square jaw suitable for a recruiting poster and shaggy blonde hair that would have gotten him kicked out of that same military in an instant.

"How?" asked the skinny man who'd mentioned the town's well. The whine in his voice told me this was Tom. "Sochi and Kate tried sneaking out and didn't even make it a mile. And I'm pretty damn sure the next wave of cultists is already gathering to swarm us again."

I looked to my companions for ideas, but Evan wasn't meeting my gaze and Two-Feathers, as usual, had both too much and too little to say. Apparently, it was up to me. From the sound of it, Shabaa had people watching the town. Why they'd let my own crew through into this trap was a question I couldn't answer but sneaking eight people back out of it wasn't going to be easy. We'd need every advantage we could get. I looked to the one member of Jules' crew who had yet to speak.

"I guess it depends on how chatty Selene's ghosts are feeling… and whether demons can see in the dark."

○○○

We waited until sometime after midnight, when the moon was low in the sky and the clouds had swept back in to hide the remaining stars. Seven people and seven horses snuck out in the darkness, skirting the edge of the town to head east.

East, because it wasn't south, where Shabaa and the bulk of his church claimed territory. Because it wasn't west, where the gate pointed, and Jules' most recent casualties had tried to flee. And because it wasn't north, where Two-Feathers, Evan, and I had come from, and where, according to Selene's ghosts, the largest grouping of cultists was already lying in wait.

Seven people and seven horses, leaving me alone on my bike to head north.

In militaries even older than the Break, there was something called a rearguard, soldiers positioned at the back to safeguard an army during its retreat. The problem with rearguards was that the people assigned there tended to end up dead. If an army was retreating—or *advancing rearward to a more advantageous position*—it was generally because they were outmatched, and yet the poor dumb bastards in the rearguard were tasked with slowing a stronger force down through bullets, blood, and their own bodies.

Tonight, *I* was the rearguard.

I waited for Jules, Two-Feathers, and the rest to disappear into the night, thumbed my bike's electric motor to life, turned on the headlight to make sure I had the attention of man, beast, and possible demon, and rode north toward the ambush Selene's ghosts had spotted.

Either these particular cultists were less devout or they had already seen what I could do up close. I was a hundred yards from the enemy camp when the first shot rang out. Despite the big glowing target I presented, their shot was laughably inaccurate.

Unfortunately, the other cultists decided that was their signal to join in.

I took three hits in the hail of gunfire that followed, but kept going, trying to close as much distance as I could, while I could. It wasn't until the first round ricocheted off my bike that I'd had enough. I spun out, leaving the motorcycle behind me in the dirt, and pushed forward. One step, then two, and my shell fell away, bullets tearing through the space leather and flesh had occupied.

The roar of a thousand shards of metal overwhelmed the dull thunder of gunfire, and the storm surged into the cultists' midst.

A few things became evident quickly.

First, these cultists had more than two brain cells to rub together. Instead of charging wildly to their deaths, they tried to encircle me, and while their bullets either missed entirely or simply added to the storm's ever-present maelstrom, the distance they maintained made killing them surprisingly difficult.

Second, Shabaa was a better Summoner than Jules had given him credit for, because there were two demons waiting in the camp. They weren't any brighter than the first had been, but their sheer mass added to the danger of the trap they had prepared.

And third?

Shabaa didn't know who or what I was, or he'd have sent some of his Powers to join this little ambush.

Flesh was weak. Bones were fragile. Bullets were but distant, wayward cousins to the storm, regarded with pity and scorn as they charted the course someone else had assigned them, soaring like bumblebees to their demise.

Not a damn thing the cult leader had sent could stop me, and each body that fell in pieces, every moment the enemy spent trying to contain the uncontainable, gave Jules more time to escape.

This time, the cultists stayed even after their demons died, after their guns ran dry and were repurposed as clubs to equally dismal effect. I formed my shell in the middle of the melee, just for the hell of it, and tore one such rifle out of an attacker's hands, spinning to strike the cultist behind me so hard that I couldn't tell if it was his skull or the barrel that had cracked.

Apparently, it was both, so I dropped the weapon and my shell, letting the storm rage across the battlefield again until there was nothing remaining but the dead.

When it was done, I reformed my shell to an unwelcome new noise: shouting and gunfire to my east. Even with my distraction, it sounded like Jules and the others had encountered a patrol of their own… and that group being smaller than the one I'd just slaughtered wouldn't matter much if a bullet went astray and ended up in one of my new crew's heads.

I recovered my bike, ran a glove over the chassis to verify the ricochet hadn't done more than dent the chrome, and tore off into the darkness.

A rearguard's job was never done.

ooo

I cut my way through three more groups of cultists—smaller ones, just like Selene's ghosts had promised—before catching up with the crew. Tom was sporting a blood-soaked bandage around his right arm, and Evan was practically comatose atop his horse, but nobody was dead yet, and I took that as a positive.

As the night wore on, optimism died a slow, lingering death. We left behind the cultists chasing us, but it seemed like a fresh group was popping up in front of us every few miles, and in the darkness, we rarely saw them coming, forced to rely only on Two-Feathers' enhanced senses now that Selene was an unspeaking lump in her own saddle.

When dawn finally broke, there were somehow still eight of us, but I was the only one not covered in blood, and only because my shell returned to its pristine original state when I reformed it. Not even Tom had the energy to bitch anymore, and everyone without superhuman durability looked minutes from falling out of the saddle.

We kept going anyway. What the hell choice did we have?

By noon the next day, we'd managed a full hour without further assaults, and Jules called for a halt. I wasn't sure whether the horses or humans were more tired, but both groups needed a rest after hours of hard riding and far too many close calls to count. I didn't have to sleep, but I'd also spent the entire night killing our pursuers, and there was a mental drain involved in all of that. I was as ready for a break as anyone.

Unfortunately, it looked like we weren't going to get one.

"What the hell?" I complained as we peered over the hill at the teeming mass of half-naked humanity that spread across the wide plain before us. "How did they get ahead of us, especially in numbers like that?"

Two-Feathers shrugged, but even he looked tense, worn thin by the long night. While the rest of us had stopped, he'd gone ahead to scout, and had only recently returned to report a small army of cultists where none should have been.

"A Teleporter, maybe?" asked Cross.

"Not a Teleporter." Jules pointed past the cultists to where dozens of demons slumbered in a pile of awfulness. I'd ignored them at first, but a second glance showed they had one obvious difference from the three I'd already killed.

These ones had wings.

"On-demand troop transport?" I shook my head. "Maybe you *should* have changed religions."

We crawled back down the hill, doing our best to avoid alerting the opposing army to our presence. At the base of that hill, the rest of the crew was waiting.

"Any *new* bright ideas?" asked Tom, once we'd shared the latest round of bad news. The skinny man was leaning against his horse and doing his best not to bleed all over it.

I didn't bother suggesting that we fight our way through. There were literally hundreds of people ahead of us. Even if I took point, they would just swarm right past me. And there was no way I would be able to keep the crew safe once they did.

"How many people does Shabaa have?" I asked Jules.

"A hell of a lot more than even I realized."

"I'm not sure we can kill all of them," said Havoc, with the mother of all understatements. So far, I hadn't been impressed with the peanut he called a brain, but even he could recognize reality when it punched him in his lantern-jawed face.

"This is a nightmare." After a long night on the run, Evan looked far older than his years, the lines in his face deep canyons.

"Can't lose them, can't outrun them, can't kill them," said Cross. "Think they'll still eat us if we surrender?"

"If we focus on taking out the demons, we might be able to get away from the cultists." Jules didn't mention that Shabaa could ultimately just summon more, and I didn't call him out for it. The Summoner had to have *some* limits, and I was betting the past night had stretched those limits as far as they could go.

Either that or he was one of the great Powers of the world, like Grannypocalypse, Dominion, the Singer, and Bakersfield himself… in which case we were just fucked.

"Pretty sure they know that," said Tom with a sneer. "That's why the demons parked themselves on the other side of the army. And haven't been attacking us directly where your friend can turn them into spare parts."

Which was both annoying and annoyingly smart. Our enemy was clearly learning from each encounter.

"Go north," said a soft voice.

Selene was a slip of a girl with a messy tangle of dark hair and eyes that focused on things none of us could see. She'd left her horse to wander over in our direction.

"The new demons have wings, Selene," Cross told her, his voice going gentle. "They might be resting now, but they're faster than we are, even carrying troops. They'll check our heading and catch up again in no time."

"They're not the only ones with wings," said Selene, her cadence changing, thin lips twisted into something hard. "Go north."

A moment later, the young Crow sagged in place, head drooping like it had gained twenty pounds. She sent us a formless smile and staggered back to slump against her horse.

"One of her ghosts?" I asked in the sudden silence.

"Yeah." Jules shivered. "First time I recall any of them speaking *through* her instead of to her, but it's the only explanation."

"Any idea what it was talking about?"

"Shit no, but it ain't like we're spoiled for choice."

"Then I guess we go north and see what happens."

"That's not even a plan," griped Tom.

"We could stake you out and leave you behind in the hopes that your torment distracts them for a few days. Does that sound more like a plan?"

"North is good." Tom adjusted his bloody bandage with a wince. "Let's go north."

Everyone ignored Evan's groan.

○○○

The horses were tired, but we pushed them anyway. Evan switched back to riding bitch behind me, and the others rotated through to try to spell their mounts even on the run. We couldn't afford to go slower than a trot though; needing to make as much ground as we could before Shabaa's demon air force woke and realized we'd changed our course.

I'd never cared much for horses, and that sentiment had always been mutual, but seeing their heads shake from side to side as they thundered on, breaths timed between each stride, I couldn't help but pity them. I had no idea what awaited us to the north, but even if we made it there, I had to question how many of these horses would ever run again.

Three and a half hours into our new route, Havoc gave out a cry and pointed behind us. High in the air, like the ugliest of birds, a few demons were winging our way. Even as we watched, additional shapes took to the air. Worse, these held nets in their clawed hands. Nets teeming with squirming bodies.

"What do you think?" Jules asked Cross.

"I'm guessing another hour before the demons are on us, boss. Assuming the horses don't collapse first; they're almost done in."

"Selene?"

The Crow said nothing, lost in her world atop a horse she didn't seem to see.

"Guess an hour will have to do," said Jules. "If you have any ammo left, take your shots when the bastards come into range. Could be we'll get lucky and they'll be less bulletproof than the landbound kind." He turned to me, eyes landing on the little man who had buried his head in the back of my jacket. "Maybe it's time for that insurance you mentioned?"

I shook my head. "It doesn't cover airborne threats."

"Well, ain't *that* fucking fabulous?" He urged more speed out of a mount already heavy with lather and then flashed the smile that had caught my eye two decades earlier. "I don't want you to take this the wrong way, Queenie, on account of knowing that tongue of yours is the sharpest edge you have… but this has been a pretty shitty escape so far."

I laughed, the smile on my visor a match for his. "Next time, you should pay for the platinum package, you cheapskate."

"Lesson learned, Your Majesty. Lesson duly fucking learned."

A few of the people in the crew looked back at us to see what the hell was going on, and that set Jules off, his laughter rising to join mine as we rode onwards, headed north on a spirit's suggestion, death winging through the afternoon sky behind us.

You only get one life before you're food for the worms or just a voice in some mad Crow's ear. Might as well enjoy it and all its attendant bullshit.

○○○

Cross' suggested hour somehow stretched into two. I thought the horses were going to simply drop dead in their tracks, but the great beasts kept going, speed slowing and eyes rolling wildly in their sockets. I didn't like horses, but damned if these few hadn't been a heroic bunch of four-hooved assholes.

For all the good it had done us. The demons were close enough behind us that we could make out individual cultists in the nets being used for transport. Hundreds of squirming bodies, if not thousands, and while I didn't think they could do a damn thing to stop *me*, I knew they'd roll right over the rest of the group like a tide, and that seed of a plan I'd started to form for taking on the Crimson Queen would never get a chance to flower.

In front, Two-Feathers suddenly leapt from the saddle, his horse taking a half-dozen strides before it slowed and turned to join him. At the same time, Selene straightened in her seat, paying attention again for the first time since we'd turned north. She too brought her mount to a halt and motioned for the rest of us to do the same.

"What the—" began Jules, but Two-Feathers was already in motion, suddenly just *there* to slap a hand over the other man's mouth.

For a moment, I was pretty sure the nomad was a dead man, but even as I stopped my bike, a noise rose all around us, and Jules' eyes widened. It was a rustling that shook the trees in every direction, despite the lack of wind.

I waited for the sound of a baby crying, even though the White Wail walked to the south, but its cry never came. Which left only one alternative. I silently cursed Selene and her ghost as I pulled Evan to the ground, seeking dubious safety in the tall grass as the others dismounted and followed my lead.

Behind and above us, the first demon saw its quarry had finally been run to ground. Two mouths opened in a roar that was soon picked up by the rest of its kind—

—and then that roar was obliterated by a screeching that shook the world. The woods around us swayed like palms in a hurricane and darkness took to the sky in numbers that blotted out the setting sun. Hooked talons and stainless-steel beaks. Wings that could break a man's spine with one strike. And above it all, that sound that dug into your brain like an ever-growing splinter.

There were three great horrors that called Texas home. The White Wail. The Hunger that Walks. And last, but never least, the Terrorbirds.

And Selene's ghost had led us right to the Terrorbirds' roost.

17

There were surely screams as cultists and demons alike fell to the earth in steaming chunks, but nothing could be heard over the Terrorbirds' awful noise. There was no sky above us, just an endless expanse of wings a dozen or more layers deep, trees torn from the earth by the backdraft of their passage.

A horse bucked and tore free from its reins, panic giving it the energy our long flight had sapped, and that started a stampede, six of the seven mounts fleeing in terror back the way we had come. They made it a dozen strides before winged shadows dropped from the sky, some almost as large as the horses they were hunting. First a few, then too many to count, swarming like locusts instead of birds, then flapping away again to leave just a wreckage of blood, flesh, and bone.

Nobody knew for sure if the Terrorbirds had to eat or if they just killed out of boredom and sheer, unrelenting malice. Given their numbers, I was firmly in the second camp… a flock this size would have otherwise scoured the land of living creatures just to stay alive.

Beneath me, I could feel, if not hear, Evan's panicked moans. The only surviving horse, Two-Feathers', was lying on its side, the nomad's hands covering its eyes now instead of Jules' mouth, and almost everyone else had gone belly-down in the grass. I wasn't sure if they were just trying to avoid looking at the carnage happening around them, or if they were smartly keeping their eyes and faces hidden.

Selene was the sole exception, lying on her back with her limbs spread like a scarecrow, hair a dark halo in the dirt, eyes wide and smile even wider as she watched blood fall like rain from the sky that wasn't a sky.

Even when Bakersfield had lost his shit and wiped out a town of innocents, along with an old friend, half the Mission, and Dr. Nowhere himself, I didn't remember him being *that* crazy.

Outside of the horses, the Terrorbirds had ignored us so far, focused on the unwitting challenge the demons had made to their aerial supremacy, but I knew Shabaa's army had to be dead or fleeing. Soon, we'd be the only interlopers left. If we were lucky, the birds would sweep on south to hunt for stragglers, and then, when the bloodshed was over, pick a new forest to roost in. If we weren't lucky, they'd return to this stretch of woods, where we'd be one more threat swiftly and easily removed.

When an individual Terrorbird dropped into the clearing right next to Tom, empty, eyeless sockets seeking out the shapes and shadows about it, I knew we were fucked. Its metal beak opened, but the expected shriek never came. Great wings started to flap in a mix of fury and panic, striking Tom with bone-crunching impact, but the air itself pinned the bird to the earth, air that had been pulled from whatever it had for lungs, robbing it of speech, motion, and breath.

Twelve feet away, lying in the grass next to Two-Feathers and his horse, Jules had one arm outstretched, sweat pouring down his heavy cheeks, bloodshot eyes fixed on the bird in our midst.

It took a long time—too long, the color draining from Jules' face as the silent struggle stretched into minutes—but finally, the bird collapsed into a heap, suffocated from a distance. I risked another glance above us and saw bare stretches of sky and stars that glowed with a distant rage as powerful as the Terrorbirds themselves.

One bird. It had almost been our death, but it had been an outlier, drawn in our direction by curiosity or greed. The flock itself had continued south in full pursuit.

We climbed to our feet, seven people and one horse, covered in fresh blood and fluids but alive in the midst of death on a scale only one of us had previously experienced. Tom, the eighth member of our crew, was dead, bones crushed in that initial flutter of wings, but there was no time for burials. We left his broken body behind, turning to follow Two-Feathers as the nomad led his horse deeper into the now-empty woods. I took up rearguard again, pushing my motorcycle instead of riding it, because even its low hum might be enough to bring death back our way.

I already made too much noise as it was, just walking.

We continued that way for hours despite not having slept the night before. People slipped and staggered through the darkness, and I lost count of the number of times someone went down hard. Initially, whoever was closest was quick to offer aid, but by the end, they were all too tired to focus on anything but their own feet.

That left things to me, but even I had my limits. When I almost tripped over the next still figure, only to realize it was three of them, tangled in a heap, I knew we'd gone as far as we could. I caught up with Jules and called for a halt. The roost was miles behind us at this point. That distance would have to be enough. It made no sense to do the Terrorbirds' job for them.

There was no pretense of making camp. Two-Feathers spared a moment to rub down his horse, now our only horse, but everyone else just dropped where they stood. Even Evan, who had spent the last hour draped over the back of my bike, making pushing it through the underbrush that much more of a pain in the ass.

I didn't have to sleep, but I was struggling to string thoughts together. If there were any threats nearby, I had to hope Two-Feathers would have spotted them or that Selene's nutjob of a ghost would let us know. I stepped away from the others, down into a gully, and set the storm free.

○○○

Everyone was still alive the next morning, which was the first damn thing that had gone right since we'd entered Texas. Alive was a long way from okay though. Other than Havoc and Two-Feathers, the two Powers with physical gifts, most people looked exhausted, physically and emotionally.

The horses had been carrying most of our supplies, which left us low on clothing, shelter, and food in a forest that was still a long way from populated, even so many miles north of the roost. Cross had thought to grab his bags when he ducked for cover, and both Two-Feathers and I had our possessions, but as a group, we were going to be living off the land until we could find a town to resupply.

The good news was that Shabaa didn't seem to be hunting us anymore, assuming he even had people left to hunt with. Between the cultists we'd killed trying to break free and the small army the Terrorbirds had savaged, he had to be low on both humans and demons for the time being. Even better, it was unlikely he had any idea where we were.

The bad news was that I hadn't held up my end of the deal with Jules. *Get us all out of here, and I'm in,* he'd said, and while I didn't think the horses had been included in that bargain, I'm pretty sure Tom was another story.

"We've got some decisions to make," I told the tired-eyed people huddled in a circle around a small, smokeless fire. "About where we're going and who's coming with."

Jules stirred from his exhausted contemplation of the flames. "We're in the middle of nowhere with about a day's worth of rations between us. Most of us have our guns still but no ammo, and there's only one horse left. Why wouldn't we stick together?"

"Because I'm headed east. And yes," I told Evan, before he could muster his usual bullshit, "you're coming with me."

He rolled his eyes but said nothing.

"The rest of you," I continued, including Two-Feathers in my gesture, "can part ways here and now."

"Why *east?"* asked Havoc.

"There's a job, big man. The target is need-to-know."

"And if I *do* need to know?" He climbed to his feet where he loomed over me and every other person in the camp.

"Christ, Havoc," said Cross, flat on his back, one hand behind his head and the other on his stomach. "Sit your ass back down before she hands it to you in pieces. You've heard the stories."

I reconsidered my stance as Havoc took his seat. There was no point in keeping secrets anymore, was there? Maybe one or two of them would think assaulting a queen in her own city sounded like fun. "I guess there's no harm—"

"Queenie, can we have ourselves a talk real quick? In private?"

Jules took me away from the camp.

"I'm not sure telling them is the right move. Not now anyway."

"It's your crew and your call," I told him. "But I figured you'd want them to be able to make an informed choice."

"I do… just not yet. Maybe let them come with us to civilization first?"

"Us?"

"I made my choice, two days ago. You got us out, like you promised. I'm with you all the way to New Memphis."

"What about Tom? And the horses?"

"Not your responsibility. Only Weather Witches and Earthshakers deal in natural disasters." He shook his head. "Frankly, I'll miss the horses more than Tom."

"I can't believe I'm saying this, but me too."

"As for the others… we can all travel together until we reach a town and stock back up on food and the like."

"You planning to rob this town?"

"With a crew of four, a few dozen bullets, and no home to call our own? Ain't no future in that." He reached into his blood-soaked shirt and pulled out a coin purse that clinked when he shook it. "I'll be *paying,* like the upstanding citizen I am."

"I thought all your supplies went with the horses."

"Got to keep your valuables close when you ride with killers. Never know when someone's going to grow a conscience and turn to thievery instead. You know," he added, "*north* would get us to civilization a hell of a lot faster."

"We'd have to come back down south afterwards anyway. There's already snow in the Ozarks; we'll need to skirt the whole range on our way to New Memphis. Besides, we have things to do before we paint the city red."

"Things?"

"Things."

He shrugged. "East it is. But can we reach that first town before you fill my crew in and make them choose? No point saving their asses just to abandon them to starve in the woods. I've seen Havoc hunt and that shit is *not* pretty."

"You still think they'll bow out?"

"I think everyone here other than you just came face-to-face with their own mortality. Even Selene's too sane to double down after that."

"But *you're* coming with me."

"That was the deal. And like I said, I always wanted to see New Memphis." He grinned. "Now, what do you say we head back before that nomad of yours gets the wrong idea about what we're doing out here? I wouldn't want him to shove his spear anywhere delicate."

"If you want to point out the *non*-delicate bits, I'll suggest he start with those instead."

Oddly, Jules seemed disinclined to cooperate.

We returned to camp and briefed the others. East until we hit a town and got everyone supplied. Then, I'd share the target, and people would be given a choice between hiring on and walking.

Except for Evan, obviously. And Jules. And from the look Two-Feathers shot me, I was pretty sure he'd be coming with us, no matter what. After all, he'd known what the job was from the very beginning.

I held his look for a moment, just long enough for something to maybe spark between us, but then he turned and went to saddle his horse. Which was a crying shame, really; he'd found a stream nearby, and after refilling our canteens, he'd washed the blood off his body… and damned if *that*, combined with the post-battle jitters, wasn't the sort of thing to get my motor running.

This celibacy shit was getting old.

○○○

Traveling with a group of seven, most of us on foot, was every bit as tedious as expected, even before you factored in the scars sheer exhaustion had left on people. You could see it in the way they walked those first few days, in the silence that settled around the fire at night. Two-Feathers and Havoc had bounced back quickly enough, but one was busy hunting for enough meat to feed a large-sized family, and the other had been put to work making camp every night.

The others all just passed right out after eating.

By the third day, even Evan started to show signs of life again, but the lack of horses still made our daily progress a pitiful thing. Two-

Feathers brought down a deer one day, and we made camp early to cook, slice, and dry it for preservation, but without salt or a smokehouse, there were limits to how long anything he killed could last. And that meant more hunting while the sun was still up and less time available for travel.

Weeks passed, the monotony only broken by two things. The first was a pack of wild turkeys that fed our crew for a few days and let us all unleash some of our avian-related anger. The second was another stream. This time, more people than just Two-Feathers had the energy to wash away the sweat, dirt, fear, and gore from our desperate flight. From their faces, that did more to restore morale than the dozen nights of sleep that had come before.

And then, the next day, as if it had just been waiting for us to make ourselves presentable, a town came into view.

Actually, maybe *town* was giving it a little bit too much credit. There were ten to twelve buildings set behind a wall even a Normal could have climbed. Outside that wall were two small fields whose crops had been recently harvested, leaving behind a mess of stalks strewn across tilled dirt.

A shout told us that we'd been spotted. A minute or so later, a handful of people with rifles peeked down from the wall.

I let Jules do the talking. Now that he was clean, he looked a hell of a lot more respectable than I did, and the bastard could be charming when he really wanted to be. Even so, it was long minutes before the gates opened to admit us inside.

The village of Greenburg—I wasn't going to call it a town again, no matter what its residents claimed—was every bit as small as it had seemed from the outside, but they did have an inn with two guestrooms above and a common room below, as well as a general store, a tanner, a smith, and a bakery. Places like this often operated solely on barter, but they were happy to accept Jules' coin.

"Merchant Haslem should be stopping by in the next week or so," explained the man who ran the general store, "both to buy goods from us and to sell stuff we can't find or make ourselves."

That was a pleasant surprise; we had the means to pay our way, even in this small of a village. Unfortunately, the villagers didn't have much that we needed. No horses beyond the handful they used to plow the fields. No cases of ammunition to replace what we'd lost to Shabaa and the Terrorbirds. Clothing and food were available in semi-abundance, but everything else would have to be found elsewhere.

After some brief discussion, we decided to wait for the traveling merchant. There was a horse breeder somewhere on his circuit of stops, and that meant he might bring fresh mounts with him to Greenburg. And more downtime didn't seem like a terrible thing, with a roof over everyone's heads, and food cooked on a woodfired stove instead of over a campfire.

When yet another storm blew through the area, that choice looked even smarter.

Of course, putting five killers, a nomad, and Evan all under one roof with nothing else to do came with its own challenges, but at the beginning, everyone was too focused on recovery to make waves.

The trouble began five days into our stay.

ooo

"Hey Jules, is it true you and the queen used to be a thing?"

Havoc's voice made its way from the common area as I left the bedroom the crew had decided I should share with Selene. That left five of them in the second room, but apparently nobody wanted to sleep anywhere near the Crow if they could help it.

A little bit of nighttime stabbing will do that for a girl's reputation, I guess.

I had left Selene behind, sprawled out on a bare mattress, blankets and pillows piled high on the floor next to the bed for some reason that neither she nor her ghosts had elected to share. That was pretty much life sharing space with a Crow. Truthfully, I didn't spend a whole lot of time in the room but had opted to stash my saddlebags there while one of the younger men in town cleaned the filth off my bike.

Either Havoc hadn't seen me come in through the common room, or he thought I was planning to stay upstairs a while. Dumb though he was, I don't think he'd have brought my relationship with Jules up if he knew I was in earshot. Then again, maybe this was his feeble way of seeking entertainment. Cross had a deck of cards that he pulled out at every opportunity, but it had been raining for more than a day, and everyone was going stir crazy.

From my vantage point on the stairs, I couldn't see the Titan or the rest of our crew, but knew they were over by the stone fireplace on the far wall, playing another hand. Evan was the sole exception, as usual; he hadn't left his room except for meals and bio breaks since our arrival.

I couldn't hear Jules' response, but he must have said something, because Havoc kept going.

"Guess I can't blame ya. Thought my eyes were gonna fall out of my skull when she walked through our gate." His voice lowered to the volume of a normal person's shout. "The helmet's kind of creepy though, don't you think?"

Again, Jules said something I couldn't hear. I descended a few steps, curiosity as much a motivator as my growing irritation.

"Yeah, but what I want to know is how she looks without it. Woman wanders around with a tin can on their head, you have to think she's hiding something. Question is, is it something horrible or something that suits that body?"

"As far as I know, she never takes it off, but you need to—" began Jules, his voice rising with his temper.

"She doesn't? Even in the act? That's some weird shit."

"We know the stuff you're into, Havoc," said a third voice, Cross. "You've got no room to speak here. Shut up and deal."

There was a loud thunk as the Titan slammed his beer mug down on the table. "I bet she's hideous. Still, for tits like that, I'd close my eyes and—"

His words cut off as a chair hit the floor. I took the remaining steps to the common room and found all four men on their feet. Jules and Cross were on one side of the table looking concerned, and on the other…

Havoc was leaning back, arms flailing, one leg barely under him, the other kicked out to the side. Holding him from behind was Two-Feathers, a hand in the bigger man's hair, and a knife pressed against the big man's throat. It would take superhuman strength to cut even a low-rent Titan's flesh, but Two-Feathers passed that bar; a thin trickle of blood lazily charted its course past the other man's Adam's apple.

"Easy, brother," said Jules, patting the air as if he was trying to soothe a horse instead of a human. "Havoc's just drunk and talking crazy. He didn't mean anything."

"You sure about that?" I finally made my entrance and watched their faces go pale. "Seems to me like your man had some things he wanted to say."

"Shit, Queenie, he was—"

"Maybe we should go answer those questions, big man," I said, the sound of metal filling the air as I slid past Jules to look the struggling Titan in the face. "Just you, me, and the storm. Blink one for yes, blink two if you'd rather not."

Two-Feathers gave me a look I couldn't interpret, but the man under his knife blinked twice, and then a few more times in case I hadn't caught the first two. I let the silence stretch as I watched that trail of blood drip down to his collarbone and shirt, then nodded.

"Just as well. I don't let stupid stick its dick in me, and that means if I ever see any part of you that's unfit for company, I'm cutting it off, and planting it in the fields like a seed. Are we clear?"

With Two-Feathers' knife still at his throat, Havoc couldn't really nod. He had also apparently already forgotten the rules of our little blink game, as he opened and shut his wide bovine eyes at least a dozen times, the panic clear on his face.

I nodded to Two-Feathers, and he released the other man, stepping aside to let the off-balance Titan crash to the floor. I turned to Jules and Cross.

"Meeting in my room tonight after dinner. It's time we talked about the job and which of you, if any, are coming with me."

"The merchant—" said Cross.

"Is still on his way, I know. We'll wait until he comes but might as well get shit sorted tonight. Anyone who bows out will need to start making plans of their own."

"We'll be there," said Jules.

I nodded, looked at Two-Feathers for a very, very long time, then pushed out into the muddy street. It was raining like someone had pissed off a Weather Witch, but at least I *understood* the storm.

18

That night, we gathered upstairs as planned, a circle of space surrounding Selene and me both. I was amused to note that the Crow's circle was larger than mine, even after the afternoon's showdown, even though that slip of a girl didn't have a single offensive power to her name.

Men didn't make any fucking sense sometimes.

I filled them in on our target, ignoring Evan's gasp, Selene's odd smile, and the way even Cross swallowed upon hearing the news. I gave some, but not all, of the information I'd learned and waited for the inevitable protests.

I was not disappointed.

"You want the *seven of us* to sneak into the Crimson Queen's capital city, invade a palace full of Powers, and assassinate the woman herself?" Cross shook his head. "What could you even offer for a job like that?"

"Gold," murmured Selene, still smiling. "Jewels."

"Who cares what she's offering?" said Havoc. "None of it matters if we're dead."

Apparently, the Titan *did* have a brain.

"I'll be going with Queenie," said Jules.

Havoc blinked. "You think this is doable?"

"Hell if I know, but I gave my word. The rest of you can decide for yourselves. Rooms and meals are paid through the end of the week, but anything else comes out of your own pockets."

"I still want to know what the pay is," said Cross.

"Selene already told you." I showed them the coins in my hand, letting the lamplight cast arcs of gold across black leather. "One of these to each of you when we reach New Memphis. Another two when we finish the job. That goes for everyone; Jules, Evan, and Two-Feathers included."

Evan just shook his head, still a picture of misery.

"That's… enough to live on for a long while," breathed Cross.

"Or to settle down and start something different," I agreed, giving Jules a look.

"Can't spend gold as a deader," repeated Havoc, before wincing and giving Selene a glance. "Right?"

The Crow smiled and said nothing.

"It would help to know what your plan is," admitted Cross.

"The plan remains need-to-know. If you choose to sign up, I'll fill you in on the basics, but until then, what you don't know can't hurt me."

"If you've already heard enough and want out, let Queenie or me know, and no hard feelings," said Jules. "Otherwise, take a few days to think about it. If you want to see just how the hell we might pull things off, we'll have another meeting like this one for the crew who's going. Is Friday okay with you?" he asked, turning to me.

I nodded. So far, nobody had left.

"Friday then," said Jules. "Try to spend some of that time thinking instead of just drinking and flirting with Greenburg's four single women. The risks are high, yeah, but the rewards are too. Only you can decide which matters more."

○○○

Later that night, long after most of the crew had gone to sleep, Jules and I sat across from one another at a table in the otherwise empty common room.

"About Havoc," he said. "He's an ass. I'm sorry."

"Did *you* ever wonder?" I asked him.

"Wonder what?"

I let the fire reflect off my helmet and waited for him to find the answer on his own. Sure enough, he got there just fine.

"Well, sure. I mean, it's hard not to. But you said I wouldn't like what I saw. Guess I never felt the need to press for more. Someone wearing a motorcycle helmet in the sack is a long way from the strangest thing I've encountered, and you're a beautiful woman."

"I was created, not born," I told him.

"So I've gathered over the years."

"This," I said, waving my hands at my leather-clad body, "wasn't my choice, but it's the shell I have and the shell I'll die in. Same holds true for this." This time, I rapped knuckles on my helmet. "It's a part of who and what I am. That's not changing, even if everything else does."

"Everything else?"

I stared into the fire and said nothing, not sure why I'd said it.

"What else is changing, Queenie?" he pressed.

"The Old Man is dead."

"What? When? How?"

"A few weeks before we came down to save your ass. I passed through Lawton looking for you and your crew. He knew his time was short and wanted to spend it reminiscing."

"Damn." His whistle was low and haunting. "The end of an era *and* an institution. I was sure he was going to outlive us all. Everyone but you, I guess. I didn't get to see him regularly anymore, but it's hard to imagine him gone."

"He's not the only one. Did you ever meet Vo Binh Raya?"

"I don't think so. Was he a friend?"

"She." Even the storm was quiet. "I guess she was a little bit before your time with me. She retired and was working as a spymaster in Kansas City. I had only just learned she had a daughter and then she was killed. Dr. Nowhere, the people of Eclipse, Raya, and the Old Man, all in the span of a few years. That's the post-Break world for you."

"Queenie," asked Jules, voice oddly gentle, "what happened to you in the City of the Sun?"

I shrugged off the non-sequitur. "Nothing of value."

"Humor me."

I looked across the table into his eyes. "I found Dr. Nowhere, like I said. He didn't have any good answers for me and then he was dead. I didn't want to kill Bakersfield, assuming I even could have, so I left. Decided to take a bit of time to think things over."

"And?"

"Turns out I'm not much of a thinker."

The young Jules would have accepted that and moved on, but this new version didn't let me off the hook. Instead, he took a sip of his beer and waited for more.

"I don't know," I finally said. "I'd been chasing answers since before the Old Man was even born. Only, when I finally found those answers, they didn't make a damn bit of difference. Maybe I just decided to sulk a bit. Take a vacation. See what life was like away from the road."

"And now?"

"Eclipse is ashes, and I have a job to do. Nothing's changed."

"It's like listening to a recording of myself a year ago."

"I'm sorry?"

"I used to tell myself the same thing. *Nothing's changed, Jules. Your hair's not thinning; it's just the lack of humidity. That knee's hurting because you slept on it funny. You're not tired; you just don't feel like staying up and drinking all night."*

"Your point?"

"One of the few things all humans have in common is our ability to lie to ourselves."

"I'm not human. You know that."

"Apparently, you're close enough to count." He winked. "It wasn't until I started losing crewmembers that I saw my lies for what they were. That I really understood what was going on."

"Dementia?"

"Fear. I've been doing this shit for half my life and have nothing to show for it. I'm slower than I used to be. At some point, I won't be able to keep up. If Selene hadn't killed that enforcer of mine when she did, the bastard would have probably challenged me within the month."

"Maybe that's why she did it."

"I don't—" His voice trailed off and he went pensive. "You know, I never thought of that. Not sure how to feel about it either. My point is that this is a young man's line of work, and with me starting to age out of it, I looked around and saw nothing but tumbleweeds. No home and no family."

"And that scared you?"

"Not really."

I was starting to think Jules was drunker than he looked. And that I should never have gone down this rabbit hole with him.

"I'm not scared of how things *are.* I'm scared of *what comes next.* After New Memphis, if we survive it. Of change I can't avoid. Twenty years went by in a flash, and I don't know who I'll be in a few more. Just another regular drinking himself to death at the Last Shot? A grumpy hermit living on the outskirts of some remote town? This life is all I know and the fear of what's next has had me trying to convince myself I could keep riding forever."

"You've got time. You're forty, not dead."

He finished off his beer with a sigh. "Forty-one, as of two months ago, with a thousand literal miles of bad road behind me, to say nothing of the blood. Guess I'm starting to wonder if it was worth it, or if I was lying to myself even back then."

"And you think this mid-life crisis has something to do with me? That I'm lying to myself like you've apparently been doing because I'm afraid of change?"

"Aren't you?"

"Of course not. I *don't* change. That's the whole fucking point. It's me, the road, and a job. Now and forever."

"You don't think hiring yourself for a job counts as change?"

"There was *nobody left alive* to hire me."

He pushed his empty mug aside, recognizing the storm in my voice. "I'm not arguing on that point. And the fact is, some people just need killing. But from where I'm sitting, you already *have* changed. I'm just not sure why you're pretending otherwise."

I said nothing, my thoughts like empty static.

"Maybe I'm just drunk and projecting," he allowed. "Maybe I'm jealous that time leaves its mark on the rest of us while you get to ride forever."

"It's not the sort of—"

"But we had something once, you and me, and even though that's gone, I still give a shit. You have a job—*we* have a job—but you're not the same woman I rode with, years ago. And when shit goes down and you're the only one left to ride away, I guess I just want to know you'll be okay. Maybe what you were created to be doesn't have to define you for the rest of forever."

I studied his face, not buying whatever it was he was selling. As much as Jules thought I'd changed, it was *his* transformation that concerned me. Not just the physical one, but what age and time were doing to him internally. It was something I'd seen recently in Raya, in Jules, and especially in the Old Man, almost like all three had grouped up to teach me a course on what it meant to be mortal. And for all my own regrets and missteps over the many, many decades, it felt like there was still some missing piece I didn't grasp. That I could never grasp.

I spared a fraction of a thought to wonder if Bakersfield knew what that piece was and if he was sane enough to even tell me. Then, I buried the question along with all those that had come before it. I had a job to do. Jules and I both did, and success depended on him being the stone-cold killer I remembered, not this would-be philosopher who seemed content to stand with one foot in retirement and a second in the grave. And whatever came after that, to either of us, was a problem we could face then.

"Fuck the future," I told him. "Live in the present. Kill whatever's in your way and the rest will sort itself out."

"I remember the Old Man's creed."

"It's not about *remembering*, Jules. I need you to fucking live it. The way that you used to."

For a moment, that angry light flashed in his eyes, and I waited for the bloodthirsty grin that fit him best. Instead, he shrugged. "The rest of us don't have eternity like you do."

"All the more reason to focus on the now instead of what's coming."

"Maybe you're right." He got to his feet, leaving the mug behind. "Or maybe the creed is just another lie we tell ourselves."

19

A day later, the storm broke, and a day after that, I was finally given access to the village's generator. I had quite a few batteries to recharge after our flight through Texas, but they weren't the main reason I'd pushed the mayor so hard for admittance. I hadn't withheld the details of my plan to kill the Crimson Queen from the others because of operational security. The plan was, at best, just a skeleton of an idea as it currently stood, and the information I needed to turn it into something worth sharing was locked away.

Greenburg's generator was my chance to finally change that.

I set my saddlebags down on the cottage's floor and pulled out the tablet I'd taken from Raya's doppelganger. By the time I'd thought to check the device, its battery had been dead as dead could be, but I was banking on the fact that the real Raya had stored her research here, that the edited docs the fake Raya had given me were just a subset of a greater whole. If I was lucky, the Body Shifter wouldn't have deleted the rest of that data. And maybe, just maybe, there'd be enough to form a plan that would make this less of a suicide mission for whoever opted to join my crew.

The generator wasn't a type I'd seen before. Greenburg didn't have solar panels or ready access to even low-grade fuel. What they did have was a mayor who was a low-grade Spark. This generator accepted the electrical charge he dumped into it each morning, turning it into usable energy that the town's few tools and appliances could run off. The Free States did something similar on a massive scale, with a small army of low-end Sparks supporting the nationwide energy grid through power stations that I had never visited or truly understood. This machine was infinitely smaller and likely far less efficient but well-suited for an individual town's needs.

I looked it over and found a stylized crown and the letters *C.E.* stamped into the metal frame.

"C.E.?"

The mayor had been hovering nervously nearby, as if afraid I was going to stomp his generator into fragments. He cleared his throat. "I believe it stands for the Crimson Empire, but you can ask Merchant Haslem when he arrives. He's the one who sold it to us; I'm not entirely sure when or where he acquired it."

I glared down at the ingenious little device. Between the car in Kansas City and this thing, it was starting to seem like the Crimson Queen had more than just armies on her side.

Thankfully, whatever mad Technomancer had modified the generator hadn't reinvented its connections too. I hooked up Raya's tablet, the tablet I'd given her years earlier, and watched the blinking light that was the only indicator something was happening.

There was nothing to do but wait.

About ten minutes into my vigil, the mayor excused himself, and ten minutes after that, shuffling footsteps announced someone coming to take his place.

"We're going to New Memphis," said Evan.

"Eventually, yeah."

"You want to take *me*. To a *city*." He bit off the last three words, the harsh tone an uncomfortable fit for his nebbish persona.

"That's right." I'd been waiting for this conversation, ever since I told Evan and the others who and where our target was. Whatever he called himself now, I'd known what the little man's response would be.

"New Memphis is one of the big cities left outside of the Free States," he said, telling me nothing I didn't already know. "There are thousands of people living there."

"Probably more, given the way the Crimson Queen's been recruiting." Armies required infrastructure, and infrastructure required numbers. I hadn't been to the city since it was just plain Memphis, but had to believe the new version was straining at the seams with all the people needed to support the queen's dreams of conquest.

"And what makes you think I would go to a place like that ever again?" I still hadn't looked at Evan, but the anger added steel to his voice.

"Because you gave your word."

"That's—"

This time, I did turn to face him. "You lost your name," I said, the metal harsh in my voice, the storm responding to anger with a fury of its own. "You lost your fame, your wealth, and even your self-respect, but you still have your life and your word. Maybe the first one doesn't mean shit to you anymore, although your actions so far have suggested otherwise. But your word? Once that goes, what will you have left? Miles or Rupert or Evan or whatever you want to call yourself, what will you be?"

He glared up at me, fists clenched at his side, but said nothing. Finally, he dropped his gaze, the fight going out of his small frame. "I'll go to New Memphis and help how I can, but I'm not using my power there, of all places. If you have a problem with that, kill me here. Greenburg is as fine a place as any to die."

The tremor in his voice gave lie to the brave front, but I opted not to call him on that. As I'd told Jules, Evan was insurance. Getting him to New Memphis was the first step. If I needed more...

Well, we'd revisit the subject when it mattered.

○○○

By Friday, the merchant still hadn't arrived. Three straight card games devolved into arguments before Jules kicked his crew out of the inn to help prepare the town for winter. And that night, we met in Selene's room again.

There were seven of us still. Jules, Evan, and Two-Feathers, each of whom either had no choice or had made those choices clear. Havoc, who had demanded to see his full payment before signing on, in case the few coins I'd shown were all I had. Cross, who I'd been sure would take an out when given it, who seemed too smart to agree to a suicide mission, even for more wealth than he'd ever had in his life. And lastly, Selene, who...

Well, honestly, I wasn't sure if Selene was on board or not. She'd just smiled when Jules asked, and my old companion had taken that as confirmation.

"New Memphis," I said, tablet in hand, "is a big city, built atop a manmade hill, and growing larger all the time. The outermost layer is mostly slum or harbor and easy enough to access, but the rest has been divided into concentric circles, radiating out from the center-point that is the Crimson Queen's palace."

"Divided how?" asked Cross.

"By literal walls. Security increases the deeper you go. Think Kansas City except with only one cartel in charge and a hell of a lot more organized firepower."

"You're not selling this at all, lady." Havoc had his arms folded across his broad chest, face twisted with the scowl that had been his constant companion as of late.

"You bought in," said Cross. "There's no folding this hand."

"The palace is in the center at the top of the hill, the first and smallest district." I referenced the tablet. "Getting there means breaching the walls of every other district below it."

"Which is something you don't need us for." Jules frowned. "I've seen you cut your way right through pre-Break bunkers. Why do you want a crew for this job?"

"The Crimson Queen has at least fifty Powers that she calls Immortals," I said, not really answering his question. "Maybe more. They aren't a part of her regular army, and she keeps some of them by her at all times. Even if I could put them all down, one is a short-range Teleporter, and several others can fly. There's nothing to stop them from just taking her away and making this whole thing pointless."

"Breaking into the palace doesn't seem necessary," said Cross. "She fancies herself a queen, right? She must make public appearances. Find the right caliber weapon, wait for her to show, and then pop goes the weasel. No muss, no fuss."

"She's a Power too," I admitted.

"Of course she is." Havoc shook his head. "Otherwise, one of her Immortals would have stomped her into people-paste a long time ago."

Jules leaned forward, eyes sharp. "What kind of Power?"

"Telekinetic. She creates some sort of shielding an inch or so above her skin. Not sure what the Free States would rank her as, but the storm couldn't pierce it. Something tells me bullets won't either."

That was why I needed a crew. Or at least the one man I'd gone into Texas to find. And from the look on his face, Jules had already figured that out.

"Before we can kill the queen, we have to reach her," I told the others. "That means breaching the security of the inner districts. And that's where Tillatoba comes in."

"What the hell is a Tillatoba?" asked Havoc.

"It *was* a town before the Break. A day or two east of the Mississippi river. A few years back, when the Crimson Queen was starting up her war, it became the first of her processing stations."

"Ore or fuel?"

"Humans." I let that sink in. "Her empire's growth has been fueled by conquest. Refugees and prisoners all get filtered through one of these stations. Those with useful skills who buy into the party line become provisional citizens, working to support the war effort. Powers who prove themselves loyal become Immortals. Meanwhile, the uncooperative Normals die there in the stations or are put to work in the fields and mines, while the stubborn Powers are broken and used as cannon fodder in the next assault."

"How many troops does she even have?"

"Enough to make Shabaa's horde look small, I think. New Memphis is her capital, but she's taken control of a huge chunk of what used to be the war-torn South, crushing other warlords as she goes. Her territory rivals anything outside of the Free States. That's good and it's bad."

"Bad because there's only seven of us," reasoned Jules. "Good because…?"

"First, because it takes numbers to control that large an area, especially when you rule through fear and power. A battalion is stationed in Memphis, but most of her other forces are spread across the land, with Immortals allocated as necessary."

"And second?"

"The bigger the empire, the greater the bureaucracy. Gate security in Memphis is largely automated, with district access based on credentials. Provisional citizens can't travel beyond District 5, full citizens beyond District 4, administrators beyond District 3, and so on, all the way to the palace itself. Proper credentials are the key to New

Memphis." I tapped the tablet against my hip. It had taken hours to recharge the tablet and days to puzzle through Raya's shorthand notes, but I'd found what I needed.

Jules caught on fast, as expected. "And the processing stations provide credentials for the people who get sent on to the capital." He popped his knuckles and grinned. "We're going to Tillatoba."

"We're going to Tillatoba," I agreed. "I doubt they'll be able to provide credentials that give us access to District 2, let alone the palace, but they'll at least get us into the city. We make our way up the hill, spend a few days mapping out the queen's movements, and then…"

I pointed to Cross, and he was happy to oblige.

"Pop goes the weasel."

"Damn fucking straight."

○○○

It wasn't much of a plan, really, but people seemed satisfied with it, or at least too busy cursing me in their heads to vocalize their displeasure. The information Raya had gathered had been mostly focused on my original ask: the identity and location of the troops responsible for Eclipse's destruction. We were fortunate that the woman had taken my request as an opportunity to augment her own knowledge of an increasingly dangerous neighbor, but there were a lot of details still waiting to be fleshed out until we got up close and personal views of both Tillatoba and the Crimson Queen's palace in New Memphis.

Jules came to find me outside after the meeting, shivering as his heavy jacket did too little to stop the cold night wind. We hadn't talked since that night in the common room, and I wasn't sure if he'd been avoiding me or if I'd been the one doing the avoiding. He plopped down next to me in the dirt, back against the inn's exterior wall.

"How do you know I'll be able to kill her?" he asked.

"She kept her shield up the whole time she was trying to recruit me. The fact that I could hear her means sound waves pass through the shield, but I don't know any Sirens to recruit. Not since the Swan died back before you were born anyway. Still, if sound travels through it, I'm guessing other stuff does too. She was breathing during all of that. Little chest rising and falling because she was just so gosh darn excited to make my acquaintance."

"And?"

"That means oxygen makes it through her shield too, or she'd have run out of air just talking to me. A normal Wind Dancer might not be able to do much with that, but you've never been a normal Wind Dancer. Sucking all the air out of one Southern belle should be a hell of a lot easier than doing the same to a Terrorbird."

"And if you're wrong?"

"Then all that time you spent worrying about retirement will seem pretty damn foolish."

It was a coin flip whether my saying that would piss him off. I was kind of hoping it would, hoping for another glimpse of the fire that had made him a killer. Instead, he laughed and shook his head.

"I always hated that classification. *Wind Dancer.* What the hell were the Free States scientists even thinking?"

"The nomads call people like you Whisperers instead."

"Wind Whisperers?"

"Just Whisperers."

"Shit. That's not half bad. Still has nothing at all to do with my ability, but at least it doesn't sound like I should be up on a stage with theme music."

"Don't knock theme music, Jules. Kill the Crimson Queen and you'll have enough money to hire a musician to walk around dropping panties on your behalf."

"You're really going to pay me the same as the others? Even though I already agreed to go?"

"Since you're the one I really need, it seems fair."

"And you like fair. I remember." He chewed on that and finally nodded. "Guess we'll see what we see. But first, I wanted to talk about Miles."

It took far too long for me to remember that was the name Evan was using, considering the heart-to-heart I'd just had with the little man two days earlier. "What about him?"

"Are you sure you want to bring him along? I don't know who he was or why he owes you a favor, but I've encountered people like him before. Something's broken, deep inside, and I'm not talking the way *we're* broken, the way that lets us do the things we do. Whatever it is you think he'll do when shit goes sideways… I don't think he's got that in him anymore. I sure as shit wouldn't hire a man like that onto my crew. Weak links get everyone around them dead."

"Says the man who was weeping into his ale a few nights ago." I turned the smile across my visor in his direction.

"Fuck you right back." Jules' grin had teeth. "I was drunk and being philosophical-like. A man's got that right, you know, especially when reminiscing with an ex."

"As long as it's only when you're drinking. I need that killer inside of you still. As for *Miles…* when we need him, *if* we need him, he'll come through."

"How can you be sure?"

"Sometimes, people break so hard that they can't ever go back to who they were. All the time and healing in the world can't do a damn bit of good. So instead, you have to break them even more, clear aside that detritus and push them to become someone new."

"And?"

"And then he'll do what needs to be done."

We sat together in silence for a bit before Jules, as always, had to ruin it. "And what if there's nothing left of him, when all that breaking's done?"

I let the empty night swallow his question, as Jules retreated into the warmth of the inn, content to have gotten the last word. I waited for the door to shut behind him, waited for the owl outside the wall to ask its own question to the world, and then turned my head to the sky above, my voice a whisper of barbed wire on bone.

"If there's anything I've learned about people, it's that the breaking's never done."

20

On Saturday, the merchant finally arrived, two horses pulling a covered wagon whose canvas top had been dyed orange and yellow in a virulent combination that would have given me nausea if I had a stomach. The villagers the mayor had sent out to gather firewood came trailing behind the wagon, and every door in Greenburg opened as families issued forth, arms laden with local goods they hoped to trade for Haslem's merchandise.

I felt Two-Feathers step up on my left as Jules matched him on my right. As usual, only one of them spoke.

"Thank fuck he brought a string of horses."

Two-Feathers nodded his agreement.

It took a while for the merchant to settle in. First, both his lead horses and his stock were led away to be fed and cared for. Then, he disappeared into the mayor's house, presumably to give the Spark news from the outside world and first crack at any screaming deals.

After he left, a middle-aged woman climbed down from the wagon, followed by a teenage boy who seemed too much a blend of both adults to be anything but their son. The pair went around to the back of the wagon and removed the long wooden board that had barricaded its entrance. Two minutes later, that board had become a table, set up in front of the mayor's house, and the mother and son were filling that table with a variety of goods, from fabric like the roll of silk I'd found for Duke's mom, Mina, to manufactured goods that likely bore the mark of the Crimson Empire.

"Take Two-Feathers with you to judge the horses," I told Jules. "And find out what this merchant knows about the empire he's clearly trading with."

He cocked his head. "You know… if we just wait for them to leave again, we could follow behind and get those horses for, shall we say, a considerable bargain."

I waited for the transactional part of me to tell me that wasn't allowed, that taking without an equal return would upset the balance. Instead, there was nothing. Not even the hint of a twinge.

What was that about?

After a moment, I shook my head and kicked the decision down the road. "Let's not make plans just yet. Go scope out the horses, buy the ammo you need, and ask them about the Crimson Queen. Everything else can wait."

I watched both men leave and turned to take in the organized mayhem that had erupted at the merchant's arrival. Truthfully, I wasn't sure how the people of Greenburg felt about our crew. On the one hand, we'd brought a welcome infusion of coin to the village, coin that was even now being used to make purchases that otherwise might have been out of their reach. On the other, we'd been there for more than a week, and I think the villagers were almost as tired of us as we were of them. And on the third hand, people like Selene and Havoc couldn't help but radiate danger, to say nothing of the six-foot-two woman in black leather and a helmet who didn't eat, drink, or sleep.

For the most part, the villagers had done their best to avoid us, leaving the inn's common room empty on a nightly basis. With the arrival of the merchant and his family, however, our crew went from concern to afterthought faster than a Speedster sprinting for the outhouse. It was hours before Jules and Two-Feathers were able to speak with the merchant, and another hour after that when the innkeeper thought to let us know that the town would be having a feast the next day and that we were all invited.

That feast began in the inn's common room and spilled out into the streets, where a pole with colored lengths of string had been hastily erected in the town square across from the merchant's wagon. Beer and ale were in great demand, and while the food was mostly what we'd been fed since our arrival, it was available in quantities that could make even our Titan happy, supplemented by a three-antlered buck Two-Feathers had brought into town the day before.

I hadn't missed the way the mayor's daughter had hung all over the nomad as she cooed her breathy appreciation for that little feat. Thankfully, neither had the mayor; the young teen swiftly found herself saddled with a chaperone and a shawl that covered the cleavage she'd been doing her very best to display.

Whether Two-Feathers had noticed the interplay or even cared remained one of the great unanswered questions of the post-Break world. Still, that one deer brought him as much good will as all of Jules' carefully spent money combined. The people of Greenburg understood commerce, but they *appreciated* generosity.

By the afternoon, the party was in full swing, drunkards populating the inn, while pretty much everyone else celebrated outside despite the chill. I watched as Jules lived up—or down—to the Wind Dancer classification he hated, joining the townsfolk in a complicated series of steps involving the pole, all those bits of string, and an ever-changing array of partners. Even Evan got pulled into the action by a rosy-cheeked, whip-thin widow whose increasingly overt advances put the mayor's daughter to shame.

When one of Greenburg's all-too-eligible young men came my way, I almost went with him. Wouldn't have been the first townie I loved and left behind, after all. Maybe not even the fiftieth, although the numbers had blurred over the decades, along with their faces. Instead, I retreated into the inn, and then, upon being greeted by a wall of noise and drunken revelry, pushed through the common room and up the stairs. Selene had stayed behind, as usual, and her blend of quiet craziness was a lot more inviting than the revelry going on below us.

I stopped, mid-stairway, as that thought set in. When the hell had I become the sort of person to shy away from parties? I'd never been able to eat or drink, of course, but the lure of fighting and fucking wasn't the sort of thing I'd ever turned my nonexistent nose up at.

After a moment's thought, I decided to blame Jules and his pointed bullshit questions. I blamed Dr. Nowhere for creating me and getting killed without cleaning up his mess, Bakersfield for doing that killing, dying himself, then turning up alive again long after I'd finished mourning his crazy little ass. And I blamed Two-Feathers for being a mystery who didn't seem interested in me unwrapping him.

I blamed a lot of people, really, all of them men, and felt better by the end of it. When this was done, when the would-be queen was dead and her debt to Eclipse paid, I would take a trip. Just me, the storm, and my bike, seeing where the road took us as we left everything else behind. No distractions. No regrets. No questions. Just a series of moments to be dealt with and then forgotten.

In the meantime, the company of a lady Crow who spent more time talking to her ghosts than the rest of us combined would have to do. I climbed the rest of the stairs and walked past the men's bunkroom and into the bedroom I shared with Selene.

On the right wall was my bed, neatly made like it had been when we first rented the rooms. On the left was Selene's ever-changing tower of bedding, then the bare mattress itself. And on top of that mattress was the Crow, although she'd finally changed position. After a week where she'd laid there with arms raised above her head and legs spread at an angle that made every man who entered deeply uncomfortable, she was now curled up on her side, one arm dangling behind her, the other folded up against the wall she faced.

It looked uncomfortable as hell, even to someone who could reform their shell at will and therefore never had to deal with lasting pain, let along something as small as a crick in her neck. Still, the one thing I'd learned about Crows was that they were going to do what they wanted, and it wasn't worth trying to change that. I shrugged and went to sprawl out on my own bed. I wouldn't be able to let the storm go, of course, not if I wanted a bed to still be there when I was done, but there was something to be said for letting furniture battle with gravity in my stead.

Only… when I gave Selene one last look on the way to my bed, I noticed something I hadn't initially seen: darkness on the fingertips of the arm folded against the wall.

I was pretty sure it was blood.

Jules and his crew avoided coming anywhere near Selene if they could help it, but I didn't have anything to fear from a woman with noodle-thin arms and a knife. I tugged her away from the wall, and she flopped onto her back. One side of her face was a mess, and though she was breathing, my not-so-gentle ministrations did nothing to wake her up.

The darkness on her fingers *was* blood. For a moment, I thought she'd done this to herself—that something she saw or heard or believed in that kooky Crow brain of hers had convinced her to savage her own face—but it didn't add up. She hadn't drawn the knife the boys worried so much about, and the damage to her face had been done by something heavy and blunt, like a hammer, a mallet, or…

I spun away from Selene, gaze darting across the room to my own bed, and the saddlebags I'd left against the wall. Even from a distance, I could see those bags were less full than they had been. A quick investigation confirmed it: Raya's treasure box was gone.

Who knew about the wealth in my saddlebags and had the strength to put Selene down before she could even draw her blade? There were only two people who fit the billing, and one of those two had spent the morning being stalked by the mayor's daughter in plain sight. The other…

Well, it occurred to me that I hadn't seen Havoc all day.

○○○

It was almost therapeutic, seeing how quickly Jules left the revelry when I came to get him. It didn't make up for his insistence on examining the scene himself, as if he'd see something I had missed, but Havoc *was* his man. I guess it made sense to be sure.

"That rat-faced, thieving bastard!"

"So, you haven't seen him today either?"

"Not since this morning. With the festival going on, it would've been child's play for him to sneak out."

"He won't get far, even with a several-hour lead. Not in land he doesn't know and not on foot."

"That's why he took a horse," said Selene.

Except, when we looked, she was still where I had moved her, eyes closed, and no evidence that she was awake. Only her bruised lips moved, and the cadence was all wrong, the words a chilling whisper that slipped into the room like winter frost.

"One of Selene's ghosts, I presume?" I asked her/it.

"The only one that matters." Selene's body pulled itself up to a sitting position, but the way it got there was all wrong, limbs moving jerkily and out of rhythm, the head lolling from side to side with each shift. Finally, it was upright, and that head tilted back to regard us, eyelids cracking open in a field of bruises like flowers starting to bloom.

"You again," it said, and for some reason, the ghost inside Selene was looking at me instead of Jules. "This does change things."

"Who are you?" asked Jules, his voice as steady as a rock.

"Ask the smiling one," it said. "She knows."

There was only one ghost who had ever spoken to me directly, through a different Crow in a small town in the Badlands. She'd carried a message from Bakersfield and the two of us had struck the deal that became the first in the long trail of dominos that led to both Dr. Nowhere and Tyrant's deaths.

I didn't say her name, not there, and not out loud, but she was right. I knew her, and I wondered how Selene, of all people, had ended up with the ghost of the Free States' greatest serial killer riding her like she was a prized steed.

"Jules, go check the stables. See if a horse is missing."

I could see the questions in his eyes, but this wasn't a friendly chat over ale. This was combat and bloodshed, and he knew better to question orders on the battlefield. He brushed past me and out the door.

"What do you want?" I asked Selene's rider.

She straightened Selene's spine, something cold and dark lurking behind the other woman's pale blue eyes.

"There is a man," she said, in a whisper that filled the too-small room, "who needs killing."

21

By the time I made it downstairs and into the street, Jules was on his way back with Two-Feathers, a scowl on his face. "Selene was right," he said. "Havoc stole one of the merchant's horses."

"Apparently, you weren't the only one with that idea."

He glanced around for a moment, eyes twitching, but the sounds of the ongoing festival made eavesdropping impossible.

"Seems so. Of course, now he's fucked that plan up unless we do the same and leave immediately."

"Is the crew all packed, with ammo and fresh supplies? Food, bedding, shelter, and the like?"

He bit off a curse. "Not yet. And I'm pretty sure Miles is too drunk to even walk, let alone ride."

"It's probably for the best. Selene will be coming with us to New Memphis and she's not in any shape to travel just yet."

"Well of course she's coming with…" He paused. "Does that mean her ghosts are on board with the job?"

"The only one that matters, yes."

"And who is that, exactly?"

"No idea," I lied. "Apparently someone I had an encounter with when they were still alive. What matters is that they not only knew Havoc had stolen, they told me the direction he took after leaving Greenburg."

"And that direction was?"

"North."

In retrospect, it was obvious. West meant returning to the area where we'd encountered the Terrorbirds. East was where the rest of us were heading. South was... well, Havoc had likely seen enough of the south lately. Meanwhile, north led to the Badlands' version of civilization, and a place to spend the riches he'd stolen.

Unfortunately for our errant Titan, it also meant a road I could follow on my bike. Five minutes later, I tore out of town, Two-Feathers on his horse behind me, the two of us chasing down a man who didn't realize he was already dead.

Jules had stayed behind, but we'd traded glances as I left, and there hadn't been a speck of mercy in my old friend's cold eyes. It was nice to see the killer resurface when it mattered, rising from where it had been hidden under exhaustion, age, and layers of human flesh. For the first time since I'd found him, I started to believe this whole assassination plot might work.

If Havoc had taken to the woods, he might have had a chance to escape. Not much of one, not with Two-Feathers' tracking skills, but *a* chance. With Selene's ghost pointing us in the right direction, and the thief himself sticking to the dirt road, that chance was gone. It was a matter of hours before we caught the first sight of trail dust ahead, of someone moving at speed for all the good it was doing him. Havoc was not a small man, and between his own weight and that of the gold he'd taken, his stolen horse couldn't compare to the nomad's.

And then there was my bike, which, even on a dirt road like this, could maintain a pace that would leave both horses far behind.

I stayed with Two-Feathers instead of accelerating to catch Havoc. If the Titan looked over his shoulder even once, he'd see our own dust, and that would be when he fled the road. Better to stick together so I didn't overshoot my prey.

Even that much thought was apparently beyond Jules' former henchman, however. We were a few hundred paces behind when he finally heard us and looked about, eyes widening to find hell at his heels. And then he did the third dumb thing in as many hours—fourth, if you considered punching Selene and stealing from me as two separate events.

He turned his horse, and dismounted to face us, large fists held before him like he was going to box his way to freedom.

"He… didn't steal any ammo?" I asked Two-Feathers, getting a shrug in reply. "Jesus. I've never minded big and dumb, but this is *way* too much of a good thing."

This time, there was something almost irritated in the nomad's shrug, and I turned the smile across my visor his way to let him know I'd caught it.

"He's yours, if you want him," I said, adding a little bit of sugar to the salt. "For defending my honor and all that."

For a moment, Two-Feathers just looked at me, as the Titan waiting for us gave out a growl. Finally, he cracked a smile of his own. Black eyes sparkling, he waved a hand in Havoc's direction, a gesture I interpreted as *He's all yours.*

Hell if I was going to say no to that.

I put my kickstand down, dismounted, and headed for the dead man, adding a little bit of sway to my hips on top of what Dr. Nowhere had already given me. I watched the stubborn anger on Havoc's face fade with every step, watched the fear come oozing out of the big man's pores, and the moment his mouth flapped open as he issued a challenge or begged for his life or did whatever it was he chose to do before he died.

I didn't hear a word of it, of course, because the storm was already on its way.

I reformed my shell, five feet past what had been a mediocre Power and an even worse man. The horse Havoc had stolen was gone, but Two-Feathers soon emerged from the woods with it in tow. His own steed waited back down the road next to my bike, as stationary as if the nomad had parked it.

Havoc's stolen horse held a saddle, canteen, and sack. I checked the last one first and found a change of clothes, a loose fistful of turkey jerky, and the box containing Raya's treasure.

"All's well that ends well, I guess." I slipped the box back into my saddlebags. "Someone this dumb would have been a hindrance more than an asset once we hit New Memphis."

Two-Feathers said nothing, as usual, but crouched down as he examined the legs of Havoc's stolen steed.

"Problem?"

He nodded and pointed at the horse's front left hoof… which helped not at all, considering I didn't know the first damn thing about the beasts. Still, I'd been around enough other riders to know that hoof problems were never good. "Are we going to have to put it down?"

He gave me a look that I could interpret even without words, and shook his head, pulling the saddle off the horse, and slinging it over one shoulder. That done, he turned the index and pointer finger of one hand downwards, wiggling them back and forth across the palm of his other hand.

It seemed we were *walking* back to Greenburg. Lately, I'd been pushing my bike as much as riding it.

I nodded to say I'd understood what he was saying, only to remember that *I* was perfectly capable of speech. "How long do you think it'll take us to walk back?" I asked.

He cocked his head, pointed to me, and made a sharp motion with his arm. A month earlier, I might have taken it as a dismissal, but now I knew he was saying it was okay for me to go on ahead.

"Nice try," I told him, raising my kickstand and pushing my bike as we went. "We left together, we're going back together."

No smile this time, but there was no hiding that sparkle.

Night fell halfway through our return trip, and we made camp, just the two of us and some horses. I waited for Two-Feathers to clear the remnants of his dinner and took a seat, next to him instead of across the fire. The woods around us were quiet except for the occasional owl noise or rustle, and I felt almost at peace.

"I don't have to breathe," I told him. "But this feels like the first time I've been able to since before Texas."

He didn't respond, but his focus shifted from the fire to me.

"Too many people," I explained after a long moment. "Sometimes, it gets old. Sometimes, the storm just wants to be free. I know that probably doesn't make sense, but—"

He stopped me, placing a hand on my arm for the first time that I could remember. When I turned to him, he gestured to a space on the other side of the fire.

"You want me to sit over there instead of here?" Inside my shell, the storm shook, as if in laughter at this ongoing hormonal shitshow.

Two-Feathers shook his head, placed a hand on my chest—if not the parts I'd been hoping for—then pulled it back and up into the air, fingers wiggling. Then, he pointed to the space across the fire a second time.

This time, I looked at the location he was pointing to. In our temporary camp, it was the only spot both open and empty, a good distance away from the trees around us, the stump Two-Feathers had tied the two horses to, and even my motorcycle and its saddlebags of treasure.

In fact, it was the perfect place for the storm to go free.

I don't have a throat, not the way humans do, but found myself swallowing past a lump that couldn't exist. I rose in a squeaking of leather and circled the fire until I was standing where Two-Feathers had indicated. The flames painted his body in warm tones, casting shadows across the hard lines of his muscular arms and chest, but it was his eyes that I focused on, dark and glittering and full of something I couldn't interpret.

I held that gaze as I stood tall on the other side of the fire, held it as my shell fell apart, and the steel and shrapnel inside burst free into the night air.

For the first time in a very long while, the storm did not rage.

It danced.

○○○

We arrived in Greenburg to find the feast long over and Jules speaking to Merchant Haslem out by the other man's wagon. As we led our horses in, he looked up with a smile that didn't quite reach his eyes.

"And here they are!" he proclaimed. "It may have taken longer than anticipated, but I told you they wouldn't let us down."

"Where's the thief?" asked the merchant, still scowling.

"In pieces along the northbound road," I said. "If you're headed back that way, you'll pass what's left of him."

"As befits someone who would take advantage of both your trust and ours," Jules added. "If we'd known that man was a horse thief, we would have never allowed him to join our pilgrimage."

I didn't know what lie Jules was busy selling, but it did its job; Merchant Haslem harrumphed and adjusted the shapeless hat on his head. "The thief was punished and my merchandise returned, so I think we can put this matter behind us, yes?"

"I'm glad to hear that," said Jules, as Two-Feathers and I bypassed the pair to lead both horses to the town's stable. "Because we're actually in the market for horses ourselves…"

An hour later, my old friend stormed into the common room and threw himself into a chair, barely pausing to wave to the innkeeper's wife for another ale.

"Fucking Havoc fucked us," he growled.

"Haslem wouldn't sell, boss?" The third person at our table, Cross was feeling positively laconic, nursing his third beer in the past hour. Over the past few months, his hair had grown out some, making him look halfway human instead of like a shaved rat.

"He'll sell, but his prices are absurd. If Havoc hadn't gotten greedy and jumped the gun, we could have just stolen the horses as soon as the merchant left town."

"We still could," said the other man. "Only three of them on the wagon, and I don't think any are Powers."

Both men went quiet as fresh mugs of ale were delivered to the table in a series of thunks, but I could see Jules thinking it over. Three guns wouldn't be much of a deterrent for our crew.

There was *still* no sign of internal protest from the transactional piece of me, but I shook my head anyway. "It's not something I'm allowed to go along with."

"Seriously?" Jules frowned. "Since when? We've done worse in trying to finish a job."

"Apparently, things change," I said, in something that was uncomfortably close to both a lie and pure bewildering truth.

"Anything I should know, boss?"

"No," we both told Cross at the same time.

"I'll buy the horses," I decided, "using Havoc's pay. It's not like he's going to earn it now anyway."

"I'm not gonna say no to that." Just like that, Jules was all smiles again. "A single one of your coins should get us the four horses we need."

I passed him two. "Get some remounts, just in case. The change can be our spending money for the road. And Jules?"

"Yeah, Queenie?"

"Make sure you *don't* buy the horse we recovered from Havoc."

He tapped the side of his nose, tossed back his ale, and headed out for a fresh round of negotiations.

○○○

Merchant Haslem and his family left the next day, seven fewer horses in the string behind their wagon, and we packed up our things not long after. For all that we'd enriched Greenburg during our stay, I thought the village was happy to see us go. I *knew* the mayor was, and not just because his daughter had tried to sneak out and find Two-Feathers in the woods the previous night.

Even with Havoc gone, we were obviously trouble, and the one thing a village that size didn't need was our kind of trouble.

Selene was up and walking about under her own power again. The bruise on her face somehow looked even worse after two days, joined by a lump that made her whole head lopsided, but whatever pain she was feeling didn't intrude on her usual empty smile. It was possible she had a concussion, but Jules and I had debated the matter at length, and neither of us could figure out a way to tell for sure. I didn't think her ghost would have allowed her to travel if there was any risk of further damage. After all, Crows didn't grow on trees, and one weak enough to be ridden by ghosts but strong enough to not crumble under that weight had to be even more rare.

I still hadn't told Jules the identity of the ghost riding Selene or the reason that ghost had decided to help us. The former seemed like a secret that might get the middle-aged Whisperer stabbed in the night, and the latter… well, that would take care of itself once we made it to New Memphis.

We spent one last day in Greenburg, as much for the horses' benefit as for Selene's, and then made our departure, six people on horses, one on a bike, with two extra mounts trailing behind. We had supplies, we had ammunition, and the villagers were neither dead nor shooting at us as we rode off.

I counted that as a win.

22

Being on the road again was bliss, even given the increasingly bitter cold and Evan's resultant bitching. Stars above us, our destination somewhere ahead, and the boys' incessant card games put aside for now. I rode in the rear by myself, and the electric motor's hum mixed with the sound of tires to make the music that I loved.

Jules might not have a theme song, but this was mine.

It didn't hurt that our first week out of Greenburg was uneventful. Only a single storm and it passed through quickly, leaving us with a scattering of showers. This far south, snow would be a rare occurrence even in the heart of winter, and the tents purchased in Greenburg were all the others needed to protect them from the elements.

Selene got her own, of course. After meeting her ghost, I no longer questioned why. Instead, I wondered just how Jules and Cross and Havoc had stayed alive as long as they had with the young Crow. Ultimately, I decided it came down to what her ghost ultimately wanted… the same reason she'd deigned to speak with me back in Greenburg. Selene wasn't a strong enough Crow to do more than stab someone and that meant her ghost needed a crew to protect her and people like me to provide access to harder targets.

None of which guaranteed safety for anyone who breached Selene's personal space. Not with *that* ghost riding her. That much I knew from the stories.

Each morning, as the others packed the tents away, I met with Jules and Two-Feathers by the remnants of the fire to discuss our route. I knew where we were going, more or less, but had only a limited idea of how to get there. In some ways, it was easy: head toward the rising sun until we hit the Mississippi. Make our way across and Tillatoba was a few days' ride further east. But the river was miles long and there were only a few spots with active ferries to help us cross it. If we came in too far north or south and followed the river in the wrong direction, we might end up in the gulf or, even worse, New Memphis, before we realized our mistake.

Two-Feathers hunted to supplement our supplies, but for the most part, our focus was on traveling as far as we could during the increasingly shorter days. With Texas long behind us and true winter yet to fall, I didn't expect to run into any real horrors, but it was clear that we weren't alone as we traveled; predators circling the camp at night or pacing us as we passed through their territories. Still, the worst dangers I encountered in those early days were the steaming piles left by the horses in front of me.

I was starting to understand why Two-Feathers rode up front. Pretty sure *scouting for danger* was just an excuse.

By the end of the week, Selene was as close to normal as she'd ever been, the bruising across her face now a shade of yellow that even the smiley face across my visor found garish. Jules had been riding behind her, one eye on the Crow in case she had any bouts of vertigo, but it seemed like she'd avoided permanent damage.

Again, as far as we could tell, anyway. It wasn't an exact science, even with Normals. Throw a Crow into the mix, especially one being actively ridden by a ghost, and we were just guessing. She hadn't fallen off her horse even once though, so I felt pretty good about that guess.

"How many more days, you think?" Jules asked me, dropping back to invade my relative peace.

"If we're where we think we are, we'll see water next week."

"And you're sure this ferry will still be there?"

"I'm not sure of anything, but it was there seven years ago, when I did a job down in Mobile. If it's gone, we'll figure something out, but at worst, I think the place will just be under different management." I spared him a glance. "You've really never been this far east?"

"Nope. Born and raised in the Free States, as you know, then matriculated over to Kansas City after a minor disagreement with Johnny Law. Never saw a need to go any further. Between the Badlands and Texas, a man could ride forever and never see all of it." He coughed. "Guess you'd know that better than anyone."

"Except for the man part."

"Is there anything we need to look out for?"

"Besides the river itself? Assassin mosquitoes, although we'll be avoiding the swamps where they tend to accumulate. Howlers, of course, and other oversized nightmare mixes, but once we cross the river, the biggest danger tends to be people like us. Powers especially. Every time a warlord gets overthrown, their armies splinter, sending out dozens of new groups of assholes to play bandit in the countryside. No offense, of course."

"None taken. I'm a businessman, not a bandit."

We both shared a laugh at that.

ooo

Three days later, we lost one of our remounts when it stepped in a snake hole, the resulting screams making even Cross go pale until Jules put the creature out of its misery with a long stroke of the knife. We took the best cuts of meat and left the rest as a peace offering for the denizens of the wood.

On the twelfth day out of Greenburg, the river finally came into sight. I'd seen oceans and been scattered across the floor of a gulf, but there was something special about the Mississippi, water snaking its way through the land for thousands of miles, from a lake far to the north all the way down to the gulf. The water was a muddy-yellow, probably a result of some tributary flooding to the north, and the east and west banks were literally miles apart.

It wasn't pretty, the Mississippi, but it had a presence to it. The Break had changed the world around it, but the river kept on flowing. People lived and died, nations rose and fell, love conquered and was conquered in turn, but the Mississippi remained as it ever was, as it had been since long before humans discovered its shores.

Crossing it was always a bitch and a half.

Thankfully, we weren't so far off course that we couldn't look downstream and see walled forts on either bank. There was no ferry out on the water, but that wasn't a surprise either. With the things that lived in the river, ferry crossings happened only when there were sufficient passengers to warrant the risk.

"Are those new?" asked Jules, nodding to the forts.

"Nope. This started out as two halves of a single town, but a river crossing is a valuable resource, especially now. The original residents built up their defenses and hired mercenaries to protect them… only to have the mercenaries betray them and take over. The new owners built the defenses up even further, then fell afoul of a short-lived warlord who made this place his home… and so on until there were two full-on citadels doing their best to pretend the right

Power couldn't bring their walls crashing down with a wave of her hand."

"Any chance the owners will give us trouble?"

"I doubt it. The value of a place like this is in making money off the river traffic. We might have to wait a day until they have the numbers needed to merit the ferry's usage—and to give their vendors the opportunity to squeeze us for whatever other profits they can—but shutting down transportation entirely would kill their income stream."

"I'm always surprised by the things you know."

"I'm not just a pretty face," I told him, the smile across my visor damn near malevolent.

"You know what I mean, Queenie."

I shrugged. "Some of it was baked into me at birth, I think. The rest is a matter of observation. Humans aren't particularly complicated creatures."

"I don't know about that. We've got us a six-man crew consisting of a Crow, a nomad, a former con man, a killer, and… whatever Miles is. And then there's you. That doesn't seem complicated?"

I let the laughter leak into my voice of iron and steel. "That's just diversity, Jules. Don't mistake it for complexity. Individually, you eat, you drink, you love, you breed, and you die. Seems simple enough from where I'm sitting."

"Well shit, if I'd known we were going to be philosophizing, I'd have gotten myself a beer." He patted the extra canteens lashed to his saddle.

"There's still time before we reach the crossing, but I wouldn't recommend it. You're the face of this party, and whoever the new rulers are, their people might take it amiss if you're too drunk to speak."

"Or they might ask where I got my alcohol and whether it came with reinforcements. Hell, we could all end up friends by sundown! Humans are complicated that way."

He sent me the grin that had been devastating when he was younger. I didn't bother telling him that two weeks' growth of beard made him look like an axe murderer. He'd have just taken it as a compliment.

"That's not *complicated.* It's just weird," I said instead.

We made our way toward the shoreline, giving the river a healthy margin of space in case anything in there had the reach to grab passersby right up off the bank, and then turned to follow it down to the fort on our side. Each half of the town had expanded over the years, now large enough to fit multiple Greenburgs inside walls that rivaled anything in the Badlands outside of Wichita. I knew men manned those walls, but they were still too distant to see.

Each fort had a single large tower rising above the walls and other buildings. They served as the last line of defense in the event of an attack, but also allowed for cross-river communication, using signal flags as large as the eighteen-wheeler that first killed me. Coded patterns indicated anything from a crossing to an attack to a need to meet in person.

Higher up, a banner flew atop each tower. The last time I'd been through, that banner had been green and white, the colors of the armed collective who had displaced the previous owners, but it looked like management had once again changed hands. Not that it mattered much who was in control; as I'd told Jules, it was commerce that ultimately ruled.

Then, a wind that barely touched us down at ground level whipped across the river. It ruffled the signal flag that I couldn't quite see on the far side of the tower, and caught the banner at the tower's crest, causing it to unfurl and fly in the afternoon sun.

A bloody skull sat atop a field of bones.

The Crimson Queen had taken control of the crossing.

ooo

I should've seen it coming. The queen had already expanded to the south, and while she had yet to conquer the lands between New Memphis and Kansas City, I knew she'd been busy making plans for just that. The Mississippi was a natural border for her capital city, but it also worked as a defensive barrier for her current territory. Controlling access just made sense.

I hated it when my enemies were halfway smart.

Only *halfway*, because if she'd been the genius she thought she was, she wouldn't have let her men burn down Eclipse. And she sure as hell wouldn't have tried to recruit or kill me when I came looking for retribution.

Regardless, this presented a bit of a problem. I rode up to the front, where Jules and Two-Feathers had stopped our little convoy.

"Gentlemen, we have an issue." I waved at the flapping banner.

"We noticed," said Jules. "You think they're preventing crossings?"

"No," I decided after a long moment of thought. "I think what I said earlier probably still stands. An empire needs commerce. She'd be dumb to shut this crossing down entirely."

"And she won't have her forces just scoop up anyone that passes through," he reasoned, "because that would kill the golden goose as soon as word got out."

"Right. But something tells me her soldiers are under orders to make an exception for Powers. The Immortals are the backbone of her strength, after all, and the shock troops that have allowed her to make so much progress."

"So, no showing our powers while we're inside the walls. Maybe it's a good thing Havoc was an idiot."

I nodded. Titans didn't blend, and the big man's presence would have brought those soldiers down on us in a moment.

And speaking of not blending…

Two-Feathers pointed at me and shook his head.

"Yeah. I stick out like a sore thumb too."

"Is that a problem?" asked Jules.

"It could be. By now, she knows I'm alive; I destroyed one of the Crimson Queen's forts *and* killed her pet infiltrator." I looked at the banner in the distance and shook my head. "Maybe the months that have passed since then have convinced her I'm done, but do you want to stake your lives on that? Because if I were her, I'd have a standing order to look out for someone as distinctive as me."

"You know that's going to be even more of a problem in New Memphis. You kind of attract attention everywhere you go."

"You can thank my so-called dad for that." I shrugged and dismounted. "You're going to have to ride my bike in, Jules."

"Why's that?"

"Because it's electric and worth more to me than you are. And dragging it through the river is a good way to make sure it never runs again. I'll meet you all on the other side." I waved at a cluster of trees a good mile or two north of the fort on the far bank. "We can meet in that grove."

"You're going to *swim* the Mississippi?"

"Something like that, yeah."

"Better you than me."

"Remember, it may take a day or two before they launch the ferry. Keep your heads down, watch out for Selene and Evan, and don't start any trouble that would give them an excuse to take you prisoner." I turned to Two-Feathers. "Especially you. I don't know how the soldiers here feel about nomads… but given the way the clans have been killing the Crimson Queen's so-called recruiters, I'm guessing it won't be a lovefest."

Two-Feathers nodded, fished around in his saddlebags, and pulled out a shirt I'd never seen before. Roughspun and poorly dyed, it must have come from Greenburg.

"If the mayor's daughter gave that to you, I want it burned when we're done," I said, not caring that the storm had filled my voice.

His eyes danced, but he didn't reply. Instead, he pulled off his usual deer skin shirt and swapped it for the new piece of clothing.

It looked terrible on him, I was happy to say, but it also went a surprisingly long way to softening his look. There was nothing to be done about his skin color or braids, but his appearance no longer screamed *nomad.*

"That might work," I admitted. "Although it's a bit tight across the chest and shoulders."

His grin was a flash of white.

"For fuck's sake," grumbled Jules. "I'm standing right here."

23

As the others continued south along the riverbank, I retreated into the woods to wait for dark. It was unlikely anyone on the walls had seen me at all, and even if they had, I would have just been a human-sized smudge at this distance. My departure wouldn't raise suspicion in a land where wilderness guides were far from uncommon.

From the shelter of the trees, I watched the rest of the crew head down the bank until they looked like dolls next to the walls looming above them. There was no way in hell I could climb those walls, and little to be gained by trying. For every guard on the wall or at the gate there were probably three or four more inside the two forts. Just getting *in* wouldn't do me any good.

So instead, I waited for night. The gate closed at sundown, but there were torches atop the wall, and the vague shapes of people on patrol. However, that circle of light barely extended past the wall itself, leaving a good mile of darkness between it and my hiding spot. I made my way to the river's edge and hugged the waterline as I headed south.

Whatever Jules thought, I had no intention of swimming across the Mississippi. The current wasn't particularly swift here, but I was far from nimble in the water, and I'd likely end up a dozen or more miles to the south by the time I finished crossing, and that was assuming something didn't drag me down on my way. Killing whatever it was and making my way back to the surface would add even more miles to the tally.

So, instead I crept down to the circle of light, close enough that I would have been easily spotted in the daytime. Then, I slipped into the dark waters of the river, just a few feet offshore, and let its current carry me south. Each fort had a dock, and those docks were shielded by the same huge walls that protected the towns themselves, constructs of stone and mortar that arced out into the river, forming two protected harbors. I couldn't swim the Mississippi, but I *could* hug the wall on our bank until I came about to its waterside opening, sneak in, and hitch a ride below the ferry when it finally departed. Once we reached the other side, I'd then let the current carry me a few hundred yards away again and slip away in the darkness.

It wasn't the sort of plan that would work for most people. Not having to breathe was a surprisingly useful side effect of my condition.

Unfortunately, when I arrived, I discovered a new problem: the inner harbor was blocked off by a portcullis, likely to prevent any of the river's inhabitants from swimming in to set up shop at the all-you-can-eat buffet. That metal grating would have to be raised when the ferry set out for the second shore, but in the near term, my only options were to climb it or hold my position outside.

Eventually, I went with the latter. Climbing increased the risk of me being spotted and didn't gain me anything other than protection from the river's current. I went the opposite direction instead, using the metal lattice to push myself deeper underwater.

If I was going to be here for hours, I might as well take a seat.

The river wasn't tremendously deep by the banks, likely artificially raised to provide yet another deterrent to the larger creatures that made the river its home, but the murky water made seeing anything difficult. By the time I reached bottom, I was confident I'd be hidden even in the daytime.

I slipped my arms through the portcullis' grate to hold myself steady and let my legs drift to the side. I'd never spent much time underwater in my shell, for obvious reasons. The water filled my helmet and saturated the leather that was both a part of me and not. If I ever had to do something like this again, I decided, I'd wait until just before dawn to make my move. A midnight infiltration had its appeal, but it also made for far too much watery downtime.

Time passed and I listened to the storm inside of me, sounds that I could feel if not quite hear. By now, the others would be holed up in whatever passed for an inn on this side of the river. I wasn't worried about Evan or Cross keeping their heads down. And Jules had always been the sort to fit in wherever he landed. As for Two-Feathers, he was smart, and strong, and capable… I just had to hope his limited disguise would be enough.

That left Selene. Women had it tough in some towns, but the Crimson Queen's men were soldiers, not the usual bandits and marauders. This near to the capital and in one of their own strongholds, I had to believe their discipline would hold.

There was some serious irony there—that I was banking on the self-control of a military that had already slipped its leash at least once, leaving Eclipse burned and buried in its wake—but there wasn't anything I could do but hope. Either things would work out or they wouldn't, and we'd adapt accordingly. Can't say that helped the time go by though, sitting there at the bottom of the river. I was underwater, catching the nonexistent sights, while my crew was walking through the lion's den above.

If I'd been with them, it would have made things worse, I knew, but at least then I could have *acted.*

I tried to distract myself by going over the plan, first for Tillatoba and then for New Memphis, but that was an exercise in frustration. Information was difficult to come by in the post-Break world, without the satellites and planes and global communication networks that had once existed. Raya's data had given us the skeleton of a plan, but we wouldn't be able to flesh out that plan until we were actually there, boots on the ground, seeing things for ourselves.

For months now, I'd been collecting random assets—Evan and Two-Feathers, Selene and Cross—in the assumption that they'd prove useful against whatever it was we would end up facing. With our destination now just a few weeks away, I found myself wondering if I would have been better off sticking with a two-man crew, just me and Jules, sneaking into the palace. A Whisperer to kill the Crimson Queen and the storm to kill everyone else.

Eventually, I got tired of wrestling with unknowns and turned to another, equally troubling issue: myself. When I'd been born, once I'd first figured out exactly what I was, I'd spent some time testing the rules that bound the storm. They had been surprisingly simple. I was compelled to seek out work, and while the ultimate decision on whether I took a job was mine, the reward always had to match the request.

At first, those rewards had been strictly material. Money for the supplies I needed. Repairs and eventually retrofits for the motorcycle. Even a small house on the outskirts of Detroit before that city tore itself to pieces. When the Break was over and the world had spiraled into chaos and ruin, my focus changed again. Driven by a need to find the man responsible for both that Break and my creation, I started to push against the confines of those rules. I took jobs that would earn me information, scraps of knowledge that might point me to Dr. Nowhere. Dream journals, newspaper articles, and stories passed down across multiple generations. And even though that information was worthless to anyone but me, it was still enough to satisfy my mental programming.

But as much as I'd bristled at the suggestion, Jules was right: I *had* changed. And not just because I'd taken this job on my own behalf. Dr. Nowhere's death had altered something, but I'd spent three long years pretending otherwise, three years adhering to the forced order I'd grown familiar with. A job. Balance in what was given and received. Rinse and repeat, as time turned the world into dust.

And yet nothing about this job had added up, no matter how much I tried to pretend otherwise.

I'd lived so long under those rules that they'd become a pattern of behavior; one I'd kept following even after Dr. Nowhere died. And now, Jules' prodding had stirred up the questions I'd been hiding from, questions I didn't know how to answer. Had I truly slipped my reins? Was I free to do as I liked, or was there some larger scheme at play that I couldn't sense, let alone comprehend? Were the consequences of my decisions just waiting in the wings, waiting to come down upon me like an avalanche?

I didn't know. I *couldn't* know, and after almost a century of structure, that ignorance was a knife in my side, digging into organs I didn't even have.

Hours passed and the sun pushed beyond its high point in the sky. I didn't make any headway on the uncertainties rising from where I'd buried them, bubbling to the river's surface in oxygen's stead. Because the bald fact was that I'd been created from an errant thought, the barest sketch of an idea, born as a creature of action with a body to match. Philosophizing, as Jules called it, wasn't a part of my toolbox.

Maybe that's going to change too, said a voice in my mind, its whisper almost lost beneath the ever-present storm. *Maybe that* needs *to change.*

And now I was hearing voices?

I'd been hanging out with far too many Crows of late.

By the time the portcullis started moving, pulling away from the silt and shoreline, I was almost grateful for the crossing and whatever dangers it might bring with it, looking forward to doing instead of thinking. If I'd been meant to navel-gaze, Dr. Nowhere would have given me a navel.

OOO

I disentangled myself from the portcullis before it could pull me to the surface. The ferry was already on its way, a dozen long oars pushing off the shallow shoreline and propelling it like the legs of an insect.

This next step had always been the questionable part of my plan. I needed to get close enough so that I could hitch a ride on the ferry's hull, yet not so close that its workers saw me waiting below. The water was too shallow by the manmade harbor, so I swam out into the deeper river, sensing as much as seeing the marine life responding to my passage.

I was not a fast swimmer, but the ferry was the equivalent of a building-sized bathtub, poorly balanced and ungainly, oars churning the water now that they could no longer reach the riverbed. I made it to my spot with time to spare and kicked my way up until I was ten feet from the surface. When the ferry came by, I swam upward again, letting the current carry me toward it.

My idea had been to simply grab hold of its keel, like a woman-sized version of the barnacles I'd seen on pre-Break water vessels. What I hadn't considered was what the underside of the ferry would be like, algae and other growth that made an already slick surface doubly so. My grip lasted for roughly three seconds, and then I was floating free again, the wash of the boat's passage pushing me back down toward the riverbed.

If the boat had been any faster, it would have left me behind entirely before I figured out what to do. As it was, I had three more handholds fail before I gave up and decided to make my own. I pressed myself against the ferry's hull, now nearer to the stern than its bow, and unleashed the storm. When I reformed my shell, a bare second or two later, I was floating free, but there were scars on a section of the hull just ahead. I wasn't sure how much damage I'd just done to the ferry, but I'd probably shortened its lifespan by a factor of years.

My heart would have bled for the Crimson Queen's men if only I had one.

I caught up yet again, found the deepest of those divots, and took hold, letting the ferry pull me toward the other shore, wondering if my added drag even registered for the people paddling.

Another hour or so and we'd be there.

The river's wildlife left us alone on our journey. I suspected the soldiers stationed at these forts included a Power or two to keep the nearby water clear of real threats. Maybe a Hydromancer, even; tasked with keeping the commerce running but far too important to pilot the ferry when manual labor was freely available.

The only moment of real concern came as we passed the deepest part of the river a mile or so into the trip, the riverbed so distant that light never reached it even on sunny days where the water was halfway clear. Something down there stirred, and that small motion sent ripples through the water, buffeting the boat and threatening to tear me free from my uncertain hold. I couldn't see the creature, but as it shifted again, I had the sensation of great size, with long, grasping tentacles that extended hundreds of feet past us along the riverbed.

Something from the greater deep maybe, an ancient horror that had swum up the river, past the long-destroyed dams and levees to slumber here. If whatever it was had truly awoken, the ferry would have been gone in an instant, and nothing I or that hypothetical Hydromancer did would have stopped it. Instead, it drifted back to sleep, neither hungry enough nor sufficiently irritated by the ferry's crossing to act.

For a moment, the storm surged inside my shell, as if responding to the unseen challenge. I held fast to both the boat and my own human-like form. This creature was the king of its domain and welcome to the title. I was just passing through.

If I'd been human, my arms would have been all but useless by the time we reached the shore, but then, if I'd been human, I would have drowned a few minutes after midnight. When the walls of the second harbor appeared out of the murk, I let go of the ferry and let the river's current carry me downstream, a hundred feet, then five hundred, drifting until I reached a natural bend and then swimming toward the shoreline. It was daytime still, but I could hide in the weeds that choked this side of the river. Once night had fallen, I'd make my way inland, circling around the fort to rendezvous with my crew.

Another hour or two passed. I reformed my shell a few times as I waited, the storm driving off an alligator large enough to be trouble but far too small to even offer a snack for the river's current ruler. Finally, the sun dropped below the distant horizon. Twenty minutes later, I was reforming my shell yet again, this time on land, my helmet and leathers going from wet to dry in the blink of the storm's passage.

This bank was every bit as dark as the other, torches on the distant wall the only source of light for miles. I pushed through the woods to the east, the route I'd chosen taking me on a wide arc around the fort. All told, that detour probably added three extra miles to my hike, all of it through foliage and terrain made treacherous by the darkness, but it was worth it to avoid detection. I reached our rendezvous point sometime before midnight, where I found my motorcycle and six horses waiting.

Six horses, but only *three* people.

Jules opened his mouth to greet me, but I was already speaking. "Where are they?"

○○○

Evan and Two-Feathers were gone, which told me precisely fucking nothing I hadn't already seen for myself. I felt the storm surge inside of me, heard its metal growl fill the grove, as Jules took a step back, hands raised. His mouth was moving but I couldn't hear the words.

Why couldn't I hear the words?

A few seconds later, the answer came to me; I'd set the storm free without even realizing it. I reformed my shell in the middle of a newly made clearing, fresh lumber scattered about me, shredded leaves falling to the ground like rain.

"Start at the beginning," I said, unwilling to admit that I hadn't heard a word Jules had said. "What happened?"

"We entered the fort on the other bank just fine," said Jules, voice tight. "Got told the ferry wouldn't be leaving until today and found a spot to hole up in overnight. We got a few looks, especially Selene and Two-Feathers, but had no real issues from the locals. Same with the ferry ride itself. Took forever, took more of the advance money you gave me, but we were on our way."

"And then?" I couldn't keep the metal out of my voice, couldn't keep the storm from raging within its shell.

"Everything went to shit when we reached this side of the river. First, they wanted more money to unload the horses. Then, they tried to take your bike as contraband. I paid those people off, but someone must have been unhappy with their cut, because we were jumped on our way from the dock. We all knew better than to fight back, so we scattered, but…"

"But?"

"Miles has got to be pushing sixty, Queenie. They ran him down and started in on him, fists and boots. And when Two-Feathers saw—"

"He went back to save him."

"Yeah. Only there was a column of soldiers passing through town from the south, and they had Immortals with them. A Beast Shifter and a Lightbringer both."

If I had eyes, I'd have closed them. Two-Feathers was hell on wheels, but he was a long way from indestructible.

"I would have gone back for them," said Jules, his tone so earnest I almost believed him, "but there were too many soldiers; they'd have taken me too. I knew I needed to find Cross and Selene and get here to tell you what had happened."

I wanted to rage, and the storm did too. The job came first, always, but you didn't just leave men behind to be—

Wait. *"Taken*, not killed?"

He nodded. "Those soldiers passing through had a wagon train with them. Three cages on wheels, chock full of prisoners to be processed. They added Miles and Two-Feathers to the final wagon. The nomad was in bad shape, but he was breathing… and from what you said about the army's need for Powers, I'm guessing they'll keep him that way."

"Tillatoba is the closest station." I turned back to the distant fort, visible only as a light on the horizon. "We'll put some distance between us and the ferry and ambush them as they come by."

He coughed. "They already did. Come by, I mean. They left the fort before we did, practically as soon as the fighting was done."

"Heading north?"

"Yeah," said Cross, speaking up for the first time. "Toward Tillatoba, like you figured."

I nodded, thinking things through. The soldiers had a lead of several hours, but we were *days* from the processing station and wagons were slow. We could catch them on horseback. And when we did... Cross and Selene would be of limited use in a full-on war, but Normals and Beast Shifters were old hat for me. And if I gave Jules enough time and space to operate, he could take down the Lightbringer before they became a problem.

I was late to the party, but the fat lady hadn't sung just yet.

24

We waited until dawn to set out, although the storm and I dug a small canyon into the earth pacing back and forth through the night. The rational part of me knew traveling in the darkness wouldn't help us make up ground if we lost a second horse to a snake hole, but the storm didn't care. I'd debated riding ahead on my bike, but even with the headlight on, the road presented its own challenges, and any damage the motorcycle suffered would slow us down more than simply waiting for daylight.

Despite the sheer shitshow the river crossing had turned into, my bike, at least, had made it through with only a few scratches. When I stopped being pissed, I'd have to remember to thank Jules for that. And to maybe apologize for the storm almost taking his head off even though the debacle hadn't been his fault.

I was a long, long way from that point though.

Finally, we broke camp and headed out, Selene looking annoyingly unconcerned with both the world around her and the twigs that had ended up in her unbrushed hair. At a trot, we figured to be traveling at least twice the speed of the wagons. Despite their significant head start, we would catch them by sunset.

We stopped briefly at noon to rest and feed the horses and then were back on the road soon after, the thunder of hoofbeats drowning out the whine of my bike and the storm's incessant grinding.

By nightfall, we still hadn't found them.

"These are clearly recent wagon tracks, and heavy ones at that," said Cross, pointing to the grooves in the dirt that continued down the road. "They're on this road still."

"How have they stayed ahead of us then?"

"Maybe *they're* traveling at night?" suggested Jules.

"Star light, star bright," agreed Selene.

I bit back a curse. I didn't know how strong their Lightbringer was, but providing illumination had to be a hell of a lot less taxing than shooting laser-fucking-eyebeams or burning through titanium with photon pulses. That made night travel feasible in a way it simply wasn't for our crew. That same light would draw attention, sure, but they had a whole detachment of soldiers to deal with any predators that came looking.

"Our horses are just about done in," said Jules, somehow knowing exactly what my next suggestion would be and moving to counter it. "We can walk them a while with your bike lighting the road, but anything faster than that is too fast, and they'll need to stop soon anyway."

"One more hour," I agreed, turning on my headlight. "Then we'll call it for the night. No fire, but we'll get the horses watered and everyone fed. And then at dawn—"

"We'll be ready," said Jules. "The processing station is still more than a day away. We'll catch them in the morning."

○○○

We did *not* catch them in the morning. Or the afternoon. And when evening rolled around, and we finally got the first glimpse of our quarry, we had a terrible surprise waiting for us.

Somehow, the fuckers had multiplied.

"Six wagons?" I turned to Jules and waited.

"And double the men too." He shook his head. "They must have gotten reinforcements from somewhere."

"We passed a second road a few hours back, boss," said Cross. "Maybe this other batch came from a different town."

"And both are headed to Tillatoba?"

"You *did* say it was the only processing station in the area."

"I didn't think it would be this active though." Raya's research had suggested the southern expansion had come to a standstill, with all the easy targets already scooped up. "I'm guessing this means another warlord just fell and the Crimson Queen is moving in on their territory. Just our luck."

"Ever worry we might be on the wrong side of all of this, Queenie?" Jules shrugged away the look I sent him. "I'm not talking morals. I'm talking *winners.* This woman is wiping out her opposition, and I don't see the Badlands, divided as they are, stopping her. Not even the nomad clans."

"Then it's a good thing we're here," I said. "We'll cut off the head and let the empire tear itself to pieces."

"Never thought I'd end up a player in continental politics."

"You still aren't. You're just a man on a job. The target being a head of state is her problem, not ours."

"Tell that to her armies," muttered Cross.

The past two days had calmed me down enough that I chose to ignore the comment. "Thoughts?" I asked instead.

"That's a lot of firepower, especially if the second wagon train brought along its own pair of Powers." Jules ran a hand through rapidly thinning hair and shook his head. "Might be too much even for us."

"If the station is where we think it is, the wagons will reach it tomorrow," pointed out Cross. "Whatever our plan was to sneak in there, it's going to be a hell of a lot harder to do so with a hundred extra soldiers in place, not to mention two prisoners needing rescue."

We all turned to Selene, but neither she nor her ghosts seemed interested in the situation; the Crow's hair covered her face as she let her fingers float on the breeze.

To Cross' point, our challenges would only mount if we waited. Maybe the soldiers with the two wagon trains would turn back once they'd dropped off their prisoners, or maybe they'd stick around for some R&R at the station, unintentionally augmenting its security. And while we waited, what would be happening to Evan and Two-Feathers? Raya's files had mentioned something called technicians, brought in to break recalcitrant Powers. While Evan probably hadn't been flagged as anything but an old Normal, the nomad's gifts had clearly been noted. That meant hours or even days of pain once he reached the station.

But Jules and the storm could each only handle small groups at a time. If we attacked now—even if we somehow won without casualties of our own—some of the enemy soldiers would escape to warn Tillatoba of our presence. That would make getting into the station that much harder… and if we weren't able to forge new credentials, we'd never even make it into New Memphis' fifth district, let alone all the way to the palace.

The math was merciless. With one option, failure was all but guaranteed. With the other, we'd have more flexibility, more time, and more options.

I sighed, and the anger I'd felt toward Jules finally faded, smothered by the knowledge that I was making the exact same decision he had.

"We'll wait and follow them in. Put eyes on the station and see if we can find an entry point. Once we know what the troop schedule and base layout is like, we'll have a better idea of what to do." I swallowed past the imaginary bile creeping up my equally imaginary esophagus. "Evan and Two-Feathers will have to hold on until we can get to them."

OOO

Either the Lightbringer had run out of juice, or the night-march's goal had been to link up with the second group of soldiers. This time, once the sun set, all six wagons in front of us stopped, and the soldiers settled in to make camp. After a brief conference, we decided to skirt those forces and keep going. Getting to the processing station *before* them seemed advantageous, and we needed every edge we could get at that point.

Sneaking past an armed column should have been challenging, but we were well inside the Crimson Queen's territory and the defensive perimeter was loose and poorly guarded. It was almost enough to make me reconsider our plan. Why not infiltrate the camp and free *all* the prisoners? If we could sneak Two-Feathers and Evan away in the chaos that followed, maybe Tillatoba would remain ignorant to our presence.

I didn't know if I was blowing smoke up my own ass or if some part of my brain really thought it was doable, but either way, those dreams died a swift death once we got a glimpse of the camp's interior. The perimeter was porous as a badly used sponge, yeah, but there were still over a hundred soldiers in place, and the prisoner wagons themselves were brightly lit by kerosene lamps. We'd be spotted long before we could make it to those wagons and then the job would be well and truly fucked.

So instead, we kept going, slipping past the camp and into the darkness, walking our horses and my bike through the night, despite the danger of terrain we couldn't see. An hour later, we cut back to the road, but our pace stayed slow. With soldiers behind us and a processing station somewhere ahead, I couldn't risk turning on the bike's headlight, and that made for a long, slow, and tiring night of travel, even for a woman who never slept.

By the time the sun was peeking up over the eastern tree line, we were miles ahead of the wagon train, and were likely no more than an hour or two from Tillatoba. Cross rode ahead in the early morning light to scout our way, while the rest of us continued to walk horses already exhausted from their nighttime trek. A handful of miles later, he was back, dismounting before his mount had come to a full stop.

"We're almost there," he said. "This road leads straight to Tillatoba, which I'm guessing is why it's in decent shape. It looks like there's some sort of trail that splits off before the station comes into view though. It might lead us to a vantage point off the road."

"I don't feel like marching up to an armed fort and dying today," said Jules, rubbing at his weary eyes. "My vote is for the trail."

"Hard to maintain the element of surprise by announcing ourselves," I agreed. "Let's see this trail."

"We'll all be dead eventually," offered Selene.

"Always good to know." I was starting to wonder if Havoc really had knocked something loose in the Crow's brain, because she'd been even weirder than normal since Greenburg.

Twenty minutes later, we were on a low hill overlooking Tillatoba, horses and bike left down below and out of sight. Selene was humming a noiseless tune, but it was too quiet to carry more than a few feet.

The processing station was twice the size of either of the forts at the Mississippi, its outer wall shorter but still far beyond our ability to scale. Inside that wall, an enormous building took up most of the space, with a handful of smaller buildings barely visible. Smoke drifted up from a multitude of chimneys.

"I'm guessing that's where prisoners are stored and then processed?"

I nodded at Cross. "And the other buildings are probably for the officers, yeah."

"No separate barracks then." He frowned. "Which means the soldiers must bunk down in that main building. How are we supposed to get in and rescue our men again once they arrive?"

I was hoping Jules would be able to answer that, but as he climbed down from the tree above us, he was shaking his head.

"Two gates instead of one, but just as secure as the forts down south. And once you put another hundred soldiers on the wall, the place will be damn near impenetrable."

"Maybe we should head in now and find a spot to hide until the others arrive?" suggested Cross. "Place that big has to have storage rooms that nobody ever checks."

"I like the thought, but how?" I waved at the station. "Both gates are guarded. And that wall is high enough that climbing it would take us more hours than we have, assuming it's possible at all."

"Head to the other side and look for trees that will get us over the wall, maybe?"

"They've cleared every tree within fifty feet of the wall," said Jules, "and there are groups out on the far side, extending the perimeter even further. At this point, it's probably more about lumber for their furnaces than security, but it screws us over just the same."

"That's our way in," I said.

"The trees? I just told you that—"

"Not the trees, the people cutting them down."

"Kill them and take their uniforms?" Cross shook his head. "You don't think the gate guards will want to see our faces when we try to enter? It's not like this is a high-traffic area; they've got time to double-check these things."

"I'll go by myself."

"Begging your pardon, Queenie, but you're the most recognizable of all of us."

"Only in my shell. Otherwise, I'm just a pile of scrap and metal."

"That's howling through the air like a cyclone," said Cross. "I don't know if I'd call that less noteworthy than your usual shape."

The storm *was* my usual shape, but I didn't bother correcting him on that front. Jules had already seen where I was going with this.

"You can keep things from spinning?"

"For a time, yeah. It's better suited for playing dead or setting traps, but if I can get into one of those carts, they'd bring me back into the station with nobody the wiser."

And then, because Jules had known me a very long time and knew the difficult questions to ask, "Do you think you'll be able to keep still long enough to make it back?"

Even Selene looked up at that, although her expression was mild and unconcerned next to Cross' visible confusion. I ignored them both and shrugged at Jules.

"I guess we're going to find out."

○○○

It took more discussion than just that, of course, but an hour or two later, I was on the other side of the station, watching as teams of woodcutters slowly worked their way in my direction. I kept as much distance between us as possible, skirting to the side to get around them and to the wagons they had left behind.

Cross had suggested I just create a pile of scrap in the woods and wait for someone to find me, but that plan had too many variables. First, they'd have to stumble across me. Second, they'd have to decide the storm's metal was worth retrieving. And most importantly, I wasn't convinced I'd be able to contain the storm's violent impulses long enough for people to move it piece by piece.

Instead, it was up to me to reach the wagons. Given my lack of woodcraft, I'd been concerned that the workers would hear me from a mile away, but the noise I made was easily lost beneath the sound of their saws and axes and the even more prevalent bullshitting that had only increased in volume since my arrival.

Maybe the gates were securely guarded, but these men worked with the confidence of people who knew, for a fact, that there was nothing dangerous nearby. It was the sort of attitude that would have gotten them killed on any day but this one. Sneaking into the station meant keeping the guards unaware of our presence and that meant all the soldiers sent out on woodcutting duty needed to return.

I made it to within a hundred yards of the half-filled wagons before I finally ran into an issue. A handful of soldiers stood nearby, having a smoke break while their companions did the work. Worse, they were directly in my path to the wagons. Going around them would have me leaving the safety of the tree line, and I didn't think the men on the wall would miss me. Nor would the smokers miss a storm of steel flying through the air to settle into one of the nearby carts.

I settled in to wait.

It took a while. Another tree had been brought down, long minutes earlier, and the branches must have already been sawed off, making it ready for retrieval, because the woman in charge marched back to the wagons and tore the smokers a collective new ass, hurling spit and invectives alike from ten paces away. Cigarettes were stomped out, shirts and camo pants were straightened, and the would-be slackers hurried off to help with the freshly fallen tree.

This wasn't the first tree I'd watched the crews cut down, strip, and then load onto the wagons; I knew I had less than a minute to cross the hundred yards of space, climb in, and dismiss my shell. I managed it in twenty seconds, the storm's sound so brief even I barely heard it before all that metal and steel and wires let gravity take its course, each piece slipping off the carefully stacked log sections to fill the wagon's floor like so much clutter.

Now, the *really* hard part began. I had to keep the storm calm for however long it took the soldiers to unwittingly smuggle me into Tillatoba.

This was already the worst plan I'd ever come up with.

25

The strangest thing about lying in pieces in a wagon like so much discarded junk was that, for once, I could hear what was going on around me. The voices of soldiers as they brought back more logs. The wagons groaning under an ever-increasing weight. The bitching of the workers, a mixture of newly minted provisional citizens and soldiers who'd been assigned shit duty.

I won't say all that noise made it any easier to keep the storm quiescent as its need to *move* grew and grew, but it did at least help pass the time.

Thankfully, the wagons had already been half-full on my arrival, and it was a matter of minutes, not hours, before the work crews decided they'd done enough for the day. Conversation was replaced by grunts and groans as they collectively worked to turn the wagons around and pull them back to the station.

Apparently, that car the Crimson Queen had sent to Kansas City was more than she could spare for her own soldiers.

It took a frustratingly long time for my wagon to make its way to the gate. Eventually, I heard someone call out a challenge. Soon after that, the wagon rolled to a stop.

"Hands clear and faces visible," said that same voice.

"Jesus, Harris, do we have to do this every damn time?"

"Protocol's protocol. You know that, Private Mar." Steps, as someone walked around the wagon, presumably checking everyone's identity as he went. "Any sign of spies or intruders while you were out there today?"

"You bet, boss," said a third man, voice dry. "We're smuggling them in on our wagons. Don't tell the commander."

"This is why you're never going to make sergeant, Van Pelt."

"And what a crying shame that'll be," agreed the other man. "I'm told I've got a face for command."

"You've got a face for something, alright," said Mar.

"Enough already," said Harris. "You're both soldiers. Try to act like it. Take your loads on through and into the north bay."

"Did he say the north bay?" Van Pelt asked.

"I always *wanted* to see the north bay." Mar's voice dripped with fake cheer.

"Clearly, we are moving way the fuck up in this world."

"I thought we always took lumber to the north bay?" That was a fourth voice, high-pitched and nasally.

"We do. Don't pay any attention to these two comedians. Something tells me they've been sniffing pinecones again."

"Why sniff what you can snort?" said Van Pelt, prompting laughter from everyone except, I was pretty sure, Harris.

"Get your asses inside so we can close up for the night," said the gate guard. "And don't think I won't have a talk with the lieutenant about your comportment."

That killed most of the laughter pretty quick. Moments later, a chorus of grunts preceded a creaking of wood and wheels. We were on our way again.

Buried under fresh-cut wood, I didn't see the north bay as much as sense it, a wide, overhead door that someone pulled open upon our arrival, and then an even greater expanse of space above and around us. We'd traveled about fifteen feet into the bay when progress was stopped by yet another guard.

"If you ever get tired of inventory and want to see how the real warriors get it done, Sanderson, you know you just have to ask."

"All that tree sap has gone to your head, Meloni," said a woman, her voice sharp. "The *real* warriors are still marching back to base, from what I heard. Maybe they'll be thrilled and amazed by stories of your little tree massacre. Now, leave the wagons here and scurry off to the showers. Get those rosy cheeks nice and shiny."

"Those two never shut up, do they?" asked a second woman, after Mar and Van Pelt had wandered off with the others.

"Van Pelt's been stationed here so long he's practically furniture," said Sanderson. "Mar isn't all bad though. You just have to get him out from under Brother Asshole's shadow."

"It sounds like there's a story there."

"Two or three of them, actually. With a fourth maybe on the way if the southern companies don't make it here tonight." She slapped the side of the wagon. "I'm all done. Looks like everyone met their quotas for the day."

"Brave deeds, no doubt, unlike any the world has seen before or may ever see again." The second woman snorted, her sarcasm thick enough to drown a Hydromancer. "I'll get the Provs to handle the unloading."

"Better them than us."

Provs, I decided, must stand for provisional citizens. Apparently, the former prisoners had a variety of ways of proving their value before getting sent up the road to New Memphis. I wasn't interested in sticking around for them to come through, so as soon as the two women had left, I slid a few loose pieces of the storm out of the wagon and then across the floor into a shadowed corner of the bay.

And then, once I'd verified that hiding spot was a reasonably decent one, I started bringing more metal my way.

The collective weight of all that lumber was more than even Two-Feathers could have dreamed of lifting, but the storm was relentless, each piece not so much shifting the pile as squirming out from under it, delighting in even this much motion after almost an hour of forced stillness.

By the time more footsteps sounded, all but a few pieces of the storm were free and hidden, though the strain to keep the collected whole from surging together again had reached new levels. I struggled to hold on as the unloading started, as wagon after wagon was all-too-slowly emptied.

"Hey, what's this?" The whisper came from nearby the last few trapped pieces of the storm.

"Metal scrap, by the looks of it. I guess the outdoor crew found more than just lumber out there today. Lucky bastards."

"Do you… do you think Corporal Sanderson already logged this stuff?"

"No, I think after two years of service and three promotions in the queen's army, she's forgotten how to do her job. You should definitely go make sure she knows about her fuck-up."

There was a long pause.

"That… was sarcasm, right?"

"Where the hell did they find you, kid?"

"In a house on—"

"Forget it. I didn't really want to know. Just put the metal aside so we can offload the lumber we're here for."

I felt a hand grasp a tiny piece of the storm and couldn't help but react.

"Fuck!"

That piece clattered to the ground.

"What the hell, kid?"

"I picked it up like you said and… I think it bit me!"

"Sure it did." A heavy sigh. "Whoever grouped us together today has some serious fucking balls on them. Let's see your little booboo."

"It's bleeding!"

"Huh. That *is* a gusher. How the hell did you manage that?" Without waiting for a reply, he continued. "Put some pressure on it and we'll get you to the medic. If we're lucky, you'll be fixed up quickly and we can come back and get this done before chow time. If we're not lucky, you owe me dinner."

"What did *I* do?"

"Kid, the list is longer than my Aunt Trudy's nose."

I gave it another minute and then pulled that errant, blood-stained shard over to the greater mass. There were still pieces stuck on the wagon, but I had enough to form my shell and get my first real look at the bay.

It was every bit as large as I'd sensed. There were two overhead doors and a human-sized regular one, all set in the far wall and shut, the evening sunlight slipping in around their edges. Crates were stacked on shelving along the bay's ends, leaving a large space in the middle that was currently occupied by wagons. A door to my left led deeper into the facility, and a ramp past the wagons led up to an observation platform about fifteen feet above me that almost definitely had a second door.

But first things first. I listened for a good twenty seconds until I was sure I was the only one in the north bay. Then, I hobbled over to my wagon. This time, my shell wasn't missing part of its boot, but a good chunk of an arm and one thigh instead, with additional cracks radiating outward in the otherwise glossy surface of my leather pants.

I'm not a Stalwart or a Titan. My shell is nothing, next to the storm, but I'm still a damn sight stronger than any Normal with my shape would be. I rolled the few remaining logs aside to free up the last three shards. They rushed into my core and then poured back out again as something flesh and fabric, filling the cracks and empty spaces of my shell.

I was in, I was whole, and the enemy was none the wiser.

It was time for phase two.

○○○

Actually, it was time for phase one-and-a-half, but that didn't sound nearly as impressive in my head. Phase two couldn't start until night fell. Phase one-and-a-half was finding a better hiding spot and doing my best to learn the lay of the land without any of the current guards finding me.

Both objectives ended up being easier than expected. Up the ramp, on the observation platform and next to the door I'd suspected would be there, was an evacuation map of the building I'd been stored in. Given the size of the bay, and the fact that it was just one of two such spaces, I already knew I was in the facility we'd seen from outside the wall, and the map helpfully confirmed that assumption. More importantly, whoever had made the sign had painstakingly—and helpfully—painted in the walls of every interior room across the building's three levels.

There were no labels for those rooms, unfortunately, but just the layout allowed me to make some educated guesses. The two largest spaces other than the north and south bay were almost definitely the mess hall and barracks, located on the first floor. The long narrow room with an adjoining space was, maybe, the bathroom and shower area, and the square rooms off the hallway were probably offices. Meanwhile, the area in the basement that had been divided into closet-sized rooms and segmented off from the rest of the building by a hall with multiple checkpoints could only be one thing: the prison.

On the other end of that no-doubt heavily guarded hallway were a set of rooms roughly the size of the offices above. Given their proximity to the cells, I was guessing those were the rooms where the queen's so-called technicians went to work.

There was no way in hell I was letting Two-Feathers get taken to one of those rooms.

The storm growled and gnashed its metal teeth, demanding action, but neither Evan nor Two-Feathers were even on premises yet. I turned back to the map. If I were the base commander, and had a basement full of prisoners, where would I put the rooms that needed to remain secure?

The obvious answer was *as far away as possible.* Meaning the second, and topmost, floor. The barracks and such would provide a buffer zone in case anything ever went wrong. Assuming the commander himself lived in one of the smaller free-standing buildings we'd seen, that meant the second floor contained the other important spaces; the communications room, the armory, the med center, and, last but never least, the citizenship room where credentials were issued.

The chances of me making it up there to determine which room was which without being discovered were abysmal, but we'd predicted that from the outset. That would be Cross and Jules' job, once I brought them into the station.

But phase two would have to wait until nightfall. In the meantime, that same map told me the best place to wait until then was back down in the bay I'd entered. There was some sort of old storage room, almost lost behind the stacks of boxes, where the worst I'd face was dust bunnies and boredom.

Maybe killing dust bunnies would help stave off the boredom.

I didn't have too long to wait. Just an hour or so spent standing like a statue, wiggling my toes to remind myself I still had them. When I finally poked my head back into the loading bay, it was empty, the wagons fully unloaded, and the daylight that had previously been leaking in now replaced by darkness.

Phase two of the plan was almost as dumb as phase one. If we'd had any stealth specialists, things might have been different, but Two-Feathers was the closest to one we had on our crew, and he was, for obvious reasons, unavailable. So instead, we'd sent me, the least unobtrusive person in existence, but also the only one who could disassemble herself into spare parts to be smuggled indoors.

And now I was the one who had to open the proverbial back door so the others could sneak inside.

I cracked open the human-sized door that led outside and peeked through. There were a handful of patrols making their way along the tops of the wall, but the streets were clear. For now, anyway. I slid out into the night before I could second-guess the decision. Lanterns hung next to a few of the smaller houses, but most of the light came from torches, mounted on poles and posted every ten or so feet.

They did a mediocre job of lighting the station and an excellent job of creating pathways of flickering shadows for me. Every step I took seemed twice as loud as usual, but there were no shouts of alarm as I crept my way toward the north gate, the one the work crews had brought me through, and the one Jules and Cross would be watching.

There were five men on duty at the gate, all armed. Two flanked the gate itself, keeping watch, while the cold wind had driven the other three into a small wooden guard shed on the right. Wary of the way light reflected off my helmet, I crouched down in the darkness to observe them.

Five Normals was nothing for the storm but tearing my way through them would be noisy and putting the entire station on alert was a good way of getting the rest of my crew killed. I'd been banking on the fact that the gate guards would be looking for external threats instead of internal and was pleased to find that to be the case. Unfortunately, their positioning still posed problems.

Thankfully, the world's best distraction was about to arrive.

Raised voices behind me had me looking for better cover, but I wasn't the one who had been spotted. The men in the guardhouse stirred and walked right past me to look to the south.

"Is that the southern companies? Finally? Sure took their sweet-ass time, didn't they?"

"Say goodbye to hot showers for the next few weeks, boys. Let's just hope some of the prisoners they're bringing us make up for the discomfort. And on that note, what do you say we go help unload those prisoners?"

"You… want to do *more* work, chief?"

"I want to see who and what we've got to work with. No point letting the men on the south gate call first dibs every time. Did you see that brunette Eckels scored last time?"

I marked the three men in my mind. Whatever happened, they would all be dead before the night was through.

One of the other men was grinning with an eagerness he didn't seem interested in hiding, but the third shook his head. "Harris would blow a gasket if we left our post—"

"Harris isn't running night shift, McKinley. I am. If you want to stay out here with Tweedledee and Tweedledum on the gate, that's your business. Rogers and I are going to go be… of service."

Apparently, McKinley did *not* want to stay behind; he joined the other two as they jogged toward the south gate, where all the commotion was happening.

That left me with Tweedledee and Tweedledum. The one on the right looked over his shoulder, sighed, and turned back to maintain his post. The one on the left didn't even do that much, ignoring the growing noise behind him.

That same noise—not to mention the fact that every eye on the wall had turned to watch a hundred men and six wagonfuls of prisoners—made the rest easy. I snuck up behind the first guard and, in one fluid move, slipped my arm around his throat even as I dragged him into the shadows. I didn't have the time to choke him unconscious, or the confidence that he'd stay that way for more than a few seconds, so instead I exerted pressure, crushing his larynx and all the small bones and other passageways in his throat.

I lowered the body to the ground and then crossed the street behind the second guard. He went every bit as easily as the first, focused more on the appearance of discipline than the reality of keeping alert and aware. Between this station and the fort back by Eclipse, I hadn't been too impressed with the quality of the Crimson Queen's military so far. The fact that she was winning battles with troops like this spoke poorly of the opposition.

Then again, as the female Corporal Sanderson had pointed out, the regulars at the station were hardly what anyone would describe as true warriors. *Those* were the ones being welcomed at the south gate.

I took up the closest torch, leaned over the gate, and waved it twice. Hopefully, Jules was watching. Our time window was narrow, especially with three guards that would likely find themselves banished back to their assigned gate in a matter of minutes.

I sensed my crew coming more than I saw them, two figures melting out of the darkness like one of Selene's ghosts. The Crow herself would stay back with the horses and my bike, ready to create a fresh distraction if we needed one.

I helped both men over the gate and they stripped the dead men, pulling on worn fatigues. Cross and I each slung a corpse over our shoulders, and I led the two back along the path I'd just come.

The north bay was still dark and quiet, but I didn't expect that to last. We dumped the mostly naked dead men in the storage room where I'd hidden, and I brought Jules and Cross up to the map on the observation deck.

"Kill the comms first," I reminded them, pointing out the room I thought most likely to be it. "Then on to the citizenship room. Both should be on this floor. I'll head for the basement."

"I don't think all of the prisoners are offloaded yet," said Cross.

"That's okay. I'll work my way down and then back up and out. It should be just the sort of noisy that lets you work unnoticed."

"You always have the best jobs, Queenie." That familiar devil-may-care grin was still missing, but Jules' eyes practically glowed with suppressed excitement. The man had no business even talking about retirement yet.

The two of them disappeared through the door. I gave them five minutes and climbed back down the ramp to find the second entrance. Based on the map, there was a stairwell nearby that would take me down to the basement and its multiple layers of armed security… men and women who took payment to stand watch during the degradation of their vulnerable charges.

The storm began to howl.

26

I hit the wooden door at the bottom of the stairwell like a pre-Break freight train, tearing it right off its hinges and blasting it through into the hallway beyond. My shell fell away as the storm poured forth, tearing through a security checkpoint that had barely begun to react to my entrance. A second checkpoint fell just as easily and then I was through into a large room where filthy, barely clad humans had been lined up against the wall.

A heavyset man in fatigues stood in front of them, backed by a dozen rifles, but my appearance had interrupted whatever orientation speech the warden had planned. I cut down half of his men before the bullets began to chatter, the rifles' noise subsumed by the storm's own clash of steel, and then he was charging my way, swinging a rod as thick as one of his legs but made of solid metal.

Seriously… they might as well wear signs saying *I'm a Titan.*

Whoever he was, he was a hell of a lot tougher than Havoc had been, but he wasn't my concern. Not yet, not with bullets flying around and twenty or more prisoners huddling on the floor just waiting to take a stray round in the face. I flowed right past the angry warden, the storm leaving superficial scrapes across his armored skin, and fell upon the remaining shooters.

They were Normals, every one of them, and they did what Normals do best against the storm.

I reformed my shell in the gore and dodged a swing that whistled through the air like a Terrorbird diving for prey, then I was the storm again, swarming the enemy Titan, finding his weak points and pressing them until they ruptured. The eyes, the mouth, the nose, the soft space behind his knees and under his arms. There weren't many Titans who could stand up to the storm, and none of those would be found wasting their lives in a dump like this. When I was done, that heavy metal club fell to the ground out of bloody fingers.

I scooped it up with one hand as I reformed my shell and plucked a ring of keys out of the mess with the other. I waved that key ring at the prisoners still huddled against the wall. Some of them were bleeding, but all of them were breathing.

"Who wants to stay alive?" I asked them.

There was a long pause and then a young woman with empty eyes and a face only a mother could love raised her hand.

I tossed her the keys.

"These should open the door behind you and the cells inside. Get everyone out. I'll clear a way. Take whatever weapons you can."

"There are soldiers out there," protested an older man who had finally found his voice. "Dozens, if not hundreds!"

I cocked my head, letting the smiley-face across the visor study him in silence, then shrugged. "Then we'd better get started."

I left them behind. Maybe they'd free the other prisoners, like I asked, and maybe they wouldn't. What mattered most was that this had clearly been the first group brought down from the recently arrived wagon train, and neither Evan nor Two-Feathers was part of it.

My men were upstairs, maybe even still out on the street, and likely guarded by at least four Powers. But if Jules and Cross had done their jobs, the radios were disabled, and we'd have credentials soon.

The Crimson Queen would know something had happened to Tillatoba but not what or who.

Stealth had played its minor role. This was a time for killing.

Soldiers poured down the stairs as I returned to the hall. I took the first one's head clean off with one swing of the former Titan's club, caved in someone else's face with the backhand, and then I dropped both the club and my shell, the storm raging through a tunnel of limbs and frail human flesh. Behind me, I could sense the first prisoners, peeking out, but they wisely stayed put, silent witnesses to the carnage being left in my wake.

The initial wave of soldiers had just broken and run when one of the doors to the torture rooms past the stairs slid open. A man in bloody scrubs and a mask stepped forth, eyes slitted as he glared down the hall at the mess I had made. I was still a dozen feet away from him when a blob the size of a small dog oozed out of the room behind him, black and tar-like, with a dozen grasping hands instead of feet.

The technician forgot about me entirely as the creature wrapped itself about his ankles, pulling itself up the man's legs even as his exposed flesh began to scorch and scar. He screamed and screamed and kept screaming, the sound tangible if not audible, and then his body simply melted, darkening until it had become indistinguishable from the thing that had grabbed it.

For a moment, even the storm was still.

With the addition of the technician's mass, the ooze formed a torso, arms, and legs, though each limb still ended in a multitude of hands with twisted, dripping fingers. Last to come was the head, vaguely human-shaped, with teeth like insect stingers, a bump for a nose, and eyes that outcrazied Selene's on the lady Crow's best day.

"Yeah, fuck that," I said in the sudden silence, not even realizing I'd reformed my shell somewhere along the way.

Whatever the thing was, it surged forward with a bubbly gurgle, not so much taking steps as flowing, a human-shaped millipede with a thousand grasping fingers instead of jointed legs. I stepped aside, giving it a path to the stairs, but it changed course to meet me, stinger teeth clicking as it moved.

I didn't know if this was some kind of Power who had been broken on the technician's table, or a dream-born horror the queen's army had thought might ultimately prove useful, and I didn't care. Whatever was left was clearly beyond saving.

I dropped my shell again as the creature reached for me, and the storm was there, steel and shrapnel cutting off pieces as fast as they came. Fifteen seconds in, and the flurry hadn't stopped, hadn't even slowed. Even as the storm continued its butcher's work, I spread my senses out to understand what was happening.

The pieces I was cutting off, the limbs and fingers and just plain carvings of dark oozing flesh, fell to the ground in waves, only to be absorbed right back into the greater mass of the creature, repurposed, and sent forth again in an unending wave of attacks. Worse, whatever made the thing corrosive to human skin was also effective against the storm… bits of ooze sticking to the many whirling pieces and beginning to smoke as they scoured the metal.

Whatever this was, I couldn't kill it… and I was starting to think the opposite didn't hold true.

I pulled the storm away and the creature chased after, the two of us crashing right into the wall of reinforcements who had been dumb enough to come downstairs. The storm cut through them, but the ooze absorbed their bodies, gaining mass as it went.

I managed some separation once we hit the stairs, reforming my shell, and joined the group of armed men suddenly fleeing for the ground floor.

The horror was on our heels, new limbs lurching forward like a Body Shifter, fingers grasping and pulling unfortunate stragglers into its bulk. The only good news was that it seemed intent on chasing me down, leaving behind the prisoners that I'd freed below. I didn't know how many people were being held in that basement, in addition to the twenty newcomers I'd freed, but their collective mass might grow this thing to the size of the ruler of the deep I'd sensed in the Mississippi.

And that seemed… bad.

I followed the terrified soldiers out of the building—as more people died behind us and were quickly absorbed—only to find a wall of rifles waiting for me. Behind them, a Beast Shifter the size of a small building raised its misshapen head and roared to the sky. Next to him—or her… it was impossible to tell, and not just because it was night—was a small woman in fatigues with chunks of solid fire orbiting her head like tiny planets, and a man with ash-white hair and eyes that glowed like the sun.

I'd found the newly arrived Powers.

The Pyromancer and the Lightbringer didn't even wait for their own men to clear out of the way. As soon as I was spotted, fiery orbs and beams of light both shot forward. The light slightly outpaced the fire, but I wasn't going to stick around and let either Power know that. I wasn't stuck at the bottom of a silo this time, and that made all the difference.

I dove to one side, dismissing my shell at the same time. That first beam of light tore through me, far too quick to dodge, but the other attacks flooded past and into the open doorway—

—where they struck the creature as it surged through the exit.

For the first time, the thing shuddered, as if in pain, smoke curling upward from small patches of rubbery tar that had gone stiff and solid. Still, it barely even slowed, pouring out the door and into the street like the world's largest and grossest bowl of jelly. The storm's offenses were apparently already forgotten as it surged toward the waiting soldiers and the Powers now frantically raining down damage from behind the lines.

I didn't know who would win that battle and I didn't care. I turned and headed for the prisoner wagons, still parked just inside the south gate. A scattering of soldiers had remained with the wagons, but they fled after I cut down the first handful without even slowing stride.

I was more than happy to see the three assholes from the north gate among the dead. They wouldn't be calling dibs on anyone ever again.

Each wagon was little more than a cage on wheels, with an exterior ledge for two drivers in front and raised out of reach of the people inside. The first such cage was already open and half-empty. As the guards fled from me, the remaining prisoners took the chance to regain their freedom. None of them were Evan or Two-Feathers, so I let them go and moved to the next wagon.

This one was still secure. I let the storm tear a hole through the wagon's wooden floor, and then backed away as people, as filthy and tired as those I'd rescued downstairs, issued forth in a wave.

Still no Evan. Still no Two-Feathers. I moved onto the third wagon, where one of the prisoners, tall and skinny, was desperately reaching for something up on the drivers' seat above him. Unless he was a Body Shifter—and he clearly wasn't—there was no way he'd be able to reach whatever it was, but he was trying anyway, the skin on the arm and shoulder torn and bloody from where he'd forced it through the bars.

I hopped up onto the cage as battle raged behind me and found a second ring of keys, helpfully left behind without me having to even shove anyone through the storm-sized blender to get it.

I scooped them up, dropped back down, and opened the cage. As people fled past me, I stopped the bloody-armed man and handed him the keys.

"For the other cages," I said, shouting to be heard over the screams and the gunfire. "Get them unlocked."

I watched his mouth open, probably to complain or ask why him, but the smiley-face across my helmet worked its magic, stopping him in mid-protest. Instead, he nodded, took the keys, and hurried over to wagon number four.

I'd have gone with him, but I'd found who I was looking for.

Evan's face was as grey as his hair, but he was on his feet, helping support Two-Feathers.

"What did they do to him?" I demanded, swapping in for the little man.

"I'm doing fine, thank you for asking."

"Evan."

He had the grace to wince and look guilty. "They broke his arm and that Beast Shifter cut him up pretty good when they first brought him down, but I think his current condition is more about the drugs they pumped him full of. Nothing fatal that I can tell and nothing that won't heal if we can get the hell out of wherever we are."

"This is Tillatoba," I said.

"*This* is the place you wanted to take us to?" He scowled, unruffled by the absolute mayhem happening a hundred or so feet away. If anyone from his old village had been present, they wouldn't have even recognized him. "What happened to it?"

"That happened." I pointed to the many-fingered ooze thing as it pushed through a wave of fire, smoldering and badly damaged, but far from beaten.

He took one look at the monstrosity and the new—or old… sometimes, it was hard to keep them straight—Evan reasserted himself, going pale and wobbling where he stood. “I think I’d like to go back to the mountain now.”

The thing screamed as a lance of light tore through it, and I handed Two-Feathers back to the smaller man.

“We’ll talk after New Memphis. Wait here.”

“Where are you going?”

I looked down at the battered nomad, at the one arm strapped to his chest, and the stitches, bruises, and swelling making a mockery of the clean lines of his form and turned away. The enemy Beast Shifter stood behind the lines, clearly unwilling to attack an enemy who ate and absorbed whatever it touched.

“I’m going to go have some words.”

ooo

The Crimson Queen’s men were discovering, just as I had, how difficult the ooze was to fight. Bullets didn’t add to its mass, but they didn’t seem to harm it either, and anyone who came within reach was swiftly killed and absorbed. What had once been the size of a small dog was now at least as tall as the two-story building behind it, and the soldiers’ efforts were spent more on keeping their distance than on actually stopping the creature.

There were exceptions, of course; one team of soldiers worked a tripod-mounted flamethrower while another had found fragmentary grenades and were hurling them from as great a distance as they could, ignoring the way the blasts shook both the buildings themselves and the people near enough to feel the impact.

Still, the Powers were, by far, the biggest weapons left in the fight. Even as I approached them from behind, the Pyromancer sent another of her orbs of flame into the ooze’s center mass, and the Lightbringer hurled something that looked like ball lightning but was pure light instead of electricity. The creature survived the dual blasts, but was smaller than it had been, its many fingered pseudo limbs twitching in uncertain rhythms.

They were *winning*.

It didn't escape my notice that the ooze seemed to share the storm's own weakness. Fire and light, abilities that also turned steel to slag, cut away pieces of the horror and those pieces stayed inert. I wasn't sure if it was something that had evolved and grown on its own in the decades since the dream or if it was another of Dad's originals, a derivation on the design that birthed the storm.

Whatever it was, I wasn't calling it brother, and the world would be better with it gone. But that didn't mean I had to sit back and give the queen's Powers the field.

With all the noise and smoke—from gunfire, real fire, and explosions—the Beast Shifter's senses were all but useless. I was within arm's reach when it spun to meet me. I stood still and silent as a clawed hand drove straight through my chest and let the Power see my smile as its victorious roar swiftly turned into a howl of pain. It pulled back a stump, but the storm followed with it, pouring forth from the hole in my shell even as that shell fell away.

Beast Shifters heal. The best of them can regrow their limbs, fight off engineered diseases, and undo the ravages of age, all at the same time… but they're ultimately mortal, just like everything else.

I didn't know how strong this Shifter was and I didn't care. No Power in the post-Break world would heal from the fingernail-sized fragments the storm left behind.

Ten feet away, the battle was coming to a close. Try as it might, the ooze couldn't overcome two ranged Powers wielding elements it had no defense against. It spun and tried to scuttle away, but if there's one thing Pyromancers specialize in, it's area of effect attacks, and a ring of flame sprung up about it, even as pulses of light whittled down that mass to the thing's original size. It reformed its almost human face in the middle of what little body it had left and gnashed together teeth whose stingers had split and torn.

And then a wave of light and fire wiped it from the earth.

The Lightbringer sagged in exhaustion and then stiffened again as the storm tore into him from behind, cutting through unaugmented flesh and bone like a chisel through porridge. Crimson light bloomed to the side as the Pyromancer brought her powers to bear on me, but she was too late, too slow, too tired, and too close.

I turned on the remaining soldiers next. No mercy, given the things I'd seen and heard. Each one I killed now was one we wouldn't have to hunt down between Tillatoba and New Memphis.

I gave the storm its reins and nothing stood in our path.

27

"What the fuck, Queenie?" Jules and Cross made their way down the street to me, the site of my recent massacre lit by torches on one side and a burning multi-story building on the other.

"This wasn't all my doing," I told them. "They caused the fires and the explosions."

"And the rest?"

"That *was* me."

With both the ooze and the Crimson Queen's men dead, prisoners were starting to make their way out of the burning building, led by the dead-eyed woman who had taken the warden's keys. Most of those prisoners stopped in horror at the sight awaiting them—and quite a few lost whatever little they'd been fed recently—but the woman herself just nodded and kept going.

"Well, we got what we came here for," said Jules, slapping the bag he'd tossed over one shoulder. "Even with *someone* starting a war out here."

"You got us credentials?"

"Yeah. They call them passports, for some reason. Maybe because Memphis is on the river? Bastards had a huge stack of them pre-filled and ready to go, so I took the fanciest looking ones in the bunch. Figure they'll be the ones that give higher level access."

"Any idea how they work?"

"Fingerprints, it looks like. Prick your thumb, make a print, run the card through a scanner in the city and compare it to your actual digit. That's as far as we got. People weren't exactly volunteering info." He looked past me. "I see you got Miles and Two-Feathers out. Are they okay?"

"They're alive. Let's—"

A loud groan interrupted us as the burning building suddenly shifted. A wall collapsed somewhere inside and fire poured from the second-floor windows like it was running from itself. The line of people exiting ground to a halt as prisoners froze in the middle of their potential tomb. Something new gave inside the building, and the whole southern wing teetered, a breath away from collapse.

There wasn't a damn thing the storm or I could do to stop it. I saw faces deeper in the building, already stained by blood and soot, look up with dawning dread, saw the recognition of their own deaths hitting them even as those closer to the door pushed and shoved to escape.

And then the ground shook, throwing us all off our feet. The building's second story collapsed in a whoosh of air and fire, but that single sharp tremor had sent it falling outward instead of inward, impacting the station's exterior wall. The people inside didn't question their unexpected salvation, climbing over fallen beams and around weak spots in the floor to stumble into the street. I knew that the prisoners hadn't all made it—that some had likely been trapped in the stairwell or incapable of leaving their cells down below—but we'd still saved a shit-ton of them.

As for those who lived up on the second floor? The Provs who had stayed inside when the shooting started? They'd made their choices long before my crew showed up.

Cross shook his head, eyes wide and a little bit crazy. "I know you told the boss that Dr. Nowhere was dead, but clearly, *someone* is still looking out for us."

I very carefully did not look over at the person I knew was responsible.

The next few minutes were bedlam as everyone put distance between them and the still-burning building. Family members found each other again (or didn't), while the more physically capable and socially minded survivors went right to work caring for the less fortunate. It was almost heartwarming… right up until the bloody-armed man I'd conscripted to unlock the wagon cages came over, followed by the dead-eyed woman who I'd tasked with opening the cells inside.

"Can we help you?" asked Jules, sliding into the face role he handled a hell of a lot better than me.

"Yeah," said the other man, in a southern drawl deeper than his frame would have suggested. "We're grateful for the rescue, make no mistake, but what territory are y'all affiliated with? Pretty sure *our* warlord's dead and there's no way he'd have had the resources or the give-a-damn to send folk like you to retrieve us anyway."

The woman with him nodded but said nothing.

"We're unaffiliated," said Jules.

"Huh. Well, okay. So, now that the rescue's done, what's next?"

Jules shot me a look and I stepped forward.

"My crew and I are going to New Memphis, alone. The rest of you are free to do as you wish."

“What?” asked a heavyset woman who’d been lurking close enough to overhear. “You’re just leaving us? What about supplies? What about guns? Where are we supposed to live?”

“There are supplies in the north bay,” I said, pointing to the part of the huge facility not currently on fire. “Take what you need from there. As for guns…” I waved that same gloved hand at the dead soldiers littering the ground around us. “We’ll want to keep some of the leftover ammo, but I think you’re still more than covered.”

“It’s almost winter.” Blood continued to drip down the thin man’s arm, but he didn’t seem to notice. “And our towns are gone.”

I let the storm echo in my sigh. “We’re headed north on a job. We don’t have the time, skills, or inclination to build you a new town and get you settled.”

“Yes, but—”

“You have access to horses, to wagons, and to lumber, not to mention supplies that most likely include both food *and* clothing. Assuming you get the boxes out before the fire spreads to that wing anyway.” I spared Jules and Cross a glance but neither seemed to take issue with my decision. We were mercenaries, after all, not social workers or philanthropists. “We’re leaving first thing in the morning. Figure your shit out.”

The dead-eyed woman scowled, and for a moment I thought she might be about to utter her first words since I found her. Instead, another wall in the facility chose that moment to collapse. All three former prisoners looked that way and then to the north, where the storage bay I’d mentioned sat, still remarkably whole.

“We’ll put together a work team.” He turned back to the dead-eyed woman. “Able bodies only, but we need to get as much stuff out of that bay as we can.”

“What can I do?” asked the heavyset woman, shooting us a glare. “I want to help.”

"What's your name?"

"Glory."

"Hi Glory, I'm Joe. Can you go talk with the people still recovering? Maybe some of them came from towns that wouldn't mind a parade of refugees if we come bearing gifts."

"What are you going to do?"

"I'm taking a few people to try and recover the horses, seeing as how they'd already been unhitched from the wagons and took off when the shooting started."

I looked over to Two-Feathers, with the idea of volunteering his services, but Evan had propped the nomad up against one of the smaller houses. Whatever drugs he'd been given hadn't worn off just yet.

"We can pitch in with pulling out the crates, don't you think?" Jules asked me, as the three prisoners went to start their separate tasks.

"You *want* to do work?"

"Well, you said we're staying here until dawn anyway. Might as well be useful. Besides," he added, dropping his voice, "I wouldn't mind a look at what the army's got for supplies. It's been weeks since Greenburg and we could do with topping up our rations. I might even have Cross go get Selene to help."

I looked at the sheer mass of humanity running about, and then back at Jules, letting my silence speak for itself.

"Or maybe she can hang out with the horses some more," he allowed. "It's not like she's big on carrying stuff anyway."

"Have at it." I waved him and Cross toward the north bay. "If anyone gives you shit about taking stuff, send them to me."

"You're not going out hunting for soldiers?"

I shook my head. "The queen's men will wait until dawn. Only a few went north, anyway, and none of them had horses. If they make tracks for New Memphis, we'll just ride them down. I've got other things to do."

He put two and two together, looked toward Two-Feathers, and winced. "He looks like he's in rough shape, Queenie."

"Yeah." There was nothing but metal in my voice.

"All I'm saying is… maybe go easy on the kid?"

In true Jules fashion, he left after having gotten in the last word, leaving me to stare at his retreating form. Did he think I was going to tear the nomad a new one? It was *my* plan that had gotten Two-Feathers captured. Worse, I had chosen to delay our rescue instead of taking on the wagon train directly. The damage Jules was talking about was on my head. The last thing I was going to do was yell at the nomad.

I shook my head as I watched Jules and Cross enter the north bay. Sleep with a man for a few months and you think you've maybe gotten a handle on each other as people. Then, a decade later, that man drops some total bullshit on you out of the blue and it turns out you're both still practically strangers.

I wove through the crowd of prisoners where the three self-proclaimed leaders were doing their best to bring order to chaos. Evan was standing nearby, white-faced and practically hyperventilating. He turned away as I came near, head down and shoulders hunched almost to his ears.

I ignored the little man and took a seat next to Two-Feathers. The nomad's eyes were closed, and it didn't look like there was anyone home just yet. In the flickering light of way too many fires, I gave him another quick once-over. There was bruising across his face and shoulders, and more than a few cuts that had at least been treated to prevent infection. His right arm was strapped across his chest, weeks from being usable even if the break had been clean, and his left was almost as battered as his face. Black hair hung in thick waves to his shoulders, stiff where blood had been spilled and long since dried, and only one of his customary braids remained intact. The ill-fitting shirt he'd pulled on as a disguise over his deerskin was wrecked, slashed, stretched, and stained, and even though I'd threatened to burn that stupid shirt, the sight of it almost pushed me over the edge.

"Evan," I called to the old man doing his best to pretend I didn't exist. "Go to the wagons and see if you can find Two-Feathers' spear."

I waited for him to shuffle off, and then waited a bit longer to make sure he was out of range. The weapon was important to Two-Feathers and recovering it mattered, but the truth was I just hadn't wanted Evan listening to this.

"You're an idiot," I told Two-Feathers. "You shouldn't even be on this job. Eclipse has nothing to do with you and neither do I. Only a total asshole would run off and nearly get himself killed for someone he barely knows. What the hell were you even thinking? You're flesh and blood, just like the rest of them!"

I was working my way into a real rant, and feeling damn good about it too, when Two-Feathers' free hand reached out and patted my arm. Only one eye opened, thanks to all the swelling around the other, but it held a world of emotion in its depths: sympathy, pain, and, most prominent of all, humor, dry as a bone.

"Maybe I'll save the lecture until you're upright," I allowed, carefully not admitting to myself that Jules might know me better than I'd realized. "Let's just sit back a bit and watch things burn."

Two-Feathers patted my arm a second time and that one eye drifted closed. As usual, he said nothing.

○○○

By the next morning, the fire was mostly out, supplies were stacked in the streets, and the former prisoners were *still* arguing about what they would do next and where they would go.

A few dozen people watched as we walked north out of the station, gazes full of a strange blend of gratitude and resentment that I was happy to leave behind. We'd saved their lives and left them with what they would need to survive; the rest was up to them. Maybe a new town would sprout up somewhere in the wilderness, or an existing one would find its population doubled almost overnight. Or maybe the post-Break world would swallow them whole, leaving behind only bones.

Either way, it wasn't any of my business. I had a job to do.

We'd left Selene with the horses and my bike, just past where I'd hatched my crazy plan to get into the station. It was a five-minute walk, but even Evan seemed anxious to put the smoking ruins behind him.

The horses had been near enough to hear the explosions and gunfire, not to mention smell the fire, but apparently, their tiny brains had already moved past that excitement; we found them, heads-down, munching their way through the grass where we'd left them tethered. Nearby were Selene's bedroll and tent, as well as the saddlebags the boys and I had left behind for our assault.

What we *didn't* find was the Crow herself.

"Well, shit," said Jules, sounding as tired as he looked. He had a brand-new rifle in one arm, and the rucksack slung over the other was bulging with whatever he'd taken from the processing station.

"Does she often go on walk-about?"

"Not that I can recall."

Two-Feathers had made a beeline for his horse as soon as it came into view, planting his spear in the earth and stroking the beast's long neck with his functional hand, but on hearing our words, he made his way back over, dark eyes scanning the campsite. A few minutes later, he knelt in the grass and nodded. He turned to make sure we were paying attention and then pointed north.

"She went north?"

At the nomad's nod, Cross came over to join us. "Did someone take her?"

Two-Feathers shook his head.

"How can you tell?" asked the other man.

What followed was a strange, one-sided conversation that meant absolutely nothing to me but seemed to satisfy Cross' curiosity and eagerness to learn. By the time they were done, Jules had broken down Selene's tent, and loaded up the horses. We followed the trail out of camp, Cross still peppering Two-Feathers with tracking-related questions as we went.

It was maybe a quarter of a mile later that we came across the first body.

He was a soldier from the processing station—the fatigues alone made that clear, but his rifle had still been on his back when he'd died, and while the gaping void left of his throat could have been done by an animal, the two dozen puncture wounds to his chest, abdomen, and crotch made it clear who was responsible.

"Where is his—you know?" asked Jules, face green.

"Maybe she planted it in the field like a seed," suggested Cross.

Mounted on his horse, Evan leaned over and lost whatever food he'd managed for breakfast.

"I guess we know why Selene wasn't at the campsite." I ignored the ruins of the body. The damage she'd done was specifically targeted, and undeniably so, but the storm literally tore people to shreds, and what it had left of the soldiers in the processing station was more soup than puzzle pieces. I was used to gore. "She was going hunting."

Two-Feathers was already moving on, following Selene's trail away from the murder site, weaving through the woods to the east instead of north. Jules stripped the wreckage of a corpse of a few items of value and then we trailed behind the nomad, continuing our macabre scavenger hunt.

By the third body, I had questions.

"Are you all sure she doesn't have any other powers?" Three soldiers, all of them dead and mutilated, and only one had even gotten a shot off, a bullet Cross found embedded in a nearby tree.

"I've never seen her do anything other than talk to ghosts." Jules shook his head. "I've also never seen her just go off and randomly kill people either."

"Other than your enforcer."

"She killed a few people in Lawton too, boss."

"Those bastards had it coming." Jules scowled. "You know the ghost that's riding her, Queenie. Any answers there?"

The obvious answer was *yes*, but I'd lied about that ghost's identity, and the boys were jumpy enough as it was without learning just who and what they'd been traveling with.

I shrugged. "She's doing our job for us, really. The Crimson Queen will learn that something happened to her processing station as soon as they realize radio communications have gone dark, but we don't want her realizing who was involved or that we're headed that way. Anyone who fled to New Memphis needs to die before they make it there."

I felt Jules' gaze on me as I turned to follow Two-Feathers and knew we'd be having a conversation at some point on the road. My old lover was too perceptive by half. He'd had time to think on what happened in Greenburg and was smart enough to know I was leaving something out, if not outright lying.

Wouldn't *that* be a fun talk when it finally happened?

We found Selene by the fifth body, caked in dried blood and sleeping like a baby. She woke as we approached, sitting up and running a hand through her stringy dark hair as if primping in a mirror.

"Is it morning already?" she asked with a smile. Even her teeth were dark with blood.

"New plan," announced Jules, in a voice like he'd just swallowed a bug. "Before we do anything else, we're finding a stream where everyone can wash up. Once that's done, we can get back to this whole *kill an unkillable head of state in the heart of her own empire* thing."

28

It took a while to find running water, but nobody complained about the delay. While Selene was obviously in a category of filth all her own, the men were ripe, dirty, and blood-covered too, from Evan and Two-Feathers, who had been wearing the same clothes for multiple days of captivity, to Jules and Cross, who had killed their way through plenty of guards while breaching the processing station.

I remained spotless, as usual, having reformed my shell not long after we tracked down Selene. I'd always thought the need to eat, drink, and shit was the biggest drawback of being human, but this trip had taught me the lack of cleanliness was a close second.

By the time everyone was done, it was afternoon. We traveled a few more miles before calling it a day and setting up camp. Given the supplies we'd stolen, there was no need to hunt, so Two-Feathers pitched in where he could. I watched as he worked, the smile on my helmet a poor match for the way I felt. Most of the nomad's wounds were superficial, but that broken arm was a real problem. New Memphis was a few weeks away, at most, and there was no way it would be healed by the time we arrived. And that meant we were down our most capable fighter.

It was an unfortunate fact of the post-Break world that modern medicine was a far cry from what it had been. Doctors were rare and Healers even more so, and that meant what would have been minor injuries before the Break could end up crippling people in the modern age. Assuming infection didn't set in and kill them outright.

I watched everyone eat, the circle of space around Selene even wider than it had been before Tillatoba, and listened to the storm, letting its noise drown out the thoughts in my head.

Later, as people turned in for the night, Jules took a seat next to me.

"Any time I can hear the metal scraping from a dozen feet away, I know you're either pissed or cogitating," he told me.

"Sometimes, it's both." I hadn't moved in at least an hour and my muscles had gone tight, but Jules was too close to risk dismissing and reforming my shell. And the pain was a reminder that I was more than just the storm or its container. I was both things and neither, and that mattered too. "Other times, I'm just listening to the storm's chatter."

"And what is it saying tonight?"

"That we have a job to do."

"Guess that fits." He rotated his shoulder, wincing at the clicking noise it made, then cracked each of his knuckles, one after the other. "You know, you never did tell me what Selene's ghost said to you back in Greenburg."

"She wants to kill a man."

"Pretty sure she just did. Five of them, to be precise."

"Four. The third body was a woman."

"It was? How the hell could you tell?"

"I've seen a few bodies in my time, Jules."

"Fair enough." He moved on to his other shoulder, then his neck, joints sounding like a high school drumline, back when high schools and drumlines were both things. “What town does this walking corpse call home?”

“That’s the best part,” I told him.

“New Memphis?”

“New Memphis. He’s high up in the Crimson Queen’s administration, apparently. Hard for a little Crow to get to all on her own. So, the ghost and I struck a deal… she helps us get to the city and I help her reach out and touch her target. And when it’s all done, Selene walks away with gold in her pocket.”

“Any idea what this man did?”

“Not a clue, and given his allegiances, I don’t care. Selene gets her man, I get the queen, everyone rides away happy.”

“Two assassinations for the price of one.”

“It seemed like a bargain.”

“And what do you think the chances are of that? Everyone riding away at the end?”

“We’ll know better once we reach the city.” It was my turn to give him a look. “Don’t tell me you’re getting cold feet already?”

“This has been a shit year, Queenie. I’m tired, I’m old, and I can’t help but feel like we’re all going to die.”

“Everyone dies. Even Tezcatlipoca, apparently.” I let the humor drain from my voice. “You know I’ll do everything I can to keep you alive.”

“Because you need me to kill the Telekinetic?” I’d gone serious and he’d countered by going droll.

“Not *just* because of that, but it does factor into the equation.”

“I bet it does.”

“We’ll sneak in with the passports you stole for us, find our way into the palace, kill my target, then Selene’s, and you’ll all end up rich as thieves.”

"I'm kind of hoping for richer than that." His lips quirked up. "I've known too many poor thieves."

"You and me both."

○○○

The next morning, we took a look at the stolen passports. They were exactly as Jules had described; heavy card stock with some kind of block code on the back and the front divided into two sides. On the right was the signature and dried thumbprint of the now-dead administrator in charge of handing out citizenship. On the left was a blank space for our own print.

IDs had still been a thing in the early days of the Break, but I'd never had much experience with them. The Free States included pictures in theirs, the prints done with ink and an index finger instead of blood and a thumb, but the idea was otherwise the same: a piece of paper that determined who you were and what you were allowed to do.

Can't say I loved it, but this was our ticket into the fifth district. Maybe even further than that, given that these passports had golden designs around the edges. Jules had said they were fancier than the others he'd found, and something told me he'd been right in thinking that meant higher tiers of access.

Everyone watched me, even Selene, as I pulled off my gloves, the pieces of my shell folding away into nothing once they lost contact with the rest of me. I ran Jules' knife across my left palm, passed the weapon back to him, and then pressed my right thumb against the wound and then onto the paper. I made sure the print was legible before I broke the silence.

"What? Anyone want to tell me what has all of you so fascinated?"

"I wasn't sure you bled," said Selene, in a dreamy little voice.

"I heal just as fast."

"Most Shifters do," she agreed. "Until they don't."

And that was enough of that. But before I could reform my shell to repair the damage and replace my gloves, Jules waved the remaining passports in front of me.

"Any chance we can use your blood for our credentials too?"

"I beg your pardon?"

"You heal. We don't. Do you want your whole crew running around with self-inflicted wounds?"

"I can think of one person that I'd be okay with, yeah," I said, making sure I was looking straight at him.

"I'm sure I'll get stabbed sooner or later." He grinned. "That's how these things seem to go. Now, hold out your hand so we can get this done before you heal up."

I was pretty sure Jules knew that's not how healing worked for me, but either I was wrong on that front or he was keeping my secrets. Either way, I'd take it.

I stretched my hand out as five people paraded by and stuck their thumbs in my open wound. I've had better days, and worse.

When the blood was dry, I reformed my shell, and we tucked our passports away into our bags. Tillatoba had been a shitshow, but it had also been an unqualified success. We were all alive, if not unharmed, and the Crimson Queen had lost four Powers, more than a hundred additional men, and whatever the hell that ooze creature had been. Most importantly of all, we had our way into her city.

The pile of bodies behind us was growing by the day, but things were looking up.

It was a week before our slowly dwindling supplies made hunting a necessity again, and this time, Two-Feathers took Cross with him. The nomad's bruises were an angry yellow but no longer seemed to trouble him. If it wasn't for the broken arm, he'd have been at full strength. Evan fussed over him a bit before he left, and then again when he returned, like a mother hen caring for its chicks, but Two-

Feathers bore the other man's ministrations with his usual quiet dignity. I wasn't sure if he was just *that* easy-going a person, or if he saw how it settled the other man down to have something to do.

Knowing the nomad, it was a mix of both.

I kept a figurative eye on the injured nomad, and a second one on our wayward Crow, but mostly left things to Jules to run. The road from Tillatoba to New Memphis was in good condition—the best I'd seen outside of the larger cities of the Free States—and the hum of the motor beneath me was a calming counterpoint to the ever-present storm.

It seemed like maybe the world had decided we'd had enough shit already on our trip. For twelve straight days, the skies were blue, the air was crisp, and every bend brought us, not fresh trouble, but new vistas of autumnal glory, vast stretches of trees whose leaves were turning red and gold. Twelve days where the biggest threat we faced was the boar that Two-Feathers brought down and Cross dragged back to camp.

I could almost feel the rest of the crew relax, the hunch leaving Evan's back, the tightness fading just a bit from Jules' eyes, even the rare grin that made its way back onto Two-Feathers' face. Cross played things close to his chest and Selene was a Rorschach test with a thousand interpretations, but after the ferry and the processing station, that stretch of peace was sorely needed and richly appreciated.

Of course, it couldn't last.

On the thirteenth day, Two-Feathers came riding in from the front like the wind itself was chasing him. He pulled us off into the woods, retreating until the road was lost behind thick layers of vegetation. There, we crouched down and waited.

And waited.

It took five minutes before anything changed, but not even Selene stirred in the interim, making me wonder if her ghost was riding her even now. Hoofbeats announced the passage of a handful of horses, and then we heard it, a dull rumble, and the noise of tires on dirt that I knew so well. Wider tires than my bike's, by the sound of it, and heavier too.

Before I could stop him, Jules disappeared into the undergrowth between us and the road, slithering like an eel through the fallen leaves and bare brush. The rest of us stayed where we were, listening as the growl of that motor grew until it rattled the trees of the forest and then slowly receded in the distance.

Behind the vehicle came a different sort of thunder, a hundred or more feet, marching in unison. Several minutes later, they were followed by another handful of horses. By the time we were certain the road was empty again, Jules was back among us.

"Convoy," he said, voice low. "No prisoners this time, just soldiers. And some sort of armored vehicle belching out black smoke behind it."

"With scouts on horses in front and behind?" I included Two-Feathers in the question, and he nodded, black eyes solemn.

"I guess they've figured out something's wrong in Tillatoba," said Cross. "Do you think the prisoners we left behind are done arguing yet?"

"It's been more than a week," said Evan, speaking up for the first time in a very long while. "There's no way the captured townsfolk will still be there."

"So maybe they'll follow their tracks instead of ours," mused Cross. "Good thinking, Miles."

"That's not what—"

"And of course, they'll want to hunt down the people responsible. That could gain us even more of a lead. We could be in and out before the Crimson Queen even knows we're coming."

Evan shot to his feet, tossing his canteen aside. "Are you serious right now? *Who cares if dozens of innocent people die as long as it works out in our favor?* Really?"

"I'm not their keeper, Miles."

"Nobody's saying you should be, but simple human decency shouldn't—" He cut himself short, bright spots of color in his cheeks. "You know what? Never mind. I'm going to take a minute for myself and pretend this conversation never happened."

He shook off Two-Feathers' hand and disappeared deeper into the woods, leaving only silence behind.

"Wasn't much of a conversation, really," muttered Cross. "What the hell got into him anyway?"

"Maybe it's that time of the month," said Selene with a smile.

Nobody laughed.

I met Jules' gaze and sighed, climbing to my feet.

"I'll go make sure nothing eats him. We'll be back in a bit."

ooo

"What part of *I'm going to take a moment for myself* was unclear?" asked Evan as I came up beside him.

"This isn't the Free States. There are things in the woods with fangs and stingers and who knows what else. Unless you go and pull another Tillatoba, you'll just be a snack to them."

"I'm not… I didn't…" His shoulders slumped. "You caught that, huh?"

"It wasn't exactly subtle."

"People were screaming and about to be cooked alive. I just… reacted. And anyone who was up on the floor above them died because of it."

"That floor held the barracks for the soldiers and the prisoners they'd turned. Maybe they all had it coming."

"Is that your answer to everything? Someone does something you don't like; kill them? Someone gets in your way; kill them? Someone sneezes; kill them? That's not just bloodthirsty. It's insane!"

"Mercy is a luxury, Evan. You already know that. If we'd let the soldiers live, what do you think they'd have done to those prisoners you helped free?"

"The exact same thing Cross is not-so-secretly hoping will happen now." The bitterness in his voice took me back almost seventeen years, to when a younger version of the man before me had railed against the realization that he'd lost everything.

"We freed the prisoners and supplied them. Everything else is in their hands now. That's how the world works."

"Only because nobody outside of the Free States fights to change it."

He seemed too old to be that naïve, but I let it go.

"We'll reach New Memphis within the week," I said instead. "And this will be over soon after that. When it's done, you can take your gold, buy yourself a town, and create whatever utopia you want."

"You're really going to pay me with the others? Even though I'm here because of a debt?"

He had a point, but nothing with this job had balanced out so far, and that transactional piece of me remained silent and still as the grave. I would leverage my unexpected freedom for however long it lasted.

"Everyone gets paid," I told him. "A tyrant gets overthrown, and you walk away rich and able to help people in your own way. What's not to like about that?"

He gave me a steady look and for just a moment, his eyes were a thousand years old, all-knowing, and deeply wearied. "What about Two-Feathers?"

"I'm sorry?"

"He's the only one of you worth a damn. The only one of *us.*"

"He'll get paid too."

"That's not what I'm saying."

"Didn't we have this conversation a while back? He's a grown man. He can make his own decisions. Hell, he's the one who invited himself along in the first place."

"And now he's injured. What are the chances of a Stalwart with one working arm surviving whatever comes next?"

That was uncomfortably close to thoughts I'd already had.

"Send him away," he urged. "Please. I know I don't have any leverage, but I'm asking anyway."

"You can't save everyone, Evan. Especially those who don't want to be saved."

"That doesn't mean we shouldn't try."

○○○

That conversation was still on my mind a few days later. Even after all he'd been through, Evan wanted to be a hero, wanted to believe that this was a world for heroes. I knew better—I'd *seen* better—but there was nothing more pointless than arguing with someone who believed they had truth and justice on their side.

The job was to kill the Crimson Queen, not to right her wrongs, save the innocent, uplift the downtrodden, or whatever the fuck else Evan dreamed of doing every night.

So, Eclipse matters, but the hell with every other town? It was the voice I'd been hearing in my mind lately, audible even above the storm.

That's different, I told it. Or myself. *I'm balancing the scales.*

Whose scales? Dr. Nowhere's? The storm's?

I didn't have an answer, but the voice kept going.

This isn't about balance. This is about revenge.

So what if it is? Don't Duke and Mina and Nathan deserve revenge? Doesn't Raya? If Dr. Nowhere dying really did free me to finally act as I want, why wouldn't I do so for them?

All this talk of freedom, and yet here you are, still following the same patterns. Using the job, any job, as an excuse for your actions. When you told Evan you couldn't save everyone, were you talking about the Tillatoba prisoners or yourself?

I wasn't sure what that even meant, but the voice went silent anyway, content, just like every other fucking person in my life, to have gotten the last word.

I shrugged it away, grateful for the silence. For my entire existence, it had just been me, the storm, and the rules we lived under. If those rules really were breaking down, I wasn't going to let some weird Jiminy Cricket-ass voice creep in to replace them.

Especially not when it kind of sounded like Evan.

Of course, that wasn't the only topic that nagged at me over the ensuing days. Eventually, I went to sit by Two-Feathers during the night watch he insisted on keeping.

"*Miles* thinks I should send you away. For your own safety."

He said nothing, of course. Just nodded, face mostly lost in shadow thanks to the fire at his back.

"I think he might be right," I continued. *That* won me a look, but I kept going. "New Memphis is going to be rough. Just getting *to* the Crimson Queen, let alone killing her. I don't know how many of us will survive to see the job done."

He turned back to the woods, eyes scanning the darkness for a threat that wasn't coming.

"Do you *want* to go? Would you leave if I told you to?"

Silence. Two-Feathers could say more without speaking than any person I'd ever met, but he was giving me absolutely nothing.

"Truth is, I still don't even know why you're here. But Miles was right about something. You're the only one of us who doesn't have blood on their soul."

He finally turned all the way around, and I had no trouble interpreting the look on his face.

"I know you've killed. Hell, I've seen it and more than once on this trip alone. But there's a difference between combat and murder, even when the murder is justified. Are you sure you want to bring that sort of burden with you back to the clans?"

He scanned my visor, as if trying to find the face that lurked inside, and then stood, all in one smooth motion that spoke as much to his powers as anything he did in battle. For a moment, he stood over me, looking down. Then, he turned and walked away.

"Good talk," I told the empty night. "Let's never do it again."

The next day, we reached New Memphis.

29

I'd ridden through the original incarnation of Memphis during the Break, back when civilization was taking its final shit and preparing to circle the drain. New Memphis was different. Still on the river, yeah, with a long narrow harbor and creaky old docks where ships were unloaded, but the bulk of the city was out east, and that was where things had changed.

There were buildings everywhere, leaving the whole place feeling almost over-stuffed. Smoke from individual chimneys mixed with the black plumes of coal-burning power plants north of the harbor. Walls divided the city into the districts I'd described back in Greenburg, concentric circles moving from large to small, with the palace sitting in the middle, like a spider at the heart of its web.

Even stranger, the new city was built on a mountain where no mountain had ever existed, each interior district elevated above its external neighbor. It must have taken teams of Earthshakers years to build that terrain up, all so that the people at the top could look down on their less fortunate neighbors.

"How the hell did the Crimson Queen get all of this done? Last I heard, she was just a kid."

With Cross being thirty at most, it was odd to hear him call anyone a kid, but the teenage warlord qualified.

"She didn't build New Memphis. She just took it over." Raya's notes had speculated that the city's previous ruler had been the queen's own father, but the spymaster hadn't known for sure. "Her reign's been more focused on conquest than construction."

"And we have to get to the top of that hill, kill her, and then survive getting back out again?"

"That's the job."

"I don't know, boss," he said to Jules. "Something that seemed doable after a few beers in Greenburg isn't looking so hot right now."

"You can always bow out," said the other man, with a smile that didn't reach his eyes. "No harm, no foul. We've reached New Memphis, which earns you a gold coin. You can take it and live like a king for a few years."

"But you're going in?"

"That was the deal." Jules shrugged. "It's not my first big city."

"So many voices, too many mouths," added Selene.

"It won't get any smaller if we wait." I scanned the faces around me, my gaze landing on Two-Feathers. "Like Jules said, if any of you want to call it quits, this is the time. You'll have to find your own way home, but I promise you won't be going away empty-handed."

Two-Feathers gave me a yawn and a look, but nobody said anything. Finally, it was Evan, of all people, who cleared his throat and responded. "Let's just get this over with. The sooner we're in there, the sooner we'll be out again."

"Actually, can I talk to you before we head in, Queenie?"

I didn't know what Jules wanted, but we had the time. I waved him to the side of the road. "Step into my office. The rest of you can take a load off for now. Just be ready to move out."

Jules followed me into a field just off the road, his rucksack in hand. For a moment, we stood there together, New Memphis spread out before us.

It really *was* a strange sight, like someone had taken some ancient medieval city and dropped it right in the middle of the continent.

"What's up?" I asked him.

"We're here," he said, running a hand through hair that looked even thinner plastered to his scalp by sweat. "At last."

"And?"

"And now would be a good time to share whether you have any sort of plan beyond *use our stolen credentials and figure the rest out.*"

"That's pretty much it in a nutshell. Raya's notes said there's some sort of resistance group in the city, but I don't know if they're even still active or how we'd contact them if they were. I figure we'll see how far these passports take us, then rent some space, lie low for a bit, and put together a better strategy."

"Fuck." He pinched the bridge of his nose, as if fighting off an oncoming headache. "I was kind of hoping you were just waiting to tell us your master plan."

"I've been working off months-old notes from a dead woman, Jules. There was a limit to what I could do without seeing the place for myself."

"Fair, I guess. Which brings me to my second question. What are we going to do about you?"

"You're going to have to be a little bit more specific."

"You avoided the ferries because you were worried the queen's men would be looking for you. Isn't that going to be even more of a problem here?"

"There's not a whole lot I can do about that. She's in the city, therefore I need to be in the city too. Unless you want to run this whole operation without me?"

"Shit no. Especially not with Two-Feathers already hurt. Can you repeat what you did at Tillatoba? Shift and let one of us carry your… uh… pieces around in our bags?"

I thought of the way the storm had cut the Prov who picked up one of its fragments. That had been after only an hour or two of forced stasis, and it would take us days to get to where we needed to go in New Memphis. There was no way in hell I'd be able to spend it in a bag.

"That's not going to work."

"There is *one* other option." His voice was so smooth and unassuming that I immediately knew he was trying to sell me something. "You could go as someone else."

"What?"

"I didn't just take ammo and food from the supply crates at Tillatoba." He pulled a wad of fabric from his rucksack and handed it over.

"This is a dress."

"Yeah. But… at least it's yellow, like your decal."

"You want to put me in a *dress* as we walk through New Memphis?"

"Not *just* a dress," he said, licking his lips in a nervous gesture I'd been seeing more and more. "Tall woman in a dress with a motorcycle helmet on won't be any less distinctive than the full outfit. But I found a matching bonnet."

"A *bonnet?* Jules, if this is you trying to fuck with me, I swear I will leave pieces of you all over—"

"If you can think of a better approach, I'm all ears."

I turned away from him, dress in hand, to study the city. The walls of each district were tall and strong. I already knew I wasn't going to be able to climb them or tear through them. That had been the whole reason we'd gone to Tillatoba.

Jules read my hesitation with his usual uncanny precision and pushed on. "These passports we almost died for aren't going to do us a damn bit of good if we pull the attention of the queen's men before we even make it *into* District 5."

"Maybe we wrap me up in a blanket and toss me over the back of a horse? Just a corpse being brought back for burial."

"You don't think that'll catch anyone's eye? Maybe not in the trade quarters or the harbor, but according to you, we're headed all the way to the inner districts. Those are for administration buildings and rich-asshole estates, not cemeteries or morgues."

"Then maybe you should have stolen a uniform and helmet instead, for fuck's sake!"

He scowled. "I probably would have, if I'd been thinking. But how to smuggle you into a walled city is a problem that only occurred to me a few days ago."

Which… was fair, given that it hadn't occurred to me at all. It did raise a rather pertinent question, however.

'Then why did you steal a dress and bonnet?"

"Why not? If we survive this, I'm going to settle down somewhere, and I don't see any point in living out my wealthy retirement as an increasingly *less* eligible bachelor. Ain't a lot of women who'll turn away a man who comes bearing gifts, especially in the Badlands."

"This is your bride price?"

"Is that what it's called? I wouldn't know." He lowered his voice, as if we hadn't already been speaking too quietly to be overheard. "Do you just not like dresses, Queenie? I know you say your outfit is a part of you, but I *also* know from extremely personal experience that you can go without it, whether it's for the old one-two or just taking your gloves off to be fingerprinted."

I shook my head again. I was being an asshole, acting out like someone fresh out of puberty instead of a woman who'd skipped the process entirely. Still, I couldn't help my gaze drifting back toward Two-Feathers. He'd rejected my naked invitation so many months earlier, and remained a broad-shouldered, square-jawed, and incredibly infuriating puzzle, but still… I was pretty sure there was something growing between us.

I took no credit for the body that had been built for me, but decades of dealing with men had taught me it was the sort of thing to get their motors running. The dress wasn't a problem, even if the thought of wearing one just seemed wrong to the core.

The bonnet, on the other hand…

The decal on my helmet was the face I showed the world, the face I *chose* to show the world, because the one hiding beneath it was a horror show, diametrically opposed to the dream-wrought magnificence that existed from the neck down. A bonnet would cover my lack of hair, but it wouldn't do a damn thing to mask the face itself.

And as dumb as it sounded, even to me, as a woman who had traversed the continent for almost a century, who had brokered deals with nightmares and waded through the blood of small armies… the truth was both simple, sad, and impossible to ignore.

I didn't want Two-Feathers to see my face.

I wouldn't need eyes to see his reaction. Wouldn't need ears to hear the sharp intake of breath that told me, as clearly as the words he couldn't speak, that whatever we might have been had just died, buried beneath a disgust even I could understand.

But that was my pride speaking. My pride and my desire. The truth was, Jules was right… I didn't see any other way to get where we needed to go. And the job—even this job, maybe the last job—always came first.

"I'm going to need some privacy to get changed," I said, the metal gone from my voice.

He just nodded instead of pushing for answers or making the sort of joke that would leave both he and his stolen women's clothing shredded in a field outside of New Memphis. "Anything else I can get you?"

"Did you steal any scarves or shawls?"

ooo

It took an hour to reach the southern gates, and at least part of that was because I was stuck riding a horse in a gods-fucked dress, a combination of two activities I hoped I'd never have to deal with again. Given the way the horse shifted nervously under me, I was pretty sure it was as unhappy as I was, but my bike was too distinctive to bring with us. After much deliberation, I had decided to hide it near the field where we'd stopped, buried with most of my wealth and possessions under a tent that was itself buried under soil and fallen leaves. It would keep until I made it back out of the city.

Assuming any of us made it back out.

Jules' stolen dress was a few inches too short, but the riding boots that stuck out from under its hem seemed more like a nod to practicality than a clue to my identity. That same dress was tight on the chest—which I doubted anyone but me would mind—and loose at the waist and hips. I felt like a fool, but I could feel eyes on me as we rode into the shanty town that had sprung up outside District 5's wall, and those eyes seemed more hungry than dismissive.

As for the rest of me? The stupid bonnet was pulled low over my forehead, and the shawl that Jules had dug up from his seemingly endless supply covered most of the rest of my face, wrapped across my eyes and nose as if to hide my sightless gaze.

Which, I guess, *was* what it was doing, even if I was the furthest thing from blind.

Even together, the bonnet and scarf didn't hide everything, leaving what passed for my lips and chin partially exposed, but short of wearing a bag—or a helmet—over my head, it was the best I could do. I rode with my head down, not looking at anyone, least of all Two-Feathers, prompting Jules to compliment my acting skills.

"Between the dress, the bonnet, and your adopted change in demeanor, I'm not sure even *I* would know who you were if I saw you on the street," he said approvingly, riding to my left where he could pretend to be leading my horse.

I reminded both the storm and myself that we needed him to finish the job, that killing him now would make the whole trip pointless.

Behind us, Two-Feathers, in an embroidered shirt that Jules had stolen to wear for his hypothetical bride, said nothing at all.

Between my ex-lover and my maybe-never lover, I knew which of the two was seeming smarter right about then.

30

The trade market that had sprung up outside of New Memphis' walls encircled the entire city, making for an unofficial sixth district. It was less of a dump than Kansas City's shanty town, but equally chaotic, overflowing with merchants and mercenaries, prostitutes and performers. The occasional guard wandered by, wearing fatigues with the Crimson Queen's logo represented by a patch on their shoulder, but the tyrant's military presence was surprisingly light on the outskirts of her capital city.

Most of the dwellings we passed were buildings instead of tents, if shabbily constructed, and a few even had shingle roofs and signs hanging out front, indications that the area was well on its way to becoming something more permanent. I hated to say it, but the people here looked more prosperous than any I'd seen outside of the rich quarters of Wichita; well fed, rarely more than half-naked, and walking the haphazard streets with little of the caution or fear you'd find in Kansas City or on the East Coast.

I kept my head down as we wound our way through those streets, but the details trickled in anyway, troubling in a way I hadn't anticipated. The queen was murdering her way across the open territories, taking prisoners and slaves as she went, but in her capital, even the non-citizens seemed secure in the civilization she had created.

I doubted they were unaware of the blood being spent to purchase that security. Most likely, they simply didn't care.

But was I any better? Kansas City was a hellhole, Wichita an autocratic stronghold, and the Free States, as a country, was a wolf in sheep's clothing, redefining personal liberty for its unknowing citizens… yet I accepted all three, content to work within their borders when I needed to, and forget them when I didn't.

So why did New Memphis trouble me?

Maybe it was as simple as the Crimson Queen being my enemy. She was responsible for deaths that remained intensely personal, and it felt wrong to find her city orderly and safe.

It won't stay that way for long, I told myself, as we passed what appeared to be a smithy, the door open just long enough for a blast of light and heat to send the horses dancing nervously across the street. *Once she dies, this whole house of cards falls apart.*

For some reason, even that thought didn't help.

By the time we neared the wall, I'd forgotten my naked face, forgotten that scared inner child that I'd never known or gotten a chance to grow out of. The storm rumbled inside of me, echoing my growing rage, feeding into it, fanning the flames.

Eclipse was ashes. Raya was dead. The Crimson Queen might be sitting up on the hill in her palace, playing benevolent dictator, but the butcher's bill was as long as one of her prisoner trains, and it was sure as fuck coming due.

"Queenie, your performance is slipping," whispered Jules. "Maybe amp the pitifulness back up a bit before we reach the gate?"

That settled it; I was going to kill his forty-year-old ass.

The closer we got to the wall, the larger it seemed. A twenty-foot gap of open space separated it from the nearest buildings and merchant stalls, and the lack of a gate told us that our unavoidably meandering path had taken us off course. Thankfully, that mistake proved easy to correct; we followed the wall a few blocks to the east where a line of people, horses, and even one wagon, all waited to be admitted into District 5.

Even the hint of inefficient bureaucracy made me feel better.

Guards stood near the gate, but the process itself was automated and as high-tech as anything you'd ever find in the Free States: a slot to insert your passport and a scanner for your thumb. Above those were two lights, one red and one green. We'd watched people go through the process, the green light flickering as each print was matched with the given passport.

Of the several dozen people in front of us, only one had seen the red light flicker instead of the green, and the guards were there in an instant to pull him away for what I assumed would be an interrogation out of sight. The rest accepted their green lights as a matter of course, retrieved their passports when the machine spit them back out, and pushed through the door that unlocked each time with an audible click.

The wagon was the biggest delay as its driver had to both pass the scanning process himself and wait as the usually idle guards thoroughly searched his vehicle. Any thoughts I'd had of stealing and using a wagon to sneak into higher-ranked districts faded about forty seconds into that search.

And then it was our turn, the wall towering above us in an unmistakable symbol of authority. In a nod to the greater volumes of traffic into the less secure neighborhoods, Districts 5 and 4 had four entry gates apiece, one for each of the cardinal directions, while the wealthier districts had only two, or in the case of the palace itself, one. That said, even District 5's gate was intimidating; solid black iron, thick, and heavy enough that one or two of the entering citizens needed help just to open it.

Once we'd reached the limits of our stolen passports, we were going to have to figure out a way past those gates. It wasn't a puzzle I was looking forward to solving.

Cross led the way, and if I'd needed to breathe at all, I might have held that breath as I waited for the light above him to illuminate. Finally, it flashed green. The door unlocked, and the first of our crew stepped inside the Crimson Queen's city.

I was next, but a guard wandered over before Jules could pretend to help me insert my passport.

"I can take care of that for you, ma'am," he said, stepping forward to support me.

I turned my scarf-wrapped face in his direction and watched that easy smile—broad and no doubt intended to be charming—flicker and die like a candle flame in a Weather Witch's tantrum. He swallowed and took a step back, eyes fixed on my lips and exposed chin instead of the now-resistible curves under my dress.

"I have it, but thank you," I said, trying to make my voice meek and probably coming off like I had a cold instead. Even that worked in my favor; he took a second step away, stumbling.

"Easy there, son," said Jules, turning to the guard after he'd made a show of placing my hands in the necessary places. "Don't want one of the queen's finest taking a spill now, do we?"

I pressed my thumb into the scanner and waited.

"What… what happened to her," asked my would-be Romeo, voice thick with horror and disgust.

"Acid spitters," said Jules in a quiet voice that I could hear just fine. "It's a miracle that she's alive, really."

"I don't think I'd call *that* a miracle," muttered the guard, slipping away to return to his post. "Don't think anyone would."

Above me, the green light lit up and a loud click announced the door's unlocking. I tugged it open with one hand and slipped through into the next district, my horse trailing behind.

The rest of the crew made it through without any apparent trouble, and minutes later, we were traipsing through District 5, walking our horses this time instead of riding them.

Jules caught up with me before we'd gone a dozen yards.

"Not sure if the guards back there just noticed that a blind woman opened their gate without even struggling," he said.

"I'd say that's their problem, not mine."

We walked side by side for a few minutes and I could feel him looking at me the whole way. Finally, he sighed.

"I'm sorry, Queenie."

I shrugged. "Like I already told you, I am how *he* made me."

"Then why didn't he—"

"Give me a face? Or at least finish it? I'm pretty sure he didn't even think that far ahead in his dream. A strange helmet, a motorcycle, and a hot body in leather and then it was on to the next nightmare." My real mouth twitched but I couldn't tell what expression it was making. "Because everyone knows *nipples* are what really matter."

"I didn't know."

"And that's why we kept the helmet on when we fucked." I tugged the scarf down, but there simply wasn't enough fabric to hide everything. "Feeling a bitter case of regret now, are we?"

"About my plan to get you into New Memphis? Yeah, I guess I kind of am. About *us?* What we used to be?" His voice went hard. "I knew you'd moved on, but I guess I didn't realize you'd always thought so little of me."

"How's that?"

"I don't care what's under your helmet, any more than I did about the helmet itself. You're the Queen of Smiles. You've done more and seen more than any person in existence and come out the other side still kicking ass. That's all that matters. Fuck anyone who says differently. And fuck you too for expecting me to think otherwise."

He left in an angry huff, moving up to join Cross in the lead. I watched him go through eyes that didn't exist, my shabby excuse for a mouth twitching from one pseudo expression to another.

Maybe I wouldn't kill him after all.

○○○

District 5 was a mixture of stone and wood houses, some as tall as three stories and squeezed together along roads of cobblestone instead of dirt. The chaos of the market was behind us, and most merchants had their own shops along the wider streets, with signs out front, and living quarters above. It was a strange mixture of modern and archaic. Gas lanterns and incandescent light bulbs, aqueducts side by side with interior plumbing. There was no greenery, but the streets were clean, and most of the houses only marginally less so.

"Are we sure this isn't heaven?" asked Cross. "Food, shelter, security..."

"You'd make it a week at best before you broke a half-dozen laws you'd never heard of and at least three you thought shouldn't apply," said Jules.

"Maybe so, boss, but it would make for a fun week. I guess citizenship has its perks."

"Feel free to move in permanently when we're done then. Just don't be surprised how quickly it all turns to chaos. Before its fall, Kansas City was supposedly a pretty nice town too."

By the time we reached the gate to District 4, the sun was down, and the guards were gone. Jules tried his passport anyway, but the machine wouldn't take it.

"You folks been away a while, I take it?" asked an old woman. Bundled in at least three layers of coats, she'd been scurrying by, but I guess our group's confusion had triggered her helpful stranger reflex.

"That we have, ma'am," said Jules. "Only just returned from abroad today, in fact."

"Then you wouldn't know." She peered past him in our direction and pulled her jackets tighter around her against the winter chill. "Her Majesty's ordered the gates closed at sundown, and the streets cleared not long after. It's those damn rebels again, stirring up mischief and making life difficult for the rest of us."

"I'm surprised they're still active," said Jules.

"You and me both, young man. I guess some folk just can't resist agitating. Hopefully, the guards will sweep them up soon so things return to normal."

"That would be for the best." He made a show of looking quizzically about him and then leaned in. "I suppose we should get off the streets then and let the guards do their jobs. Could you possibly point us to the nearest inn?"

"I thought you were from here?" she asked, suddenly suspicious.

"Our business usually takes us in and out through the north gate instead of the south, I'm afraid."

"Well, this is a *much* nicer neighborhood than what you'll find over there, let me tell you."

"I knew that the moment I laid eyes on you, my dear."

"Well, aren't you a charmer! If we didn't only have the one bed, I'd invite you home so you could teach my Harold some manners. That old coot doesn't know how good he has it!"

The smile on Jules' face became just a little bit more visibly fixed. "Perhaps we'll bump into one another again and I'll have that opportunity. But for now, I wouldn't want to cause trouble for the guards enforcing curfew."

"Quite right, quite right." She raised an arm, bones almost creaking with the effort, and pointed back the way we'd come. "If you go three blocks south, and then take a left, you'll find the Queen's Rest, a *very* reputable inn. Although," she added, voice dropping to a whisper, "I don't think Her Majesty has ever *actually* slept there."

"You are as perceptive as you are lovely, my dear." Jules threw in a half-bow for good measure. "Thank you for your help and please have a good evening."

With a broad, toothless smile and a blush that practically glowed through skin worn thin by age, she nodded and scurried off.

"Is *she* the new me?" I murmured to Jules.

"Funny."

"What was that about rebels?" asked Cross.

"Apparently, not everyone thinks this place is heaven." Jules turned to me, eyes carefully focused on a point about six inches to the left of my face. "If they are still active, they could be our way into the higher districts."

"Agreed. We'll see how far we can get on our own and then look for a way to make contact. But first, we need to get off the streets."

"I don't even remember what a bed feels like," said Evan.

"Soft like a mother's kiss." Selene smiled. "Just add bugs."

ooo

The Queen's Rest was three stories tall, with stone walls and a pitched roof, its front door open and inviting despite the impending curfew. Jules paid for two rooms using money taken off the dead in Tillatoba, but he and Cross opted to settle in at a table in the common room as the rest of us went upstairs.

Jules called it reconnaissance; I called it alcoholism.

Once again, I shared a room with Selene. There was only one bed, but I wasn't going to sleep anyway, so I stepped aside as the young Crow bellyflopped onto a mattress almost as thin as she had become. I closed the door behind us, tossed off the bonnet, dress, and matching scarf, and reformed my shell in the center of the room, my true face spread across the visor of my helmet.

Jules' disguise was necessary, I knew, but fuck if I was going to put up with it in private.

"It seems a shame to hide such a pretty face."

The different cadence, the quiet menace lurking like a blade behind each word, told me I was dealing with Selene's ghost, even before I turned to find the woman upright again, back straight and stiff.

"I was wondering when we'd see you next."

"I have been present," she said, "but there are limits to what this child can support."

"And now?"

"And now the hour is almost upon us."

Either she was speaking metaphorically, or ghosts told time differently than the rest of us. Selene's target was a bigshot in the Crimson Queen's empire and lived in an estate all the way up in District 2. I wasn't even sure how we'd get there yet, but I did know it would take days, not hours.

"What did this Councilor Becks do anyway?"

"What they always do, given both the means and insufficient accountability."

I shook my head. That told me nothing, but maybe trying to understand the motivations of a serial killer ghost wasn't the greatest of strategies anyway. This councilor was part of the queen's powerbase and that meant I was happy to remove him.

"Just don't forget your end of the bargain."

"Have I not already been of service? Five rats fled the sinking ship of Tillatoba, yet none lived to share the tale."

"I didn't know if that was you or her."

"This body is enthusiastic but hardly skilled," she said, pursing Selene's lips in a gesture I'd never seen the other woman make. "But it has me to provide."

As far as I could tell, Selene's ghost was getting more out of their deal than Selene herself. Still, I'd been burned once before involving myself in a Crow's affairs; I decided to let the matter rest.

"Did you know Bakersfield was still alive?"

"Bakersfield?"

"Damian. Walker. The boy you sent me to save in Reno."

She grew still, a too-thin statue on the freshly made bed.

"Of course. I was there when he claimed his throne."

"And?"

"And then I departed."

"Just like that."

"There are none left to punish in his domain. Just the dead, the dead, the dead, and the man they call king." Her lips contorted into a doll's smile, and for a moment, Selene's pale blue eyes went dark, like freshly dug graves. "And my work was not yet done in the greater world."

"Will it ever be?"

"That depends on them."

"Men?" I guessed.

"Humans," she countered.

"So, Becks is—"

"Next." She grabbed a fistful of her own dress, blue with red flowers blooming, and shook it. "But not last."

A knock came at our door, and I watched life and awareness seep back into the Crow's small face as Selene's ghost departed. Her eyes went dreamy and she shimmied in place.

I rolled eyes I didn't have and opened the door.

Two-Feathers stood outside.

"Selene," I said, not looking away from the nomad who filled our doorway, "could you give us a moment?"

"I'm feeling a bit peckish anyway," she said, bouncing to her feet. She rubbed her belly as she turned sideways and slipped past Two-Feathers. "I'll ask Cross to get me a bite."

I waited until she had reached the stairs and then invited the nomad inside.

"I'm not sure if it's the usual Crow madness at work or if the ghost who's riding her is accelerating the process," I told him. "Either way, that girl is not right."

He just nodded and went to stand in the middle of the small room, like a gladiator claiming the arena. For a moment, he looked as young as his age.

"At least get comfortable," I told him, taking a seat on Selene's bed and patting the space next to me. "I'm not sure what this is about, but you look like a politician about to give a speech."

He shot me a look but sat to my right anyway. The bed groaned beneath our combined weight, a noise that I was sure could be heard in neighboring rooms.

Apparently, sex in this inn was a public affair.

Not that the man on the bed with me seemed interested in anything physical, which was both annoying and depressingly on-brand. Instead, he cocked his head and tapped the sleeve of my riding jacket with his uninjured hand.

"I swapped back as soon as we came inside. Why? Don't tell me you actually *liked* the dress?"

He shrugged and nodded, but the anticipated smile never came to a face that was even more severe than normal. Black eyes glittering, he let go of my sleeve and tapped my helmet instead.

"This is the face I show the world," I told him. "My true face. Everything else is just flesh and bone."

He held my gaze but said nothing.

"I don't know what you saw," I allowed, thinking of Jules' words out in the street, "but that isn't me. Any more than the bonnet and scarf are. *This* is who I am. Take it or leave it, but I'm not apologizing."

He rested his palm against the side of my helmet, as if to cup it, looking up into the smiley-face that wrapped the visor covering a dead god's negligence. Then, he nodded, eyes as serious as the first day I'd met him in his clan's territory. He withdrew his hand from my face and wrapped that arm—his only functioning arm—around me, bringing me close.

I wasn't sure how long it had been since someone had hugged me. Even Raya's daughter, Cho-Hee, had maintained her distance, picking up on her father's reserve. Back in Eclipse, Duke had been more liable to launch himself at my legs like a cat, and Nathan and Mina hadn't been *those* kinds of friends.

Years, I decided, as I allowed myself to rest against him, enjoying the feeling of a strong arm for once offering *me* support. *It's been years.*

It wasn't sex, but I didn't hate it.

31

Everyone who stayed in the common room was hungover the next morning, with Jules the worst of the batch, looking even older than Evan and twice as grumpy. I tried not to be too smug about it as we set out.

"You're doing great," I told him. "Just be sure to keep that pitiful act going through to the next district."

His one-eyed glare was spoiled by the wince my voice at full volume had prompted.

"You're chipper today," he said in a voice like death warmed over. "Is the dress growing on you or something?"

Actually, it felt like it was shrinking, but I shrugged. My bonnet was back on, and that same scarf covered the majority of my half-made face, the cold morning air raising goosebumps on the exposed flesh of my shell.

"I'd prefer something black and slinky," I said, "and even remotely in my size."

"I'll convey your complaints to my future bride, if and when I meet her."

"There's always Selene."

"I don't like yellow," said the Crow in question, leading her horse behind us. "Maybe if you find something in lace?"

Jules shuddered, his face going a strange blend of hangover-green and ghostly pale.

"I'm going to drop back and talk to Two-Feathers," he said. "At least he doesn't talk back."

"Not in words anyway."

It only took twenty minutes to make it back to the gate, and this time, it was open, a line forming by the machine that scanned and compared thumbprints. We joined that line's slow progression and made it through without any interruptions. Just like that, we were in District 4, home to those who had full citizenship in the Crimson Queen's growing empire. The city's layout meant this district was smaller than that which had preceded it, but the streets were just as wide and every house was made of stone, brought in from the local quarry.

Raya's shirtwaist cottage would have looked old and shabby here, even before I burned it down.

Forearmed with knowledge of the curfew, we spent our first few hours in the new district locating an inn with a stable where we could leave our mounts. District 3 housed administrative buildings and the families of those who worked there, and six people leading road-weary horses would no doubt stick out like a sore thumb.

Assuming we made it into the district at all. There had been two types of passports in the processing station of Tillatoba, and with Jules stealing the fancier variety, we'd been confident they would at least grant us access to District 4. Whether they'd open the gates to the administrative level, let alone the wealthy estates above, was a question we still couldn't answer.

The inn we found was named the Queen's Jewel. I might have been flattered by the sheer number of businesses dedicated in my honor if I hadn't known they were kissing the ass of a very different queen. We rented a room—just one, since we weren't going to be sleeping there—and stored the supplies we wouldn't need again until after the killing was done: tents, survival gear, and anything else too heavy or bulky to carry ourselves. And then, because it had apparently been long enough for everyone to work off their hangovers, the crew gathered back in the inn's common room for lunch.

I abstained, naturally, although this time I wasn't hiding so much as protecting myself from the sight of Selene chewing with her mouth wide open, potatoes and mystery meat visible to all as it sloshed around inside the cage of her steadily yellowing teeth. I didn't have a stomach, but damned if my shell couldn't simulate nausea anyway.

Stabbings notwithstanding, the Crow had been significantly less crazy when we'd met out in Texas. I was almost positive of that.

Eventually, they were done, and we left soon after, our rent paid through the week. There were only two gates into District 3, and it took us hours to find the nearest one. Still, the sun remained high in the sky, and the gate was active, watched by a dozen guards instead of the six-person squad we'd found in the other districts. The soldiers here were armed and professional, a far cry from the private who'd thought he could score a date by helping me out the day before.

We'd planned out our approach back at the Queen's Jewel, and it mainly involved a single individual going ahead of the rest of us. If the passport worked, we'd meet up again on the other side. If it didn't, the distance between us would ensure we weren't linked as a group, and *that* would make it easier to act, with Jules stealing the guards' breath from the anonymous safety of the line even as our man made his escape.

Still, watching Cross make his way toward the gate, a dozen or more people ahead of us, had me nervous.

"I've got a bad feeling about this," I murmured as he stepped up to the machine and inserted his passport and thumb.

"We're surrounded by enemies and approaching the center of the enormous city your target controls with an iron fist," whispered back Jules. "What could go wrong?"

Apparently, the world didn't appreciate his sarcasm; a red light flickered to life above the armored gate.

Instead of running, Cross turned to the approaching guards waving his passport with a confused expression.

"What the hell is he doing?"

"I don't know. Maybe he saw something up at the gate that made running a non-option." Jules licked his lips. "It'll be okay. He used to do confidence work."

"Wait, *he's* the con man you mentioned back in Greenburg? I thought that was you."

"No, I was the killer. I figured that was obvious." He frowned, watching the conversation that had sprung up between two guards and our crew member. "Anyway, if anybody can talk their way out of this, it's him."

As if Jules' words had been another signal to the universe, one of the guards reversed his gun, striking Cross in the temple with the butt of the weapon. The second guard caught his body as it crumpled, and they began to drag Cross away, members of their squad falling in around them.

"That's... not good," said Jules.

"Please, for fuck's sake, just stop saying things." I shook my head, disquieted anew by the rustle of fabric as I moved. "We need to break away and see if we can follow them. Six guards should be easy enough. As long as we kill them all, nobody will know what happened. And then we can regroup and figure out our next step."

"Let's do it," said Jules, turning and making eye contact with the three remaining members of our crew. "One by one, real subtle-like, then meet back up a block over in the direction they're taking him."

That was the idea anyway. The problem was, as soon as the first of us, Evan, stepped out of line and turned to leave, the remaining guards reacted, muzzles raised and pointed in our direction. Four of them spread out to give themselves better fields of fire, while the last two started down the line toward us.

Of us all, I was the only one whose face *wasn't* showing. Instead of unleashing the storm, I pulled the revolver Jules had holstered at his back and fired at the closest soldier, hitting absolutely nothing for my troubles. Still, the crowd's reaction was satisfying; people in front of us and behind us screamed, with some dropping to the ground and others running for cover.

The rest of my crew was in that second group, taking advantage of the sudden chaos to disappear. Sadly, I didn't have that luxury. Worse, the guards were quicker to respond than I'd anticipated. A chatter of gunfire answered, and three bullets tore right through my shell. I let the slight transfer of momentum spin me around, caught another bullet in the back for good measure, and sprinted for the closest alleyway. It was in the opposite direction that the rest would be taking, but that much, at least, was by design.

Thank fuck Jules hadn't stolen dainty shoes for his hypothetical bride to go along with the rest of this outfit. Running in heels would have been a disaster.

I reached the alley, barreled through, and took an immediate right, the sounds of pursuit rising above the persistent screams. Hopefully, Evan had gotten away and the others would be joining him at our rendezvous. As for me, I needed to lose my pursuit and do so without alerting the Crimson Queen that I was in town. That meant no storm, for now. I had six guards on my trail and only five rounds left in my borrowed revolver. Worse, judging by my previous shot, it had been way too long since I'd last bothered to fire a gun. Escape seemed like a smarter plan than a second shootout.

Unfortunately, as I cut through another alley, and turned onto one of the wider streets that would give me a path toward the rest of the crew, I practically collided with a pair of soldiers coming out of the corner store. My scarf had come unwound at some point during my escape and the first soldier's eyes went wide as she saw what was underneath. Her companion shouted and pulled his pistol.

I'm not strong like a Titan or a Stalwart, but there aren't many Normals in the world who can match my shell for power; I punched the first soldier so hard that both her skull *and* my hand shattered into pieces, then rushed past to grab her companion's gun hand before his weapon came to bear. He still got a shot off, but that was all before every bone in his gun hand was pulverized. I ignored his scream—equal parts pain and terror—and elbowed him in the throat.

Through the store window, a woman in silk stood in shock, eyes and mouth wide. Maybe, it was how quickly I'd dispatched both soldiers, or maybe she was one of those rare individuals who'd somehow avoided violence all their lives. Or maybe the dress Jules had stolen for me was several years out of fashion. Whatever the cause, she wasn't trying to stop me, and so I let her be.

I broke back into a run, one block down from the store and then another right to point me back in the proper direction. The scream that came from somewhere behind me told me the woman in the shop had found her voice, but I didn't hear any further sounds of pursuit.

Mostly because they'd somehow anticipated my path and were waiting in the next alleyway for me.

Only three of the original six guards were there, but that was enough to block the street and send a hailstorm of bullets in my direction. I ducked into a doorway to avoid their fire, all too aware that the rest of the squad was likely working to flank me. I was already leaking fluids over the cobblestone road from the multiple gunshots, to say nothing of the damage I'd done to my own hand, and there was only so much damage my shell could take.

With no eyes upon me to recognize or report the storm, I could heal those injuries by releasing my shell for a micro-second, reforming it again immediately after, but doing so would shred my borrowed clothing, leaving me either naked or in the outfit the Crimson Queen's men had no doubt been told to look for. And if I did go naked, those same men would have a much easier time tracking a six-foot-two naked bald woman with a half-finished face running through the streets. It wasn't the sort of sight people forgot.

Still, it was better than hiding here bleeding all over the cobblestones. And if I was going to release the storm, I might as well make use of it for more than just a quick pick-me-up. A sprint toward the soldiers who had me pinned down, carnage for the storm, and then back on the run without this horrid dress and bonnet. Maybe someone would find the savaged bodies and put two and two together, but that was a problem for my future self. I needed to get away, rejoin the others, and help rescue Cross.

When the gunfire tapered off, I tensed, ready to leave my cover and charge the shooters, but in the sudden silence I heard three thumps, almost back-to-back, heavy weights dropping to the cobblestone road.

"Queenie!" hissed a voice.

I peeked out to find a sweat-soaked Jules standing over the soldiers' bodies. The dead men's eyes were open and bloodshot, and one had foam at his mouth.

I hurried over to join him. “What are you doing here? Where are the others?”

“They’re at the rendezvous point. Two-Feathers is watching them.” He looked at my blood-soaked dress and blanched. “Apparently, I’m going to need to steal another bride gift.”

“My advice? Find the bride first. Then buy her fancy things that you know she’ll like. You’ll have the money for custom tailoring when this is said and done.”

OOO

We had two close calls on the way to the rendezvous point, but the scrambling soldiers were searching for a single woman. Jules had given me his jacket and while he was smaller than me, that jacket was still large enough to cover most of the bloodstains. His arm wrapped around me and I leaned into him, head on his shoulder to disguise my height. Just two lovers, walking the city streets without a care in the world.

I wouldn’t have bought it, but everyone else seemed to.

Fifteen minutes later, we were at the rendezvous point and meeting with the others in a dead-end alley. By that time, Cross was long gone, leaving our original rescue plan in shambles.

“Did you at least see where they took him?” I asked.

Surprisingly, it was Evan who answered. “There’s a barracks or guard station a few blocks over. It’s a big stone building crawling with soldiers. They dragged him inside.”

“Let’s get eyes on it,” said Jules. “Figure out if there’s a way in.”

“You know they’ll be expecting that,” I said. “After the debacle at the gate, they have to know they’re facing multiple threats.”

“I’m not leaving him behind. Period. If we have to kill our way through the whole barracks, then so be it.”

"And what is that going to do to our hopes of finding a way into the next district? If the queen can declare a city-wide curfew, she can probably shut down district access entirely."

"We'll figure something out," he argued.

"There *is* another way," suggested a voice I didn't know.

We turned to find a nondescript man coming toward us, hands spread and palms up as if to demonstrate that he wasn't armed. In a world of Powers, it didn't mean much.

"Who are you?" demanded Jules.

"Just a concerned citizen. You can call me Mishan." He stopped a good ten feet away from us, offering a short bow. "I saw what happened at the gate and thought y'all might need assistance in recovering your friend."

"And if we don't have any idea what you're talking about?"

"Then I would very carefully *not* look at the blood staining your lady's dress and be on my way."

Jules didn't even blink. "Let's say you're right. How can you help us?"

"I can offer shelter. The Crimson Queen does not suffer intrusions lightly. These streets will soon be crawling with her jackbooted thugs, Immortals included."

"What about our man?"

"I may have a few contacts in the district guard. Survive until nightfall, and we'll see what can be done."

"That's a lot of assistance being offered, friend. Which makes me wonder what the catch is. Ain't nothing free in this world."

A few emotions flickered across Mishan's face, before he finally settled on uncertainty. "Well, I think that will depend upon y'all and what you bring to the table. For now, the offer of sanctuary, at least, is free. After all, the enemies of my enemy are my friends."

Which was bullshit, frankly. In my experience, the enemy of an enemy had just as much likelihood of *also* wanting you dead.

Jules looked to me for the first time. "What do you think?"

"I don't see any better options right now, especially if soldiers are canvassing the district." We could have retreated to the Queen's Jewel, but an inn seemed like the first place search parties would look.

"You're making the right choice," said Mishan. "I promise. Let's get to my safehouse."

He turned to leave the alleyway, then recoiled as Two-Feathers materialized in front of him. He looked back over his shoulder at us, eyes wide.

"If you hadn't chosen to come with me, would I have even walked out of here alive?"

"I guess it's a good thing we'll never find out."

He swallowed. "Yeah. I think y'all will do just fine."

○○○

The streets cleared out as we moved from the shopping area into a more residential neighborhood. Several minutes later, those houses were starting to peter out in turn, giving way to warehouses and larger facilities, when we finally reached our apparent destination, a one-story building that occupied an entire city block on its own. Mishan took us to the back of that building and then, while keeping an eye out for observers, unlocked the back door and ushered us inside. The lights were off, but enough sunlight came in through the windows above the entryway to illuminate a wide hallway with numerous rooms on each side.

"What is this place?" asked Evan.

"The school for District 4," said Mishan. "K through 10. Part of the queen's compulsory education program."

I traded glances with Two-Feathers. Schools weren't exactly common in the Badlands, with most towns either skipping the education process entirely or bringing in teachers for a few months at a time.

"Where are the children? And isn't it weird for a tyrant to promote education?" pressed Evan.

"Not when she gets to choose the subject material being taught." Mishan led us to a closed door, distinguishable from the others off the hallway only in that it was solid wood and lacked a window. "As for the absent children, it's a Saturday. Not even the Crimson Queen makes people go to school on the weekends."

We'd spent all our time on the road where the only thing that mattered was when the sun came up and when it went down; I'm not sure any of us had known what day of the week it was.

"There are three schools in New Memphis," continued Mishan as he thumbed through a set of keys, looking for one that fit the wooden door. "One for the Provs, one for the citizens, and one for the children of the fat cats who live up the hill. Curriculums differ, but the central goal is always the same."

"Brainwashing children into supporting their queen," I said.

"Exactly. It's a system that's helped the Laines stay in power since long before the queen's reign began."

"The Laines?"

"Our ruling family, although they were just first among equals, part of the city council. When Delia overthrew her brother and had her primary rivals executed, that changed. Now, we have a monarch, God help us."

The wooden door opened onto a dark stairwell. At the bottom of those stairs, Mishan flicked a light switch. A handful of dangling bulbs came to life, illuminating a large room empty of furniture other than a table and a dozen chairs. Two doors off that room led to destinations unknown.

"Grab a seat," he said. "I'll get refreshments and then we'll see how we can help each other."

He vanished into one of the nearby rooms, and what was left of our crew took a collective breath for the first time since Cross' capture. Two-Feathers adopted a position by the stairwell, while Evan lowered himself into the closest chair, the horrendous crunching of his knees making Jules visibly wince. Not to be outdone, Selene pulled three chairs together and laid on top of them, knees bent, and feet tucked in toward her butt.

Jules cocked an eyebrow at me. "Is he a resistance fighter?"

"That or serial killer."

Over on her multi-chair bed, Selene cracked open an eye.

"Thoughts?" he asked.

That was usually *my* line, but I let it go. "We wait and hear what he has to say. Our first priority is getting Cross back, if we can. Second priority is finding a way into the next district. If Mishan can help with both, maybe this day won't have been quite as big a disaster as it seemed."

"And if he comes back in wearing only an apron and wielding a carving knife like Cleve the Butcher?"

"Then we kill his ass and figure something else out."

"One of these days, we're going to need a better Plan B, Queenie."

"Noted. In the meantime, I'm going to slip into something a little bit less comfortable."

32

When Mishan returned, it was with a smile that didn't reach his eyes and a tray of water glasses in his hands. He stopped dead at the sight of me in my riding leathers and helmet, the smile across my visor a match for his own.

"Where did…" He did a quick head count and came to the obvious conclusion. "You're the woman who was wearing that awful dress?"

I ignored Jules' wince. "We're out of sight down here. I figured it was time to put our cards on the table."

He shrugged and put his tray out for everyone. "Okay?"

After years of notoriety in the Badlands and Free States, I'd assumed reforming my shell would be enough to move things along, but apparently, I wasn't as well known in New Memphis. I couldn't decide if that was a good thing or bad.

"The first question," said Jules, handing out water to everyone but me, "is how you're going to help us get our man out, and what it will cost us."

Mishan pulled over a chair of his own, dropping into it with a heavy sigh. Up close, he seemed to be somewhere between Jules and Two-Feathers in age, soft physically but hard-eyed in a way I recognized. This was a man who had seen some things and done even worse. Our kind of people, in other words.

He'd doffed his peacoat to reveal a checkered button-up shirt, neatly pressed black slacks, and the beginnings of a small gut. If we were in the Free States, I'd have pegged him as a middle manager or a shady small business owner. Here in Memphis, I wasn't sure what he was. Especially with those eyes.

I wondered if I'd have to kill him.

"Like I said earlier, I know a few people in the guard. Usually, anyone who runs into issues at one of the district gates just gets interrogated and then let go. Given the excitement y'all generated, I'm guessing the guards are going to take things a little bit more seriously. In all likelihood, your friend will be moved to district security headquarters tonight after curfew." He swallowed. "The head technician has his office there, and he'll… well, he'll get any information the guard interrogators might miss."

I remembered the one technician I'd seen in Tillatoba, and the ooze creature that had emerged from his torture room.

"We won't let that happen," said Jules, echoing my thoughts.

"Yup, that's what I figured. Which means you're going to have to break curfew and set an ambush along their transport route. I can tell you what that route is."

"And in return?"

"Cash. Preferably something that spends outside the city as well as in it, but I'll take chits if that's all you've got." I didn't understand conversion rates, but the price he named made Jules cough.

My saddlebags were buried outside the city, and most of our remaining possessions were at the Queen's Jewel, but I'd given Two-Feathers a stack of gold coins, trusting that he was both strong enough to not be inconvenienced by their weight and trustworthy enough to not disappear as soon as I turned my head. I didn't look over in his direction, keeping my gaze trained on our would-be helper.

"I've got a counterproposal. You help us free our man *and* introduce us to the Resistance, and we'll pay double."

"I'm sorry? The what?" If Mishan ever wanted to make it onto the Free States vid scene, he'd have to learn to lie with his eyes.

"I think you heard me." This time, I did look at Two-Feathers. The nomad had two fingers to the side of his nose, black eyes fixed on the room Mishan hadn't gone into to get our water. It matched what my own senses were telling me. "And I'm guessing the two people hiding back there did too."

Jules looked from me to the room I was pointing to, and his hand dropped to the revolver I'd briefly borrowed. As if he needed a gun to put bodies in the ground.

Mishan saw the movement and raised his hands. "Whoa! Y'all just hang on for a second. My colleagues will come on out and we'll have a civilized chat."

"What the hell did you bring down on us this time?" A small woman, as bald as I was, but with skin darker than my leathers, stalked out of the room, followed by a man twice her size with enough family resemblance to be her brother. Both wore clean, but well-used clothes. "This is supposed to be a safehouse, not a gathering space!"

Eyes sharp enough to cut, her gaze flicked around the room in an instant, cataloguing the presence and location of everyone within it. She ended with me, and something shifted in her expression.

"You know who I am," I said. A statement not a question.

"I've heard stories." The heat was gone from her voice.

"They're all true," said Jules.

"She's the reason for the security sweep?" she asked Mishan.

"They all are, Aaniyah. One of—"

"Don't use real names," cut in the man I thought was Aaniyah's brother. "You know better, man."

"I'd say that ship has sailed down the river and been eaten by a kraken." I shrugged as all three of them—four including Jules—turned to me, each one with their own expression. "I'm just saying."

"Boats are like beds," said Selene, "except the bugs have gills."

There was a brief bit of silence as we all digested that, then Mishan moved on. The middle-aged middle manager was starting to sweat.

"One of theirs got nabbed at the southern gate," he told Aaniyah. "Then she, whoever she is, took a shot at one of the guards, and killed a few soldiers."

"And you brought them *here*."

"Nobody spotted us. I guarantee it. Besides, the enemy of my enemy, right?"

"Did you actually witness the events at the gate for yourself?" asked the other man, whose name we still didn't have.

"Yeah. Why?"

"Because," said Aaniyah, answering for her brother, "the stories I hear say this woman you brought us is an assassin. And having her in our city could mean she's been hired to come after the Resistance."

"You're an assassin?" Mishan looked over at me with mounting horror.

"I also do bar mitzvahs."

Even Jules looked confused by that one. One more useless bit of information Dr. Nowhere had shoved into my brain.

"I'm not here for any of you," I told them. "I'm here for the woman on top. I'm here for the Crimson Queen."

"Someone hired you to kill Delia Laine? And you *took* the job? I can't tell if that's insane or the best thing I've ever heard."

"Why not both?" asked Selene.

"Nobody hired me. I'm doing this for myself."

"I had no idea you did that."

"Neither did the rest of us," muttered Jules.

"Shit changes." I gave my longtime companion a look that slid right off him like water on a duck's back. "A lot of people are dead and I'm here to make sure she joins them."

"And how do we even know you are who you appear to be?"

I dismissed my shell and let the storm rage for a matter of heartbeats in the school's dimly lit basement, for iron and steel to fill the too-quiet space. When I reformed my shell, Mishan was halfway across the room, but Aaniyah and the other man had held their ground.

"It's the only magic trick I do," I said.

"And it's a doozy." Aaniyah turned to her brother. "Reach out to our men in the guard. If they're moving this prisoner tonight, we need to know when and how."

"You sure you don't want me to stick around?" he asked, pointedly not looking in our direction.

"This woman here is the Queen of Smiles, El. She could kill every one of us without even blinking. I'd say it behooves us to be of value to her."

He nodded and left, taking a second stairway hidden somewhere in the back room. Mishan came back to join the group, tossing down a glass of water as his fight or flight response settled.

"What about the Resistance?" I asked.

"Why do you want an introduction?"

"Your queen—"

Aaniyah spat on the floor. "She's not *my* queen."

"Fine. *The* queen lives in the palace at the top of the hill. We can kill her if we get to her, but our stolen passports have taken us as far as they can. We need someone to provide access."

"You're sure you can take her? I hear she's unkillable."

"Nobody's unkillable."

"We all fall down," added Selene.

I gave Jules a look and he went over to calm down our resident Crow. I didn't need her brand of crazy mucking up my attempts at diplomacy.

"I've met the Crimson Queen," I continued, "and walked away unscathed. I know what she's capable of and I've brought countermeasures. As long as your Resistance—"

"Hold on there; I never said we were part of any Resistance."

"As long as *your Resistance* can get us in," I reiterated, ignoring the blindly transparent evasion, "I can take her out. And then you all can go back to whatever it was you were doing before this cloak and dagger shit started."

"I think we can trust them," said Mishan.

"Oh yeah? And why should I give a damn what *you* think after you brought an assassin right into our safehouse, along with her no-doubt very dangerous colleagues?"

"I'm Miles and I'm *not* dangerous," said Evan. I couldn't tell if he was just a great liar or if he'd convinced himself of that.

"Then what are you doing with *her*, Mr. Man?"

"I owed Her Majesty a favor." He looked well-rested for the first time since I'd pulled him out of his mountain town. Beds and interior plumbing clearly agreed with him. "She takes that sort of thing seriously."

Aaniyah puzzled that through, then shook her head, the gold hoops in her ears swaying with the motion. "Well, unlike Mish here, I don't trust any of you. But you haven't killed us yet and that counts for something. We'll see what we see tonight and take things from there."

○○○

New Memphis was almost spooky under curfew, lights shining through nearby windows to send our shadows dancing across the otherwise empty streets. Even without the threat of incarceration from the guards on patrol, I could understand why the city's citizens were content to stay indoors, clinging to the flimsy safety of their homes.

Little did they know, this was a night where death really did walk the streets. *We* were the things that went bump in the night.

I couldn't see Mishan, Aaniyah, or Aaniyah's brother, Elegy, but I knew at least one of them was behind us, silently trailing us to stand witness to our raid. Mishan aside, the Resistance members weren't eager to trust us, just yet, and that meant keeping a safe distance while they verified that our actions matched our words.

Apparently, me killing two soldiers that morning hadn't been sufficient proof.

Still, they'd given us the prisoner transport route, as well as directions to the best ambush locations along that path. We hadn't had time to scope any of those locations out, but Elegy's descriptions had been sufficient for us to settle on the second. It was an intersection where the crossing alleyway offered ample opportunity to hide and the single-story tailor's shop on the corner had a roof that was accessible and provided a solid view of the street. Almost as important, there were no residences nearby, which lowered the risk of both incidental casualties and eyewitnesses.

Two-Feathers was up front, his senses better than the rest of ours, and he led us past two patrols where none should have been. Apparently, security was still heightened after our late morning shitshow. Chances were, the prisoner transport would also have been beefed up from its usual single squad, but we were ready for that, at least; we had higher ground and the element of surprise.

Even better, this time I wasn't stuck in a dress. We were going to kill every soldier we saw and that meant I didn't need to maintain my absurd disguise any longer. We still lacked the means to access the next district, but I was confident the Resistance would have some ideas on that front.

Things were looking up.

We made it to the ambush spot without any further issues. Two-Feathers and I took up position in opposing alleyways, while Jules, Selene, and Evan climbed onto the tailor's roof with the crew's supplies. I wasn't sure what the latter two would do, if anything, during the ambush, but they'd had no choice but to come along. Our assault would poke the hornet's nest even further, and we'd be pushing on to a different safehouse rather than returning to the school.

We'd been waiting for almost half an hour when the first sounds reached me, footsteps and voices, but muffled as if they were coming from indoors or underground. The reason for that soon became clear… tendrils of thick fog crept past us like tentacles, followed by a thicker wave that expanded into the alleyway I was hiding within. Visibility dropped to nothing as the footsteps came ever closer, their numbers impossible to parse because of the way the fog muffled and magnified each noise.

There was only one explanation for fog on demand: the amped up prisoner escort now included a Power. Traditionally, Weather Witches were more about offense than defense, lightning and hurricane-force winds to batter the opponent, but fog was a pretty smart play. They'd assumed the worst and prepared a countermeasure.

What they hadn't prepared for was the storm.

Jules would be all but useless up on the rooftop, his power operating solely via line of sight. Two-Feathers would be somewhat better off, but the fog would still wreak havoc, playing tricks on even enhanced eyes and ears.

The storm, on the other hand, relied on neither.

I let the vanguard pass the alleyway, what could have been a handful of soldiers or a dozen. Cross would likely be somewhere in the middle, along with any other prisoners being transferred, but there was nothing to distinguish one figure from another, and I didn't want to kill the very man we'd come to rescue. So, I let the middle pass by too, counted to ten and then slipped into the fog, releasing my shell as I went.

Powers were just bodies to the storm's senses, so there was no picking the Weather Witch out of the mass of people either. Instead, I set to killing, and here, the fog worked in my favor. Three soldiers went down before the storm's sounds reached the rest of the guard. Voices rose in anger and fear, and guns chattered, but the soldiers were flying blind, the convoy's defense a hindrance more than help.

As if the enemy Power had realized that, wind picked up out of nowhere, and the fog began to dissipate. Figures materialized out of the dark and gloom, but the storm had sensed them long before and was already on its way. Two men to the left collapsed without being touched, clutching their throats in vain and combat erupted somewhere ahead as Two-Feathers went to work. I pushed forward, letting the storm devour everything in its path.

Soldiers had their purpose still, but when it came to outright combat, Powers ruled.

The wind picked up even further, a storm to counter my own, and the rest of the fog shredded and fell away. Two men and a woman stood in chains a dozen feet ahead of me, Cross among them. Past the prisoners, Two-Feathers was a blur even with one arm, a dagger in his hand instead of the usual spear. And directly in front of me, a cluster of scared soldiers shot at everything that moved, defending an unarmed man whose eyes glowed like ball lightning.

He saw the storm at the same time as I saw him, and even as steel shrapnel surged forward, the world around me went white. Half of the storm's mass fell away, undamaged but scattered by a blast that leapt from fragment to fragment.

It had been a long time since I'd been electrocuted.

I still didn't care for it at all.

The rest of the storm didn't stop. One guard fell, then a second, and I was on the Weather Witch. A strand of barbed wire coiled around his raised hand, a piece of rebar punctured his chest, and then came the teeth of a force that did not eat but always hungered.

I formed my shell over the Power's savaged body, pulled the scattered and electrified fragments of the storm back into the greater whole, and went to work.

○○○

One of the prisoners hadn't survived, having caught a bullet straight to his face in the chaos of battle. Thankfully, it wasn't Cross. Almost as good, it wasn't anyone Mishan recognized from the Resistance.

The trio had showed up as soon as our last body dropped, joining Jules to strip the dead of valuables. By the time we had both Cross and the female prisoner free, Aaniyah was urging us onward. A siren had started up at some point during the battle, and that meant reinforcements were on the way. Worse, given the Weather Witch's brief light show, those reinforcements would almost definitely include more Powers.

The problem with attacking an enemy in their lair was that they always, always had more cannon fodder to throw at you. I had never kept count of the people the storm and I killed, but this job must have at least doubled that number, and I wasn't sure if the Crimson Queen had even noticed.

Elegy took the lead, Jules supporting a visibly battered Cross, while Evan, of all people, gave the unknown woman a hand. I played rearguard again, but the battle had been quick enough that nobody reached the battlefield before we were gone. We vanished into the darkness, leaving only bodies in our wake.

I had no idea what role the new safehouse served when it wasn't being used to stash fugitives. The building was smaller than the school had been, but in the cover of darkness, that was the *only* thing I was able to see before we slipped inside, through a hallway, and down into another cellar. Elegy went to the far wall, pushed a stack of boxes aside to reveal a hidden doorway, and then replaced the careful camouflage again behind us when we were through.

The new room was a dead ringer for the one we'd spent the afternoon in, the lack of direct stairwell access notwithstanding. Naked lightbulbs dangled from an unfinished ceiling, two additional doors led elsewhere, and a large table dominated the room, chairs tucked in around it.

"Now what?" I asked.

"Now we wait to be contacted." Aaniyah looked tired. "El can look at your man in the interim."

"I'm not a doctor, but I have some basic training in first aid at least." At Jules' nod, Elegy disappeared into the next room, appearing a moment later with what looked to be homemade bandages and alcohol.

It would have to do. Most of Cross' injuries were superficial, but there were a lot of them, and I knew humans had a finite amount of blood in them. Our rescued crewmember hadn't said much yet, other than a quick, whispered thanks as Jules set him down. Now, he gritted his teeth, a vein in his forehead throbbing, as Aaniyah's brother started cleaning and wrapping the wounds.

I turned back to the woman herself.

"Contacted by whom?"

Her cold eyes darted over to the woman we'd rescued along with Cross. "Mishan, why don't you take the young miss here into the back for some refreshments."

"What are you going to do to her?" asked Evan, once the two had departed.

"If she's a plant, she's not walking out of here alive, old man." Her teeth gleamed in the uncertain light. "Even if she's on the level, we need to make damn sure she doesn't see or hear more than she should. Whether we recruit her or let her go, information security matters. As for who we're waiting to hear from," she said, turning to me, "I believe you wanted to have a talk with our leadership?"

"We operate in cells," said Elegy, still working over Cross. "We don't have access to anyone at the top, but there's a system in place for when we need intervention. We sent the signal on our way in. Tomorrow, a spotter will report it, and we'll see what's up."

"Just like that?" Jules frowned. "We free our man and suddenly you trust us?"

"You killed an Immortal," said Aaniyah, not even cracking a smile at the unintentional irony of her statement. "I could see the queen sacrificing a few of her soldiers in a scheme to get you into our good graces, but Powers don't grow on trees. She'll want blood for his death, and that earns you a ticket up the food chain. How far you go depends entirely on you. Once we hand you over, it's out of our hands."

My opinion of the Resistance was slowly recovering from Mishan's initial impression. Humans were fragile and I could appreciate the need for a healthy bit of paranoia.

"What is it you're fighting for, anyway?" asked Jules, as Elegy finished binding an unconscious Cross' wounds. "We have our reasons for killing the queen, but to a newcomer, New Memphis doesn't seem like it's suffering too badly under her reign."

"Unless you're a Power," said Aaniyah. "Or a second-born son, automatically conscripted into the queen's war efforts. Or someone who dares to ask for explanations or speak out against injustices in the street."

Elegy crossed the room to put a comforting hand on his sister's shoulder, but she shook it off and stalked forward, eyes hard as she went face to chest with Jules.

"We fight for freedom," she snarled up at him. "For the right to choose our own paths. An end to slavery both literal and figurative. *That* is what the Resistance is about and *that* is why we're fighting. The city's streets may run red with blood before all is said and done, but it will be free. Any more questions?"

By her tone and expression, she didn't expect a reply, but then, she'd only just met Jules. I'd known the bastard for decades.

"Just one," he said, refusing to give any ground at all as he stared down into the dark eyes. "What are you doing later this week?"

Elegy started forward with a low growl, but a raised hand from his sister stopped him in his tracks.

"I'm about to come into a lot of money," said Jules, not even deigning to look in my direction. "I thought maybe once the queen was dead, we could get some dinner."

"Food for the body, food for the soul," murmured Selene.

"Right." For the first time, Jules looked uncomfortable. "That."

Aaniyah continued to stare at him, her hands clenching and unclenching as the seconds dragged out.

"Aani…" began Elegy.

Apparently, just that was enough to end the duo's weird standoff. Aaniyah spun about and rejoined her brother, her face a mask. "Someone should be here by the morning to collect you," she said with a scowl. "In the meantime, I'd suggest taking advantage of our facilities to shower and change into fresh clothes if you have them. You all look like something that dug its way out of a grave and some of you," she added, spearing Jules with another glare, "outright stink."

I'd reformed my shell and was as right and shiny as the day I was born, so I sat back and watched Aaniyah point out the facilities to the rest of my crew. Two-Feathers had been the only one in the thick of things, but between climbing buildings, running through alleys, and robbing the dead, they were, to her point, all pretty filthy.

Still, the men in our crew—even Jules who had surreptitiously sniffed his own armpit and made a face—stood aside to let Selene shower first.

Chivalry was making an unexpected comeback.

33

I spent another night not sleeping, Evan's snores making me grateful all over again that we'd bought separate rooms in the many, many inns we'd stayed at over the length of our trip. The showers had done everyone some good, and the rough fare Elegy supplied did even more. Freshly scrubbed and in clean outfits, it was easy to pretend that the past few months hadn't happened… that we were tourists in a friendly world, here to see the sights of the big city.

Cross' wounds put the lie to that, of course, as did Two-Feathers' still-healing broken arm. And then there were our new acquaintances: the woman we'd rescued, whose name was Bluebell because her parents had apparently hated her, and the trio who remained the only evidence of the city's freedom fighters.

Bluebell was curled up in her own corner and fast asleep, having passed whatever tests Mishan had run her through. Elegy was somewhere outside, standing watch, and Mishan himself was making almost as much of a racket as Evan. But Aaniyah…

Well, she pretended to sleep, tossing and turning as if fighting the occasional dream, but no matter how she shifted, I couldn't help but notice that she kept us in her sightline. Whatever trust we'd earned only went so far.

As for me? I was leaning back against the wall, gloves folded in my lap and legs stretched out along the floor. This wasn't the time or the place to set the storm free, and that made for a long night of watching Aaniyah pretend not to watch me.

I wondered what would become of the woman if we succeeded and killed the queen. I assumed some sort of civil war would break out, with Immortals fighting for power and control, but would the Resistance pick one of the survivors to support? Or would they transfer their enmity to whoever came out on top, keeping the cause going? In my experience, rebellion was a game that consumed its players the longer it went on.

Something told me Aaniyah would stay in that game until it was far too late, and that she'd take her brother down with her.

Hours later, Elegy came back down through the bookshelf door and this time, he wasn't alone. The man with him was small and even older than Evan, with a wispy white beard doing its best to make up for the lack of hair on his head. He scanned the room with an amiable smile on his face that didn't slip even when his gaze reached me.

"I think I understand," he murmured.

"El, who is this?" asked Aaniyah, giving up the pretense of sleeping as the others began to stir.

"Names are unimportant and all too often dangerous, my dear," said the stranger. "Given what has been happening in this district over the past few days, your message was passed up the chain until it reached my desk. I thought it merited direct involvement."

"He knows the countersigns," said Elegy.

"Well, of course I do. I'm the one who created them."

"You're Shadow Council?"

For just a moment, his smile slipped. "That's… not a term we ourselves tend to use, but I suppose it is accurate enough. I've come to take your guests off your hands." He turned to me. "You wished to meet the Resistance, young lady? I am here to make that happen."

I didn't bother pointing out that I had several decades on him. Humans, when they reached a certain age, tended to fall in love with their own illusions. Given that he was giving us what we wanted, the least I could do was permit him his.

"Let's go." I caught Aaniyah's eyes and placed two gold coins on the floor next to where I'd been sitting. By now, I'd more than blown through whatever saving Eastwood should have earned me, but that transactional piece of me stayed dormant.

Still, I'd bring Jae-Sung whatever was left when we were done.

"We have injured," said Jules, coming over to join me. Behind him, Evan vanished into the bathroom, while Selene and Cross were sitting up.

Two-Feathers, I couldn't help but note, had faded over to take up position behind Elegy and the stranger, ready to cut off their escape if need be. And somehow, none of us had even seen him doing it.

The smile across my visor turned hungry. Strong shoulders were great, but his breed of continued competence was a whole different level of attractive.

"If you wish, you can leave your wounded here with this cell," said the stranger in reply to Jules' question.

"I'm going, boss." Cross looked more mummy than man, but he stood with only a low grunt.

"Are you sure?"

"You need someone to watch your back. We'll see this through together."

It was funny. I'd thought Cross was the only one of our crew still here only for the money. Jules and Evan had both given their word, Selene was here because her ghost wanted access to a different target, and Two-Feathers… well, whatever his reasons, money didn't seem to play a part in them.

Apparently, I'd misjudged Jules' second-in-command. Cross would take the money in the end—as would everyone else, of course—but he was motivated by more than just greed. Call it friendship or call it loyalty… either way, he was invested on a personal level too.

"Alright," said Jules, his voice going smooth in that way it did when he was trying not to let his feelings show. "Once Evan's done, you all should take your bio breaks. And then we can be on our way."

"That's quite alright," said the stranger, adjusting the leather satchel he wore over one shoulder. "I woke you all with my early arrival. It would be churlish indeed of me to whisk you away again before breakfast." He turned to Aaniyah. "My dear, if one of your men could fetch us something from the supplies in back, I would greatly appreciate it. And I would love a cup of tea if you have it. Coffee if you don't."

"We have water," said the other woman, not giving an inch. "And meal kits."

The old man tutted. "How tragic. Rest assured I will bring the matter up with my fellows. The Resistance depends upon stalwart cells such as your own. Providing you quality stores is hardly too much of an ask."

"I wouldn't turn down better food," said Mishan, shrugging at the look Aaniyah sent him. "What? It's the truth."

"Go get the kits." She turned to Elegy. "Help Mish."

"Only because you asked so nicely." He grinned at his sister, ducking aside as she threatened him with a raised hand.

Evan finally finished up in the bathroom—his fourth trip there since midnight—and emerged looking like death warmed over. He let Selene by, yawned, and dropped into the closest chair. "I don't suppose you all have any coffee?"

Aaniyah's death glare intensified.

ooo

When our impromptu breakfast was done, it was the stranger's turn to vanish into the bathroom, although the low *hmm* of dismay that made its way back out into the larger room told us it didn't live up to his standards.

"What do you think? Is he legit?" asked Jules, sidling up next to me. Elegy was changing the last of Cross' bandages, Two-Feathers and Evan were having one of their wordless conversations to the side, and Selene was giving Mishan come-hither eyes and stay-the-fuck-away smiles at the same time. Aaniyah stood by herself, in the center of the room, as if she could turn our chaos into order through sheer strength of will.

"He seems to be," I said. "Either that or the Resistance has been infiltrated to such an extent that their signs and countersigns are public knowledge. And if that's the case, they're all dead anyway."

"There's something weird about his smile."

"Yeah; it reaches his eyes."

"Huh." He scratched his arm and frowned. "Does that mean we've been spending too much time with people like us?"

"It might." I kept my gaze trained on the closed bathroom door. "What I can't decide is whether he's soft or just that much better at hiding what he is. Either way, keep your eyes peeled."

"Always."

When the old man was finished, it was time to leave. It was just going to be us and him; Aaniyah and her cell, including the newly inducted Bluebell, were staying behind to do more of whatever it was they did.

"Sir," Aaniyah asked, the first words she'd spoken since breakfast, "do you know if Operation Solidarity will proceed?"

"Your contact will keep you apprised of the details as always, cell leader, but yes. I would say recent developments have only amplified its importance."

"Operation Solidarity?" I asked.

"One of many things my fellows and I will fill you in on as we discuss how our two groups can be of service to one another."

Which wasn't much of an answer, really, but I could be patient.

We went through the secret door and back up the stairs we'd come down the previous night, but instead of taking a left and cutting back through the same three rooms we'd already seen, we went right and came to an exterior rear door. A horse-drawn wagon had been parked out back.

The old man knocked on the door's glass pane, and the wagon's driver made a show of stretching as he looked about. Whatever it was he saw or didn't see, he tapped the side of the wagon twice, making sure his hand was in our field of view.

"It seems the coast is clear. Out you go."

"What is this?" I asked.

"Transportation, of course. Some of you," he added, sparing me a glance, "are more memorable than others, but I have no doubt the guard has distributed sketches with everyone's likenesses by now. Curfew may be over, but their heightened vigilance will not be. Thus, a wagon whose bed is deep enough for all of you, with room to spare for a blanket and crafted goods above."

"And those same guards won't stop a strange wagon on the streets to search it?"

"They might, were they not used to seeing this particular vehicle every day, conveying products from the craftsman combine you're standing within to the storefront where those goods are sold. My presence will be remarked upon, no doubt, but given the news of armed unrest, it only makes sense that I would come down to this district to ensure my businesses have not been unduly impacted."

"You own these places?" asked Jules.

"These and many more, young man. Now then, shall we?"

I traded glances with Jules, and then again with Two-Feathers, before I slipped out the door and climbed into the wagon. We still didn't know the old man's name, but I was starting to think he knew what he was doing. And if he had come *down* to this district, it meant he lived in District 2 or 3 and might have a way to get us there.

This job had been a bitch and a half, but the end might be almost in sight.

ooo

We didn't travel far in the wagon, which was a good thing, given that the six of us were packed in together with barely enough room to breathe let alone move. Selene had been given the first spot and, by popular decree, I'd been selected to wedge in next to her. There was no way to avoid contact and I could see her fingers twitching.

I'd have survived her stabbing me—which was why the others had volunteered me for this spot—but I sure as fuck wouldn't have appreciated it. My shell *did* feel pain, after all.

If we passed any guards during our journey, they didn't see a reason to stop us, so I guess the old man knew his stuff. After ten or so minutes, almost as many bumps, some barely audible groans from Cross *and* Evan, and a half-dozen twitches and spooky smiles from Selene, our wagon pulled to a stop. There was a horrendous clatter I recognized from the overhead doors back in Tillatoba, and then a low murmur of voices accompanied the unloading of the boxes that had been stacked on the blanket above us. Once those voices had faded, the overhead door was dragged closed again, and the rest of our coverings were whisked away.

As I waited for my crew to exit, I scanned our surroundings. We were in some sort of a small warehouse, presumably at the back of the storefront the old man had mentioned. It barely had space for the wagon and a single row of crates along the wall. Two doors were set in the far wall opposite the overhead door, but the warehouse was empty again of anyone but the old man and us.

"This way, if you please, and hurry," he said. "Not all our employees know of this place's secondary role. Roger will keep them distracted with a surprise inspection on my behalf, but there *are* limits."

We were out of the wagon by the time he was done speaking, although both Evan's *and* Jules' knees decided to voice their protest, and Selene took a suspiciously long time to straighten her dress, arranging the long pleats until they fell in a way only she understood as being perfect.

It had taken days of travel before I realized the young Crow had multiple dresses, and then, only because she'd torn one on a bush with thorns as long as my fingers, only to emerge the next day with the dress magically whole once more. It turned out she had five dresses—four now—but they were all in the same color, size, and style.

The boys thought that was weird, but it's not like I was going to throw stones.

The old man took us through the left door, and down a short flight of stairs to yet another cellar. I had become something of an expert on the basements of New Memphis of late, and this one didn't impress, half the size of the ones at the school and crafting commune, and without even those places' scant comforts. No chairs, no tables, no restrooms for a species who seemed to spend half their time either eating or voiding their waste. Just rows of shelves.

"Come over here, young man." Our host showed Two-Feathers to one of the shelves in the back. "When I tell you to, I will need you to rotate that screw. Understood?"

At the nomad's nod, he directed Jules over to a different shelf and repeated his instructions. With both men in place, he went to the left wall of the storage room, and took hold of a third shelf, this one holding only a few boxes.

"Go ahead, gentlemen."

There was no audible click to indicate that anything had changed, but a moment later, he swung his shelf away from the wall, bringing a section of that wall with it. Behind, a tunnel stretched into darkness.

"In you go," said the old man. "The mechanism will reset as soon as the door closes behind us."

"Nifty." I played rearguard as usual, the last one through the door, taking a large step down from cellar floor to tunnel. "I didn't realize you had a Technomancer on your side."

"The only Technomancer in New Memphis works for our would-be queen," he corrected, losing his smile. "This was the work of an *educated* man. Loquacious always did love his traps and secret rooms."

"Loquacious? I thought names were dangerous?"

"Sadly, Loquacious shuffled off this mortal coil several years ago. We remember him now through his contributions to the cause." The old man squeezed past the others and led us onward, the tunnel rapidly growing so dark we couldn't even see the person in front of us. After a handful of twists and turns, he paused. The buckles on his satchel jangled as he reached into it.

"If you would all close your eyes for a moment? This will be a little bit bright."

A moment later, light flooded the tunnel.

Even with the old man's warning, the others took a few minutes to adjust to the sudden illumination. I was focused on the device in his hands. It was smaller than those I'd seen in Old Baltimore and lacked the techno-organic components that were Legion's signature, but I recognized it anyway.

"That's a glowtorch."

"Indeed."

"Does Legion know someone is out here copying his designs?"

"We are long way from the coast, young lady, and the Lord of Baltimore does not concern himself with affairs beyond his border."

"But how did you get it?"

"Several years ago, before we became an unwilling monarchy, a man came through the city on his way back from that place. He made some business deals with the Council of the time, trading Legion designs in exchange for future demands, and then departed." He shrugged. "He has not been seen since, but the designs he left have proven popular enough, especially once someone figured out how to reproduce them. Although," he added, "the power supply issue makes this about as large as our versions can get."

"Most of the city uses lanterns or electrical bulbs though?" asked Evan, interested in spite of himself.

"Yes, because they are cheaper and more easily replaced. Even in the administrative district, you can count the number of glowtorches in use on a single hand."

Which meant, if we'd had any doubts, that this old man was both important and wealthy. I was more interested in the story he'd told, however.

"This man who sold you the designs… did he have a name?"

"Mr. Grey."

"That's what I thought."

His affable persona dropped away. "You know him?"

"Knew him. You won't need to worry about him coming back to make those demands."

"Ah." He thought it over and shrugged. "It's just as well."

"Not to say this isn't all fascinating, because it is, but we're standing in the middle of a tunnel with one light and an injured man," said Jules. "Is there any chance we could get a move on to wherever it is we're going?"

"Of course. You have my apologies. I have at times been accused of liking to hear myself speak." Before turning about, the old man singled out Evan and sent our senior citizen a rueful smile, as if to say *Young people, am I right?*

I felt the same way sometimes… it was just my definition of *young people* that differed.

○○○

I'd known New Memphis was built on a manmade hill, but it had never occurred to me that the ground beneath would have more than a barely functional sewage system. As we walked, we passed electrical conduit tunnels, passageways that led to nowhere, and yes, the occasional sludge-filled shaft reeking of waste.

"Where did all this come from?" I asked.

"It was put in fifty or so years ago, when New Memphis was being built. The power and the sewage lines were a necessity, but the Earthshakers who did the building weren't above taking bribes to add in extra passageways. Young Delia has been blocking those routes as her forces discover them, but there are a few tunnels yet that she hasn't found."

After months of knowing her only as the Crimson Queen, it was still odd to hear anyone refer to her by name, let alone as *young Delia.* It humanized her a bit to think that she'd had a name and a family and probably a pet that drooled and shat all over the carpet of her rich person house. And then she'd wrested control of the city from her brother, claimed a throne that didn't exist, executed any naysayers, and set about building an empire.

If I hadn't already met her, I might have found something in there to admire. As it was, *human* just meant mortal, and mortal meant this job would have itself a happy ending.

"So, where does this tunnel lead?" asked Cross. He'd started laboring a bit over the past few minutes, and one of the wounds on his chest had bled through the pad again, ruining another shirt.

"We've been steadily going uphill," said Evan, who knew such things. "I mean, up and down, but predominantly up. Does this go under the wall to District 3?"

"Further, in fact." Despite being the oldest person present other than me, our guide stayed cheerful, mopping the sweat from his shiny brow, and pressing onward. "The entrances to District 3 were found and sealed off a year or so ago, but District 2 is where the elite live. Our estates are not so easily breached, even for a queen. This is one of two routes I'm aware of that lead inside."

I took note that he included himself in the ranks of elite. And didn't even hesitate when doing so.

"I don't suppose there's a side passage that we can take to District 1?" I asked. "As much as I appreciate the guided tour, a surgical strike on the palace now would wrap things up nicely."

"Sadly, I'm unaware of any remaining entrances to the palace or its district, beyond, of course, the heavily guarded gate. But we can pose that question to the others when you see them."

"Others?"

"The other leaders of the Resistance, of course." He stopped and straightened up from the hunched stance he'd adopted hiking through the tunnel. "My apologies! I had intended to properly introduce myself once we were away from prying eyes and ears, only to get distracted. My name is Tiberius. Tiberius Becks."

I sensed more than saw Selene wake from her habitual fugue state, head whipping around to focus in on the old man in our midst.

"Councilor Becks?" she asked, with a chilly focus entirely distinct from her usual demeanor.

"Not anymore, not unless you subscribe to our brave fighters' fanciful imaginings of a Shadow Council. No, the Councilor Becks you must be thinking of is my dear son and successor, Mordecai."

And just like that, shit got a whole lot more complicated.

34

Before I could pull Selene aside for a quick chat with her and—more importantly—her ghost, we turned into an apparent dead end, a rockfall blocking most of the tunnel in front of us. Tiberius didn't slow, veering to hug the right wall as he squeezed past the obstruction.

We followed him and discovered a narrow path had been laid, winding through the fallen rock. It was a tight fit—especially for me—and Selene ruined another dress in the process, but ten minutes later, we were through to the other side, and looking at the tunnel's original endpoint, a rough stone wall with an iron-bound door set in its center.

"Mind the step," said Tiberius, unlocking the door and stepping up and through it. "When this hill was first formed, it brought a lot of the existing wildlife with it. The access points were all set several feet above the tunnel floor in an ultimately unsuccessful attempt to keep vermin from climbing out."

Evan shifted nervously. We hadn't seen anything alive in our trip through the tunnels, but I could only imagine the sort of creatures that might grow to call these tunnels home after multiple decades. Apparently, Evan could too.

We emerged into yet another cellar, lit by a glowtorch mounted on the ceiling. In place of crates or supplies, there were large barrels, stored on their side.

"Wine," explained Tiberius. "The conditions are not great for grapes, but we have a low-end Druid on staff who does what he can."

I traded glances with Two-Feathers. Wine. Estates on the hill. Businesses throughout the city. Tiberius seemed to have it all. Why was he even rebelling?

"The queen doesn't press every Power into military service?" asked Jules.

"You're speaking of her Immortals?" At Jules' nod, he shrugged. "In practice, she tries to, but in reality, she pulls primarily from the ranks of the unclaimed. Prisoners taken during her conquests, individuals from the lower districts, and those who hire on of their own volition. Delia needs the Great Houses' support still to keep this city running. She won't upset that balance. Not yet anyway."

We left the wine cellar behind, climbing heavy stone steps. A door at the top opened onto the first greenery I'd seen since arriving in New Memphis: a carefully manicured grass courtyard, enclosed between the walls of a two-story mansion. Where glass was rare in Districts 4 and 5, it was everywhere here, the early afternoon sun setting the building aglow.

"My humble abode," said Tiberius, without a trace of irony in his voice. "Becks Hall. Originally built by my father's father, and then recreated here when New Memphis was built."

"Begging your pardon," said Jules, unable to keep the dry edge from his voice as we followed the old man across the courtyard and into the not-so-humble house, "but you seem to have a pretty good life up here. Why would someone like you want to be part of the Resistance, let alone lead it?"

"It's not just me, young man. District 2 is the *birthplace* of the Resistance. Its entire leadership was formed by a subset of my peers."

"Why?" I asked. It didn't really fit what we'd seen and heard from Aaniyah, and I wondered if she and her cell even knew the truth. Given the way their cells were organized, it was possible they didn't.

"Because this city does not want a queen. Nor does it need one. New Memphis did just fine with a ruling council. While not all the Laine girl's actions and policies have been ill-conceived, her insistence on being the sole authority is something we cannot allow to stand."

"You want control."

"For the betterment of the empire, of course. The concentration of power in any one person's hands inevitably leads to tyranny. Our loyal, hard-working citizens deserve better."

I wasn't sure the power being in the hands of a bunch of rich assholes was all that much better, but I wasn't here to learn about politics, let alone debate them. Behind me, Evan grumbled something to himself, but the rest of the crew stayed quiet as we followed the senior Becks down a hallway of dark wood, with furniture to match and ceilings at least a dozen feet high.

"Your arrival came as a surprise, I must admit," he told us, eyes dancing to match his wide smile. "Still, the timing could not be better! Tomorrow, I am hosting a party for my peers, and we in the Resistance will be using the festivities to mask our assembly. You will be able to speak with the *Shadow Council* then."

Apparently, the term was growing on him.

"All we need is a way into the palace," I said.

"And I assure you that will be first on our agenda. In the meantime, I have had my staff clear the east wing for your stay. I will provide libations, of course."

"I think we can live with that," said Jules, voice still dry as a bone. "Although I might request extra pillows."

"Marlena, make a note of it," he told the small woman who had emerged from the crossing hall, not even looking her way. "I do ask that you all remain in your designated space until tomorrow night. While I trust my staff implicitly, Becks Hall has its share of daily visitors, given my son's duties on the council."

"He lives with you then?" Selene's voice was saccharine sweet.

"He and his wife, yes. This is the family estate after all." He finally turned to the woman, Marlena. "Take my guests to their rooms in the east wing. You will be seeing to their needs during their stay."

"Yes, sir." Marlena was plainly but professionally dressed in a black button-up shirt and matching pants, dark hair up and in a bun. Whatever she thought of our motley crew didn't make it onto her face.

"And now, I'm afraid I must depart. As tedious as it will be, I must retrace my steps so that I can be seen returning to this district through its proper gate. It would not do for our enemy to learn that any alternate routes remain." Tiberius tipped an imaginary hat in our direction. "It has been a pleasure and I shall be delighted to discover what great things we will accomplish together."

Marlena turned to us and bowed. "If you would follow me?"

Our route took us the length of the building, down hallways filled with stone-carved busts of people I didn't know that connected with hallways covered in ornately framed portraits of those same people. Servants were in evidence everywhere, identified by the same basic uniform Marlena was wearing, but if the mansion had other guests, we were being carefully routed around them.

The east wing, when we finally arrived, was more of the same; a long hallway terminated in a sitting room that could comfortably hold twenty or more people. Doors off that room led to bedrooms, one for each of us with another four left empty. Each bedroom had its own attached bathroom, and Marlena informed us, in a voice that suggested that she had no idea *why* we warranted such extravagance but wasn't going to ask either, that the house chef would provide meals upon request.

I don't think she'd expected to be immediately inundated with meal orders, but we had spent a hell of a long time on the road over the past few months, and my crew wasn't going to pass up professionally cooked food when it was available. And free.

She left to deliver those orders, and I intercepted Selene as she tried to follow Marlena.

"Where are you headed, Selene?"

"I thought I heard a mouse." Her eyes were fixed on the door that led back into the hallway. "I want to catch it and keep it safe."

"Maybe we should hold off on that for a while." I let the storm fill my voice. "I'd like to talk with you and your ghost first."

The young Crow tilted her head, like the bird her kind had been named for, but that dreamy expression didn't leave her face. With a visible effort, she tore her gaze away from the door and blinked up at me. "Your room or mine?"

I ignored the suggestion in her tone because I wasn't dumb. "Yours."

Two-Feathers had emerged from his room—right next to mine, some part of me couldn't help but note. The nomad shot me a look, but I waved him off. This was a matter between me and Selene's ghost, and if it went sideways, I didn't want anyone else in the bedroom with us.

Selene plopped down onto her bed, a short giggle escaping her as she bounced from the initial impact. By the time I closed the door, however, someone else was in control.

"You heard the name as well as I did," said Selene's ghost.

"I did. But you need to be patient."

"Why?"

"Killing Mordecai Becks now will lose us his father's support. We need the Resistance to help us figure out a way into the palace."

"There are always reasons. Always excuses to avoid what must be done, Smiling One. But justice does not care, and justice does not wait."

"Justice won't happen at all if you lose your borrowed body."

She held herself still, forcing Selene's body to not even blink, and something ugly flickered across the young Crow's face.

"Is that a threat?"

"It's a statement of fact. Give it three days. Enough time for tomorrow's meeting and for us to figure out a way in. Then he's yours. Press early, and you'll be looking for a new host."

"That was not the deal."

"I'm not jeopardizing this job so you can get your bloodlust on early. Not now, not ever. Take it or leave it."

She studied me through eyes grown as dark as freshly dug graves, and I waited, the storm churning just beneath my shell. Judging by the corpses we'd seen north of Tillatoba, Selene was more than just a precocious young woman with a liking for edged weaponry. I didn't think she could seriously harm the storm, but I wasn't going to underestimate her either.

Finally, she nodded. "Three days."

"Three days. I got you into your enemy's home, as requested. You just need to be patient."

The darkness left Selene's eyes and a slow, languorous smile spread across her face. "Such a comfortable bed," she said, "and large enough for five. More, if you arrange the pieces just right."

Apparently, the conversation was over.

ooo

I left Selene's bedroom to find everyone but Evan in the sitting room. Jules looked my way as I came over.

"Do we have a problem?"

I waggled a gloved hand in the air. "I think I've taken care of it. As long as she stays put, we should be fine."

From the look on his face, that wasn't going to be enough. "Do you mind keeping an eye out for a few?" he asked Cross. "If Selene starts to wander off, give us a holler."

"You got it, boss." Our sixth member, the last Normal among us, stretched his legs the length of the sofa, pillows propping him up so he could keep an eye on the Crow's bedroom door. "I didn't feel like moving for a good long while anyway."

I traded glances with Two-Feathers, and the young nomad stood, following Jules and me into the bedroom I'd claimed as my own. Like Selene's room, it had a large bed, a desk, two chairs, and a dresser to hold the clothes I didn't have.

I closed the door and sat on the bed. The two men took seats facing me.

"What's going on, Queenie?"

"Did you notice Selene taking an interest in our host's son?"

"She does a lot of weird things, especially lately. If I paid attention to all of them, I'd never get anything done." Jules ran a hand through the thin layer of hair atop his scalp, and then stiffened. "Wait. You don't mean…"

"Councilor Mordecai Becks is the man she came to kill."

"Well, shit."

Two-Feathers tapped the desk to get our attention and gave us a questioning look.

"Right. I never told you." I sighed. "One of Selene's ghosts is herself a dead Crow, and the Free States' most prolific serial killer."

"Whoa, you didn't tell *me* that either," protested Jules. "You don't mean—"

"Yeah, I do."

"That's not the sort of secret you're supposed to keep from me. Not from a friend and business partner. And especially not when we're traveling with her every night!"

"If she'd wanted you dead, you'd have been so, long before I managed to track your crew down in Texas."

"That's not the fucking point."

"I made a judgment call. We can debate its wisdom when shit isn't preparing to blow up in our faces." I turned back to a still-confused Two-Feathers. "Selene's ghost revealed herself in Greenburg. In exchange for her help with this job, I agreed to help Selene reach her target."

The nomad waved a hand around us.

"Right. The owner's son, like I was saying. Our stay here wasn't planned, of course. I'd never even heard of the Becks family, and certainly didn't know the elder was involved with the Resistance. This is all one big coincidence. An unfortunate one, in my opinion. Selene and her ghost feel… otherwise."

"If she kills the son, we can say goodbye to any help from the Resistance," said Jules, telling me nothing I didn't already know.

"She's agreed to give it three days. After that, all bets are off."

"Then I'd say tomorrow night's meeting had better go well for us." Jules sighed, still scowling at me. "Shit's never easy, is it? Especially when people are keeping secrets. I'm gonna go check Cross' bandages and help him keep watch."

The door closed behind him a little bit harder than it needed to. I was left alone with Two-Feathers, the nomad gazing at me steadily, some unknown emotion in his dark eyes.

"What?"

Tillatoba felt like it had been months ago instead of a matter of weeks, but his still-broken arm told the true story. He pulled the knife from his belt and pantomimed stabbing someone with it, then followed the gesture with the same questioning look as before.

"Why does she want this man dead?"

He nodded.

"I have no idea."

He cocked his head, brow furrowed. Whatever that sentiment was in his eyes, it only intensified.

"The world is a toilet," I told him. "I'm not here to clean it up. I was created to run jobs, and sometimes, that means doing bad things along the way. The pre-Break world even had a phrase for it: the end justifies the means."

He frowned and squeezed the fist of his broken arm into a ball, passing the palm of his left hand over it.

"What about Eclipse?"

He nodded again.

"That's who I'm doing this for."

In the ensuing silence, his lack of a response was deafening.

"I don't need a conscience," I said. "I've already got Evan."

He blew out a breath and climbed to his feet, face unreadable. A few seconds later, the door closed behind him. As a Stalwart, he could have slammed it so hard it splintered into a dozen pieces. Instead, he'd pulled it gently shut.

Two-Feathers had never said a word to me but there were times his silence spoke volumes.

ooo

Soon after, everyone's food arrived. I left them to their meals, locked my bedroom door, and did something I hadn't done in more time than I could remember.

I took a shower.

I stripped everything off my shell, letting the helmet and riding gear fall into nothingness and stood for a moment in my borrowed bathroom, naked in a way that even I rarely saw myself… the handcrafted body and the unfinished face. My limbs toned and strong, my belly flat, my waist trim, my nose nonexistent, my eyes skin-covered pits of unequal size, my mouth misshapen lines of pale meat.

I was a horror show of contradictions, but that didn't matter. Jules was right. I was the Queen of Smiles, and fuck whatever anyone else thought of that, even my own companions. I didn't know what Two-Feathers wanted from me, but when this was over, when the job was over, he'd return to his clan, I'd return to the road, and this, whatever this was between us, would be done.

That's right, mocked the voice that had been haunting me of late. *Focus on the job. Always the job and never what matters.*

I stepped into scalding water, interior plumbing delivering an experience that just didn't exist outside of the Free States. I turned my face, my false face, my undone face, into the stream and let rivulets of heat burn their way down the skin of my shell.

That is *what matters,* I told the voice, heat soaking into the bones of my shell. *Another job and the road. The road and another job. It's what I am. It's how* he *made me.*

Cowardice, it said, filled with the metal of the storm. *Excuses. You are the storm and the storm goes where it will. For decades, you chose the jobs that served your needs, that brought you closer to your maker and the answers only he could give. The jobs justified your actions, and the quest justified those jobs.*

Then, he *died, and you wallowed. Eclipse burned and you seized upon the deaths of those you called friends as a distraction, as another opportunity to pretend you were still chained, all because freedom holds the one question you haven't dared to answer.*

I scowled, broken mouth twitching in the shower as I argued with the one person I couldn't leave behind, outlive, or simply kill.

Because that voice was me and I knew the question it was talking about. Not who or where or even why, but *what next.*

What next, for a life that had no ending? What next, when both the structure I'd lived under and the goal that had driven me had ended in the deserts of New Mexico, dying under a Crow's outstretched hand? What next, once jobs became just things to do, moments of accomplishment untethered from any greater purpose?

What next?

35

With little to do and nowhere to go, I assumed the crew would basically eat and sleep the time away. And Selene, at least, seemed to be doing just that. But a few hours after my shower, I emerged into the sitting room to find everyone else there. Even Evan. The carnage from their lunchtime frenzy had been cleared away by Marlena or one of the servants she commanded, and Jules, Cross, and Evan were playing yet another of their endless games of cards around a table they'd dragged into the center of the room. Two-Feathers, meanwhile, was doing some sort of complicated calisthenics in the corner—made even more difficult by the lack of a usable second arm.

I took a moment to watch the nomad and then moved on to join the others. "Is there room for one more?"

"I didn't know you played cards," said Cross, shuffling the worn deck that had accompanied him all the way from Texas. Most of his gear had been lost when he was taken, but somehow, those cards had made it through.

"She doesn't," said Jules. "At least not that I've ever seen."

"I figured now was as good a time as any to start."

"Well, you've got the right face for poker."

Once my shower ended, I'd skipped the available towel and simply reformed my shell in my bedroom, going from wet and naked to dry and fully clothed in a heartbeat. "I could take the helmet off, but the face beneath won't be any better. What are you playing?"

"Omaha High," said Cross, cutting the deck and shuffling it a second time. "And since you haven't paid any of us yet, we're playing for imaginary chits."

"In that case, teach me the rules and deal me in."

An hour or so later, my poker debt exceeded the deficits of several pre-Break countries.

"Maybe cards aren't your thing, Queenie."

The rules were simple enough to grasp, but somehow, hand after hand had ended with me either folding early or going down in flames when called. Either they were all cheating or only one of them was, and that person was making sure the other two came out ahead anyway at my expense.

Or Jules was right, and I just sucked at cards.

I was rescued by Marlena stepping in to collect dinner orders. Once that meal was both served and consumed, I bowed out of the game, ceding my seat to Selene who had woken up and wandered over. Two-Feathers had finally tired of making us all look lazy and anted up as well, adding a new wrinkle to the game with his pantomimed raises and calls.

Two hands later, Jules called it quits. He joined me over in the corner, a glass of something clear in his hand.

"Tired of winning?" I asked him.

"Nah, I just know my luck's about to change." He hadn't shaved since before we'd entered the city, and the scruff on his face was a patchwork of black and grey.

"Because Two-Feathers will notice you cheating?"

"Because all Selene *does* is cheat. Her ghosts tell her everyone's cards."

"You played two hands with her just now," I pointed out.

"And lost, as expected. If I'd left as soon as she joined, Miles and Two-Feathers would have known something was up. Imaginary money or not, I want to see how long it takes them to figure it out." He took a long sip from his glass. "And I wanted to talk to you."

"I should have told you about Selene's ghost."

"Water under the figurative bridge, my friend. I've moved on to bigger and better things." I waited in silence as he scratched his beard and drank some more. "What do you think about New Memphis?"

"It's a city," I said. "Nicer than some, worse than others. Why?"

"I think I might stick around once the queen's dead."

"I thought you were going to retire to some little village where the women would have no better options than a tired ex-raider, liar, and killer?"

"I'm keeping that plan in my back pocket," he said. "But to hear old Tiberius talk, the Resistance is looking at moving in once the Crimson Queen is gone."

"And?"

"And there's worse things than being a hero of the new regime. Women find out I was part of the crew that brought down their tyrant and they'll be throwing themselves at me. All I'll have to do is sit back and pick the right one to wife up."

"And who would that be? A saucy little blonde? A brunette with a head for business? A redhead with freckles and absurd proportions?"

His eyes went distant. "You know, I might need *three* wives. And speaking of which, do you think Elegy would take issues with me heading down to District 4 to sweet talk Aaniyah?"

Something told me the answer was an emphatic *yes*—brothers didn't tend to be crazy about their sisters stepping out with men like

Jules—but I shrugged. "I'd say it depends on how many wives you've already got at that point."

"Fair." He drained his glass. "Still, it *is* a nice city. Has its own grid. Interior plumbing in at least the bigger places. Hot water for the rich fuckers up top. When the Crimson Queen is dead, I think I'll stick around and play hero."

"You're assuming the Resistance wins the power struggle afterwards," I reminded him. "I have to imagine there will be a few leftover Powers with eyes on becoming kings or queens themselves."

"Yeah. We should probably make sure *they're* all dead too. It's hard to be a hero of the rebellion if the establishment maintains control."

"And that might prevent you from landing three wives."

"You got it."

"Just keep in mind that heroes don't always get to live to enjoy their fame. A live legend is a threat to the new order. A dead one is a story used to motivate and manipulate the masses."

"I think," he said, and the slight unsteadiness of the finger he raised told me his now-empty glass had held something a hell of a lot stronger than water, "that you might be a cynic."

"I've lived a long time, Jules. I've seen a lot of things. The post-Break world is a dark and mean place, and humans aren't exceptions to that rule; they *are* the rule."

"Definitely a cynic!" He walked over to the nearest table—not the one that had cards spread atop it and a gleeful Crow raking in her imaginary winnings—and carefully placed his glass down on it. When he returned, his eyes were bright. "I think you're right."

"About humans sucking?"

"No, about what happens to heroes. If I'm going to live to enjoy my just rewards in New Memphis, adored by all and loved by a select, beautiful few, there's only one solution."

"What's that?"

"You're going to have to stick around too."

"Excuse me?"

"*Oh, I hate that Jules*, a councilman will say. *He's just so charming and good-looking. We should kill him so the single women of our city remember we exist.*"

I shook my head, but there was no stopping him when he was on a roll. That was one of the few things that hadn't changed in the past few decades.

"*We can't!* a second councilman will say. *Even if the city* didn't *tear itself apart from grief over the loss of their bold, brave, dashing, handsome savior—*" He trailed off, blinked, and shook himself. "What was I saying again?"

"Something about the new council not being able to kill you."

"Right. Of course." He cleared his throat. *"Even if the people stood for it, you know the Queen of Smiles wouldn't. She'd ride right into our council meeting hall place on her demon motorcycle and swickety-swack, we'd all be dead."*

"Demon motorcycle? Swickety-swack?"

"And then they'll all go silent for a bit, acknowledging that truth as they remember the stories and the things they've seen. Finally, they'll shake their heads. *There are worse things than having a hero walking around. And eventually, he'll get old and die anyway. We just have to outlive him!*"

"The council sounds wildly clever."

"Little would they know," he continued, eyes gleaming, "that by the time I died of old age, my sons would be all grown up and carrying on their father's proud tradition."

"Was that straight vodka you were drinking?"

He blinked again, just one eye this time, and as deliberately as an owl. "I think it was gin."

"I'm going to have Marlena cut you off, for all of our sakes."

"You don't wanna stay in New Memphis?"

"So that I can keep you alive while you marry three women and raise a bunch of womanizing little clones of yourself?"

He grinned. "Exactly! You and I could visit each other's estates and talk shit about the other nobles."

"I'd say that's your dream, not mine."

"Well, at least *that's* progress."

I cocked my head at the non-sequitur. "What is?"

"You having dreams. Give a woman a dress and a bonnet and she starts getting all sorts of ideas."

"I will cut you into pieces so small that people will think they're threads," I warned him.

"Promises, promises." He wobbled on his feet, but his tone went serious. "All joking aside, maybe it's something to think about."

"Cutting you into pieces? Trust me, if you knew how often—"

"I mean you sticking around."

"Sorry, Jules. Once the queen dies, I'm gone. You'll have to deal with the new council yourself. That or join up with Aaniyah to overthrow them. King Jules the 1st, right up until the point someone flies by and drops a howler on your ass."

"I'd be a terrible king."

"Then make her queen. You can be the royal consort."

"Do consorts get mistresses?"

"On second thought, maybe you should forget about Aaniyah entirely. She'd kill you even faster than the council."

The card games petered out around midnight, although I'm not sure Evan ever caught on to Selene's ghostly tricks. Soon after that, people disappeared into their respective bedrooms, leaving me alone in the sitting room to keep an eye out for Selene. Some of the crew were drunk, some were tired, and some were just doing their best not to think about what was coming. After so many days and weeks and even months on the road, we were in New Memphis and only one district away from our ultimate destination. Terrorbirds and cultists and ooze creatures were behind us, but the assault on the palace remained. The palace, its queen, and however many Immortals she would have gathered about her.

Access wasn't the only thing I wanted from the Resistance. We needed information in the worst of ways. A map of the interior. Guard locations and schedules. Names and routes and everything else that would make our infiltration even possible. In a perfect world, the Resistance would just be able to smuggle us right into the queen's bedchamber, but if they'd had that kind of access, they wouldn't have needed to wait for us.

One night until Tiberius' Sunday party and the insurrectionists' meeting that it was being thrown to mask. If everything went well, we'd kill the queen on a Monday and be done by Tuesday.

Right in time for Selene's ghost to add another name to her list.

Drunk as he'd been, I don't think Jules had thought that far ahead. It's hard to be a hero of the Resistance when your crewmate has just murdered a blood relative of that same organization in cold blood.

ooo

The morning brought more of the same, if with significantly less alcohol. Tensions mounted as people woke, showered, and dressed in clothes that had been hand washed, dried, and returned to our room overnight. If you could ignore the bags under everyone's eyes, and the obvious hangovers Jules and Evan were suffering from, we looked almost respectable.

Tiberius himself stopped by just before lunch. He wore a three-piece suit, something I hadn't seen in years outside of the Free States, and his eyes sparkled. Even his beard was glossy and carefully combed.

"Friends! I hope you slept well! The festivities begin just after noon today in the main hall, but our little assembly will not occur until after night falls. Marlena will fetch you when it is time, and escort you there."

"Will they have the information we need?" asked Jules. "Your fellows on the Shadow Council, I mean."

"We shall have to see. My son is gathering what data he can, but he is yet the only one aware of your presence."

"Why's that?" asked Evan.

"Even whispers carry on the hill," said Tiberius. "By mutual agreement, Resistance business is discussed only during assemblies. We will address our usual concerns, you will be introduced, and plans will be formulated. It should be quite the unforgettable convocation!"

I traded glances with Jules. Information security was all well and good—and to be expected, given the Crimson Queen's overwhelming advantage in both military and Powers—but something told me the Shadow Council was operating on an entirely different schedule than we were.

"Our goal was to proceed as soon as possible," said Jules. "The longer we're here, the more likely we're discovered. If your queen pulls a runner—"

"Then it will be all the easier to depose her and return rule to the city's founding families," said Tiberius.

"That's your goal, not ours." The storm rumbled inside of me, as if to emphasize my words. "We're here to kill the Crimson Queen, not just scare her away."

"Well, of course you are! And to be quite frank, a dead queen suits us all far better than one in the wind, plotting her revenge. I promise you, on my name as a Becks, that tonight's assembly will not conclude without a plan of attack in place."

Since none of us had ever even heard of the Becks family two days prior, it wasn't quite the reassurance I think he intended it to be. Still, it clearly meant something to him, and that would have to do.

"I'd send over fresh clothing," Tiberius continued, "but it would take days for my tailor in District 4 to put together something suitable for each of you, and I think your impact will be all the greater in your present garb. You look," he added, with considerable satisfaction, "like exactly the sort of people we need."

From the looks on Jules and Cross' face, they weren't sure if they'd just been insulted or not. Evan was frowning, Selene was staring into space, and Two-Feathers… well, he was his usual stoic self, but I'd felt his gaze wander over in my direction more than once.

With a promise to send over freshly squeezed orange juice that would ruin all other juices for us, Tiberius departed again, leaving the six of us alone. Cross fished out his deck of cards, but this time, there were no takers.

The sight of those cards reminded me of something I had to do, but before I could speak, Evan was in front of me, Two-Feathers a step behind.

"We need to talk," he said.

"That seems to be the theme of the week," I told them both, borrowing Jules' line again as I waved to my bedroom. "Please, step into my office."

36

"What do you think of the Shadow Council?" Evan asked, almost as soon as the door closed behind us. He and Two-Feathers took their seats across from the still perfectly made bed.

"I haven't met them yet, and neither have you," I pointed out. "As for Tiberius, he seems competent enough, if prone to theatrics. Why?"

"Because I've been thinking."

"Are you sure that's a good idea, Evan?"

If looks could kill, the storm and I would be in pieces scattered across the city. "I've traveled for months with you to repay this one damn favor. The least you could do is use the name I've asked you to."

"What do you think it will change?"

"It will make me feel better."

I doubted that very much, but he was right; I'd pulled him out of his second life to repay this favor, and while he hadn't been much help so far, he also hadn't tried to run or shirk his duty.

"You're right, Miles."

A more gracious man would have appreciated my gesture. A more vindictive one would have taken pleasure in my capitulation. Evan just nodded.

"To hear Tiberius talk," he said, "the heads of the Resistance are all people like him. Members of the old oligarchy, rich and displeased that their authority has been stolen from them."

"And?"

"And I've been thinking about what happens to this city once the queen is gone. According to you, all of this, the hill and its districts, predated her reign, right? So, killing her might put a halt to the empire building, but the city's structures, political and physical, will remain the same. The rich literally on top, making decisions for those below."

I looked over to Two-Feathers, but the nomad's face gave me no clues as to what Evan was getting at.

"I ask again," I finally said. *"And?"*

"You heard Aaniyah the other day. That's not what the Resistance is fighting for."

"That's not what *she's* fighting for," I corrected. "The first lesson of any group larger than ours is that compromises are inevitable. According to Tiberius, it's the rich people who are bankrolling this would-be rebellion."

"So it's okay that they take over once the dying's done? Or do you think the queen's assassination will magically solve everything?"

"I think New Memphis has a better chance of not tearing itself apart than I'd originally expected, but yeah, there will be a power struggle as people and Powers try to fill the vacuum left by her death. So?"

"So, do you think people like Tiberius are going to wage that war? Or are they going to barricade themselves in their fancy mansions as the rest of the Resistance spends its blood for a freedom they won't get?"

"Freedom is an ideal, *Miles*, and like most ideals, it can't exist in its purest form. Someone like Aaniyah should know that already. Even the Free States aren't free."

"Maybe not, but at least the citizens have a voice."

I didn't think I'd ever hear Evan defend the nation he'd had to flee. I cast a second glance at the silent nomad seated next to him.

"So… what? You want this empire to become a democracy?"

"I just want to know we're leaving it better than we found it. That all of this will have been for something."

"The Crimson Queen is the engine that makes her empire run," I reminded him. "We're removing that threat from the board. Towns like yours won't have to worry about an army rolling up on them and wiping them out at a moment's notice."

"Until the next warlord."

"Until the next warlord," I acknowledged. "As for New Memphis and its people, or the Resistance and its leaders, that's not something I can decide. Ask the Shadow Council what their plans are. Maybe you can talk them into something better. Jules is planning on sticking around if he survives; maybe you should too."

"You and I both know a city is nowhere for someone like me."

I shrugged. "Once the queen is dead, you're a free man. As free as anyone is. Whatever you do will be up to you."

"And you don't care at all?"

"About what you do?"

"About the city and the empire you're consigning to anarchy! If the Shadow Council was going to listen to any of us, it'd be you. But you're just going to ride off and make everyone else clean up your mess!"

I knew the smile across my visor had gone flat and cold when Evan or Miles or Rupert or whatever he wanted to be called shrank back.

"I might have a face for politics," I told him, "But I don't have the patience, the will, or the desire."

He shook his head and left, a scowl painted across his face.

I turned on the nomad who had stayed behind. "Are you here to tell me what a shit job I'm doing too?"

He tapped his lips and cocked his head.

"Yeah, except you say more without speaking than other people do with all the words in both your clan's language and mine." I sighed and let the storm rumble its dissatisfaction. "This was just supposed to be a job. Kill those responsible for destroying Eclipse and move on. I don't understand why everyone's making it personal."

He raised an eyebrow and pointed at me. After months together on the road, translating that gesture was almost second nature.

"I made it personal first?" At his nod, I bit back a growl. I guess I had, even just by hiring myself for the job. "The difference is that when this job is over, I'm gone. They seem to want to immerse themselves in the city and all its problems."

He nodded again.

"And what about you? Has New Memphis cast its spell on you too? Gonna settle down and speak up for the working class or play the part of a hero?"

Two-Feathers looked at me for a long moment, something lurking in the depths of his black eyes. He tapped his broad chest, pointed at me, and then wiggled all the fingers on his hands in the same direction.

"You want to go with me? Even after the job?"

He didn't nod this time, but the look on his face was enough.

That look hit harder than any of Evan's moralizing, or Jules' drunken philosophy. Hit harder than anything but the deaths of the handful of people I'd held dear over the many decades.

"You might want to rethink that," I said, voice rough. "The jobs I've taken haven't always been ones you'd agree with. And even on the others… it's been the results that mattered. Whatever it took, whatever I needed to do. I'm not saying I'm proud of it, but I can't say I regretted it either. It just… is. Are you sure that's the sort of shit you want to wade through?"

He had the decency to give it some serious thought, and then the obnoxiousness to let that pondering stretch into multiple minutes. Finally, he held up a hand, fingers straight, and pantomimed pushing something to the side, opposite the direction he'd sent the finger versions of us a few minutes earlier.

"Put it behind us? I'm not sure that's possible either. I'm a monster of the Break, Two-Feathers, not some kind of hero."

This time, he shrugged, using only one shoulder because of the break in his other arm. He tapped his chest, eyes still fixed on the face I showed the world.

That was the sort of gesture that didn't need translation.

"When this is done," I said, all the metal gone from my voice, "you and I are going to find a room with a bed and a lack of nosy neighbors, and we're not coming back out until you're starving or that bed is in pieces on the floor."

For the first time in days, Two-Feathers smiled, his face going from stern to boyish in the blink of an eye.

ooo

"You and Two-Feathers make peace?" asked Jules several hours after their lunch had been cleared away. This time, I was happy to see, he *was* drinking water. Except for Selene, the whole crew seemed alert. The actual assault was still a day away, but we were ready to go.

"Why do you ask?"

"He's our second-best fighter, even with one arm. If I'm going to be a hero instead of a martyr, having the nomad on our side is kind of a big deal."

"Don't worry about Two-Feathers; just focus on yourself. Tonight's assembly has to go well. You and I both know time is running out."

He avoided looking at the Crow in our midst. "How do you want to play things with this Shadow Council?"

"We'll tell them what we need and when we need it and let them adjust their plans accordingly."

"The usual approach then. Blunt and bold."

"I'm not built for subtlety," I reminded him.

"That works for me." He grinned. "I should try giving this honesty stuff a bit of a test ride anyway. See how it feels."

"We'll see what your three wives think of that."

As late afternoon rolled around, Cross finally enticed the rest of the crew into another card game, with Selene and me being the two notable exceptions. As he started to deal though, I stepped forward.

"Can you afford to lose more imaginary money, Queenie?"

"I hear the second time's the charm, boss."

"Does that mean we're counting all those hands yesterday as only one?"

I ended their less-than-funny banter by dropping a short stack of gold coins on the table between them. They landed with a thunk as much a clink but got everyone's attention just the same.

"That's… a hell of an ante, Queenie."

"I'm not lining up to get cheated out of more fake money," I told him. "That's five coins. One for each of you who made it to New Memphis. As promised."

"I thought you'd left the gold back at the inn," said Cross, turning his coin back and forth as he watched how the light played off of it. "With the rest of our gear."

"I never knew you could carry items with you when you shifted," said Jules.

"There's a lot you don't know about me still."

I didn't look at Two-Feathers, who'd been carrying those coins since we'd left the inn. Sometimes, a little bit of mystery and mystique went a long way, even with people you'd known for half their lives.

"Why give it to us now?" asked Evan. "Not that I'm complaining, since I didn't honestly expect to ever be paid."

"It seemed like a good time for it."

"And the other two coins?" asked Cross.

"When the job is done."

"One cross, two cross," said Selene, gliding over to pick up her own coin. She made a show of slipping it into the bodice of her striped dress, teeth bared in a corpse's rictus. "Red cross, blue cross."

"Right." Cross shifted uncomfortably in his seat and looked away, slipping his coin into the pouch at his waist and picking up the discarded cards. "I'm not gonna complain about my sudden wealth either, but denominations this large aren't all that suitable for poker, and I'm already up bigtime in terms of chits. Let's put the gold away and deal, shall we?"

And with that, the four of them, not counting Selene or me, ignored the literal treasure I'd just given them and went back to playing each other for imaginary loot.

At a glance, I couldn't tell who was winning, but I'm pretty sure every damn one of them was cheating.

Even Two-Feathers.

○○○

Finally, it was time. We'd been able to hear the party for hours, even from the other side of the mansion, the card game slowly falling into disarray as people's attentions wandered, but when Marlena showed, it still took everyone by surprise.

"The meeting has begun," she said in the quiet but not at all meek way she had. "And Mr. Becks requests the honor of your presence. If you will follow me?"

"Should we leave our gear here or bring it with us?" asked Jules.

"These will be your rooms for the duration of your stay," came the reply. "Either I or one of the other servants will bring you back here when the meeting is done. We do ask," she added, "that any weapons are likewise left behind."

"We left our firearms back in District 4," said Jules, conveniently omitting the revolver holstered under his jacket, the snub-nosed handgun Cross had tucked into the bandages at his waistband, or even the two-shot pistol they'd given Evan, which was now hidden in the little man's boot. "So that won't be a problem at all."

"Fly away, fly away, fly away all," said Selene.

The rumors of eccentricity among the rich were clearly based in fact, because Marlena didn't even bat an eye at the Crow's non-sequitur. Instead, she gave a short bow, her first since being made our caretaker and escort, and led us back through the rest of the mansion. The route we took wasn't the one we'd followed on the previous day, winding instead towards the rear of the mansion, past living quarters smaller than the bedrooms we'd been assigned, with communal restrooms instead of dedicated en suites.

Servants' quarters, if I'd ever seen them. Marlena remained as unreadable as ever, but I could just about hear Evan's teeth grinding as we went. Maybe once he cracked the puzzle of implementing democracy in a city where the power structure was buttressed by literal walls, he'd turn his attention to fixing wealth inequality too.

Better him than me, on both counts.

Eventually, we left those quarters behind, skirting the edges of what Marlena informed us was one of three kitchens on the premises—all of them madhouses of activity due to the party—and took a stairwell down below ground level. It wasn't Tiberius' wine cellar—we'd have had to go out into the interior courtyard to reach that—but it had a similar feel to it, giving the impression of age and solemnity despite being far less than a century old.

We saw the first evidence of the Becks' house security at the base of those stairs, two men in uniform, each with a handgun at their side, and a shotgun in their hands. The uniforms looked absurd, almost as fancy as the mansion itself, but the men wearing them had the looks of hardened killers and their weapons were clean and ready for use.

I was already thinking of how we could put troops like that to use in our attack on the queen, and from the look on his face, Jules was too. They'd be next to useless against any of the physical Powers, of course, but a high-velocity bullet killed most ranged Powers as easily as it did Normals. A few dozen more men with rifles might turn the tide in battle if they were skilled enough.

The guards waved us through without any form of search, and my opinion of them dropped accordingly. Still, I'd settle for the distraction they would cause if Tiberius loaned them out for the assault.

We passed another pair of guards and then Marlena stopped outside a set of double doors, so tall that they almost scraped the basement's low ceiling. She tapped on the right-hand door, twice, a pause, and then twice again, and then stepped back and motioned us forward as the door began to open from within.

By mutual consent, we had decided I would enter first and do most of the talking. While Jules was better suited for the latter role, we were dealing with the wealthy and the powerful, and people like that tended to dismiss anyone they didn't consider an equal. I wasn't rich, but I was powerful, and if Tiberius' reaction upon seeing me had told us anything, it was that at least some of the Shadow Council would recognize me.

Fame was its own sort of equalizer. Infamy even more so.

I was also the only one of us who could take a bullet to the face and keep on walking, which may have played an equally sizable role in the decision to put me up front.

Unlike the rooms above, this chamber was lit by candles mounted along the wall. I wasn't sure if that was because the room had been built before the house was wired for electricity or if Tiberius just liked the ambiance when it came to secret meetings.

Knowing our host, it was honestly a bit of a coin flip.

The chamber was dominated by a table larger than any room in the servants' quarter above, wooden, and perfectly round. Eight people sat in chairs around that table, each with a collection of individuals standing behind them as if to lend moral support. Seated or standing, they were all looking our way. I scanned the room, noting the reactions on more than thirty different faces, those who seemed to recognize me from the stories, those who seemed clueless but welcoming, and those clearly irritated by our intrusion.

Tiberius's smile was incandescent as he rose from his chair, a chair that sat directly opposite the doors I'd come through. A round table was famous for being a table at which everyone sat as an equal but positioning yourself with the only direct view of the entrance was a way to say, rather loudly, that *some* of the Shadow Council were more equal than others.

"My friends and fellow conspirators, I told you when this meeting began that I had found the solution to our woes, and as you well know, I have always been a man of my word. I present to you the Queen of Smiles and her allies, angels sent to us by the great Almighty himself. It is tonight, with their arrival, that our resistance becomes a rebellion!"

Yeah, this was going to be awful.

37

"What are you talking about, you old fool?" demanded someone every bit as old as Tiberius himself, and twice as crusty. "When did these gatherings become social events to which strangers could be invited without so much as a by your leave?"

"He's right," said a woman with steel grey hair and a face that might cow even a howler into submission. "We are a council of equals here, Tiberius. We cannot function as we must if individual members disregard protocol and policy. Need I remind you that our lives and our names are on the line?"

From the sound of it, it was the second one that she was truly concerned over. I didn't know if that was because she was happy to give her life for the Resistance, or if she just had trouble imagining a scenario in which that life would ever truly be in danger.

"The milk is spilled," said another woman, voice flat. "And if you two have your way, it'll spoil too before anything is done. I, for one, have a fire waiting for me at home with a consort dying to show me just how attentive he can be. Let's hear what Tiberius has to say and why he thinks this mercenary will be of use." She turned to me. "With respect, of course. I'd heard you were dead. One more note in the Singer's song."

I shrugged but stayed silent. The Voidsinger was not someone to joke about.

"Thank you, Esmelda," said Tiberius. "And to the rest of you, I assure you that I both honor and obey our own protocols. This, however, was not an opportunity to be missed, and when you hear my story, you will understand why."

"Get on with it then!" The new speaker was half the age of anyone else at the table but made up for it by being twice as wide.

Tiberius' smile flickered.

"That was my intention, Thacker. If I may?"

He looked around the room, making eye contact with each of the other councilors as he waited for any objections.

"Very well then. Two nights ago, word came from one of the street-level cells under my ultimate authority. Strangers had been spotted in our city and a conflict had taken place between those strangers and the queen's guard, including one of her Immortals."

That got the attention of both the people in chairs and those standing behind.

"Which one?" asked Esmelda.

"A male Weather Witch," I replied, my first words since I'd entered the room. It was interesting to note who reacted to the metal in my voice and who did not, especially given that some of the latter included those I'd thought unfamiliar with me given their initial reactions. "He used fog to mask their presence and shot lightning from his hands."

"Sounds like Scandal," murmured another speaker.

"It does," agreed Esmelda, still looking at me. "What happened to him?"

"They had to wash what was left of him away with a bucket."

"So, the stories aren't entirely untrue."

"I'll let you be the judge when I'm done."

Her smile was barely more than a quirk of one corner of her lips, but we shared a moment of silent acknowledgment. This was a woman I could work with.

"You killed an Immortal?" asked the man Tiberius had called Thacker. "Wait… two nights ago? Was that in District 4? Christ, no wonder the place has been a madhouse since then. Getting my men in and out has been a nightmare!"

"Running low on bread again, are we?" asked the old man who had first challenged Tiberius. "I told your father to just bring that baker in house so you wouldn't spend your family money on trips back and forth."

"He tried," said Thacker. "Master Gamal 'prefers to stay in the district below.'"

"Gentlemen and ladies," said Tiberius, "as riveting as discussions of well-baked bread might be, perhaps we can table them until we have treated with our guests?"

"My point," said Thacker, "is that your *guests* have created an uproar, and some of us are already paying the price."

"What is a mercenary doing in New Memphis, and why have you brought her here, Tiberius?" The speaker who had named Scandal was dark-skinned and small within a heavy fur cape, slender hands practically dripping with rings.

Our host gritted his teeth, running one hand through his beard as if debating strangling his fellow councilors with it.

"Straight to the point then," he finally managed. "As you wish, Nero. The Queen of Smiles is perhaps the most famous mercenary in the land, and she and her allies have come here for one reason only." He couldn't help but pause, just a second, for dramatic effect. "To kill Delia Laine. They are here for the Crimson Queen."

And then everyone seated at the table and a few of those standing behind was talking at once, voices raised in a sudden bedlam that must have shaken the floors of the servants quartered above us.

I traded glances with an incredulous Jules. Was *this* what we had to work with?

Finally, the larger man, Thacker, hammered on the table with the flats of both palms, the noise loud and unexpected enough to cut through the chaos. As soon as a semblance of silence fell again, Esmelda turned to me.

"It can't be done. All of her food is tasted in advance and the only place she sleeps is impenetrable. As for direct action, we've already tried that. Even hired a Power like yourself to get the job done."

"Who?" I couldn't help but ask.

"Called himself Sidewinder," said Thacker.

I nodded, almost impressed. I'd heard of Sidewinder. He hadn't been operating anywhere near as long as me, of course, but he'd made quite the name for himself over the past few years. "What happened?"

"The same thing that happened with previous assassins. He died, she lived, and the agents who worked to get him into the palace had to be sent out of the city, so they didn't implicate any of us."

"From what we were able to gather," added Tiberius, "his special abilities allowed him to make it past the outer ring of guards, and even the queen's pet, but he died outside her inner sanctum."

"What sort of pet does a teenage megalomaniac monarch get?" asked Jules, speaking for the first time.

"Something that came from her master technician's table, perhaps." Esmelda was unable to repress a shiver. "We don't know if it was a Power they broke or something that they simply tamed, but when Delia gives audiences in the palace, you can sometimes hear it, moving about below ground."

My thoughts immediately turned to the ooze beast we'd faced in Tillatoba. If this was another of those, we were screwed. On the other hand… "The queen gives audiences? Could we use one of those to get my crew onto the palace grounds?"

"Only if you want to spend the winter. The Laine girl gives one audience a year, and it's on the first day of spring." Nero shook his head. "And what does it matter? She cannot be killed. The best we can do is to put political pressure upon her to wring out the concessions we desire."

"If we reach her, we can kill her," I said.

"What proof can you offer of that?"

"Her corpse, when we're done."

Nero scowled dismissively. "Meaning we again risk all on the word of an arrogant Power."

"Clearly, we will need to make certain we are insulated from any fallout, should she fail," said Tiberius, "but this may be our greatest chance. It is almost certainly our last. By next year, the southern campaign will have concluded. Who here truly believes that Delia will not take that opportunity to clean her own house before beginning the push west?"

That quieted the room, and our host permitted himself a thin smile before he continued.

"Cronus," he said to the man who had called him an old fool, "you still have contacts within the palace guard, do you not? Much will rely upon you."

"As ever," said Cronus, shaking his liver-spotted head. "The Laine girl seems to find and close holes in her security on an almost weekly basis, but if one of you can figure out a way to pull her guards' attention elsewhere, I might be able to create a window."

"As far as distractions go, we thankfully already have one scheduled," said Tiberius, his smile regaining its megawatt shine. "Operation Solidarity."

"Operation Solidarity? That was—"

"Our plan to stoke unrest and provoke the queen's men into the sort of violence that would swell the ranks of our street-level cells, yes," finished Esmelda. "But Tiberius is right. It will also keep Delia's eyes focused on the lower districts and give our mercenaries their opportunity."

Suddenly, we were *their* mercenaries.

"What *is* Operation Solidarity?" asked Jules.

"Riots," said Tiberius. "A public and populous uprising in Districts 4 and 5. The city guard will respond in force, and word of their assaults will only add to the growing furor felt towards the Laine girl's so-called monarchy."

"At the cost of how many of your people's lives?" asked Evan.

"It is true that there will be casualties." Our host took on a solemn tone. "The bravery of our freedom fighters, who understand these risks yet battle on anyway, is something we shall never forget."

Meaning nobody in this room was going near the riots.

"Operation Solidarity is scheduled for noon tomorrow, you fool," said Cronus, saliva spraying with every word. "How am I supposed to produce the impossible in a matter of hours?"

"We have faith, as always, in your oft-proclaimed brilliance," said Thacker. "Though I would suggest you forgo the typical post-assembly cocktails tonight."

"Mordecai will assist you," said Tiberius, nodding to the middle-aged man who stood at his right shoulder. "As a sitting member of the Laine girl's sham council, he may be able to help."

Behind me, Selene was as still as a picture, but I could almost feel the energy vibrating off of her. The younger Beck was a less polished version of his father, with a full head of dark hair to go with his trim beard and wild eyebrows.

"Yes, yes," said Cronus. "That would be helpful indeed." With a creaking of bones that put Evan *and* Jules to shame, the old fossil leveraged himself to his feet, leaning heavily on one of his aides. "If there is nothing more, we should get started. Miracles do not make themselves, after all."

"Hold a moment, Cronus," said a woman who had stayed quiet until that point. Unlike the other two ladies at the table, her hair was still more auburn than grey. "If we truly believe this desperate ploy will succeed, there are longstanding questions that must be resolved now. First and foremost, the nature and composition of the government that we shall implement once the Crimson Queen is no more."

"Surely such matters can wait until victory is assured?"

"No, Mirielle is right," said Nero. "We must be ready to act immediately upon Delia Laine's death or someone else will attempt to fill that vacuum. However, I'm sure we will be able to come to an accord in your absence—"

Cronus made just as much noise sitting down as he had standing up. "I think not."

As far as I could tell, everyone but Nero agreed that the right thing to do was to reform the old ruling council, bringing in select members from the queen's sham council to fill the spots of the men and women she had executed. Where opinions differed was on who should lead that council and which new members should be issued invitations. Meanwhile, Nero wanted representation from the lower districts with sufficient voting powers to be more than just lip service to the masses.

Needless to say, his suggestion went over poorly.

I tuned out the continued demonstration that ninety percent of politics was driven by greed and a desire for power. Jules' aspirations to hero status notwithstanding, we were here to kill a woman. All the rest of this was irrelevant. Behind me, my senses informed that Selene was abiding by our agreement, still and quiet despite the appearance of the man she'd come to murder. Evan was muttering something under his breath next to her, no doubt significantly more irritated by the Shadow Council's evident selfishness than I was, and Cross was leaning against the rear wall, while Two-Feathers had adopted his usual position by the door. Though why the nomad felt the need to guard it when Tiberius had four men standing watch just outside those doors—

Wait. Hadn't there been *two* of them when we first entered, with the other two waiting down the hall?

"It appears I was overly optimistic in thinking that we could get anything decided today," said Mirielle, the woman who had stopped Cronus from leaving. "It's a pity. I was hoping for one last moment of positivity to remember you by."

Two-Feathers dove to one side, broken arm and all, as the door behind him exploded inward, shrapnel blasting Selene and Evan off their feet, and sending Jules stumbling forward. Through the now-open doorway came four men. Three wore fatigues with the Crimson Queen's badge and had assault rifles in their hands, already blazing. The fourth was covered in a thick layer of ice from head to toe and firing spikes as long as his forearm directly out of his chest. At the same time, one of the aides standing behind Mirielle took the glass the woman handed him, shattered it with a punch, and sent a fragment flying into the throat of the councilor seated across the table. Her other two aides pulled out guns they weren't supposed to be carrying.

A Stalwart, some strange variant of a Hydromancer, and at least five armed men, all with the element of surprise. It wasn't a battle; it was a massacre.

Mordecai dropped to the floor, using the table as a shield, but his father died in his chair, genial smile just starting to slip when the bullets hit. One of Esmelda's aides tackled the older woman to the floor, using his own body as a shield, but the spikes sprouting from his back made it clear he wouldn't be getting back up.

I didn't have time to check on my crew. My shell was falling away and the storm was howling forth, swarming past the bullets that sang like tiny meteors and shredding the ice that came its way. This ambush, this execution, must have been arranged ahead of time, which meant neither Mirielle nor the forces dispatched had known I would be present.

And that was a mistake.

Half the so-called Shadow Council was already dead, and the rest would be joining them soon. That made escape our priority. The storm surged toward the door, clearing a path straight through the rifle-wielding Normals.

The Hydromancer proved a tougher foe, frost gathering on the storm's thousand blades, even as ice chipped and fell away. The cold couldn't harm me, but the longer we were stuck inside that chamber, the greater the risk of both reinforcements and a stray bullet dropping one of my crew.

Speed mattered.

The metal howl of the storm increased as its circle tightened, revolutions accelerating. Two handguns joined the chorus, and more ice crumbled under the onslaught, but I could sense the last few bodies hitting the floor behind us and knew the enemy Stalwart would be turning on us in a matter of moments.

Thankfully, our Stalwart acted first. A chair, now soaked in blood and fluids, crashed into the Hydromancer, knocking the Power to the side. More importantly, that was the blow that finally disrupted the other man's concentration. When the storm surged in, it found flesh instead of an ever-regenerating barrier of ice.

The unnamed Power fell. Another dead Immortal for the Crimson Queen. I reformed my shell, staggered as the Stalwart behind us put a dozen glass shards through my back, and held my ground, an inhuman shield as the rest of the crew stumbled through the door ahead of me.

More gunfire came from the hallway, but Jules and the others were going to have to survive for a moment on their own, because I had a Power to deal with, as well as the woman who'd smuggled him in.

Stalwarts weren't as tough as Titans or as fast as Speedsters, but they were universally considered some of the most difficult Powers to fight, the perfect blend of competence and capability. A good Stalwart was never out of rhythm, never caught off guard, and always able to use the battlefield to their advantage.

But to the storm?

They were just meat. Slightly faster, slightly stronger, slightly more annoying, but still… human-shaped meat waiting to be rendered into bits and pieces.

Not that I'd ever tell Two-Feathers that.

The hardest part was catching them, so I forced the glass-throwing Stalwart's hand by going after Mirielle instead. A smart man would have given her up for dead and gone after my own vulnerable charges, but the brain is the one muscle Stalwarts don't have automatically augmented; he cut me off in mid-charge, arms and legs flailing through what was probably a centuries-old, highly respected martial art.

He learned just how well that worked with the storm.

With her Stalwart gone, Mirielle herself was almost an afterthought. I reformed my shell in the wreckage of the Shadow Council's secret meeting place, surprised to find a few occupants still alive. All of them were aides, admittedly—Mirielle was the only councilor who had even made it out of her chair—but still, I was impressed.

One of the lucky few was Tiberius' son, Mordecai, but I'd worry about that whole situation later. There was a gunfight going on out in the hall, and now that we didn't have to worry about a Stalwart crawling up our collective asses, the crew needed my help.

I found Jules taking cover behind a pile of bodies, firing blindly with a gun he'd taken off one of my kills. Huddled behind him, Evan was a bloody mess, but I was pretty sure his wounds had all come from the exploding door, and nothing seemed life-threatening. Across the way and crouched behind his own barricade of bodies, Two-Feathers had taken out a half-dozen enemies, three with thrown knifes, the others with whatever projectiles he could find, and Cross was on his belly, crawling in the opposite direction down the hallway as he looked for a way out that we could survive taking.

I put my helmet next to Jules' face before he realized I was there, and for a moment, I thought the shock would kill him in a way a hundred flying bullets hadn't.

"Are they all Normals?"

"Yeah, but they're outside my range, and there's a shit ton of them. I'd almost rather be fighting cultists."

"And demons?"

"You had to bring up the demons, didn't you? How do you feel about killing these assholes?"

I was pretty sure his question was rhetorical. Even if it wasn't, I wasn't going to wait around for the arrival of Powers who *could* hurt me.

I kept my shell as I stepped past Jules and his macabre barricade, ignoring the bullets that tore through me like fireflies. It hurt—it always hurt—but the storm was too often indiscriminate, and that meant putting space between me and my crew. A half-dozen steps answered by twice as many bullets, spreading blood and pieces of my shell across the corridor. Then, there wasn't enough left to control the storm; metal and shrapnel, barbed wire and railway spikes pouring down the hallway like an avalanche of murder.

There were a dozen soldiers blocking the hallway. It seemed like overkill for the Shadow Council and severe underkill for our crew. The last man broke and ran, making it to the stairs before a shot from Jules slipped right through the storm to take him low in the back.

I reformed my shell and gave Jules a look.

"Please," he said, rolling his eyes. "How many times have you ignored gunshots on this trip alone? I figured I might as well start taking advantage of it."

From up the stairs, we heard more screams, but there were fewer of them than I'd expected. In all likelihood, the Crimson Queen's death squad had come right through the front door and the smarter partygoers had taken that as their cue to leave.

For the moment, things were almost peaceful, but I knew they wouldn't stay that way. We hurried up the stairs, Two-Feathers supporting Evan with his functioning arm. The nomad, too, was bleeding from fresh wounds, but his face was a mask, hiding the pain.

"Thoughts?" I asked.

"We're fucked," said Jules.

"*Helpful* thoughts?"

"Get out of here before the rest of the queen's Immortals show up," said Cross. "Did any of you see a back door?"

"There's a servant's entrance a few halls away to the left," said a new voice. Mordecai and the other survivors had followed us down the hall and up the stairs. The younger Becks was pale, his pupils enormous, and his hands shook as he spoke, but he was still keeping things together enough to be useful.

"Lead the way," I told him.

He nodded, took one step, and then staggered to the side, slumping against the wall and grasping at his neck. Blood slipped through shaking fingers in a trickle, then a river as those hands fell away, exposing the clean cut that bloomed into a gaping void in his throat.

Two feet away, Selene licked the blood from her knife and purred.

That was enough to break the survivors who'd come with us, individuals scattering in every direction, one woman even going back down the stairs at death-defying speeds. A short, strangled cry, and then a series of loud thumps made her fate clear.

Jules had his stolen gun out and pointed at the Crow in our midst, although I was pretty sure he was out of ammo.

"We had a deal," I told the ghost living behind Selene's eyes.

"My task is done," she said simply, taking small, mincing steps backwards as she widened the space between us. "Your job is too, even if you don't see it yet. My advice is that you divest yourself of these attachments if you wish to survive." She let Selene's eyes trail across the rest of our crew, making it clear what attachments she was referring to.

"I don't know why you think I'd listen to you after this," I said, the storm filling my voice, "let alone why I'd let you and your host body walk out of here."

"The balding one is out of bullets, your would-be lover is supporting his useless friend, and you… you are powerful but far from swift. Also," she added, a smile twisting Selene's lips into strange shapes, "more of your enemies are on their way."

"She's right," said Cross. "We need to get out of here."

"I'll see you around," I promised Selene's ghost.

For a moment, her eyes went dark and empty again, like freshly dug graves. "No, smiling one, you will not."

And then Selene took off down the hall, headed away from the direction Mordecai had indicated.

"We have to go, Queenie," said Jules, moving in to take Evan from a flagging Two-Feathers.

I watched the other woman's skirts disappear around the corner and nodded. "I'll take Evan. You help Two-Feathers. Cross, lead the way. Find this back door Tiberius' son was talking about."

We hobbled down the darkened corridor, five now instead of six and more than half of us injured. We were stuck in an unfamiliar district that would soon be crawling with the queen's men. Worse, my hopes that the Resistance would get us into the palace were now as dead as the Shadow Council itself.

I was not having a good day.

38

The good news was that Cross found the exit before the next wave of attackers could find us. The better news was that Jules' number two even had an idea for where we could go to lie low and regroup, courtesy of his brief incarceration and the loose lips of his jailers back in District 4.

"The queen had one of her new councilors put to death a few weeks ago," he said. "His belongings were seized, and his servants and family were sold into slavery, but the estate itself should still be standing. My guards were placing bets on who would be plucked from District 3 to occupy it."

"You think you can find a way there in the dark?"

"That part's easy." Cross paused in the middle of the empty street, a block over from Tiberius' former house, and looked about him. "It's supposed to be near the Becks manor, and it'll be the only place that *doesn't* have its lights on."

Sure enough, we could see a half-dozen estates from our vantage point, each large enough to be called a palace in its own right, and only one of them was unlit. I carried Evan in my arms like a child as I followed the others down the road. My leathers blended into the darkness like magic, but there was nothing I could do to travel in silence.

Jules looked over his shoulder at me, and I halfway expected him to make a joke about getting me new clothes before we assaulted the palace. Instead, his expression said the time for jokes was behind us, and any thoughts of pressing forward with this job might be too.

We were going to have ourselves an argument once we made it to safety. I wasn't turning away when we were this close, and I couldn't kill the Crimson Queen without him.

We hopped the fence to our hideaway house, Two-Feathers managing it one-handed despite his growing list of injuries. I passed Evan up to Jules, dropped over into grass cut short for the winter, and took the little man back. Finally, Cross led us past the estate's darkened front door to a carriage house, built just to the side and almost invisible behind the larger building. The carriage house's door was locked, but Cross found the hidden key in a matter of seconds, and shortly after that, we were making our way into the darkened interior.

"With luck, we can hide out here until things die down," he said. "You all bunk down. I'll try to find some candles or something that will light our way without telling the whole world we're here."

He disappeared into the black, and I eased Evan down onto to the wooden floor. Someone took a seat next to me, and from the noise they made, I knew it was Jules. I could practically feel him brooding from several feet away.

"An asshole, a horse thief, and a serial killer Crow," I told him. "Not sure I think too highly of the crews you put together, but at least Cross is a keeper."

"Yeah." He was silent for a moment. "He sure got us in here quickly, didn't he? I'd have broken down the door before I even thought to look for keys. And that's only if I'd seen the carriage house at all."

Something about what he was saying triggered thoughts of my own. "How did he know about the Becks family anyway?"

"Tiberius introduced himself," he reminded me. "The old man couldn't pass up the opportunity to mention his name."

"Sure," I agreed, "but that was after we rescued Cross."

"So?"

"So why would the name stick out enough for him to remember from a random conversation he'd heard previously? Especially given that he'd been tortured?" I raised my voice. "Any answers for us there, Cross, or should we ask the people who just came in with you?"

"What people—" began Jules.

"I'm sorry to admit it, boss," said his second-in-command, from somewhere to the right, "but they aren't friends."

There was a click and light blossomed around us, illuminating the carriage house and its many stalls, as well as a loft at the far end of the building, the high rafters above us, and oh yes, the twenty or so men and women in the Crimson Queen's colors with guns drawn.

"I think it's time you surrender," said the woman in front, a button-nose brunette who'd paired a beret with her uniform, like she was some kind of pre-Break fashionista.

"I'd do what she says," said Cross. "They only want you, *Queenie*. That was the deal I made back when they took me prisoner. We give you over and everyone else walks free. Even the nomad."

"You turned traitor, Cross? You?"

"They made me at the district gate, boss. Turns out they got some pretty good likenesses of us from the prisoners we freed in Tillatoba." He spared Evan a half-hearted glare. "Guess I shouldn't have hoped that convoy would chase them down after all. Someone wired the descriptions back the day after we made it into the city. We were fucked from the start; survival's the only play."

"And then you sold out Tiberius and the others," said Jules in a voice as hollow as a bird's broken wings. "Burned both the Resistance and us in the same fucking play."

"I had nothing to do with the old man; I guess they already had that other councilor on the inside. Wish someone had bothered to tell *me* an attack was coming, though," he added, giving the woman in the beret a hard look that she ignored.

"We didn't even know you or your *crew* were in District 2 until you activated the beacon a few minutes ago, Mr. Cross. You were supposed to signal us more than a day ago, and I can promise you that my colleagues still waiting in Districts 3 and 4 will be deeply irritated to hear you somehow slipped right past them instead."

"This was the first chance I—" began Cross.

"Regardless, the rebellion has been neutralized and I'm about to net a significant bonus for bringing in a walking thorn in the queen's side." She waved an idle hand in my direction. "All it cost us was two Immortals, and it's not like anyone even liked Shard or River's Child. Not a bad night, all things considered."

"Then we're square," said Cross. "I delivered her to you; the rest of us will be on our way."

I gave him a look. "Cross, how many people have you seen me kill over the past few months? People armed with guns, knives, claws, and even tentacles. Full credit for hiding how much of an asshole you were all this time, but how are a woman in a fancy hat and two dozen soldiers with machine guns going to do what nobody else has managed?"

"Queenie," murmured Jules, "something's wrong with my power."

Either sound carried in the carriage house, or the woman in the beret read lips, because she smiled and nodded. "Welcome to temporary life as Normals, all of you. No weapons, no powers, no hope."

It was like all the oxygen had been sucked out of the room.

"You're a Null."

"The only one in the empire," she agreed. "Permanently stationed here on the hill, if not in the palace, and able to bring you to heel without even lifting a finger."

Of all the Powers classified by the Free States eggheads, Crows were widely regarded as the worst, given their propensity to go crazy and murder people. As Selene had just demonstrated for all of us. They were *also* supposed to be the rarest, although recent experience suggested those numbers might be skewed. Second rarest were Healers, but just after them were the people known as Switches, individuals who interacted with the gifts of the Powers around them. One group, Amplifiers, could turn another Power's gifts way, way up, whereas Nulls… well, they did just the opposite. And given that Jules couldn't use his power and the building around us was still in one piece, something told me this Null was a powerful one.

"Now then," she said, "you have a date with a *real* queen and the rest of your men have a slightly *less* happy appointment."

"You promised safe passage," protested Cross. "I held up my end of the deal, now it's time you hold up yours. An armed escort out of town and a wagon with horses and our possessions from the Queen's Jewel. You owe—"

A gunshot interrupted Cross' speech, followed swiftly by a second. A part of me waited for our traitor to crumple to the floor, but he remained standing and whole. As a group, we turned to the source of those gunshots, an old man still sprawled on the floor, smoke rising from the two-shot derringer he'd fished from his boot.

Twenty feet away, a soldier collapsed with a groan, blood spreading from a hole in his stomach, but Evan's intended target just arched an overly plucked eyebrow.

"So, one of you *did* still have ammunition." The Null sent a saccharine sweet smile in Evan's direction. "A little bit of advice, old timer? Next time, give the weapon to someone familiar with firearms. Maybe they'll wait until I'm in range to shoot it." She straightened her beret, that smile going ugly. "What am I saying? There won't *be* a next time."

"You've got that much right." I stepped forward to place myself between the soldiers and my crew, the storm filling my voice.

"Was that supposed to be threatening? I hear you're reasonably strong, even in this form, but it's the other version of you that makes grown men quake in their boots. That's the problem with Shifters. Take away their transformations and they're just overly aggressive halfwits with delusions of grandeur. Powers are all that way, really."

"You're not wrong about that." I shrugged. "But you're operating under two misconceptions, and I guarantee the second will kill you."

"And those are?"

"First, I'm not a Shifter."

I watched her smile wobble, just a bit, and hit her with the real kicker.

"And second, I'm not a Power."

My shell fell away and the storm came out to play.

ooo

The thing about Switches is that they don't have any real power of their own. If Evan's shots had been on target, his bullets would have done for the queen's Null just as easily as the Normal he *had* hit. And against the storm...

One of the queen's secret weapons, one of the continent's rarest Powers, died with little more than a gasp and a gurgle.

The other thing about Switches is that their powers tend to function in one of two ways. Either they have to touch the target they're affecting—which is fine for Amplifiers and a little bit less fine for Nulls—or they emit a field that affects everyone around them.

Our Null had been of the second variety, which was why both Evan and Jules had been unable to access their powers and why Two-Feathers hadn't tried one of his crazy maneuvers. It was also probably why she hadn't come to the Badlands as part of the Crimson Queen's recruitment and assassination party. It's hard to fly someone who cancels out your flight powers, and I doubted the queen enjoyed sharing space with someone who could make even her vulnerable.

On the hill, if not in the palace, as the Null had said.

It also meant none of the soldiers she'd brought with her were Powers. Even with numbers and guns on their side, that made the carriage house a bad place to be. The ground shook with the mildest of tremors. *Too* mild because apparently even death wasn't enough to motivate the man who insisted I call him Miles. Still, it was enough to send the soldiers around us stumbling back, their initial salvo wildly off-target.

By the time they had recovered, four of them were collapsing to the floor, clawing at their own throats as if trying to dig a passageway for air that refused to enter their lungs. Two-Feathers had crossed the killing space in three loping strides, put his fist through the skull of one soldier, broken the neck of a second, and taken the gun from a third, spraying the flanks of what had once been a careful perimeter. Behind me, I could sense the rest of our crew, even Cross, diving for cover.

The storm, on the other hand, was right where it wanted to be.

It wasn't quiet and it wasn't quick, but between the three of us, not a one of our attackers made it out alive.

I reformed my shell, kicked a body aside, and joined the others. Thanks to the storm and the man who made me, I was unscathed. Thanks to the cover they'd found, Jules, Evan, and Cross were too. Or at least they hadn't taken any *more* damage during the firefight. Two-Feathers, on the other hand…

This time, it was Evan, still a mess from the door shrapnel in Tiberius' secret lair, who was tending to the nomad. Stalwarts were tougher than Normals or even most other Powers, but there were limits, and with only one functional arm, Two-Feathers was already well off his game. One narrowly dodged bullet had torn through his deerskin tunic and burned a bloody line across his chest. A seeping hole in the nomad's leg bore mute witness to a bullet he *hadn't* dodged and bruising across the other side of his torso suggested he'd taken a rifle butt to the ribs. If he was lucky, they wouldn't be broken, but luck seemed to be something that had abandoned us somewhere on the outskirts of New Memphis.

Thankfully, he was breathing okay, and that meant he probably hadn't punctured a lung. Nothing else looked life-threatening either, not even the bullet wound in his leg, which would have been pumping blood like a geyser if an artery had been hit. I can't say that made me feel much better though, looking down on his battered body and comparing it to the man who'd waited in silence with me on the outskirts of his clan territory. I still didn't know what had caused him to join me, all those months ago—whether he had been sent by his Elders or just decided to go on walkabout—but it felt like every blow and bullet the storm helped me avoid had transferred to him, like karmic osmosis or a parting *fuck you* from the man who'd been my creator and dad.

Evan didn't even look at me as I approached; he just tore another scrap of cloth and applied pressure with it to the next of Two-

Feathers' wounds. Nobody gave a guilt trip like an old man tending to his friend, especially when that old man was himself still bleeding.

Several feet away, a very different tableau was taking place between the last two members of our crew. Cross stood on his toes, flapping his arms about as he tried to maintain balance, and Jules was in front of him, one hand outstretched. On my old friend's face was an expression I hadn't seen since before Texas, since back when he was a twenty-year-old killing his way through anyone dumb enough to look at him sideways.

I didn't know if this was the first time Cross had seen the killer buried underneath the weight of all those years, pounds, and miles, but I was pretty sure it would be the last.

"Why?" asked Jules, in a voice empty of emotion.

"They knew everything, boss. Knew we were coming. Knew about the Resistance before we did." Cross swallowed, forcing his words past a noose I couldn't see. "You can't fight people like that. You run or you die. So yeah, I cut a deal. A deal that would save us both. Didn't think we'd even make it up here when they had so many traps set in the district below."

"And Queenie?"

"Fuck her! What has that freak brought us except death?"

"We'd have been food for Shabaa if she hadn't shown up."

"Tom and Havoc are corpses, Selene's in the wind, and you're a breath away from killing the man who watched your back for seven fucking years, boss! You think *this* is better? She saved our lives just so she could spend them when and where she wanted!"

"Maybe so," said Jules. "But the one thing she's never done is turn traitor."

He closed his outstretched hand, fingers tightening into a fist, and watched the other man's eyes bulge and his limbs kick. There were no final words because Cross didn't have the air to speak them. Within seconds, the other man became a dead weight far beyond Jules' ability to lift, and seconds after that, he was just another body on the floor.

Jules patted down his friend's corpse and turned to me, eyes cold slivers of jade. "We need to get out of here. Now."

He wasn't telling me anything I didn't already know. The Null's presence would have kept other Immortals away, but as soon as the queen's men realized what had happened, there would be hunters in the street. The problem was, this was *their* territory, not ours, and the only person who'd known his way around at all had been the one who'd led us straight into this ambush.

"We can't run far," I said. "We need a place to hole up and make a new plan."

"I'm done with plans, Queenie. We lost. I just want us to get out of this alive." He looked around him. "The few of us who are left."

"Either way, we're not going far like this. I doubt Two-Feathers can even walk and Miles isn't much better."

"We can't stay here. They're going to be all over this estate like maggots on a corpse."

I nodded, poking my head back out of the carriage house onto grounds that, for the moment, remained still and dark. Around us were more dwelling places for New Memphis' rich, but as Cross had pointed out, each was well lit and clearly occupied. Breaking into any of them would just bring the queen's men down on us even faster.

With one possible exception.

"Back to Tiberius' house."

"We just came from there!" said Evan. "Everyone's dead!"

"Exactly. It's the one place they know we're not. So, we sneak back in, find our way to the wine cellar, and hang out in the tunnels beneath the district. Rest up, recover, and figure out what's next."

Jules shrugged. "It's not like I have a better idea."

ooo

"Before the Break," I murmured to the man in my arms, bleeding all over the leather of my riding jacket and pants, "it would have been you carrying me over the threshold."

Two-Feathers said nothing, as usual, but as we slipped down the stairs of the Becks family wine cellar, a spark of humor joined the clouds of pain in his jet-black eyes.

It had taken us almost fifteen minutes to work our way back to Tiberius' estate, dodging the initial patrols that flooded the streets by crossing through carefully manicured yards and gardens with shrubs trimmed into animal shapes and people. We would never have made it in daylight, and even with the night's aid, we'd have found ourselves stymied trying to get back *into* the estate, if it weren't for one person.

Marlena hadn't fled the mansion with the partygoers when the gunfire started but had done her best to organize the remaining servants, keeping them safe and out of the way. With the entire Becks family dead, she hadn't known what to do but hunker down and wait for daylight. Our return had been unexpected, but she'd let us in anyway and even led us through the building's maze of hallways to the interior courtyard and wine cellar.

Of all the rooms we'd seen in our return to the estate, that cellar was the only one that seemed unaffected by the night's chaos. In the light of Marlena's glowtorch knockoff, the barrels stood in mute witness to our arrival. The Becks family was dead, but their wine would apparently live on.

We didn't stop there, of course. I carried Two-Feathers through the passageway beyond the barrels, around the fake rockfall that hid Tiberius' private exit, and into the tunnel that lay beyond. And then, for good measure, all the way down to the next intersection and to the right. There was no point making it obvious we were there, after all.

Once we had found a spot to camp, I lowered my nomad to the ground. Jules did the same with Evan, working to make the other man comfortable despite our lack of supplies.

That lack, at least, was something I could address. Most of our gear was down in District 4, and given Cross' betrayal, had likely already been seized by the Crimson Queen's men, but the rest of it was just one wing away.

I turned to Marlena, who had followed us down with her glowtorch. "Can you collect our gear from the room we left it in?"

"Will you use it to kill the Crimson Queen's men?" Her eyes were rimmed with red, but that was the only concession she'd made to the night's tragedy; not a hair was out of place and her all-black uniform looked like it had just been laundered.

"You'd better believe it."

"Then I will make sure it arrives." Her mask cracked, exposing the raw grief that lurked beneath, but it was only for a moment. Then, she marched off, the very model of smooth efficiency.

I hadn't lied to her. Not really. I didn't know what our next step was, what it even could be, but Delia wasn't going to give up, and that meant we'd be killing more of her people, sooner or later.

Despite a tunnel floor so rough it made camping in the dirt luxurious by comparison, Evan was out even before Marlena disappeared around the corner. Two-Feathers wasn't far behind him, fading in and out of consciousness now as the adrenaline fled his body. Both men were bruised and bloody, but I was pretty sure Evan would be mobile again in the morning.

Two-Feathers… well, even if he was, there wasn't anything he could do to help us. His powers were all physical, and every injury he'd suffered between the Mississippi and this dank tunnel under New Memphis had reduced the effectiveness of those powers. A Stalwart who could barely walk was hardly an asset, let alone a real threat.

Jules and I waited for Marlena, our backs against the wall both literally and figuratively. He didn't say a word, just breathed, in and out. Before Marlena had left, taking the glowtorch with her, I'd watched the anger fade from his eyes, leaving behind the thousand-yard stare I'd seen from hundreds of survivors over the decades.

"Would you rather I hadn't gone to Texas?"

He stirred, maybe running a hand across his face, and sighed. "Like I told Cross, we'd have been dead soon enough without you. Can't say the past few months have been easy or fun, but I'm still breathing. Maybe he would be too even if he hadn't turned coat."

"Did you find the beacon the Null was talking about?"

"Looked like more ripped-off Legion tech." He shrugged. "I left it with his body. Maybe his ghost will choke on it."

"If they gave it to him back in District 4, why do you think he waited to use it until now?"

"Cross never folded a hand if he didn't have to. Asshole was probably waiting to see how things played out with Tiberius. When that went bad, I'm guessing he decided the Crimson Queen was a better bet." I heard another shrug. "Turns out he'd have been smarter to just run, like we're going to."

"What if I can get us into the palace instead? Tomorrow? You and me. A sprint to the finish."

"Queenie—"

"Two-Feathers will be a liability with his injuries," I said, not hiding the metal in my voice. "But we're about as close to one hundred percent as people can get this late in the game. I kill everything between us and Delia Laine, and you put an end to her reign. You and me. We were *always* the core of this job."

"And Miles?"

I looked over at where my senses told me the man was sleeping, curled up in a ball on his side, and no doubt looking every one of his fifty-six years. “I brought him as insurance.”

“And now?”

“Payment is due.”

39

I hadn't convinced Jules by the time Marlena returned. She and a man she introduced as her husband came down the tunnel, staggering under the weight of their burdens. Not just the glowtorch and the weapons and equipment I'd asked for, but also bandages and medicine… needles, thread, and alcohol to kill any risk of infection.

Five minutes later, I held Two-Feathers down as her husband cleaned his wounds, doing my best to keep the unconscious nomad from lashing out and killing the man working to keep him alive. After the alcohol came the stitches, and if the needlework lacked a doctor's precision, we weren't in any position to complain. Then, pads atop each stitched wound, and a bandage around the leg or arm or chest to keep those pads tight.

Two-Feathers was a mess, but he wasn't dying on my watch.

By the time the husband was done treating Two-Feathers, Marlena and Jules had pulled the last splinters from Evan's back and legs. The whole cycle repeated itself, the old Power screaming into Jules' hand as alcohol flushed smaller fragments from his lacerations, then lapsing back into unconsciousness as the few wounds big enough to warrant stitches were treated. Finally, it was on to Jules, though none of his scrapes required more than a quick swipe of alcohol and a bandage.

Marlena's husband turned to me, but I shook my head. "I'm good. You two should be going before anyone starts to wonder where you are. I don't know how familiar you are with these tunnels, but they stretch down at least to District 4. You can make your escape."

"Only Tiberius knew the route," said Marlena. "Even Mordecai once got lost down here for almost a day as a young man. No," she decided, resting one hand on her husband's bloody arm, "our home is above. I was born on those grounds. I met and married my husband there. Whatever comes, we will face it together with those we think of as family."

Her husband still hadn't spoken—as silent as Two-Feathers on his best day—but he nodded and patted her hand in agreement.

"Tiberius was a great man," she added, "if not always a good one. Make sure she burns for his death."

I didn't need to ask who *she* was, and Marlena didn't bother to elaborate. She just stared up at the smiley face spread across my visor, holding my unseen gaze. Then, she and her husband headed back to the wine cellar, taking the light with them.

"Jules—"

"I'm going to sleep, Queenie. I'm sure you'll try again tomorrow, but I promise the answer's going to be the same. It's *suicide.* Even if you could somehow get us past the wall and into the palace, we'd be dead before we ever found the Crimson Queen. At least *I* would be. You'd just keep on doing that thing you do."

He rolled over and gave me his back, using his recovered pack as a pillow. Soon, his snores joined Evan's.

I sat in the darkness and wondered what the day would bring.

Down in the tunnels, time was more a matter of perception than science. The trickling of water somewhere in the distance. The snores of two of the three men sleeping by my feet. The air thick with odors I was glad I couldn't smell, and all around us, the earth itself.

I'd never been inside a womb, but if it was anything like this, it was no wonder so many humans emerged into our world already half-broken.

There was no light, but the darkness had never bothered me. Few things had ever bothered me. Blood and death were just a part of life. Even Cross and Selene's betrayals had occurred a thousand times over the years to a thousand different people. Life, such as it was, went on.

I waited for the voice to say something—the voice that had been haunting me, had probably been whispering in my head since New Mexico, whispering as I took up residence near a nothing town with a poetic name it had never earned—but it had gone silent before the Shadow Council's meeting. Instead, my thoughts turned to the estate where the Null had set her trap. According to Cross, the queen had killed the councilor who lived there, seized his possessions, and sold his family *and* their servants into slavery. How long would it be before the same fate came for Marlena and her husband, for all of Tiberius' servants, or those of Esmelda and the other dead councilors?

How long would Elegy, Aaniyah, and Mishan wait for word from their fabled Shadow Council, along with the other cells spread across the city, ignorant to the reality that their Resistance had been decapitated in one fell swoop? How long until the queen's men worked their way to those cells, crushing the Resistance from the top down in a way its cell-based structure had never been designed to prevent? Until the death of a few rich assholes snowballed into the death of hundreds of so-called freedom fighters, men and women who had thought they were fighting for a world where they would have a say?

The world is a toilet. I'd said it more times than I could remember because it was true. *The world is a toilet, but some people get shit on more than others.*

Sitting there in the earth's womb, waiting for my crew to wake or for our enemies to find us—and not being sure which I preferred—I carried that thought to its ultimate conclusion. It was the people at the bottom who got the largest quantity of fecal matter dumped on their heads. Mina, Nathan, and Duke. Raya's estranged husband, Jae-Sung, and their daughter, Cho-Hee. The prisoners we'd freed at Tillatoba and then left to their own devices. Even Bakersfield himself.

The world is a toilet, but some people get shit on more than others. And some part of me was tired as fuck of watching it happen.

○○○

With the sun and sky locked away somewhere above us, it wasn't light that woke my crew. It wasn't their internal clocks or any of that shit humans claim exists either.

It was noise. So distant to be unrecognizable, more waves of pressure than anything I could reliably parse as sound.

"What the hell is that?" said Jules, stirring in the darkness.

"I don't know, but I think we're about to find out." Light was making its way toward us, bouncing off the tunnel walls with a cold artificial glow. I reached out to where my senses told me Jules was waiting, helped him to his feet, and then crept to the intersection and looked up the tunnel that led to Tiberius' home.

As ever, I was anything but quiet. This time, it didn't matter.

"What's going on?" I asked Marlena. She didn't have her husband with her this time and looked torn between excitement and fear.

"You don't know?" She tilted her head. "I guess it's not so noticeable down here. Come and see for yourselves!"

"See what?"

"The lower districts," she said, hair falling free from its usual bun to frame her face. "They're rising up!"

Jules and I left Two-Feathers and Evan in the dark, following the former servant up the tunnel, through the wine cellar, out of the courtyard, and up the stairs of one of the mansion's towers. High up on the hill, we could see over the surrounding walls, all the way down to the lower districts, to people gathering in the streets. Here and there, small clusters of guards gave way before the press or even joined in with the crowd. One arm of the mob in District 4 split away and headed for the gate to District 5, and soon more people were flooding in from that district, a parade of Provs adding to the push for District 3.

"Operation Solidarity," said Jules, in a voice still fuzzy with sleep. "Nobody told them it was off?"

"Nobody was alive *to* tell them." I turned to him. "This is our chance."

"To do what? Watch them die?" He waved out the window to the troops we could see massing in District 3, reinforced by a steady stream of soldiers from District 2. "The queen doesn't have a full battalion here, but her men are armed and trained, and you know there are Immortals down there with them."

"Yeah, which means fewer bodies between us and Delia."

He spun on me. "You *still* want to go after her?"

I ignored Marlena's expression. "Damn right I do. This is the distraction the Shadow Council promised us. We need to use it."

"Those people down there are about to be meat for the grinder," said Jules. "Caught against the wall and unable to do anything but die. Unless you've found a key into District 1, we'd just be repeating their play on a smaller scale."

"We brought your gear so you could *act*," said Marlena, finally losing her cool. "What are you even talking—"

"What's going on?" asked Evan, huffing and puffing like he'd just run a mile. Behind him, Two-Feathers was still making his way up the stairs, limping badly and leaning on the spear Marlena and her husband had retrieved for him. "And why couldn't you guys wait for us? You do remember Two-Feathers is injured?!"

"Operation Solidarity," said Jules, waving to the window and the riots visible far below. "Her Majesty wants to use it as a distraction while we kill the queen."

The old man turned on me. "Are you insane? We nearly died last night, every one of us except you, and you want to keep going? We don't know where she is, or how to get to her. This is it. This is the end." For the first time since I'd pulled him out of the Free States, he stood tall, an imperious expression crossing his face. "I won't have it!"

"Boys—and Marlena—could *Miles* and I have the room?"

I wasn't sure which of Jules or Marlena was unhappier about my request, but they both acquiesced, the former wrapping an arm around Two-Feathers and helping the nomad navigate down the steps.

"I know what you're going to say," said Evan. "I owe you a favor and my life along with it. But I'm not going to throw that life away just so you can have revenge."

"What do you see out there, Evan?"

For once, he didn't bother correcting the name. "I see a lot of brave, angry, and ultimately foolish people, marching for freedom." He scanned the city below us, color steadily draining from his face. "And they're all going to die."

"Yeah, they are. Only to be replaced in a few weeks or months by fresh citizens brought in through places like Tillatoba. A whole new population to live under the queen's thumb as she turns her armies toward the Badlands. There will be murder and war and slavery on a scale that will make the massacre about to happen seem small by comparison. Unless we kill the woman responsible for it."

"The Shadow Council is dead. There's nobody to take their place except other Immortals."

"Then I'll kill them too," I said, remembering Jules' drunken words from what felt like a month ago, but had only been two days. "The empire will crumble. This will become just a city. Life can return to the way it was."

"I'm not sure that's as much of an improvement as you think," said Evan, but his eyes stayed fixed on the rioting crowds below. "But Dominion used to say that freedom was about fighting for every inch. What do you want *me* to do about it?"

"I want you to become who you've been running from for seventeen years. I don't need a fifty-six-year-old retiree named Miles. I need who you were. I need that man."

"*That man* got hundreds of people killed. It would have been more if it hadn't been for my teammates' heroics." He shook his head. "It's not just the initial jolt, you know, although even that takes on a life of its own. It's what comes after. Gas leaks and fires. Mud slides and tsunamis. Power lines and buildings alike collapsing. People starving to death buried somewhere beneath a sun they'll never see again. *That man* is a murderer."

"Yes," I agreed. "You were and you are. But if you stand here and do nothing, how many more deaths will be added to your tally?"

All the air went out of him like a tire that had been slashed. "You don't get it."

"I know what fear is, Evan. I've seen it, I've felt it, and I recognize it in your eyes."

"It's the only thing I took with me from the Free States. It's the only thing I have left."

"Then maybe it's time to change that."

"How?" His voice was quiet. Empty. Broken.

I waved at the cloud-stricken sky above New Memphis. "One of the two most dangerous people I've ever met spent his nights looking up at the stars. It took me a long time to work up the nerve to ask him why. You know what he said?"

"What?"

"That he wasn't looking at them but *listening*. That there was a music to the universe and the stars sang its melody." I shook my head. "I've tried listening on more nights than I can remember, but the truth is, I don't hear a thing. No song, no music, no sound at all. But what I *see* are distant balls of heavenly light refusing to let the years or the past or the vacuum of space steal their fire. I see defiance. I see rage."

He tilted his head to look up, though it was morning, and those stars were hours away from making their presence known again. "Defiance and rage?"

"We control our futures," I told him. "What we do, when, and why, and fuck what anyone else thinks. People are going to die, Evan. The time for fear is over. Come rage with me."

Evan swallowed, his eyes moving from the stars neither of us could see to the crowds gathering below. He breathed out, a slow exhalation that carried with it more than just carbon dioxide, and nodded. "What do you need?"

"Bring down the wall to District 1. Jules and I will do what's necessary."

"And Two-Feathers?"

"Take him with you. He's no good to us in his condition."

For the first time that I could remember, a smile crossed Evan's face, but it was a small smile and sad. "I always wondered if you had a heart; I guess now I know for sure. But he can't come with me." His eyes returned to the scene below, as if pulled there by gravity. "I'm not going to stop with one wall. I'm going to tear this whole thing open and then I'm going down to give those people a fighting chance. I don't want his death on my conscience any more than you do."

Every time I thought I had humans figured out, they managed to surprise me. Usually, those surprises were for the worse. This one… well, this was something else.

"I'll talk to him then and figure something out."

"Make it fast," said Evan, eyes hard, steel in his voice to match the storm's. "I'm not going to stand by and let those people be massacred."

Sometimes, the line between murderer and hero was just a matter of perspective.

By the time Two-Feathers climbed back up into the tower, the place was starting to feel like a confessional. Can't say I enjoyed that very much, given that Dr. Nowhere was the closest thing this world had to a God and Bakersfield had put him six feet under with a pinky.

The nomad's face was haggard beneath his usual stoic demeanor, all those stairs hell on a man with one working arm and a barely functional second leg. He glanced out the window at the noise and chaos happening far below, and turned back to me, eyebrows raised as he leaned on his spear.

"This is where we part ways," I told him. "Evan… Miles… whatever you want to call him, is going to clear a path into the palace and a second one down the hill. Jules and I are going after the queen, but I need you to get out of the city. Don't get into any fights, don't stop to help anyone, just get through the guards and the crowds to freedom. If your horse isn't at the Queen's Jewel anymore, then keep going. You remember where my bike is?"

He nodded, but the pain and fatigue on his face had been replaced by confusion.

"Take it," I told him. "And don't forget the saddlebags and extra batteries."

He set his spear against the wall, tapped his chest and pointed in my direction, eyes hard.

"You can barely walk," I reminded him. "All you'll do if you come with us is die. And if we fail, someone needs to ready the clans. They need to know the Crimson Queen is almost done with the south, and that the Badlands will be next. Your people are the only ones who have any chance of stopping her from taking the land all the way to the Free States."

He scowled and pantomimed something new, but for once, the now-familiar translation process failed me. He gave up and repeated the earlier gesture: hand to his chest then pointing to me.

"I know, but it's not going to happen. If I survive, if we win somehow, I'll find you. But you need to go. You need to live."

He tried to actually speak, managing only a noise somewhere between a croak and a groan, and I cut him off with a gloved hand on his bruised shoulder.

"I'm asking you. Please. When Evan makes an exit. Take it."

Contrary to Evan's assertions, I didn't have a heart. Not the flesh and blood organ anyway. Just the endless spiral of a tornado about to touch down. Still, as I slipped past him and down the stairs, I felt a sharp ache, like the one that had once informed me when a job's payout wasn't up to snuff.

I ignored the pain and kept going.

40

I warned Marlena and her people what was coming, then followed Jules into the estate's front yard. Evan was waiting, and something in the little man's changed demeanor had Jules frowning.

"What did you say to Miles?"

"Remember what I told you in Greenburg? About people who were already broken?"

"Yeah."

"Forget all of that. Turns out it was bullshit."

That surprised a grin out of my long-time companion. He shook his head as he looked again to the little man. "I swear… he really does remind me of someone."

Jules had said the same thing when the two first met in Texas, but the ensuing months had buried that initial impression, like bones under a winter snowfall. With Evan standing tall and hard-faced, looking nothing at all like the *Miles* we had traveled with, I could see why those earlier thoughts were flooding back.

"Picture him twenty years younger," I said. "In a three-piece suit, with round glasses."

For a moment, the Whisperer frowned, first at me, then at the old man even now stepping out into the street. I saw the light come into his eyes.

"That's—"

"Rupert Evans," I told him. "Formerly the Free States Cape known as—"

"Evan Earthquake."

The man in question, the hero-turned-killer who'd fled the Free States rather than standing trial for the deaths he'd inadvertently caused, turned to the right, to the wall that separated us from District 1 and the palace enclosed within. He raised a foot and stomped it into the ground.

The earth shook.

For us, it was a gentle tremor, less of a jolt even than the one that had sent the soldiers in Cross' ambush staggering to the side. But the further from Evan it traveled, the worse it got. The streets split wide open, a schism growing from crack to chasm to many-tongued abyss as it reached the district wall.

For a moment, that was all there was, and then something in that wall gave way, cracks spreading up its surface as the ground beneath disappeared. Twenty feet of wall, gone in seconds and the destruction kept on going, marching towards a palace of polished white stone.

"Holy shit," said Jules.

Evan had fallen to one knee, and something told me it wasn't due to a loss of balance. He rubbed his chest as I approached, ignored my outstretched hand, and climbed back to his feet, face going grey.

"I'm a little bit… out of practice," he admitted.

"You can stop," I told him. "You've done what I needed."

At five-foot-six, there was no way he should've been able to look down his nose at me, but somehow the old bastard did it. "I'm not doing this… for you… favors be damned." He turned to his left, to the district's exterior wall, to District 3 and what lay below, and stomped his foot again.

This time, the tremor was worse, but the destruction didn't truly start until it reached that wall. There, it became something out of legend. Entire chunks of wall tumbled outward, toppling onto soldiers that had been streaming through, soldiers who had stopped in their tracks with the first, far smaller shock, with the impossibility of an earthquake on a man-made mountain where no fault lines could exist.

Dozens of lives blotted out in a second, and the cracks kept going, pulling down buildings in District 3, spreading to the second wall, to District 4, where the growing mob remained bottled up like fish in a barrel, waiting to be shot. But even as the earth shook and screams rose above the roar of the mob, that distant wall held strong.

I caught Evan as he fell. The little man's chest heaved like the waters of the distant Pacific

"Evan. Rupert. Enough. You've given them a chance. That's all anyone could ask for."

He looked like someone half again his age, like the Old Man on his death bed, but mustered up a smile.

"It's not about… what they… ask for, Your Majesty. It never was. Step back… and tell Marlena… I'm sorry… about the yard."

I didn't have time to ask what the fuck that meant before the grounds to our left flowed toward Evan, leaving behind a furrow five feet, then ten feet deep, digging almost all the way down to the tunnels below. A mass of uprooted dirt, grass, and stone came toward us like an avalanche running uphill, burying Evan even as it avoided me entirely.

When the dust settled, a creature stood in the Earthshaker's place, twenty feet tall and at least that wide. It had two arms made of stone, a dozen more of tightly packed earth, but no legs at all, the ground itself moving to propel it forward. As it barreled down the street, cobblestones were pulled from the road, forming layers of armor across its earthborne torso.

Jules joined me, eyes wide. "Is Miles… I mean Evan…"

"He's inside," I said, watching the golem approach the wreckage of the wall to the lower district, gunfire joined by true fire, spears of darkness, and explosions of light, as the surviving soldiers and Immortals reacted to the new threat. "For as long as he lasts."

"I wish Cross was here," he said, "just so I could see his face. The times he complained to me about bringing the old man with us…"

As I recalled, Jules had done just as much complaining, but this wasn't the time to reminisce. I pointed away from the melee happening below us, to the first wall Evan had brought down.

"He cleared the way for us."

"I suppose he did." Jules licked his lips and ran a hand through the strands of hair atop his head. "You still want to do the job?"

"It's not about that anymore," I said, almost as surprised as he was by the words coming out of my mouth. "It's about finishing what we started."

"I guess I wouldn't be much of a hero if I let the old man's efforts go to waste now, would I? Just the two of us?"

"You and me," I confirmed. "Two-Feathers isn't in any shape to join in."

"That's probably for the best." Jules ejected the magazine of his stolen rifle, counted the rounds, and slapped it back in, hoisting the pack that contained additional magazines over his shoulder. "He's a good kid. Whole life ahead of him still. If anyone's going to survive…"

"Spoken like a man who's forgotten he'll have three wives waiting for him when this is over. Aaniyah hears you talk like that, and she might not agree to be the first."

He laughed as we left the Becks family estate, climbing over the mess Evan had left behind him. It turned out I'd been wrong the night before.

This *was* the time for jokes.

○○○

The Crimson Queen's palace must have been beautiful before Evan flexed his superpowered muscles. Gleaming white stone, multiple stories, wide windows that let in a ton of natural light, all enclosed within a decorative fence that was the delicate little cousin of the district's primary wall. That fence was in shambles now, and some of the palace was too, one wing collapsed inwards like it had taken a giant's punch. A fire had broken out up front, and the main doorway was filled with wreckage.

"It's going to be really embarrassing if we fight our way into the palace only to find out she's not there," said Jules.

"Delia has to assume we'll use the riots as a distraction to attack. She probably didn't expect Evan, but even so, she'll be ready."

"Or she had an Immortal fly her the hell away."

"I don't think so. She's half your age, Jules, and has turned a small city-state into the center of the fastest growing empire on the continent in a matter of years. Assassins haven't even been able to reach her, let alone touch her."

"You're not selling this. At all." We came across our first enemy soldier, crawling out of the rubble, and Jules brought her down with a rifle butt to the face.

"Think. Every young person believes they're invulnerable, but she has the power to support that belief. And here we are, having killed six of her Immortals and turned her capital upside down. She's going to feel like she has something to prove. To us and her Immortals, both. She *has* to be here so she can watch us die."

"You think she'll roll out the red carpet then and invite us in?"

"She's young, not stupid." I let the storm surge forward past the wreckage of the palace's fancy fence, tearing through a squad of soldiers emerging from within, and reformed my shell just past the bloody trail of their corpses. "We'll just have to make a carpet of our own."

As we pushed into the palace, several things became clear. First, Raya's information had severely underestimated troop numbers in New Memphis. Second, Evan's first, *smaller* earthquake had disrupted what must have once been overwhelming defensive positions with overlapping fields of fire. And third, Jules was going to run out of bullets long before the queen ran out of guards. He slapped in his fourth magazine, ducking behind a corner as the storm surged forward to take out the latest squad that had pinned us down. By the time I'd reformed my shell, he was a step behind, racking a round into the chamber. At some point in the past fifteen minutes, he'd taken damage from a ricochet, blood trickling down his right cheek. An inch higher and it might have blinded him, an inch to the left and it might have killed him. It was a reminder that only one of us was functionally invulnerable to Normals and their guns.

"New plan," I said. "I kill everyone we see; you hang back and save your bullets for the Immortals."

"Where the hell are they, anyway?"

"Hell if I know." I wasn't even entirely sure where we were going, other than mostly straight forward. We'd had to enter through a side door, thanks to Evan, and I'd been trying to find the throne room ever since. If there was anywhere the Crimson Queen would want to confront us, it would be the seat of her power. "Probably lining up somewhere to kill us."

"Your pep talks suck." He breathed out a short breath, wiped the blood again from his cheek, and looked my way. "Next hallway?"

"Next hallway."

We killed at least a dozen men and women, all armed and wearing the Crimson Queen's colors, before someone with a brain took over and changed tactics. I stepped around yet another corner to find a man waiting for me, a bulky pack across his shoulders and a thick-nozzled device in his hands, pointed our way.

I was moving even before it spat burning fuel in my direction. It had been literally decades since I'd seen a flamethrower small enough to be carried by one person, but the experience had stuck with me. I crashed into Jules, knocking him down and back behind the corner's cover, sending us both sliding down a hallway slick with other people's blood. Liquid fire scorched the hall behind me, licking the plaster off the wall like a hungry man cleaning his plate.

"Pyromancer?" he asked, shouting to be heard over the noise.

"Flamethrower," I shouted back, pulling him further away from the corner. The hall we'd been traveling was a long one, and flamethrowers had notoriously limited distance. Then again, they still outranged the storm. "He's all yours."

Jules measured the space, took another five feet back, and dropped to a shooter's kneeling position. "What happens if he just sets up there and waits?" he asked in a quieter tone.

"Then we'll either find another route or give you another chance to shoot blindly around corners." The smile across my visor spread as I sensed the enemy soldier creeping forward. "But it looks like that's not going to be a problem."

One minute and two bullets later, we stepped past the dead man and his flamethrower, ignoring the tongues of flame still clinging to the walls around us.

"Tom would have only taken one shot," complained Jules.

"Once I track down Selene, you can have her tell him so."

"You're joking, but I guarantee it would make his ghost smile."

○○○

More soldiers and more dead. The fires Evan had predicted were slowly spreading, linking up with those started by our enemy, by a succession of flamethrowing maniacs. Jules had put them down, one after the other, before the local forces either ran out of the weapons or realized they were simply lighting their own funeral pyre.

It had been a few minutes since our last encounter, but I could sense figures somewhere ahead. More than just a squad, spread across a space larger than an area we'd encountered so far.

"Heads up," I told Jules. "It looks like our party's up ahead."

"We finally found the throne room?" Jules had taken more damage, thanks to some overly intelligent soldiers who had used the maze of hallways to flank us, but his grin matched the one across my visor. He was a kid again, following me into some hellhole for a handful of coin and the thrill of it all.

"Either that or a dance hall, I guess. Delia seems like the sort to enjoy a good cotillion."

I stepped through into an open room.

It was *not* a dance hall. To my left, double doors opened onto the wide hallway that no doubt made a straight shot from the palace's main entrance and would have saved us a half hour of smoke, gunfire, and hell if it had remained intact. Facing us was another small door, leading into the warren of smaller hallways and rooms that made the second wing.

But to the right? Across a floor of polished onyx, black as my leathers when I reformed my shell, there was a raised dais. Atop that dais sat a throne, and in that throne sat a woman.

Just not the woman we were looking for.

I nodded to Jules and then turned my helmet upward, to the balconies that ringed the throne room and the people I could sense above. He took up position in the doorway, where it would offer protection from any shooters above. It meant he wouldn't have an angle on half the gallery, but they wouldn't have one on him either.

"Don't tell me," I said to the woman seated in the throne, letting my voice echo through the empty space. "Delia abdicated her throne, and you're here to beg for peace."

"The Crimson Queen is a busy woman," said the stranger, rearranging her black skirts as she perched on the throne. "My name is Lace. She sent me to hear your petition in her stead."

I strutted like a vid star on parade. "Is she queen or coward?"

Lace's lips thinned. She had eyes as dark as the floor, as dark as Two-Feathers' but without any sclera, and while her exposed skin was pale, she'd painted both her lips and her nails the same deep shade.

I liked black as much as the next person—maybe even more, given that it was a part of my life and my shell—but there was such a thing as taking a good thing too far. Lace made an odd contrast to what I remembered of the Crimson Queen's bubblegum princess motif.

"I'm not here for petitions," I added, letting my voice carry to the people above us. "I'm not here for any of you. Leave and you live. Stay and you die. Like Shard, River's Child, and Scandal," I added, citing the only names I had for the Powers we'd killed. "Like Red Dragon, Tyrant, and Dr. Fucking Nowhere himself."

Bakersfield wouldn't mind if I stole his thunder, right?

"I ran out of shits to give before most of you were even born," I added into the silence. "All I have left is death. Come and get it or stay out of my way."

"You heard the pretender queen, Immortals," said Lace, still perched on the throne, a black and white portrait of a woman with delusions of vampiredom. "Have at it."

Men and women leapt down into the throne room.

Jules' gun barked like an angry dog.

My shell fell away and the storm took its rightful place in the center of the chaos we had created.

41

Two Wind Dancers died before they even cleared the railing, their graceful flights cut short by Jules' rifle. Part of me traced the arc of their falls from grace, but the storm dismissed them as irrelevant, brief flickers of motion in what had so quickly become a target-rich environment.

Delia had trained her Immortals to break armies. Titans and Stalwarts and Speedsters clearing the field while the ranged Powers stood back and played the role of artillery. It must have been hell on an open battlefield, the sort of awe-inspiring display of might that could topple smaller kingdoms all on its own.

In the confines of the palace's throne room, it was a disaster.

The ranged Powers couldn't bring their abilities to bear without hitting their melee-focused counterparts, and as they tried to figure their way past that puzzle, Jules was picking his shots, putting on a display that would have made dead Tom proud. As for the infantry among the Immortal? More than a dozen danced with the storm, Titans shouldering each other aside to get at me, Stalwarts dodging blows from their own allies as they attempted to cut off my angles, Speedsters looking desperately for any space in which to run.

Tactics that worked on an enemy brigade were poorly suited for single targets, and tactics intended for single combat were impossible to implement in a mad melee where the enemy moved like nothing human. The storm cut its way through flesh and bone, armored flesh and reinforced bone, leaving bits of people in its wake.

And still the dance continued.

I had just finished impaling a Speedster who bobbed when he should have weaved, when fire filled the doorway that Jules had been shooting from. Before I could check on him, the Immortals above changed their tactics, now firing indiscriminately down upon both the storm and their own allies. Light and darkness tore through the air, too fast to dodge. Fire burned through Titans and Stalwarts alike, and just that quickly, the throne room floor became a kill zone, just like the silo I'd been trapped in back in the Badlands.

Except here, there was one end of the room that remained untouched and undisturbed.

The storm flowed past the strike of a Stalwart who'd been set on fire by her fellow Immortals, ducked under a Titan with a hole burned through his chest, and I reformed my shell, sprinting toward the throne where Lace sat in silence, as if watching a play. Beams of energy chased me down the length of the room, and the other woman stiffened, eyes going wide at the doom I was bringing her way.

Something struck the floor behind me, the explosion launching me into the air, and those all-black eyes widened even further with the realization that she was right in my trajectory.

Which was, of course, when yet another Titan decided to get in the way, swinging a massive club like it was a bat and I was the ball to be sent into orbit.

I could have dismissed my shell and counted on most of the storm sliding right past the brute's blow, but the truth was, Lace hadn't proven herself a threat just yet, and the Titan was swinging in an upward arc to meet my flight, which offered an unexpected opportunity.

This was going to suck.

I held on to my shell, and that club blasted into me, shattering bones like toothpicks, bringing with it a pain I hadn't felt since the eighteen-wheeler that ran over me on the day of my birth. The Titan's single enormous blow destroyed my shell.

And redirected its momentum.

The broken remnants of what had been a body flew back and up through the air, just like that ball from a sport that hadn't been played in a century. Through the waves of pain, I reached out to sense the positions of the Powers on the nearby balcony.

I wasn't going to land on that balcony, like I'd hoped, but I wasn't that far away either.

I dismissed my shell, and the storm rode the momentum of the Titan's blow like the weather pattern it pretended to be, steel and metal gaining an additional foot or two of distance over the less aerodynamic shell. I reformed my shell, pristine and untouched, a few seconds later, as I reached the top of the arc and began to fall.

Gloved hands reached for the balustrade.

I missed with the first hand but made the grab with the second, which was when a Shadecaster perforated my shell with spears of solid shadow. Shadecasters were one of the few ranged Powers I didn't have to fear, dangerous to my shell but not the storm inside; I pulled myself up and over the balcony, spears coming with me, and then set the storm free again.

Powers trained as superhuman mortars, I quickly discovered, lacked the discipline—not to mention the stones—for an up-close battle. The storm took its hits but left bloody carnage in its wake.

"That. Is. Enough!" The southern accent I'd heard only once before sounded odd at a full shout, but it was loud enough for even the storm to hear over its own chatter. I reformed my shell in the middle of the balcony. A dozen feet away, the Immortals still alive up there with me shrank back. On the opposite balcony, an even larger group had never joined in the battle at all. They waited in silence, their eyes turned to the throne room below.

And down there, in the midst of what was left of her shock troops, flanked by Lace and the four Powers I remembered from the Badlands, stood the woman of the hour.

Delia Lain, the Crimson Queen. Her hair had grown out since our last meeting but remained as blonde and elaborately curled as ever. She wasn't looking my way, but instead to the opposite balcony and the group who had held back as the battle unfolded.

"Et tu, Cyrus?"

The man who stepped forward wore his hair brutally short, almost like a skullcap. That hair was grey, but his body belied his evident age, visibly powerful even beneath a uniform covered in ribbons. "Like I keep telling you, Delia, I never read that book, or any other ones you've told me about. Quoting from them is a waste of your time and mine."

"I think she's saying you're a traitor," I called from my balcony. "She's probably wondering why you all weren't fighting and dying on her behalf while she hid out of sight."

"Ah." He rubbed his chin. "Given the mess you've made of the others, can you blame us? I guess the way the fellows and I see it is that we've got two people here, both claiming to be queens. Now, I like *your* crown a whole lot better than Delia's," he added, gesturing to my helmet, "but maybe this is something the two of you should settle between yourselves?"

"I'll remember this," the Crimson Queen told him sweetly, stroking the head of her muzzled short-range Teleporter. "And maybe we'll introduce you to the technician who taught Pierre here his manners. As for you, my cute little countess, you're *supposed* to be dead."

"So everyone keeps telling me." I shrugged. "It didn't take."

"Well, bless your heart! Then why don't you come down here so we can discuss this like civilized people? You already know you can't touch me, and apparently killing you is more trouble than it's worth. I'm sure we can talk things out."

"Your man, Cyrus, is right." I hopped the railing, let the storm carry me to a floor slippery with blood and other fluids, and reformed my shell ten feet in front of the queen and her guard. "The time for talking is done."

"Now, that ain't neighborly at all."

"What do you call a Telekinetic whose only power is a forcefield?" I asked her.

For the first time, she frowned. "I'm sure you're going to—"

"Useless in a fight," I answered. "The only weapons you have available are those given to you by other people. And apparently, some of them are pretty tired of your shit."

"Well now you've gone and made me sad." She pouted. Standing in the middle of a battlefield, she *pouted*, and it occurred to me that her little princess persona might not just be an act. "You come to another woman's home, stir up folk like nobody's business, put a few holes in some really expensive walls, and then you come right out and insult me too?" All expression fled a face that seemed suddenly plain without its animation. "I guess we'll just have to keep killing you until it sticks."

When the attack came, it wasn't from the queen or any of the Powers standing with her; it came from the floor itself. The tiles that I'd thought were obsidian ran like water, retreating from under corpses and their bodily fluids, leaving behind polished white stone that better suited the palace's décor.

The darkness became a puddle, then a lake twice as deep as I was tall despite the lack of any barrier to enforce its shape, and details began to appear on its surface. An amorphous mass resolved itself into a series of coils, and along the surface of each coil a succession of intricate markings appeared. They looked almost like… scales.

A head swam its way out of the darkness, armed with rows of teeth like an alligator instead of fangs, and a body that could comfortably fill the throne room—*had* filled the throne room moments earlier—surged forward.

I'd found Delia's pet and answered Jules' question to the Shadow Council at the same time: What do you get the egomaniacal teenage monarch who already has everything?

A really, really big fucking snake.

○○○

As fast as the creature was, I was faster. My shell fell away and the storm was there to meet the monster's strike, shards of steel, scraps of shrapnel, and twists of rusted wire giving welcome.

Nothing landed. Each strike found only inky smoke, flesh that disappeared and then reformed in a master class of the storm's own evasions. But when the great beast's head came around, broad and tall as a two-story wall, it hit like a battering ram, hit like ten Titans all being juiced by an Amplifier.

The storm flew apart, fragments blasted in all directions. I pulled those pieces back together, formed my shell, and this time *dodged* the coil that fell upon me like an avalanche.

And that pretty much set the course for the next five awful, pointless, fruitless minutes of battle. I was faster than the demon snake, if barely, but it had bulk and power on its side. Even worse, I couldn't touch it at all, and every blow it landed struck the storm with incalculable force. My shell was built to be disposable, but the storm was the core of my soul, and it was being battered across the chamber.

I spread the storm's fragments out as wide as I could, struck from a hundred angles with a thousand teeth, but the result was the same. Every strike that should have cut and torn instead passed through a creature that could apparently go intangible at will.

I hadn't seen Jules since the Pyromancer blasted his position, and I had no strategy for dealing with the Crimson Queen without him, but that didn't even matter, because her pet was kicking my ever-living ass. I'd never seen or even heard of something like it, had no idea how Delia or her people had managed to capture let alone tame a creature of its size, one who seemed as much smoke as monster snake.

Wait.

A thought struck me, so suddenly that the storm forgot to dodge. Another hit sent me flying across the chamber, but I pulled the misshapen fragments of my soul back together, formed my shell, and looked beyond the creature bearing down on me, to the Powers standing behind the Crimson Queen, and the woman all in black who'd introduced herself as Lace.

Not *smoke* but *shadow.*

This wasn't a creature at all. It was a Shadecaster's creation.

The weakness of Shadecasters was that anything more than projectiles, any construct that needed to hold shape for more than a moment, required a tether back to the Power creating it. It let them dump energy into their creation, maintaining its form, but it also made that construct part of them. I'd seen Shadecasters stabbed through their own shadows, seem them roasted from the inside out by a Pyromancer attacking their creations.

I didn't know how many hours and days and weeks and months Lace had spent figuring out a solution to that handicap, teaching herself to dissolve and reform her construct in an instinctive reaction to potential threats, but it was the sort of brilliance scientists in the Free States would have killed to study.

I gave her a nod from across the hall, and watched those all-black eyes widen.

Because if I couldn't kill her construct, I'd just have to take down the woman powering it.

This time, I ignored the snake entirely, letting the storm come and fly apart, like hail driven forward on a blizzard's wind. Every strike I dodged cost me a few fragments, but I landed between leaps, reformed my shell, pulled those pieces back in, and charged again. Blunt force was a far cry from fire, acid, or light. It too could destroy metal, but it took time, and neither Lace nor her construct had that time to spare.

A wall of coils rose in front of me, the Shadecaster's last-ditch effort to protect herself from the coming doom. I packed the storm together into a ball of malice and sharp edges and flew straight at that barrier. It was one thing to bat the storm aside when its rage had already been spent. It was another thing entirely to stand in the face of its wrath. Sure enough, Lace fell back on her hard-earned training, and the snake's body in front of me became smoke, saving the Shadecaster from the damage that would have been transferred through her creation.

And then there was nothing ahead of me but open space and a handful of enemy Powers. The Crimson Queen tried to block my path, but the storm's thousand fragments slipped right off the Telekinetic's personal shield and kept going, impaling the woman behind her.

I reformed my shell atop Lace's corpse and showed the world my smile as the monster snake fell apart like the smoke I'd initially mistaken it for.

The muzzled Power at Delia's side gibbered madly, and she smacked it on the side of the head, her personal forcefield protecting her own hand from the consequences of that blow.

Smoke issued from the nostrils of the Pyromancer next to her, but I wasn't Lassie's little Timmy anymore, stuck at the bottom of a well. I tore him to pieces as the first globules of fire left his mouth. The second power, the one called Venom, expelled a cloud of gas so poisonous I could almost see it, but I ignored that assault to tear through the Lightbringer instead, sacrificing pieces of myself in the process.

My fragments would grow back. Hers wouldn't.

Part of me couldn't help but notice the queen dive to the side with a curse as she avoided Venom's toxic attack. It was proof I'd been right about how her power worked. If Jules was gone, maybe I could use her own enforcer against her instead?

That plan died a swift death when I saw Venom sag to the floor, a victim of one of the light-quick blasts that had torn through the storm. Now a dozen feet away, Delia appeared, her fingers tight in the Teleporter's hair, a snarl looking far more appropriate on her face.

"And what did any of this prove?" she spat. "I'm the one you want, and you and your precious other form can't touch me. You can kill and kill and keep killing but I'll still be here, and my armies will scorch the—"

She grabbed for her throat, eyes bulging, her own hand passing through the shield she'd generated. Behind her, Jules lay sprawled out on the white-tiled floor, a bloody streak behind him illustrating the path he'd crawled. Whatever hair he'd had left on his head was gone, and one side of his body was scorched and smoking, but his other arm was extended in the queen's direction, fingers squeezing.

Delia waved wildly at the Teleporter by her side, but the man she'd named Pierre didn't react, staring through her as much as at her. She dropped to a knee, her too-large mouth flapping open and closed as it searched for the oxygen being denied it. As she swayed back and forth, I moved with her, making sure I was always in her vision, that the last thing she saw would be the face my father had given me.

I probably should have been looking for other threats instead.

He came from above, from the balcony I had decimated, a flying Power who had held back initially, knowing he was useless in that wild clash of abilities. He caught the Crimson Queen below the arms, his fingers a visible inch or so away from the woman's body itself, and lifted her into the air, over the reaching shards of a suddenly thwarted storm.

The muzzled Teleporter disappeared with a pop, only to reappear on top of the flyer. His extra weight sent the other pair careening to the side, but a moment later, he was tossed away again, howling mournfully as the queen and her last loyal subject moved beyond his evident range. I watched the Crimson Queen take her first breath in almost a minute as the flyer carried them away. Watched her eyes turn to the balcony that would lead them to freedom.

Watched the spear that came through the air like the answer to a question never asked, arcing from the blasted doorway where Jules had almost died.

It had two feathers bound to its shaft, just below the spearhead, and it took the flying Power right in his chest, sending him crashing to the floor with the woman he'd tried to save.

Delia, of course, emerged unharmed, but she'd landed ten feet from Jules, and was already gasping by the time she found her feet.

This time, I kept my senses peeled for any other would-be heroes, scanning the chamber behind me and paying little attention to the woman dying at my feet. If Delia Laine, Crimson Queen and architect of Eclipse's destruction, mouthed any last words before she went, I couldn't tell you what they were.

OOO

I was tending to Jules, assisted by the unrepentant, badly injured Two-Feathers, who had opted to ignore the curses I was hurling his way, when someone hit the ground behind us like a wrecking ball.

I turned to find the man Delia had named Cyrus standing there, unscathed by the drop. Eyes as cold as the grave met the face across my visor. I didn't know what abilities the man had, but he was backed by almost two dozen other Powers. All I had was the storm, my nomad, and a Whisperer doing his best not to pour his last fluids onto the throne room floor.

But nobody ever said this job would be easy.

And then Cyrus had to ruin my heroic last stand by doing the one thing I *hadn't* expected.

He dropped to a knee in front of me and lowered his head.

"Your Majesty," he said. "The lower districts are rioting. The people have taken District 3 and what troops remain are struggling to hold District 2. What are your orders?"

I looked at Jules, his green eyes bright with pain, and at Two-Feathers, whose black eyes gave away nothing at all. I thought of Evan, who'd run from himself for so long only to realize, in the end, that he was right where he needed to be.

For three long years, I'd continued playing my part, the role Dr. Nowhere had created me to fill, but it was time to move on. The stars could rage, and the storm could too, but I had something more.

I had my answer as to what came next.

"Pull the soldiers back to the palace," I told Cyrus. "Spread word that I will meet with the people's representatives when the riots are over." I let him see the smile across my visor and hear the answering sentiment in my metal-filled voice. "We're going to make some changes around here."

EPILOGUE

"It just seems kind of weird," said Jules, tugging at the high collar he'd inexplicably subjected himself to for the morning's ceremony. "You leaving New Memphis already, I mean."

It had been several months since the Crimson Queen's death, since the job I'd hired myself for had turned into something more, and we were a hell of a long way from rebuilding, let alone figuring everything out. Jules' burns were still healing too, the man splitting his time between council meetings, treatments from a low-ranked Healer the nomad clans had sent over, and being positively doted on by a succession of "nurses" making sure he had everything he needed.

Apparently, heroism was every bit as potent an aphrodisiac as he had hoped.

I was pretty sure Aaniyah was going to put an end to that business and quick. It had taken days to find her in the chaos after the riots and significantly more time than that to talk Elegy around, but she and Jules had been thick as thieves ever since. The next nurse who tried to find their way into his bed was going to find out why Aaniyah had led a cell in the Resistance.

If they were lucky, she'd use a knife instead of her tongue.

"I only stayed this long for the ceremony," I reminded him.

"I can't believe they built him a statue. Evan Earthquake, martyr of New Memphis? Do you know how much statues *cost*, especially with the city's Earthshakers now working for pay?"

"Who do you think signed off on the expense?"

"You mean it wasn't Cyrus?" He made a face of mock shock that was just begging to be punched. "I didn't know you ever dirtied your hands with administrative work."

"By the time I get back, I'm hoping you and the rest of the new government will have figured all this shit out for me. Then, I can just sit back and wear my pretty, and entirely symbolic, crown." I tapped the helmet that was my face.

"In your dreams, Queenie. I'm telling you now: we'll both be doing paperwork until the end of time."

I glanced out the window at a city still figuring out how to heal and an empire that wasn't sure what it would become. "I can live with that."

"Says the woman taking off on a months-long joyride."

"It's *not* a joyride. I need to see him with my own eyes."

"Walker. The Lord of the Dead."

"Yeah. We've got words that must be said face-to-face."

"One monarch to another."

"I guess so." It wasn't the only time I'd explained this to Jules, but he'd gotten sentimental of late. Give a man a house and a position of authority in some weird hybrid between a monarchy and representative democracy, and he turned soft real quick.

"There's just one thing I can't figure out."

"What's that?" Finally—finally!—I saw the sight I'd been waiting for.

"Why are you taking the nomads' ambassador with you?"

In the streets below us, Two-Feathers waited, one hand on my motorcycle, the other on his horse.

"Diplomacy is exhausting," I told Jules, watching my nomad smile up at us. "He wanted to take a road trip."

"Through the Badlands, Texas, and the Empire of the Dead?"

"With a short stop in a nothing town called Eastwood."

"He's as crazy as you are."

"That he is. And while I'd love to stay and talk, there are roads out there waiting to be ridden. We'll be back by summer."

"Fair enough and good travels to you both," said Jules, sounding almost respectable. "Just… do me one favor?"

"What's that?"

"Don't take any new jobs along the way." He gave a theatrical shiver. "This last one was murder."

"And yet here we are. The queen is dead."

"Long live the queen."

AUTHOR'S NOTE

This was supposed to be the easy book: a stand-alone story starring a well-liked character in a straightforward tale of revenge that would also serve as a bridge between *The Murder of Crows* and the new post-Break trilogy I'll be writing next year. The plan was to knock this one out with a minimum of fuss and to deliver it to beta readers well ahead of schedule.

What I hadn't reckoned with was my protagonist and the many challenges the Queen of Smiles would bring with her, as an inhuman, quasi-immortal who doesn't eat or sleep, is rarely nice, and starts out clinging to old patterns in the wake of the events of *One Tin Soldier*. Oh, and her true face just happens to be the ever-shifting smiley-face decal on her helmet's visor… while her love interest is a nomad who has a lot to say but doesn't speak.

What I'm saying is that this was *not* the easy book I'd envisioned. Every step of the way, Her Majesty forced me to rethink my usual approaches, and the book you've just read is somehow both the story I set out to write and something entirely stranger. Which is, I guess, fitting, given both the character and the setting.

Regardless, I hope you enjoyed the ride! One of my favorite things about the post-Break world is that there is no such thing as a status quo. Every change, large or small, sends ripples that might impact other characters and stories in unexpected ways. I'm excited to see where those ripples lead us next, and even more excited to announce that we *will* see more books featuring Her Majesty and Two Feathers. Stay tuned for book two of *The Storm Who Rides.*

As always, if you enjoyed *The Queen of Smiles*, please consider spreading the word and leaving a review. As an indie author, my books depend almost entirely on word of mouth and the feedback and support of readers like you.

Thank you!

ABOUT THE AUTHOR

Chris began life as a gleam in someone's eye, but birth and childhood were quick to follow. He's been fortunate enough to live in Spain, Germany, and all over the United States of America, and is busy planning a tour of the distilleries of Scotland.

A graduate of the Johns Hopkins University's Writing Seminars program, he put that degree to ill use for twenty years as a software engineer but has finally circled back around to the idea of writing for a living.

Chris currently lives in Nevada with his angelic wife and ever-expanding whisky collection and occasionally ventures outside to peer upwards, mutter to himself about 'day stars', and then scurry back into the house.

The Queen of Smiles is his eighth novel, the fourth set in the post-Break world, and the first in a new series, *The Storm Who Rides.* Chris frequently shares updates on his author website at https://christullbane.com.

www.ingramcontent.com/pod-product-compliance
Lightning Source LLC
Chambersburg PA
CBHW030952190726
48285CB00004BB/1309

* 9 7 8 1 9 5 5 0 8 1 1 3 9 *